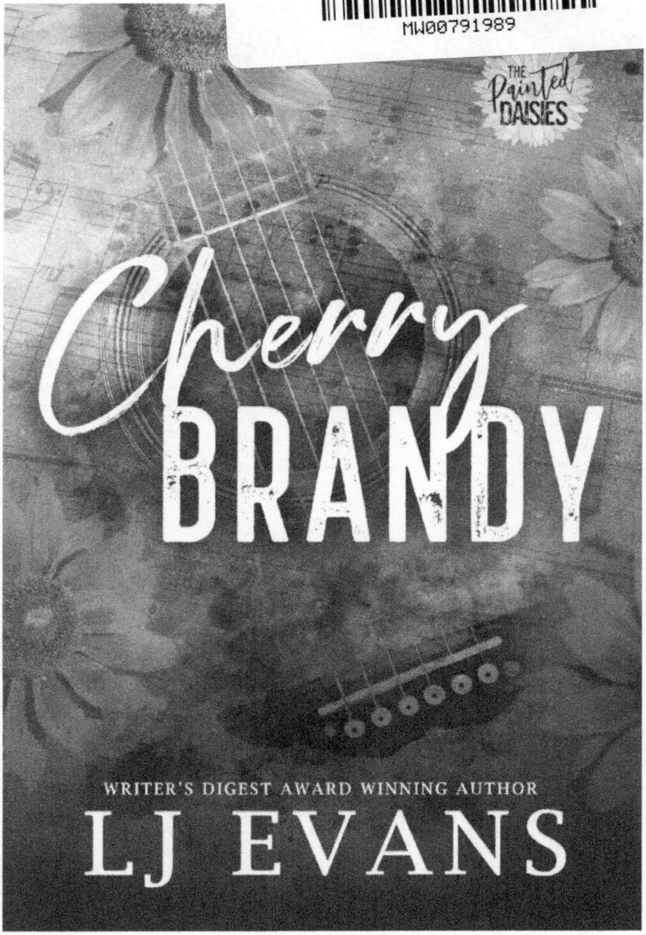
THE Painted DAISIES
Cherry
BRANDY
WRITER'S DIGEST AWARD WINNING AUTHOR
LJ EVANS

The Painted Daisies, Book III

# Cherry Brandy

L J Evans

Published by LJ EVANS BOOKS
www.ljevansbooks.com

Cover Design: © Emily Wittig
Cover Images: © Unsplash | weston m, Deposit Photos | VadimVasenin and Dekues, iStock| Punnarong, and Shutterstock | RukiMedia
Chapter Image: © iStock Vidok
Content & Line Editor: Evans Editing
Copy Editor: Jenn Lockwood Editing Services
Proofing: Karen Hrdlicka
Sensitivity Editors: Arora, Sarkar, and Patra

ISBN: 978-1-962499-13-2

Library of Congress Cataloging in process.

# Playlist

https://spoti.fi/3GDgRoj

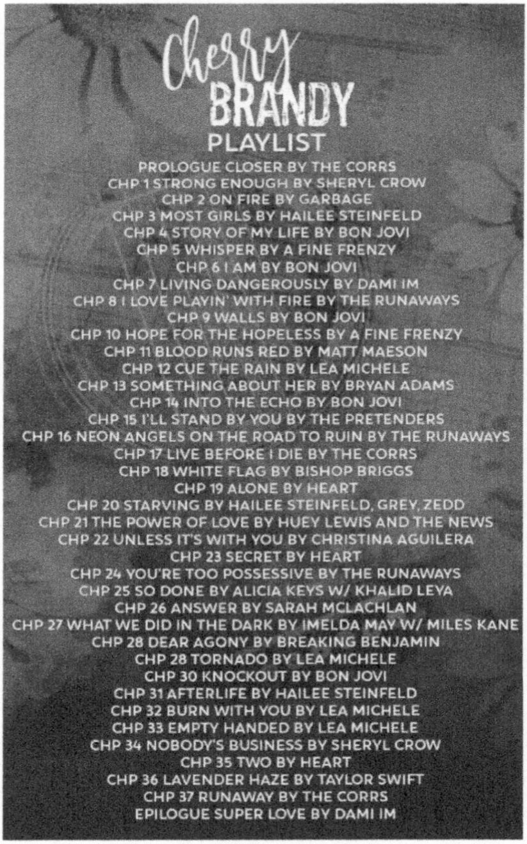
Cherry
BRANDY
PLAYLIST
PROLOGUE CLOSER BY THE CORRS
CHP 1 STRONG ENOUGH BY SHERYL CROW
CHP 2 ON FIRE BY GARBAGE
CHP 3 MOST GIRLS BY HAILEE STEINFELD
CHP 4 STORY OF MY LIFE BY BON JOVI
CHP 5 WHISPER BY A FINE FRENZY
CHP 6 I AM BY BON JOVI
CHP 7 LIVING DANGEROUSLY BY DAMI IM
CHP 8 I LOVE PLAYIN' WITH FIRE BY THE RUNAWAYS
CHP 9 WALLS BY BON JOVI
CHP 10 HOPE FOR THE HOPELESS BY A FINE FRENZY
CHP 11 BLOOD RUNS RED BY MATT MAESON
CHP 12 CUE THE RAIN BY LEA MICHELE
CHP 13 SOMETHING ABOUT HER BY BRYAN ADAMS
CHP 14 INTO THE ECHO BY BON JOVI
CHP 15 I'LL STAND BY YOU BY THE PRETENDERS
CHP 16 NEON ANGELS ON THE ROAD TO RUIN BY THE RUNAWAYS
CHP 17 LIVE BEFORE I DIE BY THE CORRS
CHP 18 WHITE FLAG BY BISHOP BRIGGS
CHP 19 ALONE BY HEART
CHP 20 STARVING BY HAILEE STEINFELD, GREY, ZEDD
CHP 21 THE POWER OF LOVE BY HUEY LEWIS AND THE NEWS
CHP 22 UNLESS IT'S WITH YOU BY CHRISTINA AGUILERA
CHP 23 SECRET BY HEART
CHP 24 YOU'RE TOO POSSESSIVE BY THE RUNAWAYS
CHP 25 SO DONE BY ALICIA KEYS W/ KHALID LEYA
CHP 26 ANSWER BY SARAH MCLACHLAN
CHP 27 WHAT WE DID IN THE DARK BY IMELDA MAY W/ MILES KANE
CHP 28 DEAR AGONY BY BREAKING BENJAMIN
CHP 28 TORNADO BY LEA MICHELE
CHP 30 KNOCKOUT BY BON JOVI
CHP 31 AFTERLIFE BY HAILEE STEINFELD
CHP 32 BURN WITH YOU BY LEA MICHELE
CHP 33 EMPTY HANDED BY LEA MICHELE
CHP 34 NOBODY'S BUSINESS BY SHERYL CROW
CHP 35 TWO BY HEART
CHP 36 LAVENDER HAZE BY TAYLOR SWIFT
CHP 37 RUNAWAY BY THE CORRS
EPILOGUE SUPER LOVE BY DAMI IM

# Dedication

*To all the girls forced into adulthood too soon.*

# Prologue

## *Leya*

***CLOSER***

*Performed by The Corrs*

*TWENTY-FIVE MONTHS BEFORE*

*LEYA: You should have told me they wanted me at the convention early.*

*CAPTAIN ANNOYING: I'm a Secret Service agent, not your personal assistant.*

*LEYA: If you were, I could fire you.*

*CAPTAIN ANNOYING: You can decline the protection of the USSS at any time. You're an adult.*

*LEYA: *** laughing GIF *** You think I'd survive either of my parents' lectures if I did? Not with everything that's going on there with Dad and here with the Daisies.*

*LEYA: No response?*

*LEYA: Really?*

*LEYA: You're a jerkwad.*

*TWENTY MONTHS BEFORE*

*LEYA: I need your assistance.*

*CAPTAIN ANNOYING: I'm not on duty. Talk to the agent standing outside your door.*

*LEYA: I'm not at the residence. I'm at EchoBar with Lincoln.*

*CAPTAIN ANNOYING: Then, you should have two teams of USSS agents at your disposal.*

*LEYA: I don't trust any of THEM to not say anything to Lincoln's dad.*

*CAPTAIN ANNOYING: Your secrets are safe with them. They're the SECRET Service for a reason.*

*LEYA: Holden...please?*

*LEYA: Holden?*

*CAPTAIN ANNOYING: I'll be there in fifteen.*

*TEN MONTHS BEFORE*

*LEYA: Do you think this is a good gift for my dad's lead agent? *** image of brandy bottle ****

*CAPTAIN ANNOYING: I'm off duty. I'm not your assistant or your mom.*

*LEYA: You're so annoying. You're an agent. I*

*want to know, as an AGENT, would this be a good gift?*

*CAPTAIN ANNOYING: I don't drink, so for me, no.*

*LEYA: Get your head out of the clouds, you arrogant jerk. I'm not buying it for you. I'm helping my mother by whittling down the long list of people she needs to buy presents for.*

*CAPTAIN ANNOYING: Sommerson brags about his expensive whiskey collection.*

*LEYA: Whiskey. Okay. Why don't you drink?*

*CAPTAIN ANNOYING: None of your business.*

*LEYA: I'll just keep asking. You know I will.*

*CAPTAIN ANNOYING: My father's partner got caught with his pants down after engaging in one too many alcoholic beverages. The woman took his USSS pin and used it for months before she was caught.*

*LEYA: Wait. You've been with me for over a year now, and I'm just learning that your father was also an agent?*

*CAPTAIN ANNOYING: We aren't friends, Leya. I'm not going to brush your hair and share our life histories. I'm part of your detail. End of story.*

*LEYA: You know every single thing about me. More than even some of my friends.*

*CAPTAIN ANNOYING: I know your facts. I*

*don't know you.*

*LEYA: Jerk. You know me. You handed me Kleenex when I cried.*

*CAPTAIN ANNOYING: One time, and that was so you could see without crashing into doors and desks and sharp edges.*

*LEYA: You're getting the gift of coal for Christmas.*

*CAPTAIN ANNOYING: How do you know I celebrate Christmas?*

*LEYA: You're right. That was very hypocritical of me. Do you?*

*CAPTAIN ANNOYING: Yes.*

*LEYA: You really are a jerk. I've just bought your coal. You can use it to cook a cow in some typical, male, barbecue ritual.*

*CAPTAIN ANNOYING: Now you're assuming I'm a meat eater.*

*LEYA: I've seen you devour a burger.*

*CAPTAIN ANNOYING: No, you haven't.*

*LEYA: You're right. In over two years, I've never seen you eat at all. You're a robot. You're like that machine in those Terminator movies. Which side are you really on?*

*CAPTAIN ANNOYING: ...*

Minutes later

*LEYA: I hate when you do that. It's rude to not say goodbye.*

*LEYA: Holden?*

*LEYA: *** picture of coal in a stocking ****

*FIVE MONTHS BEFORE*

*LEYA: How the hell does this happen, Holden? How?*

*CAPTAIN ANNOYING: He was perfect on paper. I personally ran every member of Reinard's detail as soon as I found out about the letters starting again. There were no flags, Leya. None.*

*LEYA: She almost died...and after Lan.*

Minutes go by.

*LEYA: The Kims can't lose her. WE can't lose her. She's the only thing keeping us going.*

*CAPTAIN ANNOYING: She isn't what keeps the band going. She's the spark, but you're all the fuel that keeps the flame alive.*

*LEYA: Was that some sort of backhanded compliment?*

*CAPTAIN ANNOYING: Go to sleep. You've had a long day.*

*LEYA: Now you're trying to be my mom? I thought you were ONLY my USSS agent.*

*CAPTAIN ANNOYING: I can't afford to carry your tired body around all day tomorrow.*

*LEYA: Dreaming of carrying me, Captain Annoying?*

Minutes later.

*LEYA: Someday, I'm going to be the one to end our conversations without saying goodbye, and you'll know how irritating it is.*

*LEYA: I guess today is not that day.*

*EIGHT DAYS BEFORE*

*CAPTAIN ANNOYING: This isn't funny, Leya. Where are you?*

*LEYA: ...*

# Chapter One

## Leya

***STRONG ENOUGH***
*Performed by Sheryl Crow*

*EIGHT DAYS BEFORE*

The text from US Secret Service Agent Holden Kent had Leya wishing she'd flung her phone down the toilet so he couldn't trace it. It also had her heart rate picking up in that irritating way it did whenever she had a conversation with the man. After more than two years of him being the lead—and often only—agent on her detail, you'd think her reaction to him would have faded. But it hadn't. Lately, she thought it was getting worse.

Even though she hadn't responded to his text, she knew she had mere minutes until he found her swaying on the tire swing in the yard of Number One Observatory Circle. Joe Biden had installed the swing during his vice presidency, leaving a note to his beloved wife engraved on the tree. *Beloved*… Loved... Wife.

Her stomach flipped, and nausea flew through it.

She wasn't ready to be any of those things.

And yet, the time had come for her to make a decision. She couldn't put it off any longer. Krish and his family needed a formal answer. Needed to move forward with an actual wedding and not the mere idea…the mere promise…of one that had been waiting in the background for a decade. While she understood why they needed it, the idea only made her soul curl up inside her chest as if hiding from an intruder instead of blossoming as it should. Her sister-in-law, Devleena, had been so excited when she'd married Rishik that she'd strained a cheek muscle from smiling so hard. All thoughts of marriage did for Leya was make her eye twitch.

Holden appeared around the corner, and the sunlight hit his head, turning the strands a radiant gold. With his light-brown hair, blue eyes, and wide shoulders, he looked like the epitome of the stereotypical American legend. The captain of the football team. The small-town hero. Like a superhero you couldn't believe walked in your door. He had the muscles, the bulging biceps, and narrow hips that tights would show off perfectly. But it was his beautifully chiseled jawline and the aquamarine aura that surrounded him, flickering and growing whenever they were in the same space, that called to her the most. Her fingers itched to draw every curve along a clean canvas. It had been too long since she'd allowed her other artistic side free rein, and the need welled inside her almost as large as the attraction to the man storming toward her.

He was not smiling. He rarely smiled, as if doing so would be some violation of the Secret Service code, but as he drew closer, she could see there was more than just somberness surrounding him today. His dark brows were furrowed together, and his jaw was clenched tight. It felt…grim…and her heart beat wildly for a moment, thinking of the times he'd come to her with bad news. She wasn't sure she could take more.

He stopped a few feet away from her on the tire swing, watching as she swayed back and forth, assessing her as he did every single time he came into her presence. It was as if he took in every single molecule to make sure she was unharmed.

"You should have returned my text," he said, and the deep timbre of his voice settled over her like a blanket, strangely soothing while, at the same time, her entire being danced furiously, as if called to a chorus only he knew how to sing. He put his index finger to the two-way mic in his ear and said, "Firefly located on grounds. Stand by."

"I'm allowed to move around the grounds without you following me," she replied, lifting her chin and arching one eyebrow in a challenge.

He was in a suit today, just like when he'd first shown up in Grand Orchard over two years ago after her father became the nominee for the vice presidency and the hate groups had come out in full force. It was perfectly tailored to hide his weapon. Perfectly tailored to sit across those broad shoulders like a second skin. It was a complete contrast to the black cargo pants, shirt, and military-grade boots he wore when on tour with her and the band so he blended in with the rest of their security team.

"Normally, you can," he groused, and she waited for him to finish his thought, and when he didn't, she prompted him.

"But?"

"For Greater Tomorrows has been ramping up."

Mention of the hate group had her dragging her bare feet into the grass and pulling the swing to a stop. Her chest tightened as it always did when they were mentioned.

"What have they done now?"

"There were pictures of the residence. They were of you and your family coming and going."

The tight feeling grew, fear and guilt twisting deeper, grabbing hold until she could barely breathe. Every time the group was mentioned, she was overcome with soul-crushing guilt. Terrified that the FGT had mistaken Landry for her that awful day at Swan River Pond and that her family was the reason her friend had been killed.

"What do the notes say?" She had to force the words out over the lump in her throat.

His jaw ticked again, and his hand went to the lapel of the suit jacket, tugging at it. "Does it matter? It's the normal spew of hatred. You don't want or need to hear it."

She didn't. And yet, she did. It was the same perverse reaction she had when there were negative posts or articles about her or any of The Painted Daisies. It was as if knowing what they'd said could somehow thicken her skin against them and take away the pain, but it never did.

Instead of responding or asking for more details, she just pushed the swing into motion again, sending the tire backward with as much force as she could. When she came forward, she almost slammed into Holden. He had to jump to the side so he wasn't knocked to the ground. She smirked. It was childish, but it felt good to get an unexpected reaction out of him. To prove he wasn't a robot.

She swung harder, and the limb on the tree groaned. Wood crackling.

Holden glanced up at the branch, assessing it.

"I'm not sure it was designed for a takeoff into space. Maybe take it easy."

As a little girl, one of her favorite things to do had been to leap from the swings, arms and legs spread wide, and then try to land perfectly on her feet. She rarely accomplished it, and she'd gotten a lot of bumps and bruises in her attempts. *You're not a little girl anymore.* Those had been her mother's exact words inside the private den of the residence with only the family present—well, the family and their lead agents. Like Holden. They'd been standing at the open door, within ear reach of the humiliating conversation.

She kicked back one more time, a big shove, and as she came forward, she let go, leaping from the swing and spreading her body wide. Unpracticed and much older, gravity took its hold fast. Her toes on her right foot barely caught the grass, and as she started to fall, she twisted, landing hard on her elbow in a way that made her wince and then burst out laughing.

Holden was there in a flash, feeling her arms, cursing under his breath. "Did you break anything?"

His face was so close to hers that if she leaned even slightly, she could kiss him. She wondered what it would feel like to have those stern-looking lines pressed against her soft ones. To have his focus on her one hundred percent but for a different reason. She was twenty-six, had been kissed multiple times, but never once had those kisses come close to making her feel like she did when *not* kissing him. In truth, she'd rarely felt any kind of sexual attraction to anyone, and certainly nothing like the heat coasting between them now so large and strong that if she reached out, it would burn her. Like touching the tip of a lit incense stick.

Instead of pulling back as she should, her body leaned forward, their lips nearly brushing. They were so close she could taste the wintergreen scent of his exhale. She swallowed it, longing and desire bubbling through her veins in an unfamiliar way even as her heart was screaming, *Danger!*

He stood up so fast it almost made her dizzy. As he stared down at her with brows drawn even more tightly together, his brilliant blue eyes flared with an emotion she wanted to think was something more than irritation before it disappeared. If she was going to be tormented by this ridiculous physical attraction to him, it only seemed fair he be tortured as well.

Holden's face turned into an emotionless wall, and he said dryly, "Let's not do that again, shall we?"

*Don't be so impulsive, Leya. Think before you act.*

The words her mother had said so often they had almost become a mantra rushed over her, causing remorse to roll through her. Not only because of Krish, but because she liked Holden even when he irritated her, and kissing her would end his career. She wouldn't have him in her life at all if she pulled another stupid stunt like this.

She rolled onto her back, looking up at the blue sky littered with twirls and curls of white and hints of orange as the sun began to fade. More shapes and colors tempting her to paint but also to pick up the baby sitar *Nani* had taught her to play and add the stringed notes to the air.

She felt his gaze on her, as always, and just like normal, she was confused by her reaction to it. When he looked at her…it was like he saw everything. Every pore, every vein, every muscle. But more importantly, every thought and wish—even the ones she thrust into the recesses of her mind, locking them away.

Wishes that went against everything that was right for her family. For her.

Desires she knew weren't logical and would lead to disaster.

The same disaster she feared awaited her friend and bandmate who'd let lust lead the way. Fiadh had gone from hating Asher to insisting she loved him in mere days. They'd gotten married only a handful of months after they'd started seeing each other, were on their honeymoon at this moment while the band took a break from their hectic tour schedule. It was the perfect example of letting your libido rule, and she worried what would happen to Fee when it all came apart.

Leya's friends thought she didn't believe in love at all, but that wasn't true. She believed in *jeevansathi*—life partners, soulmates—but she also believed most people confused lust for love. You didn't just stumble onto your life partner and know instantaneously they were the one. It was more complicated than that.

Lust was the reason divorce rates were so high. People let it guide them, and then when it faded—as it always did—they had nothing holding them together. There was very little Leya and her mother agreed upon, but in this, they saw eye to eye perfectly. Finding your match was a process, one that often came with your family guiding the way.

Which brought her back to Krish. The man her family and the star charts had guided her to since she was a teenager. Where once the idea of him—of them—had brought her comfort and relief, these days, it brought tension…and an inexplicable feeling of loss.

Was it just the argument she'd had with Krish at the inaugural ball that still hovered between them causing these feelings? Or was it something different…something more?

Krish was close to reaching his dream—being appointed as an associate justice to a California appellate court—and he needed his wife at his side. Needed to appear grounded in family. A married man who was stable and reliable. Not a single man looking for a mate.

But she wasn't ready to give up the band. She wasn't ready for this future that had seemed to come too fast. What would she do with the endlessness of her days in California, waiting for Krish to come home? She had her art—the other half of her flighty, creative ways that *Nani* had encouraged while her mother had frowned—but she would miss the band if she gave them up. And they needed her. The band had lost too much already.

Her stomach twisted and turned. A decision she'd made years ago, that she'd thought would always fit, now seemed like a shackle holding her back. She shouldn't feel that way about her life partner, should she?

"Are you staying at the residence this evening?" Holden asked.

He used the tone she hated the most. The one that made him sound like the robot she'd once accused him of being. Somewhere inside her, she knew it didn't fit him any more than the way his aura turned steely blue instead of flashing aquamarine at moments like these. She didn't understand how she knew these things about Holden, and yet she could barely even see Krish's aura and never understood his tones.

Her thoughts were making her sick. She needed to escape them, not only the thoughts but her emotions and expectations weighing her down.

With her bandmates off in separate parts of the world during their break, she couldn't go to them, but she still had a friend in Washington D.C.

*LEYA: Want to go out tonight?*

*LINCOLN: You feel like talking or dancing?*

As the "playboy" son of the President of the United States, Lincoln Matherton understood the pressures that came from being so visibly on the political stage when all you really wanted to do was get lost in the images in your head. He understood being the only one in your family who didn't fit the mold of the rest.

*LEYA: Can't we do both?*

*LINCOLN: Let's start at Pilot's for dinner, and if you still feel like dancing, we can hit EchoBar.*

*LEYA: I know you're trying to give up the bar scene.*

*LINCOLN: Bars, not dancing. I'll be eighty and still doing it.*

*LEYA: *** old man GIF ****

*LINCOLN: *** nag GIF ****

*LEYA: See you at 8?*

*LINCOLN: *** thumbs-up emoji****

She pulled herself off the grass, ignoring the tingling

that went up her spine as the action brought her into Holden's space. Ignoring the way his eyes trailed over her, leaving a mark.

"I'm going out with Lincoln."

His eyes narrowed, and she could almost hear his internal groan because he hated going to the clubs with them. Holden had never actually said he hated them, but it was the only time he ever trusted her to other men and women in the detail. She wondered if he'd hand her off tonight also. Wondered if, as always, she'd feel his absence. She didn't dare analyze why she missed him when he was gone. Doing so would bring her too close to that locked door in her mind. To the impulsiveness her mother accused her of and the behavior she accused her friends of—misreading lust for love.

# Chapter Two

## Holden

**_ON FIRE_**

*Performed by Garbage*

As Holden followed Leya back into the vice president's residence, only one thought was repeating through his skull—get away. He needed a break. He needed to put distance between himself and his protectee. She was driving him batty in more than one way.

She'd ignored his texts.

She'd left without him.

She'd almost kissed him.

And he wasn't sure which of those things pissed him off more.

What was worse, what had him screaming silently to himself, was the fact he hadn't pulled away immediately. The look in her eyes as she'd leaned forward, the way the natural honeysuckle essence of her had washed over him, making him hungry for everything she'd offered, had bent the last straw of his reserve. His control was fading.

He snapped himself back to the house as they approached, scanning the porch, the door, and the hedges. No movement at all. Emptiness. Her hips swayed as she mounted the steps, and his assessment fell apart. Never had he wanted to strip someone bare the way he craved doing with Leya Singh. It frustrated him and drove him right up to the edge every single day.

He should have walked away from her two years ago when the first hint of desire had slammed into him as soon as he'd walked into the recording studio in Grand Orchard. Instead of turning tail, he'd seen it as just another challenge. Admitting an attraction to his protectee on his second protective assignment would have derailed his career in a heartbeat. His boss would never have trusted him again.

Rather than admit defeat, he'd simply added, *Don't look at Leya's mouth* and *Don't stare at her hips* to the mental task list he kept in his head. It was a mix of daily to-dos as well as short- and long-term goals he'd kept running for as long as he could remember. He'd already checked off thousands to be here—on one of the most coveted assignments in the Secret Service. Protecting the president, vice president, and their families was why people joined, and if they told you otherwise, they were lying. This was the job. The suit. The earpiece. You putting your life between the enemy and the leaders of the free world.

Leya reached for the handle of the back door, and he stepped in after her, casting a wide glance over the entrance, the stairs, and the hall. He didn't have to do any of it, as there were cameras all over the place, watching twenty-four seven, but the continual assessment was a built-in habit after two years of being the only Secret Service agent on her detail. She had a private security team, one he respected even though there'd been plenty of reasons not to, but it was never the same as Holden checking the boxes himself.

When Leya had insisted on having only one agent with her, the Secret Service had balked, but she'd held firm. He never minded being a lone wolf, even preferred having the control all in his pocket. Preferred it so much that when Leya came back to D.C., and he had to revert into being a pack animal—the one who wasn't in charge—his mind and body rebelled at the idea.

As soon as they'd arrived in D.C. after Fiadh's wedding in Boston, his boss had called him in and said, "Take some time off." Most people wouldn't have balked when the special agent in charge of the vice-presidential protective division gave them a command, but Holden had insisted he didn't need a vacation.

He'd told himself it was because he didn't want to look weak, but really, the weakness was in staying. He couldn't stomach the thought of another agent watching over her, staring at the full lower lip hovering over a delightful cleft, or watching the way her hair danced around sharp cheekbones when she talked, or being mesmerized by the way her long fingers played with the rows of leather and silver bracelets dangling up and down her wrists. He didn't want another agent getting the text that begged for them to show up…

Jesus. He really needed to get a grip.

He watched her almost dance the way up the stairs, feet light and graceful. Her entire body would be tucked up against Lincoln Matherton's tonight. He'd be the one surrounded by her sweet, floral scent, and even though Holden knew her well enough to know she wasn't interested in Lincoln the way half the planet seemed to be, it would still be a challenge to stay focused. Instead of having his eyes on the room, the people, the movement of the crowd, they'd be drawn to her hips slammed against another man's.

As her lead agent, he was usually with her when she went out, regardless of the time of day. When he was the only USSS agent on tour with her, he didn't have a choice. But today, he did. Technically, his shift ended in thirty minutes, and he was suddenly, desperately in need of the space his boss had offered. He needed to get his priorities in check—his dick in check. His head back on straight.

"You'll have someone else with you tonight," he called after her.

She turned at the landing, and brown eyes ringed in deep, lush lashes looked back at him with a dash of sorrow and regret filling them. "I figured."

He frowned. She'd known he'd leave her? Why did that stab at him? "Well, now you know for sure." The snip erupted from him before he could stop it.

Her eyes flared with a hint of the anger he was stupid enough to like seeing. It happened so little. Normally, she was even-tempered, like the rest of her family. Calm in the face of the storms during the election as well as the attacks on her bandmates. But he'd been the one to see her break in her private moments. Not another agent. Not even her friends.

"You don't owe me an explanation, Special Agent Kent. Any *body* will do, right?" It was the formal use of his name instead of Holden or Captain Annoying as much as her arched brow and the emphasis on the word *body* that had him wanting to take the stairs two at a time and remove the look with his mouth pressed against hers.

He turned on his heel and exited the building.

Outside, he inhaled deeply, centering himself and attempting to clear the haze of lust and anger and frustration. He scanned the surroundings, noting the buzz of the lawnmower and the crush of steps on gravel as one of the uniformed division officers came around the house.

The first time he'd shown up at the Queen-Anne home on the grounds of the National Observatory, he'd been overwhelmed with the beauty of the place. The curved tower and pointed roof along with the wraparound porch full of plush wicker seating were graceful and elegant. But these days, he barely noticed them. Instead, he only saw what was out of place. The furniture that had been moved. The gardener who wasn't supposed to be on duty. Or the newly arrived agent, like the woman walking toward him.

Once he'd gone through the handoff checklist and stalked toward the command center, he almost changed his mind and went back. It was this reaction that pushed him finally over the edge, dialing his boss.

"I'm calling about that vacation you suggested," Holden said, cheek clenched and hating the words. Hating that he was asking to be relieved, and wanting to blame Leya for his weakness, but knowing it wouldn't be fair. This wasn't on her. This was all him.

Although, she had been the one to lean into him…to almost brush their lips together. He forced his brain to stop before it traveled farther into the realm of what-ifs.

"Ardell will take over as lead while you're out. Go visit your family. Forget the job for a few days," Roy Camp tossed back.

Camp likely knew Holden wouldn't be able to forget the job. He'd actually worry about it the entire time he was away, because they both lived and breathed the USSS. That was why Camp was forty and still single. When Holden's dad had been an agent, it had almost broken his parents' marriage. It was why his dad was watching carefully to see if Holden had reached his own tipping point. And maybe he had. But there was no item on his mental goal list beyond becoming lead agent for the president, and he was so close he could taste it. Every task he'd given himself since he was seven years old had led here. To this objective. To a life of honor and service.

As he got into the metallic-blue 1968 Pontiac Firebird he and his dad had restored when he was barely a teen, Holden debated heading home to his condo near the river. The place would smell stale after being vacant for months, and he wasn't in the mood to clean it. He needed someone to interrupt his solitude so he wouldn't wallow in thoughts of things that would never be.

So, as the engine rumbled to life, and he pulled away from the guard station at the entrance to the observatory, he headed over the Francis Scott Key Memorial Bridge to his parents' home. He let the schedule he'd had in his brain for the next two weeks—Leya's schedule and the duty roster—empty, and his stomach tightened. Uncomfortable with the blank spaces, he attempted to fill them. Maybe he'd paint the condo or refinish the scuffed wooden floors.

It was with a strange sense of relief that he pulled into the brick-and-white colonial in Arlington. It had been his parents' home for the last ten years, allowing his mom to finally see her landscape designs come to fruition—a parklike masterpiece. The mix of plants in the backyard was a bird and butterfly haven, and the enormous, multileveled patio was perfect for the entertaining his dad so enjoyed.

For as long as Holden could remember, their house had been full of his father's Army, Secret Service, and then National Guard pals—men, women, and their families who served a country that seemed to be falling to its knees these days but was still trying to raise its head proudly. Just like Leya Singh was bringing him to his knees, and he was stubbornly trying to keep himself from falling over completely.

He let himself into the house with his key, and the noise of pots and pans rang down the long hall to greet him. Despite the dark-wood floors and mahogany wainscotting, the space was still light because of the number of oversized windows the house boasted.

"Hello!" he called out.

"Holden?" His mom's face appeared at the end of the hallway as she wiped her hands on a towel.

A smile burst over her face, echoing in her eyes. Only the faint lines around them and the slight sag to her jawline proved she was over fifty—little details most people wouldn't notice, assuming she was much younger. Her dark hair was still thick and full without a hint of gray, and she was fit and tall with hazel eyes that typically showed humor more than any other emotion.

"Come give me a hug!" she demanded.

"Let me put my piece away," he said.

She nodded, retreating to the kitchen.

He slipped off his dress shoes and suit jacket before going into his dad's study where he added his Glock to the stack of weapons in the gun safe. The house was filled with the smells of his childhood, and when he found his mom in the kitchen, it was to find her adding shrimp to a pot of *fideuà*. The distinct saffron and fish stock aromas comforted him in a way nothing had all day.

He squeezed his mom's shoulders, and she draped her arm around his waist and hugged him back.

"Looks like I made it home just in time," he said. He kissed her temple and stepped away, asking, "Dad home?"

"Outside, putting together my new pizza oven."

Holden smiled for the first time in probably days, the muscles groaning from lack of use. "How long are you going to keep this one?"

She swatted him with the towel she'd had resting over her shoulder.

"I can't help it if the others were shit."

"Wow, cussing and everything. You must be serious."

She rolled her eyes.

"Go tell your dad dinner will be ready in about ten minutes." He headed for the French doors as she added, "And then you can tell us what's eating at you enough to bring you out to Arlington."

He didn't respond. He'd never understand how he could be in his mom's presence mere minutes, and she'd know exactly what he was feeling. A maternal instinct, he supposed, or just thirty-four years of living with his father who also kept his emotions buried for his job.

As Holden stepped out onto the wooden deck, the warm, heavy air hit him. It was early enough in September that summer hadn't let go yet, and the humidity was clinging to the sky even though the sun had fallen below the horizon.

His dad looked up from a large stone contraption where he was using an Allen wrench to tighten a bolt. The strings of fairy lights hanging on the latticework above the deck barely broke through the darkness, but it was enough to show the smile that hit his dad's face at the sight of him.

"Holden! This is a surprise!"

Holden rolled up his sleeves as he joined him. "How many ovens has she actually gone through?"

"I think this is the fifth one, but she swears it's the last," he said with a chuckle.

Even in jeans and a T-shirt he rarely wore, his dad still had a military aura to him. It wasn't just that he kept himself in shape, unlike some of his peers. It was a strength and power that emanated from him. Or maybe it was just the hair shaved so short you could barely notice the white that had crept into the light brown.

"Grab us a couple of beers," his dad said, waving to the mini fridge set in the outdoor kitchen.

"Mom says dinner is almost ready."

"Damn. I was almost done," his dad replied.

Holden pulled out two local IPAs as his dad rose from his work to join him. In general, Holden didn't drink, only a beer on the rare occasion, but he felt the need for one tonight. He needed to steady nerves that had been shaken by a dark-haired beauty and an almost kiss he couldn't burn from his brain.

They popped the tops and snapped the lids with identical movements into the open garbage can. They took a swig, and then his dad's eyes settled on him.

"How long will you be in D.C.?"

"Most likely till the end of the month, but I'm taking a couple of weeks off."

His dad's hand paused with the beer bottle a few inches from his mouth, taking him in, brows frowning.

"What the hell you going to do with time off?"

His dad wasn't asking because he expected Holden to be the job. He was asking because, like his mom, he knew the only reason he'd take a vacation was if something had forced it. Something pushing him to walk away. It wasn't like he had a girlfriend he was running home to or a pile of friends waiting to head to the beach with him.

He'd given all those things up for the dream he was living.

And he hadn't ever cared. Hadn't ever looked back.

When he didn't respond, the frown on his dad's face grew, and he demanded, "Want to tell me what's really eating at you?"

He wasn't sure he could. Wasn't sure he even knew the whole truth of it himself—not in any way he wanted to admit. But he was saved from responding by his mom popping her head out. "Dinner, gentleman. Before it gets cold."

They headed into the house where his mom had placed a colorful platter in the middle of a walnut table that had moved around with them for as long as Holden could remember. It had grooves and marks showing its age but was stained and polished as if it were brand new.

The three of them dished up in a comfortable silence. One that often settled down whenever his sister wasn't with them. It was Gia who normally kept the conversation going nonstop. And if she wasn't filling the house with her voice, there was usually a podcast or music blaring until someone finally hollered at her to turn it off.

"How's G?" he asked, deflecting from the conversation he didn't really want to have.

"Still floating around the globe like a waif," his dad said, the furrow in his brow growing.

"Just because you don't understand her job, doesn't mean it's not a real one," his mother scolded before turning to him and saying, "She's in Tennessee at the moment, but she's been all over the Midwest, doing a study on dude ranches."

Holden almost choked on the piece of shrimp he'd put in his mouth. "Dude ranches? Like in *City Slickers*?"

His father's deep laugh joined his. "You see my confusion. Before that, she was in Colombia, talking about deforestation."

"She's an agricultural journalist," his mom retorted. "She may not be saving the world with guns like you two yahoos, but she *is* trying to make sure we have one to save."

That put both Holden and his dad in their place. He hated to think about his beautiful little sister traveling around the world to some pretty unsavory locations, all in the name of journalism, so he chose not to think about it at all.

"You still on Leya Singh's detail?" his dad asked.

He nodded, shoveling food into his mouth so he didn't have to respond right away.

"I heard that sniveling weasel of a man heading up For Greater Tomorrows is about to announce his candidacy for president," his dad said.

For the second time in mere seconds, Holden nearly choked. He grabbed a swig of beer, and then looked at his father with narrowed eyes. "Where'd you hear that?"

"Meeting at the Pentagon. Smythe's been schmoozing military leaders to gain their support."

Jesus. Holden shouldn't have taken time off. He thought back to the images Camp had sent to the detail today of the Singhs coming and going from the residence and the white-supremacist, racist comments that had come with them. The USSS couldn't tie them to John Smythe and FGT directly, but Holden hadn't spent two years on the FGT case in Nevada without knowing what the man was capable of. His fingers itched to pick up the phone and call Ardell to check in on Leya.

Would he ever forgive himself if he wasn't there when something went down?

He already had a list of things he felt responsible for, including Landry Kim's death and Paisley Kim's attack.

"Anyone actually falling for his act?" Holden asked.

"Unfortunately, you'd be surprised."

It turned Holden's stomach. If that man was in charge of the country, they'd become another Nazi state. Holden was damn sure he'd never step in to take a bullet for the man. He'd lose his career. Having a man like that in charge was the only thing that would ever make him walk away from the Secret Service.

"He say anything directly against the vice president?" Holden asked.

His dad raised a brow at the ridiculousness of his question.

It had been absurd, but there was something eating at Holden about the pictures and the timing of Smythe's latest news. Something he couldn't put his finger on. Something that made him itch to get back to work.

As if reading his mind, his father asked, "You going to re-up for her detail next month?"

*Yes* was the instant response that came to him, born of years of wanting this, but then he remembered what had him calling Camp and making the journey over the river to his parents' place. The almost kiss.

Could he get a different assignment if he walked away from this one? Would it be a better one or a worse one? He'd been on Leya's detail for over two years. He'd joined her right before the Democratic convention, been with her in the dark months after Landry's murder, and had trailed after her to D.C. once Matherton and her father had won the election. He'd stood by as she mourned her friend and supported her family with a grace not many had, especially not in their twenties. He'd tagged after her as she went from her art studio in Truxton Circle to the bars and clubs of D.C. It had been painful to watch her bright light as it flickered, sometimes going out when she cried, sometimes shining so radiantly it was nearly blinding when she laughed and danced and sang.

It had always been easier to stay put, watching from the sidelines, when she was blinding, because he'd been less tempted to wrap his arms around her and provide comfort. Less tempted to kiss away the tears traveling down her heart-shaped face. She hadn't cried today. Her deep-brown eyes had been dry, but her light had still flickered. It had snagged at him as it had every time he'd seen it happen.

"Is it getting to you?" his dad asked. "The lifestyle?"

The unspoken reminder of the threats the Secret Service life had brought to his parents' marriage hung in the air. His father had once told Holden it was the hardest job he'd ever done, and that was no little thing. Not when his dad had spent his entire life in one form of the military or the other and was now serving as vice chief of the National Guard Bureau.

"It's not the same for me as it was for you," Holden replied. "I'm not married with little kids at home."

His dad raised a brow, knowing he'd evaded the real question. But his mom just sighed, "You'll never be married with little kids at home if you continue this way. Which means no grandchildren for me to spoil."

"Vera," his dad said, the warning clear. His parents had always let Holden and his sister make their own decisions about their careers and love lives. If either he or Gia asked them for advice, they gave it, but they never forced any expectations on them. Mentioning grandkids was probably the closest his mom had ever gotten to saying she wanted something different for him.

He'd let Gia pick up that mantle. A wife and kids did not fit with his life goals.

Neither did an almost kiss with a certain rock star.

"I'm getting too attached," Holden finally breathed out. His eyes met his dad's, and he knew his father understood what he was saying. Living and breathing someone else's life meant you knew more about them than you did anyone else on earth. You saw every emotion. You felt every emotion. And yet, your job was to be perfectly detached, stay alert, assess each possible scenario that could hurt your protectee, and stop the threat before it ever materialized.

"Damn hard not to after two years," his dad said.

"You were with Gore for two and Bush for one. Did you get too attached?" Holden asked.

"I wasn't the lead agent on either of those details. They knew me, and I knew them, but I rotated out with the rest of the team. I wasn't living their lives like you're living hers," his dad said, pausing. "And neither of them was as beautiful as she is."

"Howie," his mom tsked, but then she looked at Holden curiously. "Is that it? Are you attracted to her?"

There was no judgment in his mom's tone, just curiosity.

"No," he said, another automatic response, but he wondered if his parents could see through the lie. If they ever happened to end up in the same room as him and Leya, he was sure they'd see how every single cell in his body seemed drawn to hers. He could find her in a crowded space in mere seconds. He'd found her today on the tire swing without even looking up her phone's location. It felt wrong. And right. And the right was what bothered him the most.

# Chapter Three

## *Leya*

***MOST GIRLS***

*Performed by Hailee Steinfeld*

Even without the circle of dark-suited men and women, the customers in the restaurant would have recognized Leya and Lincoln as soon as they walked in. They were both on the front pages of the tabloids enough. Even if his dad's presidency hadn't brought him into the spotlight, Lincoln's art and his brooding good looks would have.

His dark hair was on the long side, flopping over his brows and curling below his ears in waves that looked messy and manicured all at the same time. He had his father's blue eyes and silvery aura, and if his dad had once been compared to a younger Mark Harmon, Lincoln could have been the man's twin at twenty-six. Narrow nose, sharp cheekbones, and a penetrating gaze that made you feel truly seen. Lincoln attracted human beings to him like vultures to a carcass.

Their detail tucked them into a corner booth with miles of empty tables between them and the next guest in an attempt to keep the dog-and-pony show at bay. The last thing Lincoln needed was someone overhearing their conversation and spilling more truths about him. The rumors were bad enough, varying from him being a sex addict to a drug addict, both of which were pretty much the opposite of the real man. Lincoln was almost as square as you could get.

Even when they'd danced their way through a number of clubs the year after their fathers' inauguration, he'd rarely drank. There'd only been one flukey incident that still bothered her. Instead, they'd spent hours drowning themselves in the movement of their bodies song after song. She'd been trying to forget the loss of Landry. He'd been trying to forget the loss of his girlfriend. They'd been perfect for each other in a best-friends kind of way. And yet, for some reason, it had rarely been her who'd ended up on the front pages when they were together.

Well, maybe that wasn't surprising. As a highly attractive, White male, he was much more interesting to the average viewer than the daughter of the Indian vice president. The only people interested in her were the hate groups who labeled her family *foreign insurrectionists*, no matter that her ancestors had been living in the U.S. for over a hundred years.

Once they were settled in the corner of the restaurant and had ordered their meal, Lincoln finally asked, "Want to tell me what's wrong? Has to be something pretty grim if you sought me out instead of unburdening yourself to one of the Daisies."

Leya had wanted to talk to Nikki, who was always the calmest one in the band. But if she told Nikki, she'd have to tell the others. Adria and Fiadh would have very strong opinions they wouldn't keep to themselves, and Paisley had enough on her plate from stepping into Landry's shoes. Leya didn't need to add the potential of her leaving the band when the tour was up to her burdens.

Just the thought of leaving was enough to make her queasy.

"Krish wants to get married next year," Leya breathed out.

"I thought you were happy to be engaged to him," Lincoln said with a frown.

"Not formally engaged. More like…promised to be. As in, everyone agreed to it," she said, twirling the new silver bracelet that had joined the others on her wrist. She stared at it a moment, finger sliding over the dragonfly charm. It was a little thicker than her other ones, not quite her style, but it had been an early birthday present from Adria. She'd barely had time to slide it on before the car had come to bring her to dinner, let alone call her and thank her for it yet.

"You make it sound like a business deal." He frowned, concern wafting over him, shifting his silver aura around him like a cloud. It was the same concern he'd had when she'd first told him Krish would be attending the inauguration ball with her.

Leya had liked the way she and Krish had looked together that night as much as she'd liked the pride in her parents' eyes seeing them as a couple. Krish's black tuxedo had been the perfect offset to her burnt-orange dress with piles of silk organza. He'd looked so handsome in it. His medium-brown skin and deep-brown eyes were almost glowing, his full lips turned up in a smile. But it was those attractive lips that had ended up causing them all sorts of problems when they'd completely covered hers later that night.

She shuddered. The kiss had not gone as Krish had planned. Or her.

"Are you being forced to marry him?" Lincoln asked when she hadn't responded, and his response immediately irked her.

"How could you even ask that? After all my mom and I do for Marriage by Choice?" He held his hands up in defense, but she stormed on. "Arranged marriages don't equate to forced marriages, or child brides, or any of those evil things that happen. My mom and I work really hard to put an end to those. Arranged marriages are just a beautiful way of families helping two people find the person they were supposed to be with all along. I'm grateful my family encouraged Krish and me to get to know each other. I could have wasted years of my life trying to find my soulmate and getting sidetracked by desire that I mistook for love."

Her words settled down between them, and he wasn't even upset by her vehemence. He just took her hand, playing with her bangles, and asked, "Then, why are we out having this discussion?"

All of her bluster disappeared.

"I'm not ready…to give it all up," she croaked. "The band. The things that make me who I am."

His brows raised in surprise. "They want you to give up the band?"

"It would be kind of hard to be at Krish's side as he's appointed to the appellate court if I'm prancing around the world onstage."

Lincoln's jaw clenched, and then he said softly, "They can't expect you to stop being you, Ley. That isn't a way to start a marriage or a life together."

"There's more to me than the band," she said, heart clenching because she loved her music. Loved recording and touring together with the Daisies. Loved being part of something with people who often understood her drives and dreams better than her own family did. She'd long accepted she'd never be out there saving the world like her parents or her brother, but it didn't mean she could just walk away without it tearing at her soul.

He nodded. "Would your art be enough to fulfill you?"

He'd been one of the first people outside her family she'd ever shared her art with. Black-and-white images she'd drawn with fluid and round strokes only to add a singular color at the last moment. Sometimes the color was just a flash, barely noticeable, sometimes loud and standing out, calling attention to itself. Lincoln had even modeled for her once, and she'd captured the curve of his jaw by running her hand over it with eyes closed, letting her fingers do the work. It was how she drew almost everything around her, using all her senses except the one the world expected an artist to use.

Her art gave her comfort. She craved it, but she also craved playing her baby sitar onstage. It was confusing, and she didn't have an answer for him.

To her surprise, he spoke for her. "You should be able to have both. One doesn't preclude the other. Being someone's wife shouldn't either. Someone who loves you wouldn't want you to stop."

He was right. And he was wrong. Being in a marriage meant sacrifices. Krish would make them as well. They'd make them together. It was just harder for her to see what Krish would be giving up at the moment, which wasn't his fault. She'd barely talked with him in months. A rare text here and there because the tension had never gone away since that stupid kiss.

"It's getting hard to convince everyone that the band is still worth my time. Especially with the attack on Paisley coming so soon after we got back together, and then Fee..." Leya trailed off, swallowing back the emotions that threatened to overtake her. No one was supposed to know about Fee. The media had swarmed around them after Paisley's assault. Her attacker was behind bars, but it had done nothing to shake loose Landry's killer like they'd thought it would. Just like it had done nothing to help them find Adria's missing sister. And Fiadh... Fee had looked even worse than Paisley after what had happened to her. She had a scar along her collarbone that would be there forever. Leya shivered even thinking about it.

"What happened to Fiadh?" Lincoln's brows drew together.

"Not supposed to talk about it. You know she's with Asher Riggs now, right?"

Lincoln nodded. "Think I caught wind of it, but it's not like I scan the internet every day for news about the Daisies."

It was a tease, trying to lighten her mood in a way Lincoln was good at doing.

"Someone came for him in revenge and hurt Fee instead. We kept it on the down-low because it was the last thing we needed the media to hear…another Daisy attacked. Everyone would think we were making it up for attention. Like a soap opera or a twisted episode of *Crime Patrol*."

Lincoln squeezed her hand again. "That's a lot to have had to handle, Ley."

"Which is exactly why I'm here. I don't want to think about it for a few hours," she said. "I want to dance and forget everything."

A flash went off at the perimeter the USSS had set, and one of the agents stepped toward the man wielding a camera. A whispered conversation took place, and the man stepped away, clearly unhappy.

"Your girlfriend isn't going to like it if that ends up on the internet," Leya teased, knowing he hated what was being bandied about in the press lately.

"Felicity Bradshaw is beautiful but not my type. She's the worst kind of spoiled," Lincoln groused, blue eyes flickering with something like annoyance.

"How much time did you spend with her before you figured that out?" Leya pushed her shoulder against his, trying to lighten his mood.

He sighed. "Supposedly, she wanted to commission a piece of art."

"Supposedly?"

"She actually just wanted to commission me."

Leya laughed, her heavy heart getting momentarily lighter.

"Still want to go dancing?" he asked.

She nodded. She did. She yearned to burn off some of this tension and anxiety. To let go and just feel the beat running through her. Lincoln raised his hand for the check.

Outside, their agents led them out the back door to a waiting SUV. Here in D.C., she never had her private security team from Reinard with her. It was always the USSS. Except, tonight, there was one missing. The one who'd been absent ever since she'd almost kissed him on the lawn at the residence.

It was her fault he wasn't there, and she regretted it. Not only because she'd made him uncomfortable but because she always felt naked without him there. As if he was the only one who could truly see danger coming her way. She pulled her phone out of the tiny clutch she'd brought with her, almost texting him, and then shoved it back away.

She'd been impulsive earlier—just like her mother always claimed her to be—but she wouldn't give into it again. She knew how absurd and irrational the need to have him near her was, but she also knew no one—not Krish with his dark, perfect good looks or Lincoln with his dynamic personality—made her feel the way one somber, disapproving agent did. And she didn't know how to merge that knowledge with her beliefs about *jeevansathi*, arranged marriages, and the star charts her aunties pored over to ensure she and Krish were the perfect match.

And on paper, they were. Even more, their families were a perfect blend. They fit.

But still, something inside her flinched.

Maybe that, more than anything, was what had driven her out dancing tonight. To escape from feelings she knew she shouldn't have. Lust that would never be love and yet was somehow disrupting her world and causing her to question the decision she'd made ages ago.

When they got to EchoBar, their agents circled around them as they moved through the cavernous warehouse. The crowd was thick, moving in wild flickers to the electronic dance beats as lasers shifted across the glass- and neon-filled club.

Holden had said places like this were an agent's worst nightmare. Crowded and dark. Loud and distracting. But for her and Lincoln, they were a place they could lose themselves in anonymity. Just one of the many bodies bouncing and twisting on the slab floor while their agents looked on from the sidelines, trying to blend in.

She felt a tiny stab of guilt at putting their details through it, but once Lincoln's face morphed into a stunning smile, the guilt faded. They needed this release. They needed to let go of some of the enormous pressure they lived under. Leya returned his smile with one of her own, lifted her arms in the air, and let the tangle of silver, leather, and beads she wore on her wrists slide around as they danced. Let the *ghunghroo* on the hoop earrings that had once been *Nani's* jingle in her ears, aware of the vibration more than the noise as the tingling notes got lost in the music blaring from the speakers.

She was in a black halter dress that started at her clavicle and ended mid-thigh. The silk slid across her as she swayed, adding another layer of sensations to the almost overstimulating amount of them filling the room—the heady scent of bodies and sweat and alcohol combining with the pulsing sights and sounds. Lincoln's hands on her waist were warm and comforting as he pulled her to him, joining their hips. Their movements became as smooth and fluid as her art. She wished she had a canvas. She wished she could spread dark ink over white while she moved amongst the colored lasers. She'd use bright pink to show how it stood out against the shadowy blue tones of the packed club.

As they danced, once in a while, someone would recognize them, their eyes growing wide, scanning them, and then trying to whisper to their companions even though talk was impossible. She knew what they would be saying. Knew what she and Lincoln looked like tangled together. They looked like a couple. They looked like people who would end up twisted in sweaty sheets by the end of the evening, but Lincoln's heart still belonged to another woman. Hers…hadn't been claimed yet. Hadn't been won by Krish, even if the star charts said he was the one for her.

Sometimes, she was worried the lack of sexual attraction she felt for anyone of any gender meant her heart would forever be frozen. Maybe she'd never have what her parents or grandparents or even Rishik and Devleena had. But then, blue eyes a much lighter color than Lincoln's flashed in her mind. Blue ones, not dark brown. Not Krish's. Eyes that tossed those thoughts of not being attracted to anyone right in her face.

But she couldn't have him. Not just because of who he was and his job, but because he would never fit in her world. Their star charts would be laughable. Their families would collide brutally instead of sliding harmoniously together.

Lust wasn't love. It was a flickering light that disappeared in an instant. A firework versus an eternal flame.

Lincoln's hand pulled her tighter, and she forced her thoughts aside, concentrating only on the sensations of her body aligned to his. One dance melded into the next. Faster, slower, ever-changing. Bodies colliding. She forgot everything but the rhythm shimming up her legs as the bass bounced along the cement floor. She lost herself to the voices and the beats the DJ scraped together one after the other.

She would have kept going for hours if the DJ hadn't announced a break, and the lights hadn't raised a notch so people could make their way to the bar, the bathroom, or one of the tables pushed around the rim of the room. Lincoln grabbed her hand, pulling her toward a vacant spot along a wall near the archway to the restrooms. Neither of them asked, but one of the agents thrust sealed water bottles in their direction. The last thing the detail needed was for one, or both of them, to pass out from dehydration.

The crush had moved from the dance floor to the perimeter as the crowd waited for the music to begin again. There was barely room for them to stand. Lincoln had his arm above her head on the wall, and they were tucked close together as they drank with their agents almost pressed into them.

"Hi, Lincoln!"

Lincoln, Leya, and a half dozen USSS agents turned their heads in the direction of the female voice. The woman stutter-stepped under the intense gaze of their entourage, and even in the semi-dark, it was as if her face paled. She gave a little chagrinned smile and a wave. Leya squinted her eyes, trying to place her while also admiring the guts she had to talk to them amidst a sea of agents.

"Hey, Astrid," Lincoln said with a chin nod.

An agent who'd placed himself between them and Astrid shifted sideways, catching Lincoln's eye before getting some unspoken approval from Lincoln to let her into their circle. She seemed to be a little younger than Leya and was as White as you could get. Light-blonde hair, pale-blue eyes, pale skin that was like flawless porcelain. She was short, maybe five foot four at most, with curves that were just the perfect amount. Leya doubted she had to fight them like Leya did hers.

Astrid smiled as she came closer, and her aura flickered, changing from pink to a vivid red. Whereas Leya and Lincoln were covered in sweat from dancing, this woman looked as if she'd just stepped from an icebox. Her blue silk tank was completely dry, and the A-line skirt that ended just above her knees made it seem like she'd simply shed her suit jacket and entered the club as many of their agents had. She, somehow, looked simultaneously out of place at EchoBar and also as if she could fit in anywhere.

"I'm surprised to see you here," Astrid said, eyes darting from Lincoln to Leya. "I thought you gave up the club scene."

"Just hanging with a friend," he said, eyes shifting to Leya. "You remember Leya Singh? Leya, Astrid works for D.C. Avenue Writers."

It clicked as soon as he said it. She was one of the speechwriters who'd worked for the company her father and Guy Matherton had used for at least a decade. Even though the president and vice president now had speechwriters on staff, they still used the company for one-off items the families needed. Leya and Lincoln had both used the company multiple times, and they'd even helped Leya with what to say to the press after Landry's death.

"Of course. Nice to see you again," Leya said, sticking out her hand.

"Sorry, I'm all sweaty," Astrid said, rubbing her hand along her skirt.

An awkwardness settled down between them.

"Last time I saw you at—was it the Landing?—you said you were giving up the club scene, too," Lincoln teased, and the woman preened under his gaze.

"Like you, just here for a friend," she said, and her eyes drifted out into the crowd and then back. "I guess I should head back to them…unless…you'd like to…."

She trailed off, cheeks flaring with embarrassment. It was sweet and endearing.

"Sorry, we were just heading out," Lincoln said. "We've got ice cream calling our names."

It wasn't the truth. Leya was ready to dance for another hour or two, but she'd never say that now. Not when Lincoln had used their code word they'd been using since their first foray into the D.C. nightlife.

He pulled Leya's hand back into his, tugging her up tighter into his chest. It looked possessive. The way a man held his girlfriend. Like she'd seen Fee's and Paisley's partners hold them. Astrid's eyes went wide, but she stepped away.

"Of course. Enjoy your evening. Let me know if you need any help with your next charity speech." She turned, stepped into the crowd with her blonde hair shimmering under the lights, and disappeared.

Their detail led them back to the SUVs parked right outside the club. Leya could almost hear the collective sigh of relief from the men and women who piled in around them. She felt another twinge of regret for making their jobs even momentarily harder. She wished she didn't need them at all. But her life would always require it—now more than ever—after everything the Daisies had been through, with Landry's killer still out there somewhere, and with FGT coming at her family even harder.

Her stomach fell as it always did at thoughts of Landry. She closed her eyes, resting her head on the headrest.

"Sorry, Ley," Lincoln said. "I know you needed to burn off some energy."

"Don't be," she replied. "I'm sorry I dragged you out when Astrid's right—you've been trying to avoid the clubs."

"It felt good to dance again." He bumped her shoulder. "I think we both needed a night off."

She smiled, but the full weight of all the decisions she had to make and everything that had happened to her and her friends over the last few months had already settled back onto her shoulders. The escape had been too brief. Too little. As if a mountain was still looming over her, waiting to crush her.

# Chapter Four

## *Holden*

***STORY OF MY LIFE***
*Performed by Bon Jovi*

After dinner with his parents, Holden drove back into D.C. and spent a few hours cleaning the dust and staleness from his condominium. The space wasn't very big with a loft that barely fit his king-sized bed, a tiny kitchen with a counter that could only accommodate two barstools, and a living area he'd squished a couch and a seventy-five-inch television into. The couch was black leather, the stools carved wrought iron, and the wall exposed brick, which made the condo feel modern and hip in a way Holden wasn't but still loved. Or maybe, he simply loved the fact that he'd bought the place on his own at such a young age in a city not known for its cheap real estate.

He landed on the couch at nearly midnight in sweats and a worn Wilson-Jacobs T-shirt from his college years, flipping through the channels aimlessly. What was he going to do for two weeks? He eyed the beat-up wood floors that he'd been meaning to refinish. He could head to the hardware store tomorrow and pick up what he needed, but as small as his place was, it would only take a couple of days to complete the task.

Maybe he'd actually take a damn vacation. But where to? And with whom? He literally had no one to call to take a trip with him. His stomach tightened uncomfortably at that thought before he pushed it away. He had his family and the life he'd wanted since he was a kid. The life he had no intention of giving up so his mom could have a grandchild or so he had someone to take a random vacation with.

Besides, he didn't need someone to go with him. He pulled up a bargain vacation site on his phone, searching for an island getaway where he could run on the beach, swim in the ocean, and maybe find a body to get tangled up in for a night or two. Maybe that was what he really needed. Just to get laid. It had been too long. The cravings he felt were likely a symptom of that more than anything.

His fingers hovered over the buy button.

His dad's voice came back to him. Smythe had decided to run for office just as the pictures of the Singhs had amplified. Holden and everyone else at the USSS knew that FGT was behind those pictures. The wording on them was too similar to the verbiage on their website. Analysts, with profiling skills better than Holden's mere master's degree had given him, said the images were almost a straight arrow back to Smythe. But it was all circumstantial.

If FGT ramped up even more and something happened to Leya while he was on some damn unnecessary vacation, what would he do? He'd never forgive himself. It was ridiculous because he wasn't the only agent capable of protecting her. He may have been the only one with her for months now, but he didn't have to be. There was an entire team ready to dive in, just like they had tonight, and he respected his peers with the same fierceness he respected his dad. Leya was in good hands.

*Lincoln Matherton's hands*, some primal part of him growled.

Holden's stomach flipped again, thinking of her and the president's son twined together on the dance floor with her curves fitting into Lincoln's muscled torso. Her dark eyes would be shimmering, and her long hair, with all its ranges of brown and black, would be dancing around bare shoulders in a dress short enough to expose her long legs.

Legs he'd often dreamed of being wrapped around his waist.

He rubbed his hand over his face. Jesus, he really did have it bad. Having mindless sex with someone who would understand it was just a one-night thing shifted up in priority. He should get dressed, head out to a local bar, feign a drink, and take the edge off this wild need that was building instead of fading.

And yet, he didn't move.

He just continued to flick through the channels, letting his mind fill with the things he knew about For Greater Tomorrows. He'd spent three years in Las Vegas, straight out of training, working shoulder to shoulder with other agents on a money-laundering case against the original version of FGT. They'd just hit paydirt, enough to shut them down, when John Smythe had closed up the fake charity all on his own. Then, he'd turned around and reopened shop under a new, slightly different name in Alabama, requiring the USSS's entire case to be restarted.

Holden hadn't been part of rebuilding it because he'd been sent on his first protective assignment. He'd gone back to college to spend a year with the former president's daughter at Bonin University. The USSS team in Virginia had been tiny, and the hours had been long. Hours he'd spent learning every single thing he could from the older agents, filing away the details for when he had his own team.

But it had been his experience with For Greater Tomorrows that had put him on the D.C. field office's radar for the Singhs. His firsthand knowledge of FGT and the area around Grand Orchard had his bosses sending him to protect Leya in his grandparents' hometown.

He'd done a piss-poor job of it. While she'd been safe, her friend had been murdered, and he wasn't the only USSS agent to think Leya had been the intended target. Maybe that, more than anything, was the reason Landry Kim's unsolved death ate at him so much. Or maybe it was the way Leya's eyes burned with tears and guilt every time her friend was mentioned, because she was burdened with the same notions. He wished he could ease them both of that weight.

Tomorrow, he'd go through all the information every agency had gathered on Landry's death. See if he could shake something loose while his mind wasn't full of Leya and her schedule. He shot off a text to Marco Hernandez with Garner Security, who'd been tasked by the band's label owner, Asher Riggs, to conduct his own investigation of the murder. After the attack on Fee earlier this year, the team had learned that the mystery man in the orchard on the day Landry died was one Angel Carter. But just as they'd made the discovery, Carter had disappeared again.

It was with a sense of relief, that his mind filled with tasks again. He'd spend the next two weeks hunting Carter down. That was more important than some stupid beach vacation. Having made the decision, his body started to relax. His eyes drifted shut as a rerun of *West Wing* played in the background, and he knew he should get up and move to his bed, but instead, he let sleep drag him under right where he was at.

His work phone ringing jarred him back to consciousness, and his neck screamed from the awkward position he'd been in for too many hours. For the first time in his career, he almost let it go to voicemail and then hated himself for even considering it.

He answered in a voice raspy with sleep, "Kent."

"FGT sent another note." Camp's voice was equally sleep-ridden at five in the morning.

"Is it the same old crap?" Holden asked. His stomach tightened as if he'd done a hundred sit-ups in a minute instead of the fifty that had given him his excellent rating during training.

"This one targeted Leya specifically."

His heart squeezed, and his stomach did another series of crunches as Holden sat straight up, hand going through the short bristles of his hair. It was longer than he liked these days because he hadn't found time to get it cut while on tour with the band.

"What did it say?"

"Leya's asking for you," Camp said, ignoring his question. "Go assess the situation. Tell us what we're missing."

"Yes, sir." The phone went dead, and his blood slammed through his veins as he jogged toward the bathroom.

*Fuck.* Leya had been threatened, and he hadn't been there. It was his worst nightmare. She'd be scared, her band members would be worried, her family would circle in closer, and she'd need the lead agent on her detail at her side. The person she relied on the most. The person she begged to come get her when things went haywire.

And he'd taken a damn vacation.

What had he been thinking?

Holden showered, put on his suit, fastened his USSS pin on the lapel, and was out the door with his Glock at his waist and his all-purpose utility knife in his pocket in less than ten minutes. His mind kept going back to Leya, imagining the shock in her eyes—the fear. He'd seen it too many times since he'd been on her detail.

While it had been her mom who'd swept Leya up into her arms when he'd delivered the news about Landry's murder, there'd been no one but him to keep her from collapsing when he'd told her about Paisley's attack. She'd leaned into him, holding on desperately while quiet tears dripped down her face. And then, she'd pulled herself together, demanding to see her friend with anger overriding her fear. He'd been there to see the same combination of emotions take over when they'd learned about Fiadh's situation just months ago.

He admired Leya's strength. All of the Daisies'. He'd promised he wouldn't let anything happen to her or them again, and he'd meant it. But how could he do that with FGT out there? How could he do it with Landry's murderer running free? He slammed his hand against the steering wheel, frustration and anger brewing.

The ride to the residence felt like it took twice as long as it should have, and as he inched closer, all he could see in his mind was Leya's wide eyes, frightened and sad, looking for him. And he wasn't there. It felt like something inside him had cracked. As if the glass wall he stood behind was splintering, brittle boundaries trying to tumble down, while he frantically tried to fill it with adhesive.

The holdup at the guard station irritated him when normally it reassured him. Once he'd parked his car, he strode purposefully into the command post, signed in, picked up a two-way mic, and caught an update from Ardell.

"Family's in the den," Ardell said, straightening her impeccable black suit.

"Where was the note found?" Holden asked.

"In a copy of *The Exhibitor* delivered in the morning packet."

The packet was a sea of newspapers and magazines brought to the residence for the vice president each day. It seemed old school when every single one of them was available digitally, but Ved Singh said he wanted to feel it while he absorbed it. The note being placed there meant it had been done so by someone who knew his routine.

Holden barely stopped himself from asking Ardell how Leya was doing. Instead, he bit his cheek and headed toward the residence. Inside, the home was as stately as the outside. Plenty of crown molding, white wainscotting, and beautifully maintained dark wood floors. The last time it had been redone, the decorator had used classic early-American pieces, plenty of gold-and-cream wallpaper, and heavily patterned furniture. The Singhs had done very little to it, except for the addition of a small shrine for the family and their staff to use for their daily prayers.

He took the stairs two at a time. Normally, the detail was almost invisible at the residence, but today, there were agents everywhere, including one outside the door to the den.

Holden didn't recognize the man, but he obviously knew Holden as he simply stepped aside to let him into the room. Even though the other occupants held a much more commanding presence, it was Leya who Holden took in first. Dressed in leggings and an oversized yellow tunic, she was curled into an armchair, as if trying to shrivel up. Her thick hair was piled on top of her head, and her slender neck seemed as if it would collapse under the weight.

When his gaze met hers, he saw a million emotions swimming in them. Anger. Fear. Frustration. Sadness. Her look flitted over him, shoulders sagging ever so slightly, as if in relief, and it sent a spiral of feelings through Holden he couldn't afford. Her look lingered on his lips, and the almost kiss filled the space between them again until he forced himself to turn toward the others in the room.

The vice president was standing at a side table, a delicate china coffee cup in his hand. He was a large, broad-shouldered man with an aristocratic nose, thick black hair, heavy brows, and medium-brown skin. Leya had gotten very few of her features from him, looking like her mother instead.

Zaira Singh was on the couch with her own cup in hand. She was tall and curvy with much lighter brown skin than her husband. She had the same straight, thick brows of her daughter and the same arched curves to her eyes, but she'd long ago cut her wavy hair into an elegant, tapered bob that swung around her heart-shaped face. Nearing sixty, she didn't look it. She had an intelligence to her gaze and a steadiness to her hands that served her well in her practice. She was a respected neurosurgeon, but she rarely performed surgery anymore, leaving the day-to-day to her son to manage now.

"Kent," Special Agent Sommerson, lead agent on Ved Singh's detail, greeted him with a clipped tone, drawing Holden's eyes. Sommerson's navy suit fit him like a glove, and his crisp white shirt stood out against skin so dark it was nearly black. The man's entire muscled frame was quivering with restrained anger.

"What do we know?" Holden asked.

Sommerson waved a paper evidence bag in his direction. Holden crossed the room to take it from him. He used a glove Sommerson offered to pull the note out and read it. His stomach and chest churned violently.

> *Your inferior bloodline makes you unfit to even be seen with Lincoln Matherton. For Greater Tomorrows will not allow you to spread your impure genes by aligning yourself with the president's son. If we see Leya Singh with Lincoln again, there will be dire consequences for the entire Singh family.*

Holden's head jerked up, but Leya wouldn't meet his gaze. Instead, she looked down, fidgeting with the hem of her bright top. What had happened with her and Lincoln the night before? Those thoughts made him almost as nauseated as the note itself.

"It came inside a copy of *The Exhibitor*?" he asked Sommerson.

With a gloved hand, Sommerson drew the morning edition of the tabloid from another evidence bag, and Holden took it. While it wasn't quite known for spouting alien babies, *The Exhibitor* did spread celebrity gossip like it was truth instead of supposition. Holden was surprised it was even in the vice president's stack of magazines. But then again, it was probably the way his staff kept tabs on any rumors about Leya and The Painted Daisies.

Today, the cover of the magazine held an image of Leya and Lincoln clearly taken at EchoBar. The bluish hue of the club's dim lights was streaked with a pink laser that cut across Leya's skin. She was tucked up against Lincoln, dancing—if you could call it that. Their bodies were aligned at almost every curve with her arms around his neck and his hands spread wide along her back and hips. Her eyes were closed. Lincoln's weren't. His were focused directly on Leya's face, an intensity there that dripped from the page.

The image was worse than anything his mind had conjured up the night before.

Holden's stomach turned again. It had been pounded into him from an early age, and then again in the USSS training, that words mattered. They created an image of you lasting long after you'd left the room, so he'd always been determined to use ones reflecting who he wanted to be. It meant cussing was a rare part of his vocabulary, and yet, he wanted to string a host of them together, back-to-back, while shredding the damn magazine.

He handed it to Sommerson before he was arrested for destroying evidence.

"Was the article leaked to them on *The Exhibitor's* end, or did someone from FGT follow Lincoln and Leya?" Holden asked.

"We don't know yet," Sommerson said.

"What do we know?" Holden snapped, and Sommerson's eyes narrowed.

"We're tracking the packet backward, every pickup and handoff. We're also interviewing every member of *The Exhibitor* staff who was in the office last night."

"No one at the magazine is going to reveal their source," Holden grunted out.

Sommerson didn't respond. He didn't need to. The Secret Service battled against the freedom of the press regularly. Warrants would be served, and it still wouldn't get them what they needed.

"You know how I feel about giving in to any terrorist organization, including FGT," the vice president said, directing his gaze to his daughter huddled in a chair. "But this is an easy enough fix, *beta*. We just announce your engagement to Krish and put an end to the rumors."

Leya flinched visibly at her father's words. "Dad, not this way."

The words were quiet and respectful, but Holden could also hear the steel beneath them. He wondered if her father could hear it as well. He wondered if she'd decided to not go through with the marriage, and he hated the tiny sliver deep inside him rejoicing at the thought. The piece of him that didn't want to see her tucked up against any man—Lincoln, Krish, or anyone else. Anyone except him.

# Chapter Five

## *Leya*

***WHISPER***

*Performed by A Fine Frenzy*

*SEVEN DAYS BEFORE*

Her father's words and her response hung in the air like a challenge she wasn't sure she'd meant. After getting home earlier than expected last night, she'd lain awake for hours, trying to unravel her feelings. A large piece of her didn't want to give up on her family's plans. Joining the Arya and Singh families felt right. Krish was everything she could want from a husband. *Nani's* sister, Aja Aunty, had insisted their star charts were perfectly matched. And the pride her mother showed when she talked of the marriage…that alone was enough to make Leya wish she could take the words back. If she gave up on Krish because of one argument—one kiss that had gone awry—was she walking away from her *jeevansathi*? The person the gods had already marked for her?

And yet, every time she thought about saying yes and setting a date, her body and heart rebelled. It might not have been logical, but it was the truth.

A conversation she'd had with *Nani* came back to her. It had been on the trip they'd taken to India with the Aryas where this entire plan for her and Krish had first been put into motion. *Nani* had said the only time people made mistakes was when they didn't listen to the voice inside them. "Your inner truth will never lead you astray, *beta*. Open yourself up to it, and you will always find your way."

How long had her inner voice been tapping at her without her listening? She wasn't sure, but she did know she wasn't ready to become Krish's wife.

It was her mother who finally broke the awkward silence that had settled over the room. "It is time, *beta*. We cannot, in good conscience, tell the Arya family no, and after this debacle"—her mother waved a hand at the paper Special Agent Sommerson held while her soft mulberry hue shifted about her—"we're lucky they still want to tie our families together."

This raised Leya's hackles, and before she could control her emotions, she'd snapped back, "Dad is the Vice President of the United States. It's not like it's a hardship."

"But you're a challenge, no?" her mother demanded.

Leya's stomach rolled over. There were so few things she and her mother would ever agree on. Their charity work against child marriages and her agreement with Krish were it. Beyond that, her mother considered Leya impulsive, flighty, and emotional. When she'd first joined the band, it had been tolerated. When the band had signed with Lost Heart Records, and she'd made music a career, it had baffled her mother completely. To her logical, science-driven mom, music seemed…inconsequential. A bit of fluff. Worse, it put Leya's inner self on display to the world in ways her mother would never allow anyone to see her…not even her own daughter.

"If he is truly the partner to journey through all seven *janams* with me, what I do for a living shouldn't matter," Leya shot back.

Her mother's nose flared. "That ridiculous notion of my mother's—"

"Perhaps we should discuss this later," her father interrupted in a way he rarely did. His jade halo was strong today, almost a solid line hovering around the edges of him as his eyes shifted between them and their Secret Service agents. He didn't want an audience for this very private discussion. Leya didn't blame him, but it still hurt to hold her tongue. "Until we can resolve this somehow, you'll stay on the grounds. Away from the cameras and Lincoln."

Leya rose from the chair, feeling like an eight-year-old being grounded instead of the almost twenty-six-year-old woman she was. She felt bound and caged in ways she never had before. Even when her parents hadn't understood her, they hadn't held her back. She fingered the tinkerbells on *Nani's* earrings that she wore almost every day, trying to find some of her grandmother's strength. "I agree to stay out of sight, but I need access to my art studio as well as the residence."

Her parents exchanged a look, and worry shifted through her. Lincoln's gallery was in the same building as her studio, but it didn't mean they'd see each other. She'd duck in the back and not even tell him she was there.

"I promise I won't see him," she said, trying desperately to sound calm.

It was the almost apologetic look on her mother's face that told Leya something was wrong, because Zaira Singh never apologized.

"We gave up the studio. Mirabel moved everything into the extra bedroom upstairs," her mom said softly, glancing at her assistant who'd been standing quietly at the back of the room. Mirabel's gray eyes grew wide, and her pale skin became almost translucent.

Shock rippled through Leya, and she barely held back a curse. Her fingers went from her grandmother's earrings to the layers of bracelets on her wrists, pushing them up and down, hoping one of the movements could soothe the fire burning inside her. "That was my space. It wasn't yours to give up."

"It wasn't practical to spend the taxpayers' money protecting it while you were off gallivanting with the band," her mother explained. It was so logical, so perfectly stated that Leya would only sound like a selfish, spoiled rock star if she argued it. But it had been her money paying for the loft, not theirs, and it had been more than just a place for her to paint. It had become her refuge, her saving grace, after Landry's death. She'd grieved and found her feet again there.

Leya lifted her chin and sent a betrayed look in her father's direction. "I didn't ask the Secret Service to guard it. I hardly make any demands of the taxpayers. I have one agent with me when I'm gone and a security team I pay for that has nothing to do with the U.S. government."

"Enough. It's already done. You will stay here, Leya." Her father's voice held a finality. The fact he'd said her name instead of *beta* was more telling than his tone.

Waves of emotions winged through her veins—ugly ones that weren't healthy. If she stayed in the den with them, she'd say something else she regretted, so instead, she left. She felt rather than saw Holden step in behind her, but her father's voice held him back. "Special Agent Kent, if we could have a word."

The heavy knot in her chest grew. She needed to let it out before it consumed her and made her into something she wasn't. She'd barely made it to the upper floor, headed for the extra bedroom where her art supplies had supposedly been placed, when her phone buzzed.

Fiadh.

"Hey," Leya said. "How's the honeymoon going? And why are you calling me in the middle of it?"

Fee chuckled. "I'm not sure those virgin ears of yours can handle the truth of it."

Even though she knew teasing was Fiadh's way of showing love, it still made her sigh. In a moment of weakness, she'd told her friends that the first time she'd seen a man's junk had been at a strip club Landry had taken them to years ago. Fee had somehow turned that into Leya knowing nothing about sex. She may not have gone all the way home with anyone, but she did have experience. She wasn't a sheltered eighteenth-century debutant.

What she hadn't told any of them was that the times she'd engaged in any kind of kissing and foreplay, she'd felt nothing. Certainly not the wild passion books and movies portrayed. She hadn't been filled with an overwhelming longing to strip the person bare and touch every part of them. The thought of seeing their hairy body parts actually turned her gut a bit. So, maybe it was just her and sex. Maybe she wasn't cut out for desire and lust. As if taunting her, the reaction she had to Holden danced through her veins. Whenever he was near, it was as if she'd been caught in an electrical storm, her entire body bursting with energy, zapping around like the lasers at EchoBar.

It was confusing. It was just one more reason why formally announcing an engagement to Krish and setting a date felt wrong.

She wanted to talk to Fee about all of it because as much as her friend teased her, she'd also understand. She'd help because it was Fiadh's nature to do so. To give of herself so others could be happy. But for the first time in a long time, Fee was allowing herself to be happy. Leya couldn't unburden herself while her friend was on her honeymoon, so she simply said, "You're ridiculous. Why are you really calling me?"

"Have you seen *The Exhibitor* today?" Fiadh asked quietly.

She swallowed hard and said, "Yes."

"I knew I was right about you and Lincoln Matherton," Fee teased.

She sighed as she opened the door to the bedroom that would now be her studio. "Nothing is going on between Lincoln and me."

"Are you sure? He looks like he's ready to throw you down on the dance floor and devour you."

"I'm sure," Leya returned. "We're just friends."

She was tired of having to repeat this over and over again. Bone tired. And not just from the conversation, but from all of it. From her mother's harsh words. From the fear that she'd sever the tiny bond she had with her mother if she turned down Krish. From the terror that had funneled through her as she'd read the note this morning. From the heavy guilt that settled in her veins whenever she thought of the FGT, because she couldn't shake the idea they'd come for her and killed Landry by mistake. What would Paisley and Fee think if that was proven to be true? Would she lose them? Would she have anything left?

"Ley." The single syllable expressed all of Fiadh's concern. "You were the first to tell me I shouldn't have kept what happened with Asher a secret. Don't keep them from me now."

Leya's chest tightened because Fee was right. All the Daisies had been hurt when they'd realized Fiadh had been keeping secrets from them. Not only about the role she'd thought Asher had played in Landry's death, but the private investigator she'd hired who no one could now find—not even the Secret Service. So, instead of holding back as she'd initially wanted to, Leya spilled it all, from the Aryas and the marriage request to the threat and Lincoln. She shared everything except the almost kiss with the somber Secret Service agent who was basically her shadow. That she couldn't admit to even herself without feeling as ridiculous as she'd called Fee.

"Don't stay in D.C.," Fiadh finally said. "Asher can get you out, anywhere you want to go. Hell, you can simply go back to his place. It's like Fort Knox there these days."

The entire band had spent a few nights at Asher's family's home outside Boston for the wedding. It was Gothic and gloomy and yet so utterly perfect for Fee and Asher that the entire band had laughed about it.

"I can't run away from my parents," Leya said softly. "I have to give them and Krish a decision."

"Then, tell them no. Break it off. You deserve to find someone who will worship at your feet," Fee said. There was a deep voice on the other end, and Leya knew it was Asher—the man who worshipped at Fee's feet.

"I don't believe—"

"In love. I know," Fiadh said. "But it's real, Ley."

"It isn't that I don't believe in love, Fee."

"Wait, what?"

Leya laughed softly. "I just think..."

She trailed off, worried that in expressing her thoughts, Fiadh would finally understand her concern for Fee and Paisley. What her friends had found was visible—tangible, even—but was it love or just lust? Would it fade? Would they still be ready to fight demons for each other if the passion had gone? Or would they end up fighting each other instead? Would they divorce and go their separate ways, searching for the next high that desire could provide?

"You just think?" Fiadh prompted.

"There's more than one way to find it. For you, finding Asher was like running into a burning building. I don't want that. I want to know that the person I tie myself to is right for me in all my lives. Right for my family."

The pride and joy in her mother's eyes the day she'd agreed to the Aryas' idea of Leya and Krish someday marrying had been one of her happiest moments. But she'd also found a great comfort in knowing she didn't have to search out a soulmate, making mistake after mistake. Her partner had already been found for her. And yet, all of a sudden, the decision she'd made felt like wearing a shoe that no longer fit. Too tight. The wrong color. Out of fashion.

She wanted to blame her doubts on a certain broody agent and the feelings he raised by just being in the room. To blame it on the heady rush she felt when he took her in, inch by inch. But that would be unfair. He certainly hadn't done anything to encourage her. Still, there was a tiny part of her brain wondering if what she felt with Holden was something she should feel for her *jeevansathi*? Not that *he* was her soulmate, not that lust was love, but shouldn't she feel more than the wave of disgust she'd felt at Krish's touch? Could she ever just simply get past her initial reaction to him? And if she didn't, how would that be fair to either of them? A lifetime of barely tolerating someone's caress seemed like a prison sentence.

"Love isn't always logical, Ley, but that doesn't mean it's wrong. Sometimes, allowing yourself to explore all the options helps you see more clearly when the right person comes racing into the burning building."

"Do you have a particular option in mind?" Leya asked dryly.

Fee laughed. "There's a hot son of a president."

Leya growled in protest.

Fee continued to chuckle. "Okay, how about the somber Captain Avenger you call an agent."

That caused Leya's heart to leap and jump in all the wrong ways. The idea of exploring Holden was too much for a body that already longed to do just that, but there was no way she'd ever admit it to Fiadh.

"You really are ridiculous, but I'm still glad you called," she said. "I miss you. I miss everyone already, and it's only been a few days. I can't imagine three more weeks without you."

"We lived eighteen months without each other," Fee replied, and her voice was purposefully light, but Leya heard the hurt behind the words. Leya, Adria, and Nikki had all but disappeared from Fiadh's life after Landry died. They'd all returned to their families, grieving in their own ways, and left Fee with Paisley and Landry's parents. What none of them had known was that Paisley had retreated into a deep shell, and the Kims had been so lost in mourning that it had fallen on Fiadh to try to keep the family together. There'd been no one there to hold her up. It tore at Leya now…the thought that she'd essentially abandoned her friend to find her way through the dark times by herself. Worse, Fiadh was so good at hiding what she really felt that none of them had truly understood just how alone she'd been until Asher had pointed it out to them this year.

It brought tears to Leya's eyes, and she said softly, "Never again, Fee. I promise."

"If you marry Krish and leave the band…" her voice broke.

"I'll still never let it be so long before we're together again. I swear it on all the stars."

Fee sniffled, and a gruff voice on the other end let Leya know Asher wasn't happy that her friend was upset. It brought a small smile to Leya's face. Fiadh had Asher now, and she could only hope and pray that it was more than a rush of lust. That what they had would become permanent…lasting.

They hung up with more I love yous, and then Leya stood, staring at the room her art supplies had been moved into, fingering the bells on *Nani's* earrings. She wished she could conjure up her grandmother's spirit and ask her what to do about all the things that were coming apart in her life. But there was only silence.

She'd been longing to paint for a few days now, but this room wasn't going to work as it was. It had been emptied of all the antique furniture, and in its place were her art supplies. They'd been set up in almost a replica of how they'd been arranged at the downtown studio, but the problem wasn't with the supplies. It was the lighting. Tucked into the gables, there was very little natural light, whereas her studio had been flooded with it.

She'd have to buy some heavy-duty lamps. She turned on her heel, heading for the door, only to find Holden standing in it, watching her.

The quiet intensity in his look stopped her in her tracks, breath catching and heart slamming into action. This… she never felt this with Krish. If it was lust…she still wanted it. She still wanted to experience it, just like Fee had suggested. But she couldn't. Not with him. Not with her

Secret Service agent. That knowledge sliced like a knife in her gut.

She wanted to look away, but she couldn't.

Instead, she let herself take in every piece of him, as if she was getting ready to draw him. He was powerful and calm all at the same time, full of a tightly coiled energy that he held back with ease and would only release in carefully measured doses, as if not even a bullet coming at him would cause him to panic. He'd just step to the side to avoid it. Even now, with one hand gripping the lapel of his jacket and the other swinging loosely at his side, ready to grab his weapon, he appeared confident and in control. Always watching. Always ready.

The longer she stared, the more awkward she felt, and it frustrated her—the way he made her feel and the way those feelings had her acting entirely unlike herself.

She stepped toward him and said, "I need to go to Kringle's Art Supply."

He didn't react, except for the smallest narrowing of his eyes. "I understood you were staying here today."

She had to admire him for not telling her directly what to do. In his role, he couldn't—and didn't—stop her from doing whatever she wanted. His role was simply to let her know the risks and then protect her whether she followed his suggestions or not.

"This isn't going to work." She waved a hand around the room. "I need to buy some lights."

"If you tell me what you want, we can have them delivered."

"It isn't that simple. I need to see them. Try them out. Get a feel for how they'll cast shadows across the space. This isn't something anyone can do for me."

This time, she saw his jaw tic in addition to the tiny tightening of his eyes.

"I have to agree with your parents. Keeping a low profile for a few days is what's best."

"You think some member of FGT is going to be hanging out at the art store, just waiting for me to show up?"

"I think you've received a threatening letter and that it's better for you to stay put until we get our arms around it." His tone remained calm, but now his hand was gripping his lapel with a little more ferocity, indenting the cloth.

"Like any one of a gazillion agencies has gotten a hold on Landry's death? Or protected Paisley? Or stopped Fee from getting hurt…" her voice cracked.

He stepped into the room, the distance between them shrinking even more, and she felt it immediately, the crackling of energy that drifted between them.

"I promise no one is going to lay a hand on you," he growled. An actual growl that sounded like a wolf sending his possessive howl up into the sky.

"I'm not afraid for me," she said. And it was strange because she wasn't. Not when Holden was there. This fear was all for her family because the note had said they would suffer…

She swallowed hard, tears pricking her eyes at the thought of something happening to the people she loved, and she knew he saw them, because he took another step toward her. He'd comforted her several times—after Paisley and after Fee. But this…this was something more. The flickering between them increased until she was sure if she put her hand between them, she'd get zapped.

Once, when she was little, she'd touched an electrical socket, and her hand had tingled for hours as if it no longer belonged to her. That was how her entire body felt now—as if it wasn't hers. She hated it, and she loved it all at the same time. She wanted to tease and tempt it, to explore it even when she knew it was the last thing either of them should do.

"You may not be afraid for yourself, but I'm afraid for you," he said quietly with his gaze boring into her. "And me." Her heart did a little leap at his words and then crashed into pain at the ones that followed. "If something happens to you on my watch, I'd lose my job. I'd be the laughingstock of the Secret Service."

Maybe it was the way her heart had leaped and then crashed, or Fee's encouragement, or just the way she was tired of being logical and wise instead of rash and emotional, but she poked at him instead of retreating. "Of course. This is about your job."

His shoulders went back even farther, rigid and uncompromising. "Excuse me?"

"It must be nice, being able to use your job as a shield. You can stand there, in the little bubble you've created, and let others live and love so you don't have to take risks with your heart and soul."

It was unfair because hadn't she been doing the same thing for years now? Hadn't she used the promise of an arrangement with Krish as a shield? An excuse to not live? To not risk? Maybe he knew it, or maybe he was just upset she'd called him out, but for the first time ever, she saw his anger directed at her. In truth, he rarely showed any emotion, and some twisted part of her reveled at having been able to force any feeling onto his blank face.

"You know nothing about me, Leya," he said, and his voice was dark with something she wasn't sure she understood but ached to discover. "The risks I take every day."

"To be here. With me?" she breathed out, the innuendo and undertone clear.

They just stared at each other, the energy screaming so loud she was sure anyone on the floor would hear it. But then, she realized she'd pushed too hard, as he carefully hid every single emotion until there was nothing left but the somber intensity he wore while guarding her. He retreated, glancing away and stepping back until he was outside the door.

"If you insist on leaving," he said, "I'll get a team ready."

It was a quiet rebuke, not only for wanting to leave but for the words she'd said when they both knew she shouldn't have. What had she expected? For him to risk everything for a random kiss that could never be more? For her? For someone practically engaged and completely off-limits to him as anything but his assignment? Stupid. She was so stupid sometimes, but especially when she let her emotions rule.

Her parents, her brother, and her little sister were all geniuses, with IQs off the charts and logic ruling every decision. She was the outlier. The flighty, creative one. Only *Nani* had thought otherwise and had encouraged her love of music and painting.

*"Intelligence comes in many forms,* beta. *The tests that attempt to measure creativity only score how you think, but creativity is not thinking. It's something bigger. Something tied to our souls. Who can measure a soul?" Nani had said.* "*Your genius is maybe even more important than your mother's or your brother's. You'll take yours with you into the next life, and they'll have to leave theirs with this brain and this body."*

She missed *Nani* in a way that grew stronger instead of weaker as she navigated all the important milestones in her life. She missed having someone who saw her as being perfect and whole and valuable regardless of her emotional decisions. Her grandmother would never want her to give up her art. Even more than the music she made with the band, Leya's paintings were part of her. She found peace in them. Truth.

And that was what she needed more than anything right now.

A respite only getting lost in a painting could give her.

# Chapter Six

## *Holden*

***I AM***

*Performed by Bon Jovi*

Holden's heart was pounding as if he'd just done a twenty-mile run. Hard, fast, sucking the air from him. He fought every nerve ending in his body that was straining to pull Leya into him instead of push her away. The amount of control it took to not prove to her how little he was keeping himself inside his bubble was at an all-time high. Only his training kept him from taking action.

He saw the moment she defied him and all the people in her life. Her chin went up, and her deep-brown eyes sparked with fire.

"Then, get a team because I'm going out," she said.

She breezed out of the room, and he took two giant steps back to keep them from colliding. He couldn't afford for his body to touch hers. He'd lose the fragile hold he had on himself.

As she stepped into the bedroom two doors down, he cleared his throat, put a finger to the two-way mic, and ordered one of the USSS vehicles to be waiting for them. He'd taken her to Kringle's many times when she'd been in D.C. It wasn't one of the huge box stores she could get lost in. Instead, it was a small, intimate place where the staff knew her well. But it also meant she'd be close to the gallery Lincoln Matherton ran in the same building as her old studio. Which meant it was the last place she should show up at.

He ground his teeth together.

When Leya came out of the bedroom, he saw she'd taken her hair down, and it was cascading around her in long waves, a kaleidoscope of bronzes and onyx shimmering like strands of precious metals. Strong. Vibrant. Leya.

She barely acknowledged him, swaying her way down the hall on light feet. Fluid and smooth, her movements reminded him of her art. Long, spiraling strokes. Motions he wanted to replicate on her skin.

If only she knew the risks he took every day just by being in the same room with her, then maybe she wouldn't have tossed out her careless words. She could destroy everything he'd worked for, every future goal he still hadn't achieved, and yet, he still showed up every day. But maybe she did know, and that was why she'd said them anyway. A challenge to them both.

Outside the residence, one of the bulletproof SUVs her father normally used sat waiting for her with an agent he truly respected at the wheel. Holden held the door, she got in, and he slid in after her. Marv took off, and they headed out the gates and onto the streets of D.C. The detail consisted of a single vehicle containing two agents besides himself, and it didn't feel like enough. He would have an entire cavalcade of vehicles, like when the president went anywhere, if he'd had his way. But if he'd requested more coverage, Camp would have thought he'd lost his mind, which in some ways he had. Ever since he'd heard about the threat this morning, he'd felt his hold cracking. His chest hadn't loosened once, and his stomach still felt sick. He wanted to bundle her up and run away.

The vehicle double-parked outside the art supply store, and Holden told Leya to stay put. He got out and scanned the street, getting a sense of the overall activity. First with a wide-angled look, assessing any outliers, and then with a more focused glance journeying over every person and burning their faces to his memory. He noted every posture, every flick of the hands, and every eye cast sideways. He hesitated on a guy twirling his cell phone while waiting behind a woman on the corner who kept switching her tote bag from shoulder to shoulder before moving on to a teen who kept looking at his watch.

No one looked toward the vehicle. In D.C., protection details were a dime a dozen, and this quaint area, filled with restaurants, boutiques, and galleries, saw their fair share. After skimming the street one more time, he strode into the store.

The owner was behind the old wooden counter where a TV hung, playing the news. The man looked up with a chin-nod greeting. He took in Holden's suit, as if knowing he didn't fit there. Then, he lost interest, turning back to the sketchbook he had open on the plank surface. There were two other customers in the tiny shop crammed with tall shelves and oversized easels, canvases, and frames.

Once he'd evaluated the situation, Holden returned to the vehicle, opened the door for Leya, and followed her inside. She greeted the owner by name with a warm smile. They chatted for a few minutes about the Daisies' tour, what she was working on, and the outlandish sketch the man was doodling. When Leya told him she was looking for studio lighting, he started jabbering about temperatures in units of Kelvin. He took Leya to an open space at the back, pulling folding lighting from shelves. It reminded Holden of the lights used in photography studios.

The owner and Leya talked size of the room at the residence and LED bulbs while Holden continued to do what he did best. Scan. Assess. Repeat. The two other customers, one male and one female, had watched Leya move through the store, and it made him itchy. The back of his neck crawled in a way he recognized as feeling out of control. A feeling he didn't care for—ever.

"Hey, Trent, can you ring me up?" the male customer hollered.

"Hold your pants, Radio. I'm coming," the owner replied with a grouse in his voice. Trent turned to Leya. "This one? Shall I haul it up front for you?"

She nodded. "I guess it's my best option."

She grabbed a set of bulbs he'd shown her, and the three of them made their way up front with Trent carrying the larger box.

As they reached the counter, the newscast changed topics. "And now, breaking news on the political front. Seems like the president and vice president might be more than political allies these days. Speculation is running rampant that they may soon be in-laws. We want to know your thoughts, so head over to our social media page and cast your vote."

Holden's heart snagged, and Leya froze completely as the image of her and Lincoln from the cover of *The Exhibitor* flashed onto the screen above the station's social media handles.

The reporter continued, "The official response from both the president's and vice president's offices has been, 'No Comment.' But we have a reporter in the field today at Lincoln Matherton's gallery in downtown D.C. What have you found out, Macey?"

The screen flipped to a black-haired, brown-skinned woman in a suit outside the gallery just a few blocks down the street. Holden tensed, and he shot a look out the store windows to make sure they hadn't been discovered before pulling his eyes back to the television and the reporter. She was standing in front of the gallery's windows. A few steps away, two USSS agents stood at the door, sunglasses reflecting the puffy skies and tall buildings.

"While a source close to the executive office said neither Lincoln Matherton nor Leya Singh will be talking to the press today, we also learned there was a threatening note delivered to the vice president's home early this morning, demanding the two stop seeing each other or else there would be consequences."

Leya stiffened beside Holden, and he felt like the air had been punched from his gut.

How the hell had she gotten ahold of that information? Who inside the circle had dropped it to the media? Anger swelled. A need to throw every person who worked for the president and vice president into a room and grill them overtook him along with a contrasting need to get Leya as far away as possible from all of this. The urge to pick her up and run that had filled him earlier was only growing stronger by the moment.

Trent and his two customers both darted glances in Leya's direction, their eyes going wide before the reporter's words drew them back to the screen.

"What everyone in America wants to know, Ralph, is whether the two are actually a couple," the reporter continued. "Leya Singh has been very vocal in her rejection of forced marriages while remaining a supporter of arranged ones, and it's been assumed her family would announce their plans when they were ready. I doubt they ever intended those plans to include the president's son. But as you can see from this painting hanging on the wall in Lincoln's gallery, I think love has bloomed where no one expected it. Like a fairy tale where the prince and princess of two kingdoms collide."

The camera zoomed in on a painting through the windows of the gallery.

You couldn't see the woman's face because she was turned away from the artist. Her spirals of dark-brown and black hair were pulled partially up by a warm brown hand. Dozens of bracelets in different mediums of leather and silver and beads traveled down the woman's arm. Her back was bare, scraps of deep-orange silk barely seen along her sides before it gathered just below the divot at the base of her spine. It looked like she was in motion, hips swaying, skin glistening. You could almost hear the music she was moving to coming from the painting.

Even if people didn't know Leya Singh personally enough to recognize her from the back, they might still remember the press images of her dress from the inaugural ball. But Holden had both her and the dress burned into his brain. This painting put it all on display. What was even more telling than the beauty of the woman was the reflection in the mirror that had been painted above her shoulder. You couldn't see much more than the dark-blue eyes as a man watched her dance, gaze full of longing, but everyone knew the Mathertons for the brilliance of their blue eyes. So, even though the painting didn't name either Lincoln or Leya, it was clear to the world who the people were.

The woman in the art store brought Holden crashing back to reality as she started throwing questions in Leya's direction. "Are you going to marry the president's son? Are you engaged? Did your parents arrange the marriage, or did you fall in love?"

"Get out of my store, Linda," Trent growled.

Linda turned wide eyes to him. "Excuse me?"

"Get out before this Secret Service agent tosses you out."

Holden wouldn't toss her. Not unless she posed a physical threat to Leya. But the woman clearly didn't know that as she turned her gaze to him, eyes growing larger in her pale face. She threw down the basket of supplies she'd been holding and stormed out.

"I'm going to ring Leya up first, Radio," Trent said.

The man just nodded and stepped away from the counter.

Holden could feel the emotions simmering in Leya, much as they had when he'd first arrived at the residence this morning. The anger and fear and frustration were back, but she stayed calm while finishing the transaction. As a rule, Secret Service agents didn't carry bags. This was so they had their hands available at all times, but today, he needed to get her out of the store and off the street as quickly as possible. So, he grabbed the box with the light, flung it over his shoulder, and tapped his mic as he opened the door with Leya right behind him. He caught movement at the streetlight out of his peripheral vision. The news crew was making their way toward them with the woman from the store pointing in Leya's direction.

Inside, his heart was panicking, slamming in his chest, but his body reacted with the cool calm he'd been trained to have. He threw the damn light into the back of the SUV and all but tossed Leya inside just as the reporter reached them.

"Leya, what's the story with you and Lincoln Matherton? Are you on the way to see him? Why isn't anyone commenting? Do you know who sent the note? Was it Felicity Bradshaw? Is she upset that you've upstaged her?"

Holden slammed the door shut, and the outside sounds became muffled and indistinct.

"Go, Marv," he said.

Marv hit the gas, and the wheels all but spun out. Horns honked as they sped away from the store.

When he turned his gaze back to Leya, she was shaking. "What have I done? Dad is going to be furious."

"You couldn't have known the press would be there. Couldn't have known—" He shut up as the agent in the passenger seat cut a glance his way. He didn't know the man at all. What he did know was that Holden had no right to console her. No right to make sure her life, which had already tipped slightly over, didn't turn itself completely upside down. He was there to protect her, and he'd done that.

Except, his job was also to protect the integrity of the office of the president and vice president. That meant the integrity of their families. And this… The media would make this into exactly what it hadn't been—one lover sneaking over to see another. It would play right into the FGT's hands, spur them on, bringing havoc and chaos.

As if on demand, her phone buzzed.

She glanced down, clearly expecting one or both of her parents, because her face was already grimacing, but then shock rolled over it, and the phone slipped out of her grasp.

He grabbed it before it could hit the floorboard.

*UNKNOWN NUMBER: We warned you.*

It buzzed again just as the voices in his earpiece went nuts. A video came across the phone's screen, showing the gates to the high school Leya's sister attended. In the video, an explosion tore through the air that had him jumping in his skin even though he wasn't anywhere near it. The brick pillars supporting the gate burst apart, and the heavy wrought iron was flung from its hinges.

In his ear, the entire USSS detail protecting the Singhs went nuts. A lockdown order was issued. Marv pressed on the gas, zipping through crowded streets, heading for the bunker under Number One Observatory Circle.

Leya's phone vibrated again, and he was tempted to throw it from the car, except he knew they needed every single ounce of evidence and information they could get. If this was FGT, they'd just started a war they wouldn't win.

*UNKNOWN NUMBER: Next time, it won't be a gate. It'll be a body.*

Chills coated his spine, fear reaching up inside him and strangling his lungs until he almost couldn't breathe. Could barely think.

The same thought he'd had all morning returned. He needed to get Leya out of D.C.

Out of the damn limelight.

Somewhere no one knew her.

Somewhere safe.

# Chapter Seven

## *Leya*

***LIVING DANGEROUSLY***
*Performed by Dami Im*

Something was wrong. Something worse than what the reporter had said on the news. Something worse than the text message. Something Holden had seen on her phone after it had slipped from her hand. Leya tried to get it back, and he just tucked it into his suit jacket while their driver sped through the streets. She gasped as they barely slipped by a sedan on the right side, hitting the sidewalk and still going.

"What is it?" she demanded, fear reaching up into her throat, strangling her and making the three words almost unintelligible.

"We're going into lockdown."

"Why? What happened?"

None of the agents talked.

"Tell me, damn it! I have a right to know."

Silence.

She was fuming. At herself. At them. At FGT and all the damn hate groups.

The arm of the gate at the observatory opened as they sped toward it, letting them in without question. Holden hauled her out of the car, practically draping his body over hers while the other two agents surrounded them. They hustled her through the main doors to an elevator that was already sliding open. It led to a level she'd only seen one other time—the day they'd first arrived at the house and been assured of their safety.

They were going down into the secure bunker.

Her heart was galloping so fast she couldn't breathe. Her vision got spotty, and she sagged against the elevator wall. Then, Holden was there, wrapping an arm around her waist. Heat spiraled through her at his touch, pulling her back from the edge of blackness.

"Don't pass out, Leya." Holden's voice was gravelly, deep, and full of emotions he normally hid. Anger. Fear. Worry.

The doors had barely shifted open before they were hurrying her down a cement hallway to another set of metal doors thicker than a bank vault. As she was pulled inside, she saw her mother, her assistant, and her detail were already there.

"Firefly secure," Holden said next to her, the code name he rarely used sending a shiver up her spine as the heavy doors clanged shut.

"Where's Dad?" Leya asked, the fear inside her ratcheting up another notch.

"In lockdown at the White House. Safe. Whereas Ria…" Her mother's voice trailed off, real terror showing on her face, and Leya's heart plunged and dove again. "Why could you not do this one thing, Leya? All we asked was for you to stay put. Instead, you did what you are always doing. Running off impulsively. This time straight to Lincoln! What is going on with you?"

"What's wrong with Ria?!" she cried.

"They threw a bomb at her school," her mother said, tugging at the cuffs of her suit.

"*Nahin*!" Leya exclaimed, shock and horror reeling through her. Her knees finally gave out, and she sank to the floor. The carpet there was thick and luxurious because it was rarely stepped on. The softness was a complete contrast to the harsh words—the harsh reality of a bomb at her sister's school.

"Genius is secure. She's here," her mother's lead agent said, and relief spiraled over her mother's normally impassive face, whereas Leya's heart still banged wildly.

Just moments later, the enormous door swung open again, and Ria burst into the room, followed by her detail. Her mom rushed toward Ria, wrapping her in a hug that spoke of love and relief. It was the exact opposite of the welcome Leya had gotten, and it ripped a hole into her already shredding heart.

"You're safe, *beta*," their mother whispered in Ria's hair, rubbing her back.

And then, as if she'd heard Leya's tortured thoughts, her mom held out her hand to Leya. She took it, pulling herself up from the ground and surrounding her mother and sister in a fierce hug.

"Is Rishik okay?" Leya asked softly.

"He was in surgery. They're letting him finish," her mother uttered, the comforting scent of her mother's Chanel perfume wafting over her, soothing her but also filling her with guilt.

"I'm sorry. I'm so sorry," Leya said, her words mixed with a sob.

"Hush, *beta*. It'll be okay." Her mother's voice held regret. A rare apology for the ruthless words she'd thrown out when Leya had walked in. A phone rang, her mother's familiar tone, and Mirabel scurried forward to hand the cell phone to her mom before stepping back and tightening her blonde ponytail.

"They are both here, Ved," her mother's voice cracked again. "Safe. We're all safe."

Leya pulled Ria into her once more. Whereas her hair had always been a mix of browns, her sister's was almost black. She had a full oval face, their father's nose, and thin brows she highlighted with liner. She was shorter than Leya and rounder, fuller, with a cotton-candy aura. She looked like an adorable doll, but she was the smartest of them all. Ria could do advanced math in her head in the blink of an eye and used it to study the universe, even though she was only in high school.

"Are you okay?" Leya whispered, palm to her sister's cheek, while their mother stepped away to continue talking to their father.

Ria nodded, but her voice shook as she replied, "It was scary, hearing the bomb go off and having the agents pretty much carry me to the car. But they said no one got hurt."

Her sister shuddered just as a phone started chiming again. It was a Painted Daisies song. Holden took Leya's phone out of his suit pocket.

"We need the texts," he said. "Don't delete them."

Then, he handed her the phone. It was Paisley on a video call. She hit the screen, and her friend's face came into view with her dark-brown eyes drawn together in a frown. Her sleek black hair was up in a messy bun, and she had her finger on the star birthmark at the corner of her eye. It was a nervous tell Paisley had all but stopped using these days. "Leya, what's going on? Are you okay? Is Ria okay?"

Behind Paisley, Jonas's face appeared. His green eyes were drawn together as much as Paisley's. His hair flopped in front of his eyes as he leaned into the phone before he pushed his bangs aside with a large hand. He had Paisley tucked up against his chest, and when they were together like this, their auras blended into an almost metallic shimmer.

"We're all okay," Leya said. "Ria is fine. She's here with Mom and me. Dad is at the White House. Rishik is at the hospital."

"Is it really because of what's going on with you and Lincoln?"

Leya let out an irritated breath. "There is nothing between Lincoln and me. You know how the media likes to chase him and blow every person he's friends with into a love interest. We're friends. That's it. But yes, I think the hate group targeting Dad is responsible. You know, they don't want my unclean brown hands touching his pale white ones."

"Fuck that," Jonas muttered.

"Your father wants to have a family meeting," her mom said, bringing Leya back to the room and away from the call. "We'll have to do it virtually while he's stuck in the White House bunker."

"I have to go, Paise. I'm okay. Can you please let everyone know? Tell them I'll call as soon as I can," Leya said.

Paisley nodded. "I love you. Please…" her voice cracked. "Please stay safe."

"Love you, too. I'm in the safest place I can be at the moment."

Jonas's eyebrow raised. "The bunker, right? There's really a bunker."

It lightened the stranglehold on Leya's heart ever so slightly. "I can neither confirm nor deny."

Jonas and Paisley both smiled.

"Talk soon! Love you," she said and then hung up.

The room was designed as a combination of a living space and a command center to be used in case of an attack. It was loaded with supplies, oxygen tanks, and every possible thing that might be needed to stay underground for weeks, and yet it was a weird combination of luxury and simplicity. Rich linens and cold cement. Behind her, Mirabel futzed around with a keyboard sitting beneath a huge screen and brought her dad's face into view. He was in a similar location below the White House grounds.

"*Achaa*, you are all okay," her father said, relief dripping from his voice even though his expression was somber.

Leya's eyes filled. She'd done this. She'd sent the evil after them, made them all worry, and put an even bigger target on their backs. If she'd just stayed at the house like they'd asked her to, none of this would have happened.

"I'm sorry," Leya said again, her voice breaking.

Silence hung in the air between the family and the agents waiting behind them. Having people listening to every word was the hardest thing to get used to when you had security around you all the time. Nothing was really private.

"We need to stop the rumors, *beta*, by announcing your engagement—unless there is something you need to tell us about you and Lincoln," Dad said. His eyes assessed her carefully, but she had nothing to hide.

Leya shook her head. "No. We're just friends. Good friends." She didn't miss the look her parents shared. "What?"

"The painting…" her mother said. "Plus, the photograph. Are you as sure of Lincoln's feelings as your own?"

Leya wanted to roll her eyes and scream yes, but then she paused. She'd been certain there was nothing between them but friendship. A connection because of their similar situations. He was still pining his lost love, wasn't he? She swallowed hard.

"I can only know my own feelings," she said softly. "Lincoln is just a friend."

"I'll call Sid Arya. We'll have a formal announcement made by tomorrow and let the press know the engagement party is next weekend," Dad said.

Leya was already shaking her head. "It will look like a cover-up, Dad. And I am not ready to marry Krish."

"An engagement does not mean you have to marry right away," Mom replied, irritation showing in her voice. "This needs to be handled quickly, Leya."

Back to her given name and away from the term of endearment her parents preferred. She swallowed hard, and the words that had been bouncing back and forth inside her since her parents had first mentioned the engagement yesterday finally broke free. “I don’t think I’ll ever be ready to marry Krish.”

Silence again. Leya’s mother put her hand to her forehead, frustration causing her brow to wrinkle. “It’s okay to be nervous. It’s a commendation to you that you are. Marriage is not to be entered into lightly, but you agreed years ago. You told us this was what you wanted. If you changed your mind, you should have said so before now.”

“I didn’t know my own heart until now.”

Her mother grimaced but didn’t speak. She didn’t have to. Leya knew her mother’s thoughts. The word heart was almost as bad as *Nani* using the word *jeevansathi*.

Dad frowned. “Is there someone else, *beta*?”

Leya immediately shook her head, but her entire body prickled with the awareness of the silent agent behind her. She could practically feel his steely gaze boring into the back of her head. They could never be anything, but for the first time in her entire life, she was determined to explore this physical reaction. If it couldn’t be with him, there had to be someone else who would make her entire being light up in the same way, wasn’t there? Was it fair to her or Krish if she went into their marriage already knowing it was less in even one way? A significant way, even though the physical aspects of a marriage were not the most important.

“There is no one else, Dad.” She swallowed hard. It was the truth and not. “But I don’t believe we would suit. I’m not ready to give up my career for his, and he needs someone who can be there at his side for every election and every political event.”

“I didn’t give up my career for your father’s. You can certainly do both.” Her mother’s voice was softer, cajoling, as if she could still convince Leya.

“Have you heard Krish’s opinion about this?” Leya asked. “The last he and I talked, he wanted someone who was there every step of the way. He asked me when I would be ready to stop playing rock star."

She'd held that conversation close to her chest, certain he'd said it in a moment of frustration after she'd pulled back from his kiss. She hadn't schooled her expression closely enough. But the kiss had been…so cold. So dry. It had repelled her in a way she hadn't expected, and he'd seen her response. His words had been in retaliation, stemming from a hurt ego. She'd forgiven him because there would always be bumps in a new relationship, a period of getting to know each other both physically and emotionally. But the truth was, her body had already rejected him.

Her parents exchanged another look.

"We're putting together a statement about the bombing at the school," Dad said. "Domestic terrorism will not be tolerated. We will come down on those responsible with the full force of the law. But we need to make sure we don't aggravate the situation."

He was telling her to stay away from Lincoln. That was fine. She hadn't heard from him at all. He was likely as upset about everything being thrown at them as she was. She'd been the one to ask him to go dancing the night before. This was on her.

"I suggest the Secret Service take Leya out of D.C. Somewhere she isn't known and the press won't easily find her. I also suggest that, until we know who leaked the information to the reporter, we keep the people with the knowledge of her location to a bare minimum," Holden's voice rang through the room from behind her.

When she risked looking at him, she saw a grimness to him she'd never seen before. A look she couldn't quite fathom. He'd stepped into what was essentially a family conversation, and while it wasn't unusual for the USSS to offer solutions in situations like this, somehow Holden's statement felt deeper…more…

Leya couldn't afford to think that way. Couldn't afford to let her impulsive soul get wind of even a hint of hope. She'd pushed him earlier, and he'd been clear that she was a job and that was it. She already knew they could never be anything. And yet, the idea of disappearing from the world with him for a few days, escaping the rules and boundaries that bound them, was tantalizing.

It would be bliss and disaster rolled all into one.

And she certainly couldn't afford another disaster.

Not after the multitudes she'd already made.

# Chapter Eight

***I LOVE PLAYIN' WITH FIRE***

*Performed by The Runaways*

*THE SAVIOR: What did you do?*

*BLOCKED: Something. The inaction was killing me.*

*THE SAVIOR: You don't get to decide when we come out of the shadows. I've been planning my moves for decades with patience and an eye on the long game. It's a chess match, not a fucking game of UNO.*

*BLOCKED: But now I've placed all the wild cards in our hands.*

*THE SAVIOR: I won't have some blonde Barbie ruining a lifetime of planning.*

*BLOCKED: Better Barbie than Ken. The emasculated plastic toy could never execute something like this. You trained me to find these opportunities.*

*THE SAVIOR: You've thrown yourself into the wind for nothing. For a goddamn crush. You're out. For good this time.*

*BLOCKED: Are you sure? If I burn, you burn.*

*THE SAVIOR: Honey, that's a game you don't want to play. I was setting this board before you could piss without getting it all over yourself. Just remember, you started this.*

*BLOCKED: You're scared. ***Laughing emoji.*** You're actually scared. Is that why you've done nothing for decades? All bark and no bite. Well, I bite. I bite hard, and I leave marks. Sit back and watch. Maybe you'll learn something.*

*THE SAVIOR: When you get arrested, I won't be bailing you out. And just remember, I have friends. In prison. In law enforcement. In every walk of life. You open your mouth, and I'll close it for you.*

*BLOCKED: I've been underestimated my entire life. I thought you already learned that about me. I guess I'll have to show you.*

# Chapter Nine

## *Holden*

***WALLS***

*Performed by Bon Jovi*

As soon he'd suggested taking Leya away from D.C., Holden knew he shouldn't have—not without running it by his boss and an entire Secret Service team who would assess the situation and offer solutions. But he also knew it was the best way to keep her safe, and that was all he really cared about. Getting her out of town, out of view of the public. Away from the FGT. What had happened today was already too much. He'd promised her she'd be safe with him, that she could trust him, and look at the crap that had gone down.

If something happened to her…he couldn't even think it. It tore holes in his gut that went well beyond the idea of failing on the job, went beyond not protecting the person you'd sworn to serve. This reaction was visceral. One he didn't have the time to analyze.

"You have a place in mind, Special Agent Kent?" the vice president asked.

"We can have something for you in an hour or two at most."

The quiet had been heavy and prolonged every single time it settled down in the room. Leya had her arms around her sister again, looking like the weight of the world was on her shoulders. The consequences of her actions were tugging at her even when she'd done nothing overtly wrong. Nothing that should have resulted in this even if she'd gone against her family and his wishes.

"Are you sure about Krish, *beta*? Shall I hold off with the Aryas until you have more time to think?" her father asked.

She shook her head. "No. I'm sure."

A sense of pride Holden had no right to filled him. She was standing up for herself in a way he doubted many people would have the courage to do. Years of planning by her family were disappearing with those three simple words.

Her mom huffed, but Leya simply continued, "It is not a good match, Dad. I should have…I should have said something after the inauguration, after he… I wanted to give us a chance to…" she trailed off.

Her father's eyes grew dark and stormy at her words, and Holden felt a similar reaction building in him.

"Did something happen?" the vice president demanded.

"Nothing of consequence. Nothing that matters. A misunderstanding. But we have not been able to get past it."

The vice president turned his gaze toward Holden. "Make it happen."

Holden stepped toward Leya, trying hard to keep his voice and face emotionless, as he held out his hand and said, "I need your phone."

She looked uncertain as she gave it to him, as if he was severing a lifeline, and in many ways he was. He'd sever them all if it kept her safe.

He turned, heading for the door with a well of conflicting emotions scouring him. He felt Leya's eyes on him as he left, and all he could hope was that no one else in the room noticed the same thing he did every time she looked at him—like he was somehow both the problem and the answer to everything in her life.

♫ ♫ ♫

Inside the command center at the residence, five people had been gathered. It was one too many people, in Holden's opinion. Obviously, Camp and Sommerson had to be there, and Marv Bitty had been tapped to join him in this madcap escape, but he didn't know why Daringfield, as the head of the president's detail, had to be there. Regardless, he kept his mouth shut as he'd already caught hell from Camp for his suggestion to take Leya out of D.C.

"How about Camp David?" Sommerson suggested.

"Gibbs is due there next week with the Israeli prime minister," Daringfield replied, referring to the president by his code name.

For some reason, the idea of Camp David niggled back to life the conversation he'd had with his parents about Gia's latest article. He could only imagine the reaction he'd get if he suggested a dude ranch, but it also made him think of his grandparents' place. The remoteness of the farm could be perfect.

"My grandparents own a farm outside Grand Orchard," Holden offered.

Even though not a single one of the men's faces changed, Holden knew they all flinched inwardly at the mention of the town in upstate New York.

"No offense to your family, Kent, but I don't think any of us trust Grand Orchard," Sommerson said dryly.

Holden's stomach tightened, knowing the man was both right and wrong. But the last thing he could afford was for any of these men to consider him a joke, so he crossed his arms over his chest, narrowed his eyes on Sommerson, and snapped back, "It's not like we'd be hanging out in town. No one but my grandparents would even know she was there."

"They got people coming and going on the farm, helping them out?" Camp asked.

They did. A contingent of managers and farmworkers. His grandparents were too old for the day-to-day activities, so it was handled by people they hired. At one point, his granddad had hoped Holden would take it over, but even though he'd enjoyed working with his grandparents while attending Wilson-Jacobs, farming was never going to be something he loved. Nothing but his job with the USSS ever would be.

His lack of response was enough for Camp to move on. "I'd prefer a location within easy reach of an airport and a hospital. A city would be better than a small town." Camp looked over at Daringfield. "Is that safe house in Knoxville still up and running?"

Daringfield didn't respond. Instead, he just stepped to the side of the room and raised his phone to call and check.

Camp opened the conference room door and shouted at a techie at a desk nearby. "What do we have on the call made to Firefly's phone?"

"Tracking it now, but I can guarantee it's a burner. I can trace its last location, and that's about it until we find where it was bought," the woman hollered back.

"We know who's behind this," Holden growled. "John Smythe and the rest of the For Greater Tomorrows assholes. They declared it in the note and then followed it up with action."

"Which is exactly why I don't like him for it. The FGT has never put their name on a note. This feels like someone using their known hatred for the Singhs as a decoy," Sommerson grunted back.

"The number one goal on their website is to put the vice president out of commission."

"They never say his name directly, nor do they actively threaten lives, which is why the site is still up and running."

"Enough!" Camp barked, slamming the door shut and eyeing Holden for a long moment. "You need some space, Kent? Too close to this?"

Holden's stomach shredded as if he'd swallowed glass. "Not any closer than Sommerson, sir."

Camp's gaze narrowed, assessing them both.

Marv, who'd been as quiet as always, cleared his throat and said, "No matter where we send her, she's going to be recognized. Her face is everywhere, along with the rest of her band. It's a nightmare,"

"You got a better option?" Camp demanded.

"Leave her here. Inside the compound. The bunker has a bedroom. We can put out a release saying she's left and then just keep her here," Marv suggested.

It wasn't a bad idea, but Holden had an overpowering urge to get her as far from D.C. as possible. Away from the family who'd upset her. Away from the leak that had shared top-secret information with the press. Away from Lincoln Matherton and the longing looks he sent her way. Jesus, those kinds of thoughts were the exact reason he should have been walking away from this detail, and yet he couldn't. Wouldn't.

He'd see her safe or die trying. It wasn't just his job. It was what he'd promised her he'd do.

Daringfield hung up his phone and rejoined them. "Knoxville is a go. They just finished the undercover op last week."

"I'll run it past Lantern," Sommerson said, heading for the door and looking over at Daringfield. "Do you need to run it by Gibbs?"

"I can safely say he has other concerns today. He'll be relieved if we can solve at least one of them," the president's agent said with a note of sarcasm that irked Holden. Just like Sommerson, the man was too cocky for his own good. Too sure of his place in the food chain. Holden would never be that way if he ever got a chance to lead one of the top two teams. But a sinking feeling in his gut told him the likelihood of him even having a job when this was over was disappearing with every hour he spent next to Leya.

"I'll be back in twenty minutes, and I need transport plans, logistics for the stay, and an extraction plan in case things go south," Camp said before he stormed out.

Holden and Marv confiscated laptops from the command center's stack and sat down at the conference room table to pull together, in a handful of minutes, an op that should have taken weeks to arrange.

"A standard-issue Secret Service vehicle is going to stand out like a fly on ice cream in Knoxville. We've got some undercover vehicles at the depot. I'm thinking a pickup truck."

"Agreed. Go get it while I update Camp," Holden told him, and when the man hesitated, he added on, "Last I checked, I was still the lead agent on her detail, Marv. Let's just make it happen."

Marv headed out just as Camp entered. "Where's Bitty going?"

Holden explained about Marv's truck idea before running through the plans they'd come up with. Camp signed the authorization form without another word. It was as close to a "good job" as Holden expected to hear from his boss after everything that had happened in the last few hours.

"Firefly on board with this?" Camp asked.

Holden's chest tightened, dual emotions running through him. Part of him didn't care if she was on board. That part wanted to shove her in an armored tank, drive her to a remote Alaskan bunker, and never let her out again. But the other part of him, the part that knew her almost as well as he knew himself, realized that dictating to her would only result in rebellion. Exactly the shitshow that had happened today when her parents had demanded she stay at the residence.

"She'll agree," he said, standing up and heading toward the door. He'd convince her. But to do so meant being in her presence again, and he was unsure if he was ready for it. Not when the cracks in the walls he'd held up for so long were now splintering around him. How long would it be before he was unable to hold it together? Especially when just looking at her, just being close enough to get a hint of her honeysuckle scent, was enough to make his pulse hammer and his body tighten.

The assistant director called his name before he could escape. "Kent." Holden looked back at him. "You didn't get the downtime you've been long overdue for. I need to know if you're a hundred percent."

Holden didn't even hesitate as he bit out the lie. "More than a hundred percent, sir. She won't be harmed on my watch."

They continued their stare-down, and it wasn't Holden who blinked first. He couldn't afford to be. When Camp turned back to his laptop, Holden made his way to the residence, thankful for only one thing—with Marv tagging along, there was no chance of any moments like the ones that had happened on the lawn yesterday or upstairs in her studio earlier to happen again. He might actually be able to get through this, protect her, and hand her off, before his career was completely ripped away.

# Chapter Ten

## Leya

***HOPE FOR THE HOPELESS***

*Performed by A Fine Frenzy*

*Everything from her old phone had* been converted to a new one by some techie on the Secret Service staff, but in handing it over, she'd felt as if another layer of her privacy had been removed. Her text messages had been sent to the USSS to be scrutinized as well as her call history and photos.

She should have been used to these kinds of violations, not only because they'd had very little privacy during any of her father's campaigns, but because her career choice removed even more. The Painted Daisies were known everywhere they went. Every action was dissected, haters calling out every single thing that was wrong with them as well as adoring fans sharing each sighting with glee.

But today…today was worse, and she had no one to blame but herself.

As the hours went by with no further retaliation, her family was allowed out of the bunker but asked to stay inside the residence. She went upstairs to her newly appointed art room, setting up the light she'd risked everything to buy and suddenly hating it.

She walked out of the room without turning it on, stomach turning nastily.

As she stepped into the hallway, Holden found her.

"We've found a location to take you off-grid and can leave within the hour if you approve," he said.

Leya's stomach flipped. "Who's we?"

He looked confused.

"Which of the Secret Service agents are coming with us?"

"Marv Bitty and myself."

"How long will we be gone?"

"I don't know. Hopefully, this will be over quickly once we have the person or persons who placed the bomb in custody," he said calmly but with a gentle coax, as if he expected her to argue.

How could she? Not after her impulsive decision had already put her family at risk.

"What happens…" she broke off. "What happens if they aren't found before I'm due back with the band?" Worry twisted with the guilt turning her stomach into a web of acid. She couldn't let her bandmates down, not after everything they'd been through. This tour wasn't just for them. It was for Landry, honoring her and what she'd built.

Holden's face flickered, the bland, emotionless mask turning into empathy or sympathy, she wasn't sure which, before it closed off again. "We'll find them."

"No one has found Landry's killer, Holden. That was over two years ago."

More guilt rushed through her…maybe her friend really was dead because of them.

Holden's Adam's apple bobbed, and he looked away before returning his gaze to hers, steely blue eyes trying to soothe her. "This is different. We know who did this. We just have to find one individual in a small stack of them."

"You're that sure it's FGT?"

"Yes," he said without hesitation.

She sagged against the wall, wrapping her arms around herself. He took a step toward her but stopped short of touching her.

"I hate that I brought them closer to my family." It was almost a whisper, a beg for him to disagree with her, but he didn't—couldn't. He'd told her not to go out, and she was just glad he didn't say the "I told you so" aloud.

Instead, he tried to comfort her. "I know it doesn't seem it at the moment, but this might be a good thing. If we can prove it's FGT, even one single member acting on their own, it will give us what we need to legally shut them down. They won't come after your dad or your family again."

It did soften the hurt some. Bringing down the FGT would be a victory, but Leya wasn't naïve enough to think there wouldn't be another hate group filling the void. It was a never-ending battle. The sad truth was White supremacists would forever be a part of America's landscape, and the more they felt cornered, the harder they fought.

She turned toward her bedroom, going into the walk-in closet and pulling down the suitcase she'd barely stored. It was one of the things she hated most about being on tour—living out of suitcases. Feeling like there was never a place you could land that felt like home. Even being here, at the vice president's residence, she felt like a guest. Temporary. Fleeting. She ached to find something permanent.

She could have had it with Krish.

But then she'd have to give up something else. The chance to find her real *jeevansathi*. She'd been so eager to please her mother, to do at least one thing that brought pride to her mom's eyes, that she'd not once questioned whether Krish was really the right one. Aja Aunty's star charts had said they fit. Their families respected each other. She'd liked Krish as her brother's friend even before they'd become friends themselves. She'd believed their friendship would bloom into love. But looking back now, she realized she'd simply wanted him to be the one because it was easier.

If she'd listened to *Nani* telling her to trust her instincts, she would have paid more attention to her body's reaction to Krish rather than her brain's. She should have ended things a long time ago. But the idea of being without him, without the assurance of having someone already picked out who would marry her, care for her, and whom she could take care of in return…it made her feel lost. There was no relief in having called off the arrangement. Instead, she was now flailing in a sea of unknowns, a ship that had lost its navigation system. And she wondered if, just like her mom insisted, her flighty, emotional soul would now lead her the wrong way.

Would it lead her to the man whose gaze was boring into her even as she packed, sending arcs of awareness down her spine? There was nothing right about the idea of Holden. Not a single thing. There could be nothing long term between them. Not only because he was Secret Service, but because she knew nothing about him or his family beyond the fact that his dad had also been an agent at some point. Their families would never mesh.

But who said exploring these feelings of lust and desire had to lead to love? Couldn't it just be that—exploration? The handful of guys she'd fooled around with was an abysmally small list. The lack of passion she'd felt with them had led to her disinterest. She'd never felt what she did when Holden was near, but she'd also never really pushed to find it, to see if she could stoke an ember into a flame. She'd been happy to save the idea of the physical aspects of a relationship for marriage while she concentrated on her career and her art.

Now, she craved the feelings Holden raised in her, seeking them out, even when it could only end in misery. It would be selfish and unfair to even tempt him. It would be her impulsiveness at its worst. The best she could hope for was that she'd cross paths with someone else who would light her up in the way he did. And if not…then maybe she wasn't meant to have it. Maybe it was penance for sins of her past—or her present.

The weight of the day settled back over her again. The guilt was the heaviest. She'd failed her friends, her family, and even herself. The remorse inside her was so large it felt like it would choke her.

"Ever seen a ghost in this room?" Holden's question drew her eyes to him. When he raised a brow, she realized exactly why he'd asked the question. Because regardless of how they didn't fit, he was still one of the only people who could truly read her. He saw past the calm exterior she'd learned from her mother to the chaos underneath, and he was trying to ease her discomfort, just like he'd once soothed her tears with a warm embrace.

She looked away, shoving more clothes into her luggage. "Don't be ridiculous."

"No, seriously. Eleanor Mondale hit her panic button and brought her security detail into the room, guns blazing. Then, she admitted she'd seen an apparition. Not many of the men on duty believed her."

"I bet they were pissed. Gave her the 'Don't misuse your privilege' speech."

Holden snorted. "I'm sure they did."

She watched in fascination as his lips twitched ever so slightly. She wondered what it would look like if he really smiled. How would it change his face? Would he have a dimple? Would his eyes crinkle, or would they stay wide and open like the sky?

"I've never seen a ghost. I don't believe in them," she finally breathed out.

"You believe in reincarnation."

"Are you belittling my beliefs, Special Agent Kent?"

He looked shocked. "Not at all. I actually find it a relief. The entire idea of living your life over again in different iterations so you have a chance to get it right."

"I'm definitely going through a few more rounds," she said, and then wished she could take it back.

He looked like he wanted to disagree, but then his hand rose to his ear. "We'll be down in five." He looked over at her. "You ready?"

"I need to pack a few things from the bathroom, and I want to say goodbye to my family."

He nodded, reaching over and picking up the large suitcase she'd just stuffed with more things than she'd probably need. It wasn't his job to carry it, and he rarely did. He left it to the many workers shuffling the band's suitcases and instruments between hotels and venues while on tour. So, the fact that he was doing it today caused a weird flutter in her stomach. It felt…tender…like the way Dad had never let any of them carry shopping bags when they were little.

"I'm assuming I can't bring my sitar?" she asked.

"You shouldn't bring anything that will tie you to Leya Singh."

"Who will I be?"

"Lita Rae."

She laughed. "Who came up with that name?"

His lips quirked. "I remembered you said you liked Lita Ford."

"Rock legend," she said, nodding. "The Runaways, Lita, Joan…classics."

"Someday, musicians are going to be saying that about The Painted Daisies. Leya, Paisley, Fiadh," he said, his lips curling up ever so slightly more. She itched to reach out and touch the corners. When she looked up from his mouth to his eyes, there was a look there that had the heat returning to her chest and spreading down through her lower limbs.

"I'll meet you at the bottom of the stairs," Holden said before turning and leaving.

She placed a few things from her bathroom into a messenger bag and then, at the last minute, went back to the hodgepodge art studio and tossed a couple of sketchbooks and pencils in as well. She'd need something to pass her time.

Leya passed Mirabel with her purse on her shoulder and her car keys in hand, a dangly flag charm swinging against her suit sleeve, as she entered the den. Ria and her mom were both waiting for Leya inside. Her mom rose to hug her fiercely, the scent and warmth of her a balm to the tormented swells inside Leya.

"I truly am sorry," she told her mom, squeezing back tightly. "For Krish…for today…I—"

*Hate disappointing you*. She couldn't say the words.

"I just want what is best for you. I want to see you settled. To find solid ground instead of flitting away. If it is not with Krish, we will find someone else. I'll have Aja Aunty pull together some biodata sheets. She's helped many people in our family find suitable matches."

The idea should have made Leya feel better. It should have given her the relief and steadiness she'd been seeking now that she'd abandoned the idea of Krish. But instead of easing her emotions, they caused them to swirl into bigger knots, as if she was a bird being thrust into a cage when she needed to practice flying.

But if she rejected her mother's idea of Aja Aunty's help outright, she would only return the frown to her mom's face. She would only prove once again that she was irrational. So, she simply smiled and teased, "If it's an impossible task, I'll just remain single. I can be the amazing auntie who spoils her nieces and nephews."

She started to pull away, but her mother's cool hand cupped her cheek. "No. You will have your own family, *beta*. I need grandchildren to spoil."

Leya snorted. "You already have one on the way with Rishik and Devleena."

"I want a dozen at least."

"Then, you should have had more children yourself." She smiled at her mother.

They hugged each other tightly again. "You have time. Just don't wait too long. You don't want to have crow's feet on your wedding day."

Ria laughed behind them, and it lightened Leya's heart a teensy bit. They were all okay. She'd screwed up, but they were okay. She just couldn't do it again.

Leya's smile faded. "I can only say again how truly sorry I am."

She meant for everything that had happened, but her mother thought she was still talking about the engagement. "*Maa* told me she didn't agree with Krish for you."

"*Nani* did?" Leya asked, surprise settling over her. "I thought she approved? When we were in India together…she was always pushing Krish and me together."

"I think she wanted you to say something. Wanted you to tell us then that he was not the man for you."

Leya laughed. "That sounds like *Nani*. So ornery."

"You're just like her—telling the world the sky is green when everyone knows it is blue. But promise me…" Her mother stopped to collect herself, emotions she never liked to show all but bursting from her. "Promise me you will listen to your Secret Service detail. I need to know you are safe wherever they are taking you."

After the disaster of today, listening to Holden was exactly what she intended to do. That wasn't the problem. Keeping her distance from him was another matter. But if her mother even suspected that was the case, she'd worry more—or worse, she'd insist on a different agent.

"I promise," she said. She squeezed her mother again and then turned to pull Ria into her arms. "Be safe, Jujube." Leya tickled Ria's ribs.

"You too, Skittles."

The lump in Leya's throat returned. They hadn't used their candy nicknames in ages, maybe since they'd been living in California. A lifetime ago. Someone else's life.

As she headed out the door, she had the oddest feeling that when she returned to them, her world would be different again. She would no longer be the same person, but one she couldn't yet see.

At the bottom of the stairs, Holden waited for her. He eyed her up and down in a way only he had ever done. A mix of assurance that she was all right and appreciation of what he saw. She ached to see just the appreciation—or rather appreciation and lust—which had her almost tripping on the bottom step.

He led her out the door and onto the drive. The vehicle waiting for them caused a chuckle to escape her. It was a four-door pickup truck painted silver with black trim and a black roll bar. She looked over at Holden to see his lips had tilted upward again, like they had in her room, and it did nothing to ease the craving deep inside her to see more of it. To see his full smile.

"Marv believes we'll fit in better this way than in the Escalade," he responded to her unanswered question with a sparkle in his eye that was infectious. That made her want to absorb it and make it her own.

He opened the rear passenger door for her, and after she'd climbed in, she realized she could barely move. The seat was tight, crammed up against the front bucket seat. It was hardly what she was accustomed to, but she supposed that was the point. They didn't want her to be Leya Singh. She was Lita Rae for now. Her heart tugged. Maybe Lita Rae would have better luck when it came to love and lust. Maybe she'd know how to take advantage of one without losing the other.

Ridiculousness.

Instead of heading out of town as she'd expected, Marv headed to the riverfront and stopped outside a condominium building where Holden got out. For a minute, even though he'd already said he was going with her, she panicked, thinking he was finally walking away from her, leaving behind the temptations that put them both at risk.

He read her emotions in the annoying and comforting way he always did, saying, "I just need to grab a bag. Marv's going to take a drive around the block and pick me back up."

She mustered every ounce of her mother she could find as she tossed out, "I'm not going to fall to pieces if you leave my side, Holden."

Marv made a choking noise that sounded a lot like a laugh he'd barely held back, and Holden's lips twitched again. Her fingers clenched with a need to touch the corners, to feel them with one hand while she drew them on canvas with the other. She wondered if he'd ever model for her. If, on this trip filled with endless days, she could convince him to stand still while she drew him without her eyes. Just the idea of it gave her a little thrill she knew she couldn't afford.

Touching him couldn't happen. Not even for art.

He shut the door, and Marv put his foot on the gas, shifting them out into the traffic as he made to circle the block.

"How long will it take to get to Knoxville?" Leya asked him.

"Almost eight hours."

She sighed. She hated being stuck in a car. Bad enough when they were traveling on the band's tour bus, but at least there she could walk around, get a snack, and watch television. Here, she could barely move a muscle.

"We'll stop for the night in Roanoke, about halfway," Marv said on hearing her sigh. "I'd prefer not to drive at night anyway. It's easier to see what's coming at you in the daytime."

Her body tensed back up. The momentary relief she'd felt at the idea of leaving D.C., of making sure she didn't put a heavier target on her family's back, flew away. There were still so many people who could get hurt. Because of her. Because of the people who hated her and her family.

She turned her head to look out the window as they stopped once again in front of Holden's building. She wondered what his place looked like. Was it all bachelor pad, or did he have a knack for decorating? What surprises about his life would she find if she was inside? Would it reveal secrets about him she'd never been able to unravel? A glimpse at the real man he held tightly behind the Captain Avenger aura he wore like a shield?

A large man covered in a black hoodie drifted past the side of the pickup, momentarily blocking her view before he dropped to a knee to tie a shoe. He rose and kept going, and something pricked at the back of her brain. She never saw the man's face, and yet he felt vaguely familiar. When she glanced at Marv, she could tell he was watching the man in the side mirror as he walked away. They both jumped as Holden threw a large duffel into the bed of the truck.

She let out a shaky exhale as he climbed in. He'd changed into jeans and a T-shirt, and the clothes seemed oddly surreal and appealing on him. She'd rarely seen him in anything so normal. He was either in a suit or the black uniform their private security team wore. Now he looked…younger. More relaxed. As if the three of them were just a little group going on vacation together. A couple and their friend.

Except, they weren't a couple. They weren't anything.

They couldn't be, and her body and brain needed to get that straight before she did another rash, stupid thing and ended up hurting more people. Ended up costing Holden his job because she didn't have a damn ounce of self-control.

It was all too much for her tired brain. Too many deep thoughts at the end of a day that had been full of intense emotions. She couldn't sit there swimming in a pool of them anymore. She needed to find a release, so she pulled out her earbuds and turned on her music. It wasn't the truth and peace she found in her art, but it was still an escape. She listened to the chords and rhythms, letting them pull her into a deep meditative trance. Not sleep, but at least rest.

# Chapter Eleven

## *Holden*

***BLOOD RUNS RED***
*Performed by Matt Maeson*

*Leya had put in her earbuds*, closed her eyes, and lost herself to the sounds as soon as they'd driven over the same bridge he'd used the day before to visit his parents. He and Marv were silent, watching their mirrors, listening to NPR on the radio. The bombing had thrust the Singhs into the spotlight, and every past rumor was being shoved to the surface. Every political stance her father had taken and everything that had happened to The Painted Daisies was tumbling around all over again.

Holden's jaw tightened as the newscaster hinted at what things were happening behind the scenes with the Daisies in order for so many bad things to be associated with the band. It irritated him that everyone was looking for reasons to pin this on them instead of blaming the assholes who'd actually done the unspeakable deeds.

Twice on their drive, Holden thought he spotted a vehicle trailing them, and twice he had Marv get off the freeway, take some evasive maneuvers, and then get back on. Other than these clipped conversations, the radio was the only discussion in the car for hours.

As they neared Roanoke, the light started to fade, turning the puffy clouds into a series of oranges and grays and reminding Holden of being at his grandparents' orchard. He wasn't sure why their place was on his mind so much today, but he couldn't seem to shake it. Once, in late summer, he'd caught the aurora borealis shimmering in the sky there. A rare glimpse at something spectacular. His eyes journeyed to the silent woman in the back seat. As much as he fought thinking it, he knew she was spectacular too. Someone you were privileged to catch sight of in real life.

"Ten minutes out. Want to get her into the wig?" Marv asked. The words were almost harsh after the hours of quiet.

Holden pulled out the plain brown bob they'd brought with them. One of the first things they'd been taught about undercover work was you didn't do anything to attract attention. So, no vivid blondes or brightly colored wigs. Even though Leya's hair was dark brown, almost black, the fake hair was dim and dull compared to the hundreds of different shades that shone in hers.

He tapped her knee, and her eyes opened, meeting his with a startling heat that almost made him gasp.

"We need you to put this wig on," he said.

She grimaced but didn't question him. She sat straighter, pulled a hairband from her tangle of leather and silver on her wrists, and did her best to pull her luxurious waves into it before struggling with the wig. He unhooked his seat belt, leaning back to help her. Every place his fingertips touched her, flames leaped, burrowing into him. She went completely still, just watching his movements with the same heat she'd had when she'd first opened her eyes.

"I think I've spotted another tail," Marv said.

Holden jerked out of his locked gaze with Leya to the back window.

"About four cars back. It's a black Camaro, a two-thousand-twenty model or sooner. Not exactly rare but not exactly something you expect to see multiple times in the same day."

Holden noted the car. No front license plate.

"I'll call it in. Have a local pull him over for no plates."

He picked up his phone just as the newscaster's voice turned into an excited trill. "Sorry to interrupt, but we're going over to Jeannie who's live outside Lincoln Matherton's gallery where he's answering questions for the media." Another voice came over, shouting a question out in a sea of chatter. "Lincoln, what do you have to say about the bombing today?"

"Hate never wins," Lincoln's voice drifted through the cab of the truck. "If I love Leya Singh, that's my business. No one has a right to tell me who to love and who not to love. She's talented, kind, generous, and smart. Any person would be lucky to call her their partner. For Greater Tomorrows and anyone else who wants to throw literal and figurative bombs at the Singh family had better be prepared for the consequences."

"What exact steps is the president taking?"

"I have no idea what my father is doing. I'm not the President of the United States. I'm a man who just had a person he cares about crucified for no reason, and I personally will see to it that whoever is responsible is held accountable. I won't stop."

"Fuck," Marv muttered as he drew up at a light at the edge of a roundabout inside the city limits.

Holden swore to himself and shifted slightly to look back at Leya. The wig did nothing to disguise her. She was still Leya Singh, world-famous Daisy. She was glowing, even after everything she'd gone through in the last few hours.

"Are you sure there's nothing between you and Lincoln?" he asked, keeping his voice as level as possible and hating the jealousy raging through him.

"If Lincoln had feelings for me, he never acted on them," she said, chin lifting in defiance. But it hadn't really answered his question. She knew it, but she was putting him in his place. He didn't have a right to ask about her love life. It still twisted his gut, a knife digging farther into the wall he was barely holding up between them.

He'd turned halfway back around in the front seat when their truck was slammed from behind. Marv cursed, and the truck jerked as he slammed his foot onto the brake.

Holden ripped his head toward the back window just as they were hit a second time, even harder, and the unexpected force pushed them into the roundabout and the slew of oncoming cars. Horns and brakes screeched as the driver's side was struck with a sickening crunch of metal on metal. A scream tore through the air. Feminine and high. It joined the unforgiving squeal of twisting metal and shattering glass. The truck spun as they were hit several more times from different angles as the cars in the roundabout continued to plow into them and each other.

The truck was pushed toward the center curb, bouncing on the edge, and then the entire world rotated as the vehicle flipped onto its side. Glass rained in on him, and his body slammed into the console right before his face connected with the exploding airbag. Pain radiated through his nose and head, and everything started to go dark. He ground his teeth together, fighting to not pass out.

They'd finally come to stop on the driver's side door. The smell of bug spray and powder from the airbags was joined by the scent of steaming oil and gasoline. Holden's eyes drifted shut, and he forced them open again. *Jesus*. Blood dripped down into his mouth from his broken nose. His ribs felt like death, and pain radiated from his right elbow. He drew his Glock with his left hand, glad for one of the first times in his life that it was his dominant hand, and turned toward Leya in the back seat.

Glass littered the wig that was slightly askew, but there was no blood on her. She was still strapped in, chest and stomach pushing into the belt that held her tightly in the air. But her eyes were closed, and he couldn't help the well of panic that rose within him at her unmoving form.

"Leya!" he called her name, tapping her cheek gently.

She groaned, eyelashes fluttering, and relief coursed through him. *Thank God!*

He turned to Marv. The entire driver's side was crumpled inward, and Marv was pinned between the seat, the door, and the steering wheel with an airbag that hadn't deflated. Blood dripped from a large slash on his forehead, and his eyes were closed.

"Marv," Holden growled. The man's eyes flickered. "Hey, man, wake up."

"Is he okay?" Leya's voice was shaky and scared. Like it had been earlier in the day when they'd gotten the news about the bomb. "You're bleeding, Holden." Her voice grew more panicked. The last thing he needed was for her to lose it.

They had to get out of the truck.

"It's just my nose. They bleed like a waterfall when they're barely scratched. I'm okay, but we have to get out. Can you unlatch your seat belt?" When she reached for it, he shot a hand and had to bite back an expletive as pain dragged through him. "Careful. You'll fall."

She seemed to brace herself and then slowly unlatched. He caught her the best he could as she came down on the side, trying to evade landing on Marv. Every movement sent new waves of agony through his body that he continued to ignore. He kicked out the rest of the windshield and dragged himself through before reaching back in for Leya.

The roundabout was chaos, cars turned every which way, people hurrying to check on each other. Sirens already filled the air. The last thing they needed was for Leya to be on the news in a major accident with her two Secret Service agents.

He pushed her behind the truck, farther into the shrubs and bushes in the center circle of the roundabout, and then he returned for Marv. The man's eyes met Holden's, a surety in them Holden had never seen before in the quiet man.

"Get her out of here, Kent. They're going to need tools to get me out. She can't be here when they do." His words were sure, but his voice was breathless as the steering wheel dug into his chest. Holden's gut sank again. He didn't want to leave him. But that was the job. Protect the protectee at all costs—to you or anyone else on the team.

"Go!" Marv said as the noise of the sirens grew closer.

Holden did a quick scan of the area, noting the people who'd already whipped out cell phones to video the accident. Damn. He lifted his T-shirt to wipe at the blood on his face, causing the light blue to turn a nauseating hue. He looked around for their bags that had been in the back of the truck. He spotted his duffel and Leya's smaller one in the street. He picked them up, biting back another grunt of pain, and joined her in the bushes. He grabbed her hand and drew her through them to the other side of the island.

"What are you doing?" Leya demanded, concern rippling through her. "Marv is back there. He's stuck."

"And the first responders will get him out."

She tugged at him, slowing her feet, and it shot a stabbing sensation through his side.

"Holden!"

He turned to take her in. She had a knot on her left temple, and she was pale and shaky, but other than that, she looked fine. That didn't mean there wasn't internal bleeding. She could be injured from the seat belt, from slamming her knees into the back of the seat. Jesus. He should probably have her looked over.

"Leya. Listen to me. You cannot be here when the police show up. Do you get that? Not after everything else that happened today. They can't find you here." Her face went paler than it already was. He grabbed her hand again, hauling her toward the street. "Keep your head down, try to look like you're just another bystander, but keep up with me."

The pileup had stopped traffic completely, and he weaved through the tangle of vehicles, thankful for the darkening sky. He pulled out his phone, attempting to appear like any other onlooker, all the while knowing if anyone really took him in, they'd see the blood. They'd know he was involved. He had to get them off the main thoroughfare.

They made their way back to the street and the light they'd stopped at. There were black skid marks on the ground from where Marv had tried to hold the pickup steady. Holden glanced back at the circle, and his stomach fell as smoke spiraled from the truck's engine. He ground his teeth, turned away, and headed for the parking lot of a nearby strip mall.

He didn't slow down at any of the open shops, heading straight for the alley at the side instead. Once they'd stepped into the darkness and were no longer visible from the street, he dropped his bag and yanked his T-shirt over his head, barely holding back a groan as both his arm and ribs objected. He wiped his face again with the bloody shirt, grabbed another one from his duffel, and pulled it on.

He turned toward Leya. She was watching him with eyes wide. She picked up the bloody T-shirt and stepped closer. She found a clean spot on the sleeve and leaned forward to gently wipe at the side of his face. Cuts he hadn't felt before stung at the touch.

The air was cool around them, but he was sweating profusely. Pain spiking. He had to get her off the street. A hotel. Somewhere safe. Because if he passed out, she needed to be locked away.

Holden pulled the shirt from her hands, dropped it into a dumpster, and picked up their bags. He'd just grabbed her hand and started toward the rear exit of the alley as a car came zooming toward them down the narrow space. Holden twisted to put himself between Leya and the vehicle, drawing his weapon and aiming at the black Camaro barreling down on them. Brakes screeched as it skidded to a stop next to them. The passenger door was shoved open, and a huge man in a hoodie ducked down to look at them from the driver's seat.

"Get in," the man said.

Holden kept his gun trained on him.

"I don't think so."

Holden knew the man as soon as he pushed his hoodie back. Knew him because he'd stared at the grainy black-and-white photo for days after Landry Kim's death. Just like he'd stared at the sketch artist's rendering made from Fiadh Kane's description for more hours than was sane.

"You know who I am, right?" the man asked. His voice was almost impossibly deep, like listening to Michael Clarke Duncan from *The Green Mile*, and he was so dark he blended in with the night, his tan face the only hint of light.

"Yes. And as much as I'd like to haul you in for questioning, I'm not exactly in the position to do so at the moment." Holden's voice was smooth, calm, nothing like the anger that was roiling through him at the audacity of this man to follow them and then pull up and casually demand they get in.

"You need to get her out of here, right? You going to go on foot? How far are you going to get before someone spots you?"

"Don't know, but we sure as hell aren't getting into the car with our number one suspect in the Landry Kim murder."

Angel Carter actually looked surprised for a millisecond before his face turned into a stone wall.

More sirens screamed behind them. The front of the strip mall became a mass of flashing lights. The only exit was out the back. Holden pushed Leya toward the driveway behind the dumpsters, eyes and gun still on Carter.

The car rolled forward with them.

"Don't be a fucking idiot. Get in the car. I'll drop you wherever you want, but she's not safe out here."

"How would you know that exactly?"

"I wasn't the only one following you."

Holden's entire body cried out with each step, the spots kept coming and going in front of his eyes. Marv was an expert driver who knew evasive maneuvers, and yet Carter had followed them. Not only him but the other vehicles they'd ditched repeatedly today. Uncomfortable doubts filled Holden about his team. About the men and women he served with.

"I didn't kill Landry Kim," Carter said calmly—a fact—no beg in his voice to be believed. A voice that held a hint of an accent Holden wasn't sure he would have noticed if he hadn't been trained to do so, and yet still couldn't place. "I want proof of who killed her as much as you do. It's why I was helping Fiadh. If I'd intended to harm any of the Daisies, I could have done it a hundred times before now."

"Who do you work for?" Holden demanded as they continued to inch their way down the alley. He could feel Leya's body up tight against his. She was shivering and shaking. The cool air and the aftermath of the adrenaline were going to have them both crashing fast. They needed to get out of here.

"Hey, come out from back there." A police officer stood at the other end of the alley, shining a light toward them. Holden turned his face away instinctively, making sure Leya was completely hidden behind him.

His body clenched tightly as the realization hit him—they had only one choice. His heart and mind objected, but he had to get Leya out of there. Holden stepped toward the open car door, sliding inside it and pulling her onto his lap. He hadn't even slammed the door before Carter was hitting the gas and squealing out the back exit.

Holden kept his weapon trained on him.

"Who are you?" Leya's voice shook as she asked the question.

Carter flicked his eyes at her and back to the road. "A friend."

Holden scoffed. “I don’t think so.”

The man’s eyes narrowed ever so slightly. “I just saved your ass back there.”

“Offering us a ride when you know we can’t refuse and being a friend are light-years away from each other.”

Carter drove fast, but not fast enough to draw attention. He followed the rules of the road, stopping at every streetlight and every stop sign until he was merging onto the highway heading south. It was the action of a trained operative, and it only spiked Holden’s concerns over the man.

Holden’s phone vibrated in his pocket. He had to move his hips to drag it out, forcing his body into Leya’s. She tried to pull herself away, but the quarters were just too close, and the movement was far too personal…intimate…sensual when, given the situation, it should have been anything but.

He ignored the agony shooting through his bones as he put the phone to his ear.

“Kent.”

“Status,” Camp demanded.

“Firefly is safe. We’re on the interstate, heading south. I’ll call back once I have her secure. I had to leave Marv.”

“He’s en route to the hospital. Are you injured?”

“Nothing that will stop me from doing my job.”

“Firefly?”

Holden’s gaze glanced from Carter to Leya’s face, eyeing the knot that was growing on her temple.

“Small head injury I’d liked to have checked out once we get somewhere safe.”

“She’s awake and mobile?”

“Yes.”

“You need a vehicle,” Camp stated.

“I’ll rent one in the morning.”

"We're suppressing all images we can of the crash and who was in the truck, but I don't expect it to last long. Someone will have noticed her."

"Agreed. If we can get where we're going before it breaks, that would be best for everyone."

"Dye your hair, Kent. Get a goddamn hat. Blend the fuck in."

"Yes, sir."

"I need status every hour until she's secure in Tennessee."

The line went dead, and Holden lowered the phone, meeting Leya's gaze, trying to reassure her with a calm his insides didn't feel. She was frightened, the look in her eyes clear as day, and it made him ache to pull her even closer. To wrap his uninjured arm around her shoulders and force her head to his chest. Movements he had no right to. Movements that meant he was as screwed as he'd thought when she'd almost kissed him on the lawn.

He tore his eyes from her and placed them back on Carter, the safer choice at the moment, and that said way too much.

"You owe us answers," Holden said to the silent man behind the wheel.

"There is only one person I serve, and it isn't you or the fucking United States government."

"Who's that?"

Carter's eyes drifted from the road to Leya and back. A surprised exhale escaped Leya as Holden's stomach turned again.

"Me?" her voice was a shocked whisper. "I don't even know you."

"Not you," he said with his deep voice going even lower, so low it was almost nonexistent.

Silence settled down among them. Holden knew he needed to be peppering the man with questions. Needed to be demanding Carter head to the closest police station or field office. But at the moment, he could barely think. He was running on instinct, and that instinct told him to get Leya somewhere safe. Away from the press, the accident, and the people who were coming after her.

"That wasn't an accident," Carter said as if reading Holden's mind.

"How could you know that?" Doubt and anger filled him in equal measures.

"I watched that car ram you from behind. Not once, but twice. After you were hit, they pushed you farther into the center divide."

Leya let out a gasp, and Holden's entire body grew tighter.

"Did you see who was at the wheel?" Holden demanded.

"Woman. Blonde. Mid to late twenties."

Holden cursed inwardly again. Of course it wouldn't be John Smythe at the wheel, but every vein in his body knew this had to have been related to the events of the day and FGT's threats. He'd gotten cocky, secure in the fact that he'd spotted the earlier tail, and yet he and Marv had missed the last one. He'd messed up.

And he knew exactly why. His mind had been on the news report and Lincoln Matherton basically claiming he loved Leya. Holden needed to be pulled from this detail. But the thought of leaving her was like a knife to his heart. Worse than any of the pain that was creeping through him from the accident.

"We'll need you to come in and identify the woman. Plus, we have some questions for you," he told Carter.

They were at least two towns over from Roanoke, and Carter took an exit boasting a cheap motel and a chain restaurant no one ate at unless they were desperate. He pulled into the motel, backing into a space at the back of the lot where the streetlight didn't shine into the vehicle. More proof that he was a trained operative. Holden's gun went up again, pointing right at Carter's face.

The man didn't look the least bit concerned. He shoved his hands into the pocket of his hoodie.

"Hands on the wheel," Holden commanded.

Carter brought them out of the pocket slowly, a business card in his fingers.

"I need to know if For Greater Tomorrows killed Landry thinking she was Leya or if whoever did it thought she was one of the other Daisies," Carter said.

"You aren't in a position to ask for anything," Holden bit out.

"Asher Riggs owes me. Now, you do too."

Carter reached for the door, and Holden couldn't do much about it without either shooting him or tossing Leya out onto her butt. Instead, he reached for the handle, pushed open the door, and let Leya ease out of the car. The loss of her closeness caused something akin to panic to run through him that he fought to put away. He dragged himself out with a hiss and turned to block her from Carter's view with his weapon pointed once again at the man, this time over the top of the car.

"How did you follow us?" Holden asked.

"Tagged the truck outside your condo. Your place was easy to find once I knew you were her lead agent. I also knew you'd be back home before you took off. Predictable." Carter said it with something close to disgust in his voice, and Holden's stomach turned yet again because it had been. He'd led this man and whomever else right to them.

"How long was the other vehicle behind us?"

"They switched off several times. Ended with the woman in the gray sedan that rammed you."

It matched some of what he and Marv had seen. At least they hadn't missed all the damn tails. It wasn't a comfort.

The rush of cars on the highway mingled with the sounds of a television in a nearby room and the zapping of the streetlight a row over as it flickered while he and Carter continued to glare at each other. The man lifted his hands slowly, setting the business card on the roof of the Camaro and placing the car keys on top of it.

"The car's clean. I'll be in touch."

He started to walk away, and Holden tapped his gun on the roof just to get the man's attention, to remind him that he had a weapon trained on him. Carter looked over his shoulder for half a second and then simply pulled up his black hood and lost himself in the gloom of the trees at the edge of the lot.

"Shit," Holden uttered quietly.

He couldn't risk shooting the man, and Carter knew it. The shots would call the cops they'd just evaded. He couldn't run after the man and leave Leya unprotected, and he damn sure wasn't dragging her with him in pursuit. That left letting the man walk away, and it added a new layer of disgust to the one already sitting like paint thinner inside his gut, eating away.

# Chapter Twelve

## *Leya*

***CUE THE RAIN***
*Performed by Lea Michele*

*Leya's entire body was shaking. She* felt nauseated, and she wasn't sure if it was from the tender knot growing on her temple or from everything that had happened that day. Or maybe it was because of the man, Angel Carter, who'd just disappeared with the dark, smokey gray of his halo blending into the night as he left them with his car and a calling card.

She needed to lie down, and she was pretty sure Holden needed more than that. He was doing a valiant job of pretending he wasn't injured, but he was holding his right side stiffly, and she'd heard the sharp inhale every time he'd used his right hand.

Holden pocketed the keys and the card, reached into the car, and grabbed their two bags. After he'd flung them both over his good shoulder and tucked his gun away, he took her hand and led her toward the hotel office. The normal awareness that wafted over her whenever they touched returned—inappropriate as always, but even more so as they'd just survived a car accident and a run-in with the man the authorities thought might have killed Landry. Her heart hammered fiercely at that thought. Fear and anger simmered, but beyond it all, an intense exhaustion waited to drag her under.

They paused outside the main entrance, and Holden opened his duffel bag to pull out a baseball hat and sunglasses. He slid the glasses over his eyes and handed her the hat. She attempted to pull it down over the wig, but it felt like it was going to spring off any second like in a cartoon.

The lobby smelled like fast food and cigarettes and was barely large enough for the two of them to stand at the reception desk. There was a rubber duck on the counter next to a sign that said, "Squeeze me for service."

"Keep your face down," Holden whispered before reaching over and squishing the toy a couple of times.

"Hold your horses," a man's voice growled. A smoker's cough was followed by heavy footsteps, and a man with so many wrinkles his features almost disappeared came around the corner. His glazed eyes barely registered them. "Seventy-five a night. Cash only. Pay in advance."

"We just need one night," Holden said, fishing through his wallet and coming up with five twenty-dollar bills he placed on the counter.

The man pushed a hotel register at them. Holden signed them in as Mr. and Mrs. Green. No first names. The man didn't seem to care, even though it had to break a whole host of state and local laws.

The clerk ran a card through a card reader on the back counter and then slid it across to them. "Room 201."

As they stepped outside, Leya realized Holden hadn't gotten his change, and when she said as much, he simply responded with a calm, "We paid for the anonymity and his silence."

She swallowed hard, wondering if this was forever going to be her life now. Running. Hiding. Remaining silent when she really wanted to scream.

Holden led her up a rickety metal staircase on the outside of the hotel to a cement landing that probably hadn't been cleaned in a decade. Old gum, food wrappers, and pigeon poop lined the way to a door that was once white and was now blackened with fingerprints.

After glancing toward the parking lot below them one more time, Holden unlocked the door and hauled her inside. He placed her right at the entrance with an authoritative, "Stay there."

He looked under the bed with a tattered comforter before opening the tiny closet that could barely hold a child. He moved to the bathroom with its pedestal sink right on top of the toilet and a stall shower she doubted Holden would be able to stand in without half of him outside it.

In her entire life, Leya had never been in a place like this. It wasn't just the worn-out appearance. It was the fact that the walls were dirty, the carpet was stained, and there was a scent of smoke and stale food in the air.

"I think I'd rather sleep in the car," she said as another shudder rippled through her that had nothing to do with the night air that had permeated the room.

"Carter could have another set of keys, and I can't afford for him to catch me unaware again."

Holden's gaze settled on her, doing that top-to-bottom assessment that would forever send cartwheels through her stomach.

"I'm hoping the ice machine works. Stay here and lock the chain behind me. I'll be right back."

The realization hit her. She was alone with him in a hotel room, seedy or not, that had one full-sized bed. It caused her heart to slam, joining the cartwheels in her stomach. Holden opened the door and looked back at where she remained fixed in place by the cheap dresser with a drawer hanging at an angle.

"Leya," he called softly.

She shook herself out of her daze. Their eyes met as she shut the door, concern causing his brow to furrow before it disappeared behind the wood. As she heard him walk away, fear spiked through her even though she knew he'd be back.

She leaned her forehead on the door and yelped as the swollen knot connected with the wood. She moved to look at herself in the mirror above the dresser. The wig was atrocious. Heavy bangs slid over her eyebrows, the sides landing at her chin in a cut that would never be flattering on her. She pulled it off, and her own hair came tumbling loose from the hairband. She pushed it aside to eye the puffy knob on her temple where a slight bruise had already developed. When she pushed on it softly, it made her eyes water and white lights flash.

A sharp knock had her jumping back from the dresser as Holden's voice came through the door. "It's me."

She looked through the peephole and could see nothing but unlocked the door and swung it open anyway. He was glaring at her.

"Did you even check?"

She didn't respond, just stepped back, and he slammed the door behind him, the entire room shaking with the force of it. Her mouth dropped open slightly. For the second time that night, he was shirtless. The muscles on his chest and back rippled like moving water as he stalked into the bathroom. Her breath caught at the beauty of him, and her fingers itched once more to draw the fluid lines of him.

The T-shirt he'd put on in the alley was now in his hand, twisted up in a ball that he opened to pour the ice he'd retrieved into the sink. "No buckets," he explained, his gaze meeting hers in the mirror's reflection.

He pulled a frayed facecloth from the shelf, piled some ice into it, knotted it, and then approached. He held the makeshift icepack to her forehead, and she tried not to wince. She was hardly hurt, whereas he'd taken a full beating. He hadn't had his seat belt on when they'd been struck, because he'd been helping her with the stupid wig.

He'd been hurt…because of her.

It made tears prick her eyes. She closed her lids, holding them back.

"Are you hurt anywhere else?" he asked. The gentleness of the words was almost too much to bear. Her eyes fluttered open, meeting his hooded gaze. His nose was swelling, and black had appeared below his lashes. He was ten times as injured as she was, and yet, his complete focus was on her, and she wondered what it would be like to be the center of his attention all the time. Wondered what it would be like if they were skin to skin with his intensity washing all over her.

And then the guilt she was so good at feeling rammed back into her. Not only because he'd been hurt because of her but because of her traitorous thoughts. She hadn't been willing to give up her life, her dreams, for a lifetime with Krish. She'd felt caged and burdened by the idea. She could hardly expect anyone to give anything up for a mere moment of time with her, and that was what would happen if they pursued these emotions. He'd lose everything.

She was greedy and selfish to even think it. She was so far from reaching *moksha* and being rejoined with Brahman that it was likely her soul would be reduced to its worst reincarnation yet after this life.

She settled her hand over the top of his where he still held the icepack. "Holden…" She inhaled sharply at the blaze that ran through his eyes as she said his name. "I'm fine. It's you we should be worried about."

She dragged her gaze from his injured face to his bare chest. A large bruise was growing on his right side. Her fingers skated over it gently, and he shuddered. There were so many things wrong and forbidden about this moment, but she couldn't stop herself from continuing to brush circles over the injury marring his fiercely defined body. He stopped her hand with his own, and she noted the tic in his jaw and the grinding of his teeth as he held on to his control.

"You need the ice more than I do." Leya's voice didn't sound like her own. This was husky, almost like Nikki's…like Landry's had once been.

She pulled away from his grip, pushing on his chest and trying to direct him toward the bed, but he didn't budge.

Her hand settled above his heart, feeling the rapid-fire banging of it beneath her palm. The collision of skin and the wild rhythm of the beat triggered a yearning in her so strong she could almost see it visibly in the room.

She swallowed hard, forcing herself to focus on the bruises covering his body and away from her secret desires. Softly, she said, "Please, Holden. Let me help. You got hurt because of me."

His jaw ticked, the stubborn set of his jaw flaring an equally stubborn reaction in her.

"I can always call Dad and have him tell your boss you're injured."

His eyes flashed with anger and something else—fear. Her stomach flipped.

"I'd rather you be the one with me," she pushed. "I trust you. I won't trust any of them."

"You shouldn't," he said and then clamped his lips shut as if wishing he hadn't said it. He sighed and backed away from her, his warmth going with him, leaving her shivering again. He pulled back the comforter to reveal sheets that had probably been white but now were a dingy gray. She tried not to think about it as he lay down, and she went into the bathroom to fill another towel with ice. They only had one more hand towel and a single bath towel left.

She retraced her steps and stopped. He had his gun laying on his bare stomach over the lines of an eight-pack she'd never seen in real life. His jeans were hung low on his hips, encasing legs so long they hung off the edge. He took up so much space it made the bed look child-sized. He was exactly the superhero her friends had teased him of being. It was nothing that had ever appealed to her in the past. Not until he'd shown up in Grand Orchard and announced with a calm command that he'd been assigned to her.

She'd been annoyed by the way her body had reacted to him back then.

And now…now she couldn't get enough.

She forced herself to move, to stop gawking like one of their fans, and sank cross-legged next to him on the bed. Her knees were almost touching him, causing goosebumps to coat her skin. She placed the larger towel on his ribs, and his stomach rippled in response. A motion that was fascinating, mesmerizing. She forced her gaze upward, placing the towel he'd given her onto the bridge of his nose, partially covering his eyes.

"What else can I get you?" she asked. "Do you have any pain medicine in your bag?"

"No. It dulls the senses. I don't use them on the job."

She swallowed hard at his words. A bitter reminder, once again, that this was exactly what she was to him. A job. The protectee. The person he'd give his life for but not someone he'd lose everything for. The distinction in words was small, but the meaning enormous.

She couldn't think about it now. It caused more pain than she cared to acknowledge.

"Why did you agree that I shouldn't trust anyone else from the Secret Service?" she asked.

"They found us too easily, just like the note got into your dad's mail too easily. Something isn't right," he said. His voice was tired and worn.

"There's someone on the inside?" she asked, fear spiking again. "Is my family safe?"

"I don't think it's with the Secret Service." But she could hear the shred of doubt in his voice.

"Do you think it's Angel Carter?" she asked, thinking of the man in the car. His eyes had appeared black in the dark of the vehicle, but Fee had said they were midnight blue. He'd been scary as hell, and she wasn't sure how Fiadh had ever dared to meet up with him. Leya would have run away the very first time she'd seen him. He was bigger than Holden, bigger than any of their bodyguards, and they had some pretty big men on their team.

Holden's phone rang on the dresser where he'd left it. He started to sit up to retrieve it, and she pushed her fingers into his chest. "I'll get it."

It was a testament to how much he was hurting that he didn't argue. She brought the phone over to him, noting the name Camp on the lock screen.

"Kent," he said, pausing for a response. "We're in a hotel for the night under the name Green. I've got a vehicle, and we'll head out at dawn as planned."

He listened again. "You've got an APB out for her already?" He gritted his teeth. "I'll keep an eye out. There should be no way for her to find us. Not unless…"

The man on the other end growled loud enough that Leya could hear him but not decipher what he said.

"Understood, sir."

He clicked off, placing the phone next to him and meeting her gaze.

"Do you know an Astrid Barrows?" he asked.

Leya's eyes widened. "She works for D.C. Avenue Writers. She's a speechwriter. Why?"

"She was the one driving the car that pushed us into the intersection. They caught her on a camera a few blocks before the scene."

Leya let the shock roll through her as the image of the thin woman who'd approached her and Lincoln at EchoBar came back to her. She kicked herself for not thinking of their weird interaction earlier, but her mind had been filled with other things. With Krish and marriage and FGT and a bomb…and Holden. Maybe he was the biggest distraction of them all.

"They're doing a deep dive into her life," Holden continued. "But she was roommates her freshman year with Penny Waylin. That's John Smythe's daughter. Penny and her mother have supposedly had no interaction with Smythe since she was a toddler, but it's too much of a coincidence to think Astrid could be connected to FGT any other way."

"She wanted Lincoln to dance with her at EchoBar last night…*hey ram*, was that really only last night?" She shook her head in disbelief. "He rejected her and used our code word to let me know he wanted to leave."

Holden muttered something under his breath that she thought sounded a lot like he was kicking himself for not being with her at the bar.

"She thought you were together," he said, and underneath the layer of calm he forced, there was a growl, as if he hated the idea of her with Lincoln. It sent a decadent thrill through her.

"When she came up, he held my hand and put his arm around me. We've both done it before—as a deterrent, you know. If someone thinks you're together, then you don't have to deal with them asking you out or making a scene. It's like our code word. We've used them both as a way to get out of sticky situations."

"Except, this time, it thrust you into one," he said dryly.

The towel on his face started to drip along with the one on his side. The trail ran down over his ribs, drawing her finger to it and setting off sparks that felt larger than a fireworks display.

"If she's part of FGT, this could be the break we need. We just have to find her," he said softly. He'd said something similar earlier, but she wasn't confident that anyone would save them. Not after everything the Daisies had been through.

She stared at him for a long moment, then grabbed the makeshift ice packs and returned to the sink. Guilt and anger and frustration rolled through her. Hate groups made no sense to her. She didn't understand their lack of compassion. Their utter determination to not see that, below outer appearances, everyone had the same two hundred and six bones and over six hundred and fifty muscles. All people were made up of the same components, just assembled differently.

Leya should have been used to it by now. But how did you ever acclimate yourself to illogical taunts and insults? Her family tried to be prepared for it…her band tried to ignore it. But it still hurt. It still struck the inner core of her.

She wrung out the towels, filled them back up with ice that hadn't melted, and returned to Holden's side. A question that had burned in her brain for two years, that Angel had hinted at, and did nothing but ignite the remorse and grief and pain inside her burst from her lips.

"Angel…he thought maybe Landry was mistaken for me." She swallowed hard, catching a sob and looking away. What would she do if it was actually true? That awful night her friend had died, Holden and her mother had both hinted at it in a whispered conversation they thought she couldn't hear, and ever since then, she'd lived on this weird edge of wanting to know and not. How would she forgive herself if it were true?

"None of it is your fault," Holden grunted out, and her eyes returned to his face to find he'd been watching her, reading her thoughts in the way he was so good at doing. "Even if it ends up being the reason she died, it still isn't your fault or your father's fault. The only person to blame is the one who wielded the knife. I highly doubt that was Astrid Barrows."

Her eyes grew spotty. She unwound her legs and lay down next to him, their elbows brushing, fire racing through her at the simple touch.

"You didn't tell your boss about Angel," she said quietly. "Why?"

His body stiffened slightly. "Because Carter was right. He could have killed Fiadh any of the times he'd met up with her. He could have killed us tonight in that alley. He certainly didn't have to drive us to a hotel and hand over the keys to his car. I don't understand his motivations, and I certainly don't trust him, but right now, there aren't many people I do trust."

Lying down had been the wrong thing to do because her exhausted body reacted to it, forcing her eyes to shut, even though she desperately tried to keep them open. She felt like the towel she'd wrung out in the bathroom. Tattered and weak. Twisted and cold. Except for the warmth of Holden that was leaking into her. Comforting. Soothing.

She wished things could be different. Wished she was allowed to experience passion and desire with the only man to bring it out in her and that he wouldn't have to give up anything at all to share it with her.

Wished she could just have a taste of him.

And that singular thought followed her into her dreams. Sensual ones where her lips and hands were tangled with Holden's and where his voice growled out her name as they slowly consumed each other.

# Chapter Thirteen

## *Holden*

***SOMETHING ABOUT HER***
*Performed by Bryan Adams*

*The ice had melted and started* dripping again, and yet Holden was reluctant to move. Leya was asleep next to him, her breathing even, her face tucked into his shoulder, and her thighs curving gently into his side. It was utterly intoxicating. But unless he wanted them to wake up in a wet mess that was opposite of the one his traitorous body wanted, he had to do something. Slowly, he used his left arm to remove the towels and place them on the side table. Then, one-handed and awkward, he set an alarm on his phone, using the vibrate mode so it wouldn't wake her but he could still check in with Camp.

He needed a different phone, and he needed Leya to lose hers as well. The USSS could track these, and for the first time ever, he found no comfort in that thought. Not when there were too many unanswered questions. Too many holes to fill up.

In an attempt to keep awake and stop himself from thinking about the woman tucked up against him, he made a mental list of things they needed to get in the morning. Cash. Disposable phones. Clothes. Hats. Ammo. Toiletries.

Astrid Barrows may have rammed into them, but she wasn't the person pulling the strings. Someone had sent her after Lincoln Matherton at EchoBar and after Leya today.

He highly doubted a twenty-four-year-old college grad had the means to get a note into the vice president's packet or the training to track a Secret Service detail down.

Leya's body completely relaxed, molding into his even more. Not even the exhaustion and pain scouring him prevented his dick from hardening, the scent of her embedding itself into him in a way he'd never be able to shake.

He'd known back in the command center that going with her threatened his future. He'd sworn to himself, to his dad, to anyone who'd challenged him, that there was nothing he'd give up the Secret Service for. Not his family. Not friends who had come and gone from his life. And yet, here he was, on the verge of doing just that…giving it all up. He had mere moments to pull the pieces back together before it shattered forever.

Not telling Camp about Angel Carter could easily be the final straw, but something had held him back. The inner instinct his dad had always told him to listen to had made him bite his tongue. Something that made it feel like the past and the present were somehow tangled together.

He hadn't heard back from Marco Hernandez yet, so he repeated the text he'd sent the night before.

*HOLDEN: What did you find on Carter?*

*MARCO: I was just pulling together the latest for you. We found his room in Boston and have been trying to make sense of what we found.*

A slew of images appeared on Holden's screen, taken from inside a studio apartment. The living space was empty except for the large wall where an evidence board of sorts had been set up—pictures of people, reports, and maps all with text and lines drawing them together. Close-ups had been taken by Marco, or his team, of everything on the board. It was a picture of Landry's body by the pond that stopped Holden from scrolling. He zoomed in, something nudging at the back of his brain as he looked at her body curved in an almost fetal position. Finally, it clicked, and he barely held back a muttered curse.

*HOLDEN: He was there before Paisley.*

*MARCO: Was wondering if you'd catch that. Yep. That shot is before Paisley rolled her over. As Paisley and Jonas were the first ones on the scene...means he was there.*

Chills went up Holden's back, and he hated again that he'd let Carter walk away tonight. He didn't know what he could have done differently to detain the man. Not in his condition with Leya to protect. He debated telling Marco about what had happened, but it would mean giving away their location, and if Holden didn't fully trust the Secret Service, there was no way he trusted the security detail on duty the day Landry was murdered.

*HOLDEN: Have you been watching for him to come back?*

*MARCO: He's not coming back. Sent the landlord a final check.*

*HOLDEN: He saw you?*

*MARCO: Maybe, or maybe he just moved on.*

Holden thought back to the conversation in the car and the weird look he'd sent Leya.

*HOLDEN: He's not a lone wolf. He's working for someone.*

*MARCO: We've been canvassing the area between his apartment and the library, talking to whoever is willing to chat. People remember him because he's a big mother, but no one remembers seeing him with anyone else.*

His mind reeled through everything that had happened today. FGT. Astrid. Carter. Could they all be threads being pulled from the same source, or were they just overlapping weaves? He'd never be able to pick it apart until his mind was clearer, until he'd gotten at least a few hours of sleep, but every inch of him fought it.

Even still, his lids grew heavy until they finally shut, his body giving in to pain and exhaustion. It felt like mere seconds had passed when the vibration of his phone alarm jolted him back awake. He sent a text off to Camp, reset the alarm, and repeated the process throughout the night—making lists, sleeping, jerking awake. He wouldn't be firing on all cylinders tomorrow, but he'd been trained for these exact scenarios. He'd done it before. He'd do it again. It was the job, just like he'd told her.

His inner critic scoffed. This was way more than a job. If he was lying next to Ved Singh or, hell, even the daughter of the former president he'd first been assigned to, he wouldn't have thought twice about their scent or the way their curves felt tucked up against him. But lying next to Leya, a deep, animalistic craving made him want to flip her over and take a bite. Lick and kiss and caress every inch and swell.

He really needed to get laid, but he had a sinking feeling it wasn't the act that would ever fix what was happening inside him. He wanted to hate it. Wanted to hate her for making him feel this way, shredding the goals he'd held firm in his mind for the majority of his life. Jesus. He had to get out of bed. Put distance between them. Pull back those splintering pieces before it was too late.

He rolled slightly away from her, and his entire body groaned. As he pulled farther away, Leya's hand trailed after him in her sleep, as if seeking the heat of him, and damn if that didn't hit him in the chest like a bolt of lightning.

He swung his legs over the edge and sat there for a moment until the world stopped spinning. His ribs throbbed. He was pretty sure they weren't broken, but he was way more injured than he'd let on to Camp. If he'd said anything, his boss would have yanked him, sending someone to replace him, and Holden wasn't trusting her to anyone else. He pushed himself up off the bed, and his stomach roiled at the agony. Like it or not, he needed some over-the-counter pain meds. He added it to his mental list, a new schedule for their day replacing all his other plans.

When he turned back around, his heart skittered around in his chest at the sight of her. Dark lashes were closed, thick and lush resting on high cheekbones. Long strands of hair feathered across her face, landing on full lips delightfully ripe for kissing. Deep inside him, a roar to consume her tried to break free, but he forced himself away instead. Forced his feet to the bathroom where he stopped suddenly at the sight in the mirror.

His nose was larger than normal, swelled enough to make it hard to breathe, and black bruising extended from the top of the bridge down under both eyes. He looked like he'd been punched in the face.

He turned the shower on, got in, and almost groaned in relief as the heat spread over him. He stood, head bent, letting it loosen his tight muscles. But as his muscles relaxed, his gaze went to where he could still see Leya through the open door. He hadn't dared shut it, obsessively needing to keep her in his line of sight. His dick reacted to the early morning, the shower, and the vision she made. Aching and hard. He almost reached down and took himself in hand, but it felt wrong in a way masturbating never had before. Wrong because she deserved better than some idiot jerking off while staring at her.

He turned the handle to cold and let it do the trick, suddenly furious with himself for his thoughts. For this situation. For not being able to protect her better.

He stepped out, wrapped the single towel around his waist, and turned to see her sitting up in bed, watching him, and his body responded all over again. Her gorgeous hair tumbled around her shoulders, and her deep, dark eyes were sleepy and lust-filled. Her mouth was parted slightly, and the tip of a pink tongue snuck out to wet her lips.

The entire space between them became a charged wire, lurching back and forth, zapping them both. She was as affected as he was. Even if the almost kiss on the lawn hadn't already proven it, the look in her hooded gaze screamed it.

She rubbed her eyes softly, smudging the limited makeup she'd worn for too many hours, but it did nothing but add to the temptation she presented. Because he wanted her smudged and swollen and aching but from a night lost in his arms and not from an accident that had nearly sent her to her death.

She rose, pattering across the stained carpet toward the bathroom door, pulling her hair out of her face as she moved. She leaned against the frame. His fingers twitched, longing to settle on her hips, craving to have those curves she'd had tucked up against him all night pressed into him once more.

He tore himself out of his trance, a scowl taking over his face because he was an asshole who wasn't worthy of the trust and confidence the USSS's motto demanded. He started to slide past her, snarling, "Get ready. We're leaving."

Her eyes narrowed, unhappy with the command.

She reached out, long fingers resting on his bicep, and he stilled, unable to stop the wash of images that flooded him, wanting her fingers on other parts of him.

"You've got the only towel," she said.

He closed his eyes, teeth clicking tightly together. Here he'd been lost in scandalous visions, and all she wanted was the goddamn towel. But when he opened them again, her gaze was strolling down him, taking in his flat stomach, and the Vs at his sides, and the hair that led down below the white cotton.

"Leya." His voice was deep and gravelly, loaded with meaning in that one word, and it jerked her eyes up to his, mouth parting again. "I need to protect you. Do you understand that?"

She frowned, confused by his words.

"I can't do that. I can't protect you if you keep looking at me like that."

Surprise lit her face because these words acknowledged his attraction even more than the ones at the residence the day before. The ones he'd covered by reminding her she was his job. They both knew it was more than that. But putting it out there, calling them both out, was his attempt at strengthening the barrier between them before the cracks running the entire length of it finally let go.

"Maybe protection isn't what I need," she said, and his heart slammed into action like he'd done a ten-mile run. "Maybe what I need is to be treated like a woman someone can't live without. A person worthy of someone throwing everything else in their life away for, not because it's their job but because it's the only viable option. The only way they'll be able to breathe again."

His entire being responded to her words. He suddenly wanted to give her exactly what she desired. Ached to be the one who gave up everything to center her at the top of their world. And that single reaction had him stepping backward into the room.

*How could he even think it*? Give up everything for what? A chance to fuck her senseless? No…not fuck her. Make love to her. Worship her. Show her exactly the goddess she was. But it would end. End brutally because even though she'd tossed aside Krish Arya, their worlds were light-years apart.

If his barrier came tumbling down, she was right. It wasn't her who would lose. It would be him. But he'd lose more than just his job. He'd lose his integrity. His belief in himself. Everything that made him who he was would be gone.

He took five more steps away until the bed hit the backs of his legs. "Shut the door, Leya. I'll get dressed and get you a towel."

She stared for a long time, disappointment in her eyes, and it made something deep inside him scream at his stupidity. At turning her away. Denying her what both their bodies craved. But she did as he asked before he could change his mind, turning away and shutting the door with a quiet click.

He dragged his hands over his face, the pain of the motion to his nose, elbow, and ribs jerking him back to reality even more. He reached for the single duffel he'd brought, the clothes already dwindling, and pulled on a clean pair of jeans and a black T-shirt before slipping back into his sneakers. He found the pair of sunglasses he'd set on the dresser, slid them on, and ducked out of the room, locking it behind him.

A different person was at the desk in the office as he demanded more towels. When he returned, the shower was running, and thoughts of her on the other side of the door in absolutely nothing almost catapulted him into it with her.

He needed space. He needed to get her out of his skin and head, but there was nowhere for him to go, not unless he abandoned her completely, and he'd never do that. When he heard the shower turn off, he knocked on the door, turned his face away, and thrust the towels inside. She grabbed them from him without a word.

When she emerged, she had her hair pulled back in a long ponytail, baring her slender neck in a way that tempted him to litter it with kisses. Her face was scrubbed clean, and the knot on her forehead stood out, tinged with black and purple. She wore the same clothes she'd had on the day before as he hadn't been able to grab her suitcase from the crash.

He handed her the wig and the baseball hat. She ignored the wig but pulled the hat on, tugging her ponytail through the opening at the back and then tipping the brim low enough that she hissed when it hit her injury. They didn't say a word as they both threw their meager belongings into the two bags he'd rescued and headed out the door. He stopped to scan the area. A couple of people were in the parking lot, loading trunks or heading for the restaurant. Everything else was quiet.

He continued to sweep their surroundings as they went down the stairs and headed toward the Camaro.

"Keep your head down," he growled when they reached it. Instead of opening the door, he cast another glance around the parking lot before sliding underneath it. He used his phone light to examine the undercarriage, searching for not only bombs but tracking devices.

When he rolled back out, she brushed at the back of his shirt. He opened the passenger door, and she slid inside. As he walked around to the driver's side, his heart slammed in his chest. Hard and fast. He took in a deep breath. He was teetering on a balance beam, knowing he was going to fall but unsure which side he'd end up on. He was caught between duty and desire, unable to walk away but also knowing that staying only promised hell…or heaven…or both.

# Chapter Fourteen

## Leya

***INTO THE ECHO***
*Performed by Bon Jovi*

*SIX DAYS BEFORE*

Leya's body was still humming from every touch and every brush of a hand that had occurred since waking up with the vision of Holden getting out of the shower. She'd been unable to look away, slowly taking in every piece of him. Carved lines and rigid curves that sent fire licking through her veins. Whereas other bodies had left her disinterested, he'd left her hot and throbbing without a single touch. Her brain was screaming at her that it was just lust—desire at an intensity she'd never felt—but her heart was chanting something different.

Which was why she'd impulsively, stupidly, challenged him. A dare she'd known he couldn't accept. Not only because of his job but because of who he was at his core. How could she even think of asking him to give up everything he wanted and believed? For what? A kiss. A night twisted together in the sheets? How dare she ask anyone else to give up their life for even less than she'd been offered and turned down with Krish?

The feeling Leya was most accustomed to in her life swept back over her—guilt. Remorse for pushing him. He was in this untenable situation because of her, and she'd only made it worse. She just needed to box up the feelings she had when he was near and lock them away. She had to hope some other man would come along and free the feelings when it was right. But somewhere, deep in her soul, she doubted there'd ever be someone else. Not when the handful of others she'd kissed had left her feeling dry and frigid.

The car jerking suddenly to the right brought her out of her thoughts as she gripped the handle, panic slamming into her veins instead of lust as he sped down an off-ramp. She glanced over at Holden to see his brows furrowed together above the mirrored glasses he'd slid on.

"What's wrong?" she demanded.

He didn't respond but took another sharp right down a side street, followed by several more quick turns until they came to a main street blocked off with temporary barricades. People were lining the sidewalks as if waiting for a parade.

"Jesus," he muttered, turning at the last minute into the lot of a box store. He backed into a space near the back.

"What's going on, Holden?" she demanded.

"It's probably nothing."

"Were we followed?"

His jaw clenched. "I'm just being cautious."

But she knew he wasn't telling her the truth. He'd seen something that had bothered him. He got out of the car before she could say more, rounded the hood, and opened her door. When she stepped out, his mirrored glasses met her eyes for a moment, and she wished she could see what he was thinking. Wished for once his face wasn't the mask he wore as an agent.

"I want to make this as quick as possible, but you need clothes, and we need different phones, so keep your head down, and stay right by me. Got it?"

He grabbed her hand, twining them together as if they were a couple, and it sent waves of mixed emotions through her. The sparks of desire she always felt were there but also a deep longing to be part of a couple. She wanted to find happiness and love. Wanted exactly what she'd tossed out this morning—someone who saw her, with all her impulsive, creative, flighty ways, and still desired her.

Inside, he grabbed a cart and walked at a fast clip through the store, dragging her with him. Pre-paid phones went into the cart first, followed by boxes of ammunition from the sporting goods section that made her stomach flip. Then, he whirled her into the clothing department. She could feel his impatience as she tried to find things that would fit her curves without trying them on. He shifted uncomfortably when they hit the lingerie department, and she couldn't help the small smile that lit her lips.

She waved two packages of underwear in his direction. "Cats or hearts?" He had his glasses tucked on top of his head now, and she could clearly see the way his eyes narrowed at her taunt. Her smile grew. "You act as if you've never seen women's underwear before, Special Agent Kent. Don't you have a mother? Or a sister? Maybe a girlfriend?"

He stepped closer into her space, bending slightly so his mouth was close to her ear, his warm breath coasting over her skin as he said, "I'm Miles Green. You're Lita Rae Green. And yes, I have a sister and a mother. Just put the panties in the damn cart, darlin', so we can move on."

Her heart skittered at the term of endearment. Had it slipped out, or had he done it on purpose to make her uncomfortable? A returned taunt? Their eyes met for a long, lingering moment. He grabbed both packages and tossed them with the other items before backing away and leading them to their next stop.

They added clothes for him, pain medicines, a couple of duffel bags, and some water bottles to their growing pile, and then he abruptly changed course, turning into the Halloween section.

"What are we doing here?" she asked.

He scanned the shelves, but she didn't miss the way his gaze lingered at the end of the aisle. Her heart sped up again. Had they been followed again? Into the store?

"Holden?" Her concern could be heard in the breathless whisper of his name, and his pale-blue eyes met hers again. He didn't respond to the unasked question. Instead, he grabbed a cowboy hat from the rack, slid off her baseball hat, and placed it on her head.

She snorted. "I don't think this is me."

"We're going to Tennessee. You'll fit right in." His lips quirked, and her heart stopped for a different reason than panic and fear. She'd been aching to see his full-blown smile almost as much as she ached to kiss him.

She turned away, eyes catching on a Captain America mask. She grabbed it, stepped closer to him, and rose onto her toes to tug it on him. She was rewarded with another twitch of his lips.

"What?" she said, barely unable to contain her smile. "You need a disguise almost more than me."

He huffed out a sigh as he pulled the mask back off. "No one knows who I am, Leya."

She shook her head slightly. "Maybe not *who* you are, but definitely *what* you are." When he turned around from putting the mask back, she could tell he didn't believe her. "When you stride into a room, Holden, everyone notices. You take up the entire space. You command the room almost as much as my dad and Guy Matherton. Maybe more."

He started down the aisle, but she didn't budge, and he turned to look at her with a brow raised.

"It's the truth," she told him. "I noticed it the very first moment you walked into the studio in Grand Orchard. My entire being noticed it…" she faltered, taking a breath and then changing course, trying valiantly to do what she'd told herself was right and lock up those feelings and throw away the key. "It was irritating, which is why I called you Captain

Annoying even though everyone else in the band called you Captain Avenger."

Their eyes stayed locked for too long. So long she could feel every molecule in her being turning toward him, waiting to bask in his rays as if he was exactly the superhero she'd always thought, demanding she notice him. He was the one to turn away first, grabbing a second cowboy hat, one that matched hers, and placing it on his head.

While she probably looked preposterous, he looked absolutely perfect. It flipped the superhero-like image he carried around, turning it into boyish, country charm instead. Her mouth dropped a little, causing the upward lilt of his lips to return and hypnotizing her with their pull. Her heart jumped and kicked and pattered wildly.

"Maybe I should call you Captain Cowboy instead."

And then, something magical happened. His face broke into an enormous smile. It pushed his cheeks up and curled the corners of his eyes, adding a sparkle to the blue depths that caused her racing heart to stop completely for a nanosecond before slamming back into action. It made him even more gorgeous. Stunning. She wanted desperately to have her sketchpad open so she could capture it before it went away, before he returned to the somber agent he normally was.

"Maybe we'll stop at a thrift shop and find some used cowboy boots too," he said and then winked.

Every attempt at locking away the lust and desire crumbled with that single motion. How could she deny it when her body reveled in it? She wouldn't dare him again. She wouldn't because it wasn't fair to him, but she could at least savor these feelings while they lasted, couldn't she? She could give herself this much? Yearning that would never be satisfied, but at least experienced.

"Let's go, Lita Rae," he said, smile remaining as he pushed the cart to the end of the aisle. But it disappeared as he scanned the main corridor and then led them toward the checkout stand. He paid with cash, loaded their bags back into the cart, and then headed for the door.

As the store's automatic doors swept open, Holden's feet stuttered. From the time they'd gone inside until now, the parking lot had completely changed. Instead of a dozen or so cars, it was now packed. Several parade floats were parked there with what felt like hundreds of people milling about. Teens in band, cheerleading, and football uniforms huddled together. Teachers and parents bustled around, trying to put the kids in some kind of order. A banner on one of the floats read *Wayland High Homecoming*.

Holden had parked the Camaro at the back of the lot, but now it was surrounded by cars and people.

"Jesus," he muttered. "Keep your head down."

He grabbed her hand and pulled her between him and the cart handle, caging her in. To the casual observer, they would look like an adorable couple who couldn't stand to not be touching even for a few seconds. His front was up tight against her back, his arms on either side, and she felt him wince as her elbow collided with his side. He'd been hiding the pain better than he had the night before, but the black and purple tucked beneath his sunglasses were a clear reminder.

As they moved toward the car with their bodies touching in multiple places, energy zapped through and around them, making her warm all over again. Hot and loose and pulsing. It wasn't just her body responding. It was her soul. A sense of complete rightness settled over her when she was locked in his embrace like this. As if her feet had finally landed where Devi Maa had always planned for her to be.

As if she'd found her *jeevansathi*.

And that scared her. Scared her because how could this be more than just passion and lust when she knew so little about him? She didn't know how his stars meshed with hers. Didn't know more than the fact that he had two parents and a sister. If this was more than just passion and lust, they still couldn't be… But would the gods really lead her to her life partner only to forbid them from being together? Maybe that was really what made love different than lust—the sacrifice. The willingness to abandon everything to be together.

She hadn't wanted to do it for Krish, but did that mean she would never find anyone she was willing to sacrifice for? Would she be willing to do it for Holden? Her heart squeezed tight, knowing her mother would never approve of this. Of him. Of a family that was nothing like theirs being joined to them. Would she give up any chance of seeing pride in her mother's eyes so she could be at Holden's side forever?

Did it even matter if he wasn't willing to take the same kind of leap?

When they got to the Camaro, he moved away, and she almost cried because it felt so unfair. To have had him like that and yet not really have him at all. She ached for more than his protection. She ached to be his. Not just physically, but in every way possible.

It was ridiculous.

Impulsive.

Everything her mom had always accused her of being.

But could she fight it? Did she even want to?

Holden had popped the trunk, and she realized he was shoving all the items they'd just purchased into the two new duffel bags while she stood there having a crisis of her soul. She shook herself out of it enough to help him add the items.

"Give me your phone," he said.

She frowned but did it. He looked around surreptitiously, dropped to his haunches, hiding behind the car, and smashed her phone with the butt of his gun.

What the hell are you doing?" she demanded. Everything was on her phone. Her friends. Her family. Numbers she didn't even know.

"Don't worry. All your information is backed up on a cloud. But I can't have them tracing us. From here on out, we only use the pre-paid phones and only when we absolutely have to."

He repeated the process with his own phone, and it sent a chill up her spine. He thought they were in danger from far more than just the FGT. He'd insinuated it last night and then backtracked. But it was clear as day—he didn't trust his own people. Fear rattled around in her chest, spinning through the lust and lodging itself like a block of wood.

He stood up, scanning the crowd as three cheerleaders bounced by them, and one of them turned her smiling face in their direction. As the girl's smile slipped and her mouth rounded, Leya realized she wasn't looking down anymore. The girl made eye contact and then turned in a rush to her friends.

Holden saw it at the same time.

"How many times do I have to say to keep your head down?" he growled.

He unlocked the door, took her bag from inside, and tossed it over his shoulder before picking up the two new ones. He grabbed her hand and headed on foot through the people gathered around the floats. He led them at a steady pace. Fast enough to get them out of the lot quickly, but not enough to draw too much attention.

"We're l-leaving the car?" she asked, desperately trying not to stumble as she kept her eyes peeled to the asphalt.

"Yes."

She swallowed. Was it Angel who'd followed them this morning? Or had Astrid shown up again? It seemed ridiculous that the tiny blonde was chasing them. But as Holden strode toward the street that was even more packed than the parking lot, she could tell he was trying to lose someone.

Families waiting for the parade lined the sidewalks, laughter filling the air, little kids chasing each other around, and waving school banners. Holden stopped in a storefront, pulling her up against his chest as a boyfriend might do, and even as part of her banged happily at being tucked up against him, the other part was flooded with fear. He waited, scanning the way they'd just come before tugging her back onto the street.

A little kid burst from a coffee shop in front of them, almost tripping them. His dad apologized before they rushed past her and Holden. She glanced back over her shoulder and caught sight of the top of an ice-blonde head, the hair up in a high ponytail. Leya's blood went cold.

"Is that her?" Leya muttered.

Holden didn't look. Instead, he dragged her forward again. At the intersection, he drew her quickly around the edge of the building, pushing her back against a brick wall. One hand went above her head, the other to her waist as he stepped so close his thighs brushed against hers, forcing their hips and groins to align and causing that nonstop buzz to overtake her once again.

He bent his head, tilting it slightly so their cowboy hats didn't collide, and met her eyes with his, a look there she couldn't quite name.

"I'm going to kiss you," he uttered in a deep guttural tone that caused her pulse to flutter more than his words did. "Don't read anything into it. I just want them to lose interest in us. I want them to see a couple and not a rock star on the run." Her heart banged fiercely in her chest as his mouth slowly eased toward hers. It brushed tantalizingly close, his breath coasting over her lips as he asked, "Leya, do you understand?"

Enticing, tingling sensations shuttered through her, but somehow, she choked out, "Yes."

His lips lowered until they touched hers completely and lightly—a mere brush of soft, silky skin against skin. But it sent a thundering wave of desire through her. With that tiniest of touches, she was already lost, drowning and being pulled under. His hand moved from the wall to cup her jaw as the one at her waist drew her closer. The pressure of his mouth on hers grew, moving from a simple taste to an insistent demand. *Give me every part of you*, it seemed to chant. And she desperately wanted to.

She moaned, but it seemed far away, as if it was someone else. With a returned growl, he took the kiss from light and insistent to frantic and unbridled. His tongue swept along her seam, and she let him in with an aching sigh. She met his wet, hungry lunges with urgent flicks. Heat traveled from her core, through her chest, and upward until she felt like, somehow, she'd been joined to Holden with a simple glide of mouths and tongues, as if the fire ritual had already melded them together.

When Krish had kissed her like this, open-mouthed and passionate, at the inauguration ball, she'd pushed him away, disgusted by her own lack of reaction but also with his intensity. His persistence. With the pure wetness of it all and the way he'd tasted like champagne and garlic.

The opposite was true with Holden. Every lick, every glide, every twist made her warmer, made the flickering flame inside her seem to grow wider, stronger, faster until it felt like an inferno that couldn't be contained.

He went to pull back, and she couldn't let him. She didn't want the moment to end because she was terrified that the additional piece of her soul she'd just discovered would disappear with him, and she'd never feel this alive again. She placed her hand at the back of his neck, holding him in place, the pads of her fingers dancing along the short hair below his cowboy hat. The harshness of the bristles was a delightful contrast to the softness of his mouth, much like the hardness of his body up against her gentle curves was a dichotomy that felt completely perfect.

That felt so damn right.

Her hips shoved into his of their own accord. Needing the friction. Needing him. But the action seemed to bring him back to their reality. His back had already stiffened, and he'd started to draw away even before a tiny voice nearby said, "Gross. Get a room," and a very adult voice said, "There are kids around. Maybe take it somewhere else."

And then, he was gone, and if the loss of him in the parking lot had been painful, this was pure torture. She barely registered him pulling her down the street, away from the crowd gathered for the parade. She moved in a haze as they took one street and then another. She was almost panting, trying to keep up not only with his pace but with the kiss and her reaction to it. Her mouth felt decidedly and delightfully bruised. Her cheeks felt hot and flushed. Her core was clenched tight, needing a release she was unsure she'd ever get from him.

They found themselves back on a major thoroughfare, the sounds of the parade and the crowd left behind them. This street had cars zipping past them across four lanes of traffic. Holden brought them to a stop at the crosswalk, and when the light changed, he drew them across to where a fast-food restaurant sat next to a used car lot.

He went inside, shoving her into a booth where there was both easy access to the door and he could see almost three-hundred-and-sixty degrees around them. She went to take her hat off, and he shook his head.

"Keep it on."

They stared at each other for too long, eyes falling to mouths and back. Nothing had prepared her for the earth-shattering kiss. Not anything she'd read. Not anything her friends had said. And certainly not anything she'd experienced.

"I'm sorry," he uttered. "I thought it would give us time to blend in, let anyone who might be following us slide past."

The words were forced, as if he was trying to justify it to himself as much as to her. But those instincts *Nani* had told her to trust told her that he'd wanted the kiss too. Had lost control while doing so. And maybe to a man like

Holden, whose entire life was about control, that was the worst thing that could happen to him.

But to her, it had been the best.

"What do you want?" he asked, head tilting toward the registers and the overhead menu.

"I'm not hungry," she said, turning her face away from him, twisting and turning her bracelets in an effort to soothe herself. Her feelings were all over the place. Panic at being cut off without her phone. Anger and frustration at being chased. Hope that was irrational after a singular kiss. And below it all, a great big pool of fear. Not only because of who was after them but because the truth from earlier was pounding its way across her veins. She might have to give up more than she'd ever been expected to give up with Krish in order to have Holden…and there was absolutely no guarantee that he was willing to make any kind of sacrifice in return.

# Chapter Fifteen

## Holden

***I'LL STAND BY YOU***
*Performed by Pretenders*

*Holden's gut was flexed tight, his* ribs ached, and his vision was still spotty at times. But nothing hurt like his heart. He'd kissed Leya, stepping so far past the line he'd been taught to keep that even though he'd retreated, it still mocked him. The truth was, he could have lost the tail he wasn't even positive they'd had in a different way. He could have simply kept them moving through the crowd before ducking through the side streets like the ones that had ended with them here.

But he'd been full of the smell of her, and the feel of her tucked up against his chest, and the smile she'd sent his way in the store. So, instead of following his training, he'd kissed her. It had been a mistake not only because of the boundaries he was supposed to keep but because it had been fucking beautiful. Magic. Like sipping from a well at the gates of heaven. Sweetness and lust all bundled together.

He would have gone on kissing her for hours…days…a lifetime…if her hips ricocheting into his groin and the cold disgust of the adult behind them hadn't jolted him from the bliss.

Even now, he was still gone.

Over the edge.

Beyond recovery.

Nothing but shattered glass around him.

Staying with her put her in danger because he wouldn't be calm and collected if someone came after her. He'd be frantic. Enraged. Desperate. He couldn't adequately focus on their surroundings and possible threats because all he could do was focus on her. Most attacks happened in under ten seconds. But his job wasn't to respond to the attack. It was to stop it *before* it happened. And that meant concentrating, not on one particular face or movement, but thousands, if not millions, at once. It meant absolutely no distractions.

And he was completely distracted. Even now, he should have been concentrating on the people in the restaurant and the cars driving by, but all he could do was stare at her. Even in day-old clothes, a hat that didn't fit right, and exhausted, she was still stunning. Shining exactly like the firefly her code name labeled her.

There was a whole class of female fireflies called *femme fatales* who, unlike the rest of their species, lured unsuspecting males and used them as dinner in order to acquire the toxins needed to protect their eggs. He'd let her if he was the duped male. He'd gladly give over his body to protect her and whatever family that came along.

He'd choose her over duty.

He already had.

So, what the hell did he do now? He should just call Camp and tell him to send a goddamn replacement. But he wouldn't. Which was all sorts of screwed up.

He needed space. A moment to figure this out. So, he got up and ordered food for them at the counter, all the while keeping her and the entrances in sight. While he waited, he started compiling the facts in order to make a new checklist. He was almost certain they'd been followed from the motel this morning, and his neck had been itching every moment they'd spent in the store. It was why he'd left the Camaro and their phones behind. There was no other way people could be tracing them.

When their order came up, he brought it back to the table, sliding a veggie burger and curly fries her way. She mumbled a thanks, and he was relieved when she ate it, but the silence between them grew heavy as they finished the meal. He'd told her the kiss was nothing, but they both knew he'd lied.

After they were done, he tossed their garbage, eyeing the used car lot next door. He didn't have enough cash on him, but he had an undercover credit card with no limit. It would leave a money trail he wasn't sure they could afford, but he was determined it would end there.

"I need to use the restroom," she said, coming to stand next to him.

His stomach twisted. He directed her down a back hallway, darting a glance back to make sure no one was watching as he swung the women's bathroom door open and ducked inside. There was no one else there. She moved past him, and he stepped back out, hoping just his hulking presence would keep anyone else from going in.

Dread clung to him as he opened a duffel, grabbed some aspirin, and swallowed them dry. Then, he broke open one of the pre-paid phone cases and dialed his boss.

"Camp," the man growled into the phone.

"It's Kent."

Cussing burst out on the other end. "Where the fuck are you? Your phone went dark, and you didn't check in. I almost had to tell Lantern we'd lost her. Explain."

Every instinct in Holden told him he could trust Camp, but there was someone in the chain they couldn't. Something they were all missing. But after all the missteps he'd made in the last day, he needed someone else's opinion, and he needed to try and salvage the slim chance he had left of keeping his career by coming clean.

So, he told him about Carter, the tail this morning, and the fact that he'd ditched everything, including their phones. Silence followed his confession, and it lasted so long Holden wondered if he was going to be fired on the spot.

"Why the hell didn't you tell me last night? We could have tailed him."

"And then the entire Secret Service would have known where I was at with Firefly."

"This isn't us, Kent. We've never had a goddamn traitor in our entire history, and there isn't one now." Holden wasn't sure who Camp was trying to convince more, but the words were forced. The truth was they'd sent Leya into hiding with only a handful of people knowing, and they'd still been found.

"Once we're out of here, I'll text you the location of the Camaro, and you can send a team to look it over. I'm going to buy something at a used car lot that's old enough it doesn't have a computer that can be traced. I'm going to use one of my undercover credit cards, but I'm tossing it after this." Camp grumbled something he couldn't decipher, and Holden continued, "I'll call from a pre-paid phone, but it won't be hourly. It may not even be daily. What's the status on Astrid?"

"Nothing. She's gone underground. No one at her job has heard from her. Smythe told our agents he's never heard of her before and that she certainly wasn't working for his organization. His daughter, Penny Waylin, told us a different story. She admitted Astrid was her roommate but said they didn't really get along. Astrid was clingy and jealous when Penny made other friends. She was furious when Penny didn't want to be roommates their sophomore year."

"A bit obsessive," Holden said.

"Here's where she contradicts Smythe. Penny told us he showed up at her dorm room in the middle of her freshman year and Astrid was in the room at the time. Penny told him to get lost, just like her mother had for eighteen years, and she said Astrid flipped out. Astrid never knew her father and would have given a right arm to know him. She screamed that Penny didn't know what she was doing, was an ungrateful human being, yada-yada. Penny went and stayed with a friend for the weekend to let it blow over. My guess—Astrid went after Smythe, and he's been grooming her ever since."

"Jesus, Camp. She's been working at D.C. Avenue Writers and had direct contact with the president's kids and the vice president's family. How the hell does that happen?"

"She was an intern in a sub-contracted company. It's not like she's working for the government and had to file a national security clearance form and pass the personnel security interview."

"Maybe that should change."

The bathroom door opened, and Leya emerged. She'd replaced her ponytail with a loose bun that barely showed beneath the cowboy hat. It still exposed her long, slender neck, and he fought the urge he had every time he saw it to bury his face in it. To lick and nip and suck until he left a mark like some damn vampire. It was the opposite of the control he desperately needed to rediscover.

"I need to go," he said to Camp.

"This isn't just any old rock star you're babysitting, Kent. This is the vice president's daughter. I need updates. Regular ones, or it'll be my ass and yours on the line. Feel me?"

His boss's words hit him hard in the gut. It was an honor to do this job. He had a whole list of people, from the vice president on down, who were counting on him to keep his shit together, protect her, and keep his damn hands to himself.

"Find out how we were followed, promise me they won't show up again, and you can call me every five minutes." Holden knew he'd crossed the line as soon as the words were out, but did it matter when his career was already burning down around him?

"Watch yourself," Camp hissed.

He didn't respond. He just hung up and turned off the phone before Camp had a chance to call back.

"Everything okay?" she asked, eyeing the phone in his hand. The only reason he knew she was uneasy was because she played with the row of tinkerbell beads on her hoop earrings. Just like twirling the dozens of bracelets on her wrists, they were physical tells he'd read in her long before he'd been able to see past the serene presence she showed the world. The same calm her mother showed.

He nodded, wanting to soothe her nerves with an embrace. With his lips or his body.

But that was one way to get them both killed.

He had to force himself to stay on guard, just like in training when they'd stood at a door for two days straight. You learned how to focus through the exhaustion. Now, he just had to use that training to focus through the attraction.

♫ ♫ ♫

It was over another hour before they were able to get on the road. Holden had picked out a 1976 Chevy C10 step-side that glistened in the sun like root beer on ice and had a special-edition 454 engine under the hood. Perfect if he needed to gun it. The best parts were the old-school computers that no one could hack and how it smelled like his Pontiac. Like oil and old vinyl and miles.

Holden did a couple of loops around the town before he got back onto the freeway headed toward Knoxville. Every time he looked in his rearview mirror, Leya glanced out the back with him.

"You're afraid they're still following us?" she breathed out.

He didn't respond. He didn't need to.

"I want to call my parents and my friends. They're all going to be worried about me."

"I'd like to put some miles between us first, if that's okay?"

She didn't like that answer and went back to fiddling with her bracelets. She reached over and turned on the radio, switching through stations but only finding country music. She shut it off, and they rode in silence for too long, but he didn't know how to break it. Especially not when his thoughts and feeling were still all over the place. Not when he was trying his best to focus on the job he'd been trained to do and keep them both safe.

"Who's your best friend?" Her question came out of nowhere, surprising him.

He shot her a confused look. "What?"

"We've got hours more to go. I can't talk to *my* friends, and I don't have my music because you broke my phone. I need something to keep my mind off everything, or I'll come apart at the seams. That leaves you. So, tell me. You do have friends, right, Special Agent Kent?"

Her question wasn't one he could readily answer. One he didn't want to because his response bothered him in a way it shouldn't.

"I'm Miles Green. You're Lita Rae Green. Don't forget that," he grumbled, procrastinating.

Her lips quirked, and her eyebrows raised. "You're avoiding the question. Who's your best friend?"

None of his high school friends had gone to the same college as him. And once he'd landed at Wilson-Jacobs, his focus had been on getting his degrees in record time. Once he'd been accepted into the Secret Service, he'd been driven only to prove himself. That meant the few friends he'd still had after college had disappeared along the way. It took two people to keep any kind of relationship going, and he hadn't put in the time or the effort. So, he gave her a half-truth. "My job doesn't really leave time for friendships."

"You've put the job above everything else." She seemed sad at the thought, and he felt the need to dissuade her from feeling bad about it.

"No one forced me to give anything up. This job, doing what I do…it's the exact life I wanted."

"Did you know what the sacrifice would be when you signed on? Did you know you'd have to become a machine? A robot who doesn't have love or laughter or friends?"

"I'm not a robot," he said, irritation spiking through him.

"Besides me, who was the last person you hugged?"

"My parents," he said. "Just this week, by the way."

It was her turn to seem surprised. "They live in D.C.?"

"Virginia. My dad is vice chief of the National Guard Bureau."

She smiled again, and it made driving difficult because it was like a blinding ray of light filling the car.

"That explains so much," she said.

"Did you get a psychology degree I don't know about?"

She laughed, and he hated that he loved it. Or maybe he didn't hate it. Maybe he just loved that he loved it. He didn't know anymore.

"The most I've taken is a handful of art classes. What did you major in?" she asked.

"I got a B.S. in criminology at Wilson-Jacobs in Grand Orchard and a master's in forensic psychology online with Purdue."

When he glanced over at her, her eyes had widened. It was his turn to smirk. "Not just a dumb jock."

She blustered. "I never thought that."

"Didn't you?"

She flushed. "Well, we've already established you look decidedly superhero-ish."

A chuckle tore through him. "There are quite a few times I could have used some superpower skills, but I'm disappointingly human."

Her gaze settled on his mouth. “I think you’re underestimating the power of those lips.”

His pulse thudded in his veins, and he ignored the warning his conscience was screaming as he taunted, “Yeah?”

“Don’t fish for more compliments, *Miles*. That’s all you’re getting from me today.”

“All day? I can’t squeeze even one more out of you?” The tease came spontaneously, as if he was talking to Gia instead of rockstar Leya Singh, the vice president’s daughter.

“What are you going to do to earn it?” she asked breathlessly, cheeks flushing.

He pretended not to pick up on the innuendo even though he thought of a million ways he could earn her praise as he slid into her inch by glorious inch. His voice was gruff as he asked, “What could I be good at that would surprise you the most?”

Her finger rested on her full lips. Pink and soft and beautiful. Ones that tasted like a sweet treat he’d never had before. A sweet delicacy.

“Sports are out. I’m assuming you’d be good at all of them. You just told me you have a master’s degree in psychology, so you’re probably decent at word games as well. I want to say dancing, but…” Her gaze strolled down his body, and he almost shivered, clutching the steering wheel and swallowing hard. “That’s more physical activity. I think you might want me to say something musical. Did you play an instrument in school?”

“Saxophone.”

“Band nerd.”

“My high school was small, so everyone did multiple activities. I was the quarterback, first chair in band, and valedictorian, but believe me, no one thought I was a nerd,” he responded with a wink.

“So, humbleness is definitely not your hidden talent.” Her eyes sparkled, thoroughly enjoying their exchange, and he tried not to like it equally as much and failed. “Okay, Mr. Quarterback-First-Chair-Intellectual-Avenger Man, I want to see you paint.”

“Did I mention my mom is an artist?” he lied, just to get under her skin and see the shock come over her face again.

“You are a robot! Inhuman robot!”

He chuckled, a moment of joy bubbling through him. When was the last time he’d felt it? When was the last time the weight of the world hadn’t sat on his shoulders? When had he even had a halfway normal conversation with anyone who wasn’t his parents or his sister?

Maybe he was a robot. Maybe his goals and the drive that had driven him blindly forward in his career really had left him missing the things most humans needed to make life worth living. Not only the love and laughter she’d mentioned, but sex and lazy Sunday mornings spent in bed. Children laughing and calling him Dad. He’d never imagined wanting those things. He’d had girlfriends in high school, hookups in college, but he’d never wanted to keep any of them.

Is that what he wanted now? To keep Leya Singh? It was laughable. Preposterous.

They had not a single thing in common. Just a wave of desire that was sure to leave them both scorched and bleeding.

He’d vowed to protect her. So, he would. Even if that meant saving her from himself.

# Chapter Sixteen

***NEON ANGELS ON THE ROAD TO RUIN***

*Performed by The Runaways*

*THE SAVIOR: You used my men. I told you to leave me out of this.*

*BLOCKED: I'm doing this FOR you.*

*THE SAVIOR: This does nothing for our cause. She's disappeared, and they've circled the rest in bulletproof glass. Leave it alone, and you may make it out of this.*

*BLOCKED: It's not a battle if there aren't scars, right? Besides, I know where she is.*

*THE SAVIOR: Bullshit!*

*BLOCKED: I'll bring her to you wrapped in a sparkly bow, and then you can say the word. You can give us the future you promised—a land free of their disease.*

*THE SAVIOR: Stay the fuck away from me! I'm warning you.*

*BLOCKED: You've strayed from our path, Father. What happens when people stray?*

*THE SAVIOR: ...*

*BLOCKED: You can't ignore me forever.*

# Chapter Seventeen

## *Leya*

***LIVE BEFORE I DIE***

*Performed by The Corrs*

Holden had laughed. Which also meant his entire face had lit up into another glorious smile like the one at the store. It was impossible to ignore. Impossible not to feel in the very depths of her core. But then it disappeared, as if laughter wasn't allowed, and she hated that. She wanted to see what she could do to bring it back. To make him smile one more time. So, she pushed past the silence that had settled down, hoping that, in talking, she'd find a way to make it happen.

"So, your dad's in the military…your mom's an artist…what about your sister?" she asked.

"Gia is an agricultural journalist. She travels around the world, shining a light on issues with our water and food supply and the impacts of over-farming on the environment. She works for a scientific journal focusing on ways to feed our growing population in an earth-friendly way." His voice rang with the pride he felt for her.

"That's pretty amazing," Leya told him. "You're both superheroes. A whole family of them."

"Says the daughter of the Vice President of the United States with two of the top neurosurgeons in the world in her family," Holden responded.

She fidgeted with *Nani's* earrings. Whenever the comparisons between her and her family had weighed on her too much growing up, it had been her grandmother who'd told Leya about the good she could see in her. But *Nani* had been gone for too long—nearly nine years—and it made it hard to hear her words anymore. She'd encouraged Leya in her artistic endeavors even when, for a long time, Leya hadn't even known what she wanted to do with it. She'd just messed around, drawing and playing her instruments. Then, Landry and Fee had invited her to join the band, and she'd felt like she'd found a little home. While she loved what they did together, it wasn't the same as saving a life or changing the entire fabric of a country.

"At least four out of five isn't bad," she said sarcastically and then wished she could have taken it back.

"What's that supposed to mean?" he demanded.

"You know what I meant. Everyone in my family does something…life changing. Even Ria, at seventeen, has more potential than me. I'm like that *Sesame Street* song. You know…'which of these things doesn't belong with the others.'"

"That's bullshit," he said with a growl, and it surprised her because Holden rarely cussed. She met his gaze before he darted it back to the road. "I can't believe you don't see exactly what you do for others. I'm a heterosexual, White male in law enforcement. I'm the epitome of privileged. I can't blink without seeing more people like me. But you…you've given a whole host of individuals a chance to see themselves in the spotlight, to believe that everything they want is a possibility. You save something much more important than just a random body part. You save their dreams."

Tears welled in her eyes. Next to *Nani* telling her that her creativity may be more important than her family's intellect, his words were about the sweetest thing anyone had ever said to her. Her parents and siblings had never tried to make her feel less than them because of what she did. And she wasn't stupid. She knew being on the stage and on the cover of magazines, being a celebrity, allowed people like her to see themselves in roles they hadn't always been in. But it felt so much smaller than anything her family accomplished.

"You need a brain in order to dream. I think what Mom and Rishik do tops even Dad," she said softly.

"It wouldn't really be living if you could think and breathe and eat but you couldn't dream. You might as well have nothing if you don't have something you're striving for."

She swallowed hard, tears pricking her eyes, fighting the well of emotions he'd raised, wondering again how someone so different, so far removed from her world could see her so clearly. Better than her family. Better than even *Nani,* who'd known her best. Maybe it was their differences that made it possible.

She looked out the window, seeing nothing of the trees and towns that flew past, feeling, instead, her connection to this man growing in leaps and bounds. She'd left Observatory Circle with a premonition that she wouldn't be the same when she came back to her family, and it was already true. One kiss—one life-altering kiss—and she was different. She'd never be able to turn back to being the old Leya. Instead, she'd had an invisible string tied around her heart that now anchored her to another human being. Made out of some impermeable material, the string would never break. It would bend and twist, but it would always be there, even if Holden strode miles away from her and never looked back.

Losing her family to keep him would be like severing an arm. But losing any chance at having him? It felt worse. It felt like she'd fade away into nothing. She'd be the Leya her mother wanted, living without emotion. All logic and no heart.

"My turn," Holden said, breaking the silence, and she turned to look at him. He was facing the road, his profile to her. Even with a swollen nose and black eyes, he was still beautiful.

"Why don't you do more with your art?" he asked.

Lincoln had wanted to know the same thing. He'd repeatedly offered to hold a show for her at his gallery. He thought she was afraid of the critics, and that was part of it, but not the whole thing. So, she tried to explain it the best she could, hoping Holden might actually understand. "With the Daisies, our music has become the world's. It doesn't really belong to me or the band anymore. In some ways, it's always belonged more to Paisley and Landry, even though I participate in crafting it. What I do on canvas…it's mine and mine alone. If I put it out into the world, people will share their thoughts, whether they're positive or negative, and that will force it into a different shape, regardless of how I try to ignore it."

"It won't be just yours anymore."

Relief coasted through her. Relief and joy and a little bit of something that felt so much deeper than the lust she'd tried to convince herself she felt for him. This…it felt like a partner who understood the very core of you. It was heady and fast and all wrong, just like what had happened to Fee and Asher. Or maybe it wasn't fast at all. She'd been ignoring her feelings for Holden for two years, hiding behind her promise to Krish. Keeping herself safe. She didn't want to be safe anymore. She wanted to feel fully alive, like she had when Holden had kissed her.

Their eyes met for a long moment. So long that he had to jerk the steering wheel to put it back on course. The silence settled down again between them, but it didn't feel quite as heavy anymore. It actually felt like the most peace she'd had in days.

♫ ♫ ♫

They'd stopped for gas and snacks and had just started back toward the freeway when Holden flipped the turn signal and pulled into a strip mall. Her heart immediately jumped into panic mode, looking around her for anyone who might have been following them.

"Did they find us?" she asked.

"No, sorry, we're just making a stop," he said, and his lips twitched, pointing to one of the shops.

She eyed the thrift store sign and then said dryly, "You weren't serious about the cowboy boots, were you?"

"Damn straight I was."

He backed the truck into a spot across from the store and got out. As he opened her door and she slid to the ground beside him, she said, "I'm not sure how I feel about wearing used shoes, Holden."

She barely repressed a shudder, and it caused a grin to light up his face.

"Trust me. With cowboy boots, you'll never even know."

A bell over the door jingled as they entered. "Holler if you find something you can't live without," a woman's voice shouted from the back.

Holden steered them to the clothes section, finding an entire row of shoes from sneakers to high-dollar designer pumps.

"Size eight, right?" Holden asked, and she was surprised again by how much he knew about her when she probably shouldn't have been. She felt like she had a long way to go before she knew him even half as well.

He pulled a pair of tan boots off the shelf that had teal stitching and metal tips. As much as she never would have expected any version of a cowboy boot to appeal to her, she had to admit they were pretty.

She slipped off the canvas slip-ons she'd been wearing for over a day and stuck her feet into the boots. They should have looked ridiculous with the leggings she'd had on for way too many hours, but she was surprised to find that, instead of looking all wrong, the boots dressed up the rest of her outfit. She didn't want to admit to liking them, but as she twirled in front of a mirror, she heard Holden's chuckle and turned in time to see the smile on his face.

*Hey, bhagwan*, was he beautiful like this—relaxed—with the aquamarine of his aura glowing around him like a sea god.

The air between them crackled again before he turned away to grab a pair of black boots out of the men's section. They had a lot more scruffs and scrapes than hers but were still in relatively good shape. When he slid into them, he grew an additional inch he didn't need.

"You're lucky. Those just came in this morning," a tall woman said, emerging from the back and eyeing the boots on Leya's feet. "I knew they'd be snapped up in a heartbeat. If I'd been able to slide my feet into a size eight without bending my toes backward, I would have kept them myself."

"We'll take them both," Holden told her.

On the way to the counter, Leya passed a rack of coats where an old aviator jacket was hooked. She grabbed it, slid it on, and looked up at Holden with a grin. "It's like I'm channeling Tom Cruise *and* Kevin Bacon."

Holden's chuckle tore through him, and she almost patted herself on the back for making it happen. She'd count every twitch of his lip, every smile, as a triumph.

"You look damn good, honey," the woman winked.

"I guess we're taking the jacket too," Holden told her.

"Smart fella. The best way to a woman's heart is to say yes to all her shopping needs."

"Don't tell Lita Rae that. I'll be broke before morning," Holden said, a twang Leya had never heard in him coming out. When she joined him at the counter, his smile seemed to grow, causing his eyes to sparkle. He reached out and tapped the brim of her hat in a sweet move that made her heart and stomach flip.

The woman grinned at them, happily taking the cash Holden handed her before he hustled Leya back out to the truck. She started toward the passenger door, but he pulled her to the driver's side instead.

"Slide in, Lita Rae. I have a feeling Miles Green would expect his woman to ride in the middle next to him."

Leya laughed, a weird joy coming over her that she didn't know what to do with. Maybe for a short while she could actually be Lita Rae instead of Leya Singh. Maybe she could wear cowboy boots and hats and talk with a twang. Maybe she'd even line dance and sing a sad song about a dog dying and a truck breaking down—as long as the one they'd bought didn't.

Sitting in the middle meant her thigh and knee kept touching Holden's as he pulled out and headed down the road. Every touch sent a hum of energy through her, building like a static-electric field that would eventually need a release. But how? Would it be with a sharp zap when she touched a metal surface or with a delightful zing as his skin glided against hers? She'd always been afraid of letting lust and desire rule her. Thought it would lead to a mistake. And now she was wondering if she should have followed her natural instincts for decades.

What would her mom think of emotional Leya running rampant? It would have made her chuckle if it didn't hurt so badly. She was sure her mother would never understand a decision to explore something with Holden when it could never be what was right for their family.

She fiddled with the old radio again. She'd found nothing but country stations earlier, and it was more of the same. One song caught her attention, the rhythm and beat halting her hands. Then, she started singing her own made-up words over the top of the ones on the radio. "Got a dog chasing me, a man at my side defending me. Who knows what the night will bring, but all I want is to get lost in this feeling." She glanced over at Holden. "Zap me once. Kiss me twice. Let's see if his fire can melt my ice."

His eyes darted over to her, the truck veered, and he had to swerve to get it back in the lane. A grumble of a protest lodged in his chest that he didn't fully voice, and it brought a smile to her lips. She slid her hand onto his thigh, and it stiffened beneath her fingers, but he didn't push her away. She removed her hat and tucked her head up against his shoulder. She felt his chest contract and expand as he let out a shaky breath.

She made this superhero of a man unsteady.

Something about that pleased her to no end.

"Leya." His voice was a deep plea and command as he said her name, and she wondered if it would sound the same if he was inside her moving to a rhythm slow and then fast as they chased the high at the end, all the while trying to make the sensations last forever.

She forced her voice to be a light tease as she corrected him. "Lita Rae, don't forget it. And you're the one who said Miles would want Lita Rae tucked up against him. Just playing the part you gave me, Avenger-man."

They rode for several minutes before he asked in a tight voice, "Tell me more about Lita Rae. What does she do? What does she want from her life?"

Leya's heart sped up. "Well, as you witnessed, she's a good songwriter and has big dreams of singing in Nashville, but right now she's waiting tables while Miles works as a mechanic so they can pay for their little one-bedroom apartment in an iffy part of town."

"Miles believes in her. She doesn't know it, but he's saving up every penny so he can help her record her album."

She looked up, surprised he'd picked up the thread of tale she'd woven.

"It's a good thing she has Miles, because her family disowned her for living in sin with him." The pang of truth to the words hurt, but she ignored them. "They wanted her to follow in their footsteps, in the family's used-car lot, and attend church on Sunday, leading the fundraising bake-off."

"He wants to buy her a ring but knows the recording is a bigger way to her heart."

It felt like Leya's entire soul clenched for these two made-up people, but also for her. "He's the only one who's seen the truth of her," she said softly.

The radio was the only sound for a long time again.

"Is that why you originally decided to marry Krish Arya? Because it was what your family wanted?" His voice was gravelly and deep, but when she looked up at him again, he'd clenched his jaw. "Never mind. I shouldn't have asked."

But she suddenly, very much wanted to tell him. To have him understand.

"Ever since my parents told me Krish was interested in getting married, I felt an overwhelming sense of relief. I wasn't going to have to go through the entire *rishta* process of circulating bios and pictures, being dissected by families. Aja Aunty had insisted our star charts predicted a successful match. It was like knowing the end of a romance story before it began, I guess. I knew Krish and I would be together. But when Rishik and Devleena got married, I was surprised by the deep affection they showed each other. Krish and I had never acted that way when we were together—not even after I was old enough for him to show me…affection. I thought Krish and I just needed to spend more time together. I was sure we'd be like my parents, or my brother, or even my cousins and their partners. Everyone seems so… happy."

"What changed your mind?" he asked.

She fidgeted with the row of tiny *ghunghroos*, the tinkle joining a new country song in a strangely appealing way. Finally, she breathed out, "He kissed me." His hands tensed on the steering wheel, gripping it so tight his knuckles turned white. She squeezed his thigh, and it flexed underneath her touch. "It was nothing like yours. I mean, physically, it wasn't any different. It was still mouths and hands touching."

His jaw clenched, and his voice was deep and dark with what her heart hoped was jealousy when he asked, "If it wasn't different, then what?"

"I said there was no physical difference. It was something else…unexplainable almost. Having him touch me felt…odd. I'd been kissed before, and while no one had ever made me want to tear my clothes off, they hadn't repulsed me either. Krish's kiss…it was practiced and smooth but also wrong. Like…kissing my brother. I jerked away from him, which of course was not what he'd been hoping for."

She moved the bracelets on her wrist back and forth again, the dragonfly snagging on the beads of another one. This wasn't a memory she liked. Krish had always been a perfect gentleman. He was handsome and smart. Kind. But she'd seen a side of him that day she hadn't been able to reconcile.

"What did he do?" Holden's voice simmered. The protectiveness of the tone sent a thrill up her back. This had nothing to do with his job. This was simply a man looking out for someone he cared for. Wasn't it?

"He told me I wasn't a child anymore, and that sex was a healthy part of every marriage, arranged or not. And of course, that made *me* angry, him treating me exactly like the child he'd just said I wasn't, and so I told him next time he touched me to make sure he'd brushed his teeth and put on deodorant, and maybe I'd react differently."

The tension in Holden's shoulders released, and he chuckled. She smiled up at him, and their eyes caught for two seconds before he turned them back to the road.

"The truth is, if Krish were being honest with himself, he'd realize he wants someone much more traditional than me. He deserves that. Someone who will be at every campaign rally, entertaining the other judges, and maybe even working in his office. There are plenty of women who would love to be that person for him. It's just not me. I could never be the doting wife, giving up my dreams for his. I don't even know why I thought I had to, because my parents never expected it. My mom certainly didn't give up her career for Dad's. They want me to get married because they believe it will make me happy. And maybe they want a few dozen grandkids to spoil."

He choked a bit. "Dozen?"

She laughed. "Don't worry, Captain Annoying, no one is asking you to father a herd of kids."

Leya had always thought she'd have kids, but it was in that vague "someday" kind of way that felt far into the future. But she wondered what it would feel like to have Holden's baby inside her. To have him doting over her, maybe being a bit overprotective and commanding. It sent a thrill up her spine. It wasn't nearly as terrifying as the idea had been when she'd envisioned Krish as her partner. Her heart settled a little bit more.

Even if the feelings she'd experienced all day with Holden hadn't already told her the truth, she knew now that she'd made the right decision in breaking the arrangement with Krish. She still felt panicked, but it was for a different reason. It wasn't because her future was unclear and unknown. It was because she could distinctly see two versions of it. One with Holden and one without, but in both versions, her mother would be displeased because even if Leya never had Holden in the way she truly wanted to have him now, she wasn't going to marry someone else. Aja Aunty could find hundreds of men and families to parade in front of her, but her heart had already been tied to another's, and she wasn't going to be able to walk away from that, even if he did.

It made her inexplicably sad.

She turned, watching Holden's profile. The sun had faded, dropping below the mountains and casting them into the in-between world of dusk. He looked golden in the twilight. A bronzed statue with an aqua hue that made him glow.

"Lita Rae's pretty lucky," she whispered, her voice deep with longing.

His throat bobbed, and he shot her a heated glance full of everything she was feeling—and maybe more. For so long, her experiences had taught her that sex was just sex. A motion like brushing your teeth or jogging. Muscles and bones being brought together. And it certainly would have been that way with Krish. But what she felt with Holden…when he'd kissed her, when her side was pushed against his right now, when her palm rested on his leg…it was enormous.

If she drew the feeling, it would be large ripples growing wider and wider from where a pebble had been tossed into a lake. The singular color on the painting would be darker than his sky-blue eyes, more aquamarine, like the flickering of his aura. Blue was the color of the hottest flame before it turned pure white, and that was how she felt when he looked at her. Like she was about to combust into fiery flames.

Instead of running from her emotions like she'd been taught to do for years, she wanted to race headfirst into the thick of them. She wanted to be engulfed by them until there was nothing left of her but ash. But she'd rise from it, like a phoenix, and she'd be everything she'd ever wanted to be. More than the quiet, impulsive daughter. More than the Indian rock star the world saw. She'd be the person *Nani* had convinced her she could be when she'd looked into Leya's future. Strong and brave and confident.

# Chapter Eighteen

## *Holden*

***WHITE FLAG***

*Performed by Bishop Briggs*

*His body was screaming from his* injuries, and his eyes were trying to droop by the time he pulled into Knoxville. He'd been watching their mirror since getting the truck, and he hadn't seen anything suspicious, but instead of going straight to the safe house, he made several right turns, a U-turn, and a complete circle of a block. Even having done a whole series of evasive maneuvers, a strange sensation still returned to his gut as he pulled onto the street where the house was located.

As he pulled into the driveway, he scanned the neighborhood. It was a newer development with sea upon sea of similar houses, cookie-cutter fashion. The block was quiet, likely because everyone had headed in doors as the sun had dropped and the temperature with it. When he slid out of the truck, he could see his breath, and he cursed himself for not getting a coat at the thrift shop like Leya had.

He risked meeting her eyes as he held out a hand to help her from the truck, and every emotion he'd been fighting came slamming back into him. It felt much deeper than desire. For a brief moment, he wished he actually was Miles and she was Lita Rae. That he was bringing her back to their first house where they'd make love in every room and spend weekends locked behind doors, wearing nothing but each other.

Even though he'd never wanted a relationship like that before, the way it settled over him felt like it was a longing he'd had for a lifetime. As if he'd always been searching for her. Wanting her. Needing her.

Ridiculous.

Dangerous.

Forbidden.

He swallowed hard, dropping her hand to grab the duffels from the back, handing her one as he made his way to the lockbox on the door. The hairs on his arms and neck raised as he flipped the combination in place and took out the key. Anyone in the Secret Service who'd needed a safe house in Knoxville would have the code, and it made him itchy and uncomfortable. He opened the door, pulled out his gun, and told Leya to stay put as he planted her just inside the door.

As he cleared the three-bedroom, three-bath house, the size of it set his teeth on edge almost as much as the lockbox. There were too many windows and doors for a single agent, and his gut continued to twist as he jogged back down the stairs to where Leya waited for him in a bomber jacket that was way too large and cowboy boots that somehow looked perfect on her when they shouldn't.

"I'm going to check in with Camp. There should be some food in the kitchen. Why don't you see what they've got?"

She nodded, and he stepped outside. He moved to the side of the garage, letting his eyes adjust to the dark and watching the length of the street as he pulled out the burner phone and called Camp. "We're at the safe house."

"The car was gone when we got there."

"What?" Holden grunted out.

"The Camaro wasn't in the parking lot where you left it."

The tension in his body grew, and he ran a hand over his face, surprised to find a thick coat of stubble. He'd run out of his apartment early the day of the bombing, and today had been a shitshow. His fatigue was barely being kept at bay by the pain spiking through him.

"Who had access to our communications?"

"No one but the five of us who were in the conference room yesterday," Camp barked back.

"And every damn admin you, the vice president, and the president have. Plus, the IT folks who have access to your phones," Holden all but hissed.

"You let a wanted man hand you a vehicle and then expected a clean getaway?" Camp reminded him. "You're lucky you weren't blown up on the drive there."

A strange and unexpected fear crawled through Holden. He couldn't remember a moment in his life when he'd truly been frightened to his core. Growing up, he'd felt safe with his father looking after them. As he grew older, his dad had taught him how to fight, how to use a gun, and how to protect his family when his father wasn't around, and he'd always felt confident that he could handle anything that came at him. Facing criminals in Vegas hadn't frightened him, and having a gun shoved in his face undercover had only pissed him off.

But now…thinking of someone coming after Leya, of losing her bright light, it filled him with cold dread. Like sinking to the bottom of a frozen lake. His job, his goals, his dreams, none of it would matter if he let something happen to her. None of it was as important as this one task. Making sure she lived. Making sure whoever was behind this was put away and never came after her again.

"What's the status on Barrows?" Holden asked.

"Nothing. Not a peep. We've got some agents interviewing people from D.C. Avenue Writers and some of the known FGT members here in Washington."

A V8 engine rumbled down at the far end of the street, and Holden stepped deeper into the shadows. It wasn't the black Camaro he'd half-expected. Instead, it was an Escalade that seemed to slow as it drove by the safe house before going to the end of the block and pulling into a driveway. No plates.

His hackles went up another notch.

He couldn't see the driver, and the person didn't get out of the car.

Jesus.

He couldn't stay here.

"We're leaving," he told Camp.

"You just got there."

"Dark Escalade, no plates, parked at the end of the street. Driver is just sitting there."

"That could just be someone finishing up a conversation, Kent. Some suburban cheater not wanting his wife to hear him talk to his mistress. Don't panic."

A second car, a smaller-sized SUV, came down the street from the opposite direction and parked in front of the house with the Escalade. Neither driver emerged, and Holden was already moving toward the front door, keeping to the shadows.

"Second car just parked. I'm not waiting to be ambushed." Anger flared through him at the audacity of the damn group to continue following them and at the fact that they'd been able to do so.

"Fuck," Camp grunted out. "Where do you plan on taking her?"

His mind flashed to Gia and her dude ranch research, just like it had momentarily the day before. No one would think to look for them there, and he was glad, for the second time, he hadn't mentioned it in the command center the day before.

"I'm not telling you or anyone else," he growled. If Camp fired him on the spot, he'd do this anyway. They couldn't stop him from protecting her. They'd have to arrest him, put him in a cell, and throw away the key.

To his surprise, Camp didn't scream or holler. Instead, he said in a voice that was far too serious, "Watch your ass, kid. Watch the news. If we catch up to Barrows, I'll make sure it's all over the place so you know it's safe to come home."

Jesus…the assistant special agent in charge was basically telling him not to trust the USSS. The one agency that had never in its history been penetrated. The men and women he trusted with his life. That the president trusted with his…

He hung up, pulled out his gun, and reentered the house, locking it behind him. The kitchen was quiet. No Leya. Panic coursed through his veins, heart hammering. He bit back the automatic instinct to call her name and instead eased down the hall with his weapon leading the way toward the main bedroom on the bottom floor.

Water was running. The shower?

The lights were on in the bedroom, and the shutters were closed, but the windows still faced the street, giving away their location. He flicked them off and went to the bathroom door. It wasn't the shower running but the sink. He put his hand on the door and hesitated. He didn't want to startle her any more than he wanted to walk in and see her without a shred of clothing. Which was a lie. He wanted to see her completely naked, but right now it would be just another damn distraction. Just like the talk of Lita Rae and Miles and the way Krish Arya's kiss had done nothing for her while his had.

He turned the handle silently, easing the door open a crack and keeping his eyes down as he called her name, "Leya."

She pulled open the door, and he swallowed hard at the image she made. Her face had been scrubbed, the skin a soft pink, and her long hair was curving over her breasts that were covered in a pair of thermal pajamas that seemed inappropriate for both rock-star Leya and the country-singer-wanna-be Lita Rae. The cotton covered every inch of her and yet put all her curves on display as it clung to every single one of them. His mouth went dry, and his heart galloped even harder as forbidden thoughts swirled through his mind, visions of sliding his hands underneath to the soft skin below it.

He'd already tasted her. Tasted her and not gotten his fill.

He tore his gaze from her body and lifted his eyes to the ceiling. This was the exact reason he shouldn't have been the one on her detail. He was going to lose focus, and someone was going to get hurt. Her. Him. Both of them. His entire being clenched tight at the thought.

"We need to leave," he said, trying to keep the panic from his voice.

"Wh-what? We just got here."

He pushed open the door and swiped all the items she had on the counter back into her duffel.

"Holden? You're scaring me."

He walked back into the bedroom and saw the bomber jacket thrown on a chair in the corner with her boots sitting next to it. He tossed the boots in her direction. "Put these on."

"I'm in pajamas."

He stopped, heart pounding violently as he took her in again.

"We don't have time for you to change. Put the boots on. Let's go."

Her hands shook as she did what he asked. Her face was pale, and by the time she stood back up, he was at her side, helping her into the jacket. Then, he handed her their bags so he could have his hands as free as possible and led her out the door, whispering, "Stay behind me."

She made a little noise in her throat, and her eyes turned wide, but she did as he'd asked. He eased into the hall, keeping them tight up against the wall, gun pointing ahead of him. There was no motion, no sound in the house.

He kept them moving as quietly as he could with both their cowboy boots banging on the wooden floors.

The great room was empty. Maybe they were still parked down the street. Maybe they'd be waiting for them once they left the house, but he had to get them into the truck and out of here. He didn't have a choice but to exit the building.

Outside, he slid the key into the lockbox and then stood in the darkness, letting his eyes adjust once more, listening for signs of anyone near them. There was music playing loudly in the house next door, and a dog barked at the opposite end of the street from where the two vehicles had parked. He eyed the cars again. There was movement in the driver's seat of the Escalade. At least one of them was still there.

"I'm going to have you get in on the passenger side. Once you're in, stay low. Keep below the dash," he told her in a voice so quiet he wasn't sure she could even hear him, but he felt her nod.

He drew them down low, hunched over, walking as fast as he could to the side of the truck. He unlocked it and put her inside, shutting the door behind her as quietly as possible. Then, he dropped to the ground and rolled under the truck. It had been parked outside for too long. Damn. He didn't want to use his phone light, but it was either risk that or something worse. A tracer. A bomb.

He kept the light as close to the undercarriage as possible, cupping it to block the shine the best he could. It took too long, many more minutes than he felt he could afford, but he moved down the truck slowly. Nothing. He flipped onto his stomach, looking from behind the back wheel well at the two vehicles parked down the street. More movement, this time in the smaller SUV. Either they'd gotten out, cased the safe house, and gotten back in, or they were waiting for someone or something.

He wasn't going to stick around to find out. He dragged himself out, unlocked the driver's door, and slid behind the wheel. When he looked over at Leya, she was hunched completely over, and her eyes were huge and luminous in the dark.

He didn't say anything. He just turned the engine over without switching on the headlights. He backed out and took off down the street. It took a beat, and he wasn't one hundred percent sure, but he thought the SUV pulled out to follow them minus their lights as well.

He sped up, ran two stop signs, weaved in and out of cars, took random streets and alleys, and lost them on the back roads. He needed a place to go. He needed to talk to Gia.

"You can sit up," he said.

"How could they hate me this much?" Leya whispered, the agony in her voice clear.

She was right. This went beyond the norm he'd expected from even FGT. Especially when they'd gotten what they wanted. They'd gotten Leya out of D.C. and out of Lincoln Matherton's reach. He was missing something, and he hated it. Hated that every agency that had come in contact with The Painted Daisies had missed something along the way, and the band had paid the price for it.

He wouldn't let Leya be another one who got hurt.

He cleared his mind, thinking of everything he'd ever known about John Smythe, FGT, and what had happened over the last two days. He thought about what Camp had said about Astrid freaking out on Penny, and what Leya had told him about Astrid asking Lincoln to dance. His profiling degree and his gut told him this woman had an obsessive personality. First with Smythe and then Lincoln.

"I think this is personal to Astrid. She's using you to prove a point. To Lincoln. Hell, maybe even to Smythe."

Leya didn't have her bracelets on. They'd been on the counter when he'd swiped everything into the duffel bag that now sat at her feet.

"Wh-where are we going to go?" she asked.

He searched the street for a place to pull over. They

needed gas, but he hated to be anywhere near the bright lights of a station at the moment. Instead, he drove into a bank parking lot, backing into a space near the rear where he could see all the driveways and yet was still hidden from the street. He shifted in the seat, dragging the burner phone from his pocket, and his body protested. He needed more painkillers and about fifteen hours of solid sleep, but he wasn't going to get either.

# Chapter Nineteen

## *Holden*

***ALONE***

*Performed by Heart*

His sister picked up on the second ring, her voice hesitant, most likely due to the unknown number. He was lucky she answered at all.

"Hey, G, it's Holden."

"Big-bad agent man calling from a burner phone. What's wrong?" Gia greeted with a slight tease, but under it was a layer of concern.

It struck a nerve that this was her immediate reaction, that he'd only called because something was wrong, and below the anger and frustration he was feeling over the situation they were in, guilt settled down. Gia's job, just like his, required significant amounts of travel and had a wild schedule, which left very little time for family. He wondered what would happen if they lived this way for another ten or fifteen years. Would they even know each other anymore? Would they have anything to talk about, or would they drift apart completely?

He swallowed back the regret and handed her the closest truth he could possibly give at the moment. "You're right. Things are pretty intense, and I need a favor. Mom says you've been working on a piece about dude ranches?"

"If you didn't sound so serious, I'd give you shit for teasing me about it."

"I wouldn't dare, even if I wasn't serious," he said, and she snorted, which brought a small smile to his lips, easing some of the guilt that had built up inside him. "I need something remote and private to duck out of the limelight for a while. Any recommendations?"

"All the ranches are pretty remote with the amount of acreage they take up, but none of them are likely to have openings at the drop of a hat."

Holden's stomach flipped. "Somehow, I didn't expect them to be booked. Who knew vacationing at a dude ranch was that big of a draw?"

"It'll be even more of one if I have anything to say about it," she huffed, and his lips lifted upward, imagining her raised brow and the attitude flying off of her.

"So, you're telling me we're out of luck?" Holden asked, mind already spiraling to figure out an alternative. Maybe he'd just keep driving until he found an abandoned cabin somewhere.

"No…not completely. Where are you?"

He hesitated, not wanting to tell anyone, but this was his sister. Who the hell could he trust if not her? "Knoxville."

She hesitated for a moment too, and he didn't know if it was because of his reaction or something else, but her words were calm when she spoke. "The Hatley Ranch in Willow Creek isn't far from you. It's a dinky town, and they're pretty good at keeping their celebrities off social media."

"Someone famous lives in the backwater of Tennessee?" he asked disbelievingly.

She laughed. "Yep, the band Watery Reflection and a pro-football player. But, like I said, the town keeps a close lid on their celebrities. But…"

"But what?"

It took another beat for her to respond, and his stomach curled back up. He wasn't sure if it was big-brother instincts or his training.

"Nothing," she said. "Lucky for you, I was slated to be back there yesterday. I called Eva and asked her to hold my reservation while I worked out a few kinks in my schedule. You can take my spot. I was going to be there for a week."

"You're not going?"

Gia hesitated again.

"Tell me what's wrong with the place," Holden demanded.

"Seriously. It's nothing. The ranch is perfect. The town is like a greeting card. The surroundings are gorgeous. One of the owners and I didn't exactly see eye to eye is all. He's a little too full of himself and has a chip on his shoulder when it comes to women. He'd be fine dealing with you."

"What did he do?" Holden growled, letting his big-brother reflex finally take over.

Gia laughed. "Absolutely nothing, Golden-Holden. Seriously, don't get your underwear in a bunch and go all He-Man. I'm used to handling all sorts of folks. Don't tell Mom, but when I was in South America, I hung out with a group of guerillas for a day and handled them just fine."

"Jesus, G. You want to give me a heart attack?"

"I was trained by Dad on how to protect myself. And I'm never alone."

"You talking about Gary? He's gotta be at least fifty years old and almost fifty pounds overweight. He probably couldn't ward off a mosquito."

"But he's really loud. If he screamed, an entire jungle would come running."

Holden didn't know whether to laugh, growl, or cry. "G…"

"I said too much. Don't tell Mom."

"Does Dad know?"

She hesitated again. “Dad knows enough.”

Silence settled down between them, and Leya shifted in the seat next to him, drawing his gaze back to hers. She was only hearing one side of the conversation, but even that much put his life on display in a way he wasn’t used to sharing with anyone.

When he didn’t respond, Gia piped in again. “Stop worrying like Mom. You don’t hear me complaining about you putting your life on the line every day, even when there was a bombing at Ria Singh’s school.” She let her words hit home, a quiet rebuke for not texting her. “I’ll call Eva Hatley and tell her to expect you instead of me. How many of you will there be?”

“Just two of us.”

Concern filtered into her voice, all teasing gone. “You’re on your own?”

“I’ve gone underground.”

She inhaled sharply. “Holes…”

“Who’s worrying now? I’m okay. Promise.”

But he wasn’t sure it was true. And it had as much to do with the people chasing them as it did the stunning woman sitting next to him with her eyes glimmering in the shadows. He was screwed. He’d thought it so many times since leaving D.C.—since that moment on the lawn—but it settled in his chest with a certainty he hated. He could practically see his life goals being erased as he sat there. His mind swarmed with endless, empty calendar days that would never be filled, and it hurt as much as his bruised ribs and broken nose.

“Who should I tell Eva to expect in my place?” Gia asked.

“Miles and Lita Rae Green.”

“Does Lita Rae look a whole lot like Leya Singh?”

“You know I can’t talk about it,” he grunted.

“Right, right.”

"Thanks for giving up your reservation for me. I owe you," he said quietly.

"Send me one of Eva's pies, and we'll call it good."

His chest ached in a funny way. For his sister. For him. For things he couldn't even name and his life that had spiraled out of his control in a way he'd never allowed it to do before.

"Hey, G."

"Yeah?"

"We need to line up our schedules soon. I miss you." His chest eased again at the thought of having at least one future event on his calendar. A date with his family. A barbecue on the back deck. Mom making pizza in her new oven. But before he could stop it, another body emerged next to his in the yard. One who shouldn't have been there. A woman with soft curves, a luscious voice, and hair a hundred different shades of brown and black.

"Aw, is big badass agent man going to cry?"

He snorted. "Can you feel the middle finger I'm sending your way?"

She chuckled and then said softly, "Love you, too."

They hung up, and Holden immediately pulled up the Hatley Ranch on the burner phone, letting his immediate tasks of keeping Leya safe stall the empty spaces looming in his mind. The website was professional, and the image gallery showed a majestic landscape set in the middle of nowhere. It was perfect.

He memorized the directions, turned the phone off, and pulled the SIM card out before swinging open the truck door and smashing the phone and card with his cowboy boot. It had been mostly a joke when he'd pulled into the thrift store parking lot, a way to lighten the mood and get out of the truck before he lost all sense, but now the shoes seemed completely appropriate, given where they were headed.

When he started the truck back up, Leya put a hand on his arm, halting him.

"I'm sorry," she said quietly.

His heart squeezed tight at the true remorse in her voice. "I've said it before, and I'll say it again until you believe it. This isn't your fault. You've done nothing wrong."

She stared at him for a long moment, finger skimming over her hooped earrings, bells tinkling through the cab of the truck, and he could practically feel the guilt dripping from her. He'd do just about anything to have back the teasing, taunting, smiling Leya who had squeezed his thigh earlier. He pulled her hand away from the little bells and dragged her body across the bench seat until she was up against him again. Pain rippled through him at the action that he ignored. It was going to be more painful to have her that far away, lost in her own thoughts, beating herself up for other people's actions.

"How does Lita Rae feel about taking a vacation at a dude ranch?" he asked.

To his utter relief, she laughed, and then her eyes grew wide as she realized he was telling the truth.

"Well…she is a country girl, so I'm sure she'd be happy to go. What about Miles? How does he feel about mucking cow dung and riding horses?"

Holden nodded. "His grandparents owned an apple orchard he worked at during the summers. He'll do just fine."

He started the truck, glancing both ways along the streets at the end of the drive, looking for any sign of the two vehicles that had been parked near the safe house. When he saw neither, he pulled out, heading for the freeway and the road into the hillsides of northern Tennessee.

"Didn't you say you went to Wilson-Jacobs in Grand Orchard? Do your grandparents really own an apple orchard?" Leya asked.

He nodded. “I stayed with them while I went to school. Between working on the farm and the scholarship I got, it allowed me to get my bachelor’s debt free.”

She tilted her head against his shoulder like she had earlier, and it felt so right he wondered how he’d ever lived without riding in a truck like this with her.

“This is a side of the Avenger-man I didn’t expect,” she said, stifling a yawn. “Farm boy. But maybe it’s your secret identity.”

He shook his head as if disgusted, but his lips twitched.

“Is that why they sent you to me at first?” she asked. “Because we were in Grand Orchard, and you knew the town?”

He nodded. “I’d also been deep in the trenches with FGT while on assignment in Las Vegas, so I was versed in the folks coming after your dad.”

Her head turned on his shoulder, and when he glanced down, she was staring at him with a look of awe on her face. “All the pieces of your life came together to bring you to me.”

Jesus…was that true? Had everything in his life that he’d thought was leading him to a position as a lead agent on the presidential detail really been bringing him to her door? He couldn’t respond. Didn’t know how to with his heart lodged somewhere in his throat.

Silence settled down again as they rode in the dark. The radio was playing some damn country song about love that felt too poignant. Too pointed. Too real in ways he’d always scoffed at.

Her body sagged against him some, and he’d thought she’d fallen asleep when she lifted her head and broke the quiet by saying his name softly.

“Yeah?” he responded.

“Thank you. For being here. For keeping me safe.”

His throat nearly closed at the tender words. He wanted to respond with the fact that it was his job, but they were well past that now, and she knew it as much as he did. Because if it was truly just his job, he wouldn't be there at all. He would have handed her off to someone else.

"Go to sleep, Lita Rae," he said gruffly.

She settled back against him, hand on his thigh, breast pushed into his arm, breath wafting over his neck. The hum of the energy that always zipped between them flung itself back and forth as the hint of honeysuckle that always surrounded her filled his senses to bursting. He ached to lose himself completely in her.

Or maybe he already had.

# Chapter Twenty

## *Leya*

***STARVING***

*Performed by Hailee Steinfeld, Grey, and Zedd*

*FIVE DAYS BEFORE*

The truck rolling to a stop pulled Leya out of her semi-sleep. She'd drifted in and out as Holden had driven along roads that seemed to get darker and darker the farther they got from the city. The shock of the last two days had settled hard into her chest. Every time she'd thought they'd finally reached somewhere safe, she'd been rocketed back into fear. The only thing keeping her from losing it completely was the man at her side, because she knew, without a doubt, that he would do anything and everything to protect her.

She raised her head from Holden's shoulder as he pulled into a driveway blocked by a wrought-iron gate set between two large stone pillars. The words *Welcome to Hatley Ranch* were scrolled across the top with an outline of a bucking bronco below them. There was an intercom on the driver's side pillar that said to push for service after hours.

Holden pressed the button, and after a minute, a woman's light voice came across. "Hatley Ranch. The restaurant's closed for the night. Are you trying to check in?"

"Yes. Gia Kent called and explained we'd be taking over her reservation," he responded.

"Oh, yes. Come on back. We'll meet you in the lobby of the restaurant."

The gates swung inward, and Holden drove down a winding drive lined with trees. A large, light-blue house with white trim and a slate-gray tiled roof came into view. The windows reflected the headlights above a wraparound porch that reminded her of the one at Number One Observatory Circle in some ways. Old, Southern, refined.

The road led around the house to the rear where a large addition jutted out from the back of it. A pair of golden oak doors etched with stained glass greeted them with a sign that read *Sweet Willow Restaurant* in curving, vine-like letters.

There were several parking spots between the restaurant and an enormous barn that was painted light-blue to match the house instead of the stereotypical red. Holden backed into a spot at the edge, slid out of the truck, and did his normal scan of the area, but Leya didn't see another soul.

He grabbed their bags and held out his hand for Leya. When she'd landed at his feet, he tapped the brim of her hat like he had earlier, the sweet motion landing in her chest almost as if it was a term of endearment.

"Remember, keep that gorgeous face down."

Her heart thudded at the compliment. She'd been called beautiful, gorgeous, unique, and even the cringe-worthy exotic, but she'd never believed the words as much as she did when they came from his mouth. She didn't respond, and he led them up the wide stone steps of a building teeming with ivy. Inside, the place was quiet, a soft clank of dishes from somewhere off to the side of the dining area, but no customers.

"Hello. Welcome again." A vivacious brunette in her twenties with a pixie haircut, bright-blue eyes, and tan skin greeted them from behind a long walnut desk. Her eyes widened as she took in Holden's battered face for two beats, but then she added on, "Even though I'm glad you're here, I'm a little disappointed it's not Gia, because now I've lost my bet."

"Sadie," an older woman scolded as she approached from the dining room, wiping her hands on a towel. Her brown hair was woven with gray, and her face was lined with a few more wrinkles, but her blue eyes sparkled with the same liveliness of the younger woman.

"What? It's true. You know you were hoping I'd win—"

"I'm Eva Hatley." The woman stuck out her hand, cutting off the younger woman's comment, and her eyes did the same widening thing as she took in Holden's bruises.

"Miles Green," Holden said, engulfing her hand in his much larger one.

Eva thrust a thumb in the young woman's direction. "This is my youngest, Sadie. The most exasperating of the entire bunch."

Leya's heart squeezed for the girl because she knew what it felt like to be the one your parent saw as different, but Sadie didn't seem offended at all. She simply laughed it off. "That's just because the rest of my siblings live very boring, monotonous lives."

What would it feel like to be able to laugh off her mother's words about her impulsive, emotional nature?

Eva turned back to Holden. "Ignore everything she says."

"Except when I tell you where to go to have some fun," Sadie said with a smile that Leya found drawing one from her in return. She was still semi-tucked behind Holden, watching everything from beneath the brim of her hat, and Eva finally shifted her head to the side to take a look at her.

Leya was sure she looked utterly ridiculous in her mix of pajamas, oversized bomber jacket, hat, and boots.

"This is my wife, Lita Rae," he said, and her heart hammered at how true it sounded. A lie that couldn't have felt more right.

Both women looked at Leya as her eyes barely greeted them. Her stomach squished, waiting for them to recognize her and say something, but if they did, they didn't acknowledge it.

"Gia said you could use some downtime, and I can see that it's true." Eva's eyes settled back on Holden's injured face before continuing, "You've come to the perfect place. Fresh air and the quiet of the outdoors are just what you need. And if you happen to get bored"—Eva shot a glance in Sadie's direction—"we offer a host of outdoor activities from fishing to white-water rafting and even caving. The only outdoor sport we don't offer is hunting because my granddaughter promised to disown me if we let anyone kill a wild animal."

Leya's lips twitched as Holden responded, "Quiet sounds perfect to us."

"Meals are included in your stay, but as this is a working ranch, the times are determined by our employees' schedule. Breakfast is from five until nine, lunch is from eleven to one, and dinner is from five until eight. We can provide room service, but that's at an additional fee, and it normally ends at nine each night. If you're hungry now, we can wrestle you up something."

Holden glanced at Leya with a raised brow. They hadn't had anything since the gas station snack near the thrift store hours ago.

"We wouldn't want to put you out," Leya said quietly.

"Sadie, go get them one of our picnic boxes for tomorrow, we'll make another one first thing."

Sadie moved away from the counter, walking with a limp it seemed like she was trying valiantly to hide. Eva watched her daughter's movements with a hint of sadness before turning back to them with a wide grin. Leya wondered again about this mother-daughter relationship.

Had her mother ever looked at her that way? Sad and wistful? Normally, her mom was calm, rarely expressing love by the actual words even though she knew she felt it. The emotion she'd seen the most from her mom was disappointment.

Eva came around the counter with an old-fashioned key and said for them to follow her. Holden grabbed Leya's hand, shouldering their bags as they followed the woman out toward the barn. For a moment, she wondered if they were going to be sleeping with the animals. But then, Eva stepped onto a path that wound around the side, and an ornate, wrought-iron staircase came into view. They followed her up to a golden oak door similar to the one on the restaurant. She unlocked it and handed Holden the key.

"There's a map of the ranch, the hiking trails, and vista points on the table as well as a brochure of the activities I talked about," she said.

Holden took the key, but Leya felt his entire body grow taut.

"Does anyone else have a key to this room?" he asked.

Eva's eyebrows jumped.

"There's one more. It's kept in the safe, and only my family and the cleaning folks ever have access to it."

Leya could almost feel the indecision wafting from him as he rocked slightly on his heels before pulling something from his pocket and showing it to Eva. It wasn't the Secret Service pin he normally wore when on duty. This was a badge she'd never seen.

"I'd prefer if no one had access to the key while we're here," he said quietly.

Eva's eyes widened, flicking to Leya and then back to Holden. "My son Maddox is the county sheriff. How about I ask him to hold on to it?"

"I suppose that'll work. I'd actually like to talk to him. Maybe you can arrange it?" he asked. Eva gave a curt nod. Footsteps on the gravel path made Holden stiffen even more, reaching for the gun he had tucked beneath his T-shirt. Sadie stepped around the corner with a wicker basket, and his hand dropped.

Eva hadn't missed a single motion, and she was frowning by the time Sadie got to the bottom of the stairs. When her mother started to go down to grab the basket, Sadie groused at her, "I got it!"

She climbed up and handed the basket to Leya even though it seemed to take quite a bit of effort. Eva put her arm around the younger woman and said, "We'll see you in the morning," and then proceeded to pretend not to be helping Sadie back down.

Holden exhaled, but Leya could feel the tension still radiating from him as he placed her just inside the door in order to clear the apartment. Leya's gaze swept over it while she waited for him to come back out of the bedroom. Even if they hadn't stayed in the worst motel on the planet the night before, this room would have looked elegant. It had brown leather furniture, warm woods, and brightly colored linens. The cream-colored walls were littered with black-and-white shots of what was likely the surrounding countryside, and there was a small kitchen off to the side done in teal-colored, fifties-style appliances with white, farmhouse-chic cabinets.

It was a lot nicer than the drab track home the safe house had been, but she wondered if they'd be any better off here than they'd been there. Her pulse picked up again, thinking of the way he'd all but shoved her into the truck. Would she make it home? Would she be able to get back on tour? She missed her family and friends, ached to see them almost as much as she ached to have Holden's lips on hers again.

When he came back out of the room, she said, "I'd like to call my parents."

"Camp's been giving them updates."

She swallowed hard, suddenly feeling close to tears and not knowing exactly why, hating that it was the exact opposite of the confident, brave, smart woman she wanted to be and had thought she'd stepped closer to just hours ago in the truck. In two strides, he'd crossed the room and wrapped her in his arms. The heat of him settled over her veins, soothing in a way that was addicting.

"You've been through a lot," he said softly.

"We've been through a lot, and you're not breaking down." Her voice was muffled, buried in his shoulder. He smelled like the old truck and sweat and that uniquely Holden scent of mint traced with honey that tugged at her insides.

He didn't respond, but he stepped back, and the loss of his heat and his comfort sent a shiver through her. He dug through one of the bags he'd dropped by the door, cracked open a new pre-paid phone case, and handed it to her.

"Try to keep it to a minute or two at the most."

He took the rest of their bags and headed for the bedroom again.

She dialed her mom's number, hoping she wouldn't wake her as it was close to eleven. But the worry was for naught because when she answered, her mom's voice was rushed and clipped, as if Leya had caught her going into surgery.

"Mom. It's me."

"*Beta*!" The tears Leya had held back pricked once more from the relief and tenderness in her mother's voice. "Are you okay?"

No. Yes. What was the right answer? "It's been a long day. Are you all okay?"

The tenderness was gone so fast Leya thought she'd imagined it. "Your father is dealing with your mess and the bombing, the Aryas have been calling nonstop, and I'm having to cover for you tomorrow at the Marriage by Choice gala."

Her stomach fell. She'd completely forgotten about the fundraiser. Not only was she slated to be the keynote speaker, but she was supposedly bringing several auction items, including a guitar signed by all the Daisies.

"I'm so sorry," Leya said, truly meaning it.

"It's fine. Ria's helping as Mirabel got called away on a family emergency."

More guilt rammed through Leya. They were picking up the pieces from the fallout she'd caused with the Aryas, FGT, and now this. Why hadn't she done what they asked yesterday and just stayed at the residence? Why had she let her emotions force her to the art store? None of this would have happened, she wouldn't have disappointed her mom one more time, and her mother wouldn't be scrambling to fill her shoes without even an assistant to help her.

"Mom…" her voice clogged with tears.

"*Arre*, crying won't help," her mother said, her tone even sharper than normal, and it stabbed at Leya more.

Holden came out of the room and tapped his wrist where a watch normally sat and then moved to the basket Sadie had given them.

"I have to go," Leya said softly. "I just wanted to hear your voice."

Her mom was silent for a moment and then asked, "You are safe, no?"

What would her mother say if she told her everything that had happened? Would her face turn sad and wistful as Eva Hatley's had following her daughter? Or would she be frustrated at all the choices Leya had made that could have been different?

"I'm safe," she said softly, eyes finding Holden's.

"Do what Special Agent Kent says, and we will see you soon."

"Okay," she said.

The call ended abruptly without a goodbye. It was the way her mother had always hung up, but maybe because Leya's emotions were so high, it felt harsher in some way.

She joined Holden at the counter, handed the phone back to him, and eyed the plates with sandwiches he'd removed from their wrappings. Her stomach turned at the thought of putting any food inside it.

She was exhausted. More so than she'd been after nonstop weeks on The Legacy tour. More so than even after sleepless nights with guilt eating at her after Landry's death. She was feeling a thousand different emotions. Fear and hope. Heartache and love. Desire and pain. But what she really needed was a respite from it all. She needed to be numb for a few hours. She needed her yoga mat and meditation videos and a place to drift away while she restored some sort of balance to her mind and soul.

She needed a life that wouldn't continually disappoint the people she loved.

"I'm going to bed."

"You need food," he said.

"I need sleep. I want to wake up and for this to all be over," she said and regretted it when he winced. This wasn't his fault. He was doing his job the best he could after she'd continually made it harder for him. She hadn't listened when he'd warned her not to go out. She'd taunted and teased him until he'd broken his own moral code and kissed her.

She turned, leaving the coat and boots by the door and heading for the bedroom.

She barely registered the luxurious purple linens, gray walls, and rustic furniture as she pulled back the covers and crawled inside. Her eyes shut, but her mind was whirling. So many thoughts tormented her, including the way her body had felt when Holden had kissed her, and how it had felt to ride next to him as if they belonged to one another.

She was still awake when the bed dipped, but she pretended not to be.

Earlier, she'd thought she was ready to rush into the burning building and declare herself his. To be turned to ash and rise again as a new bird—stronger, more vibrant, claiming love as if she'd somehow earned it. But if she gave in to it all, she wouldn't be the only one left as burnt embers. Her family, her friends, and Holden would be as well. So, she ignored every instinct telling her to turn around and wrap her arms around him, every desire to lose herself in his scent and his touch, and tried to find enough calm that sleep would overtake her.

♫ ♫ ♫

When Leya woke and didn't immediately recognize her surroundings, it almost felt like she was on tour again. Bouncing from hotel to hotel. But then, the terror of the last two days slammed into her, and her pulse quickened. She reached for Holden as if she was already used to him being next to her—as if it was normal. When he wasn't in the bed, she sat up, panic flying through her.

She heard a murmur of conversation from the other room and recognized the deep gravel of his voice. Relief flooded her veins. It was so strong it propelled her from the bed, desperate to see him. To touch him. To dance along the ravine that divided her soul between instincts and logic.

She walked out to find him shutting the door behind Eva. The sunlight shining through the window surrounded him in a glow, and she was struck by the beauty of him all over again. His hair was wet, and he had on a blue T-shirt the same color as his aura—a shimmer of pale aquamarine she wanted to lose herself in. Her hands itched to paint him in strong, vivid lines of black that would curl over the page, but even more than that, she wished she could walk right up to him and kiss him.

He drank her in as he always did, and that combination of assessing and appreciating set fire to her veins.

"Eva brought more food." He waved to a pink box on the counter. "And there's coffee in the pot."

Neither of them moved, and yet it felt like they had, the tension that always existed between them banging at the doors of her heart, waking her nerve endings completely.

Yesterday, she'd wanted these emotions, needed them desperately in order to feel alive. She'd told herself she was already tied to him forever, and yet she'd let one call with her mother drag it all away. How pathetic was that? To walk away from someone who could be her *jeevansathi* just because she was afraid of disappointing one person?

The truth was, she'd never be what her mother wanted because she *was* emotional. She did let her feelings and instincts guide her more than logic. But listening to herself, that inner core, had brought her many wonderful things. They'd brought her the band…and Lincoln…and her art. And now…now they were bringing her Holden. If only she had the courage to take the leap, and if he had the courage to take it back.

Mom would say it was impulsive…but it wasn't. Impulsive would have been kissing him that very first day on the lawn at the residence. Kissing him now was going into it without blinders. Understanding what she was giving up…what he would have to give up. They'd have to risk enormous parts of themselves for a mere chance at something bigger. Something that may not last even if they both wanted it to.

She stepped toward him, eyes falling to his mouth, and he mirrored the movements until they were close enough that he could tug gently on a long strand of her tangled hair. The bruises under his eyes had turned even darker, and it stabbed at her. She reached up with both hands, gently running the pads of her thumbs over the marks while almost cupping his face.

"I wish you hadn't gotten hurt because of me."

He grunted out his disapproval. "It isn't—"

"Because of me. I know. And yet…it is, right?"

She eliminated the little bit of space left between their bodies, breasts grazing the hard planes of his chest. His lips parted as he watched every movement she made with an intensity that left her breathless. She wasn't short, but she still had to go up on her tiptoes to place a gentle kiss on his cheekbone. First one side and then the other.

He grabbed her wrists, pulling her hands away and shifting so there were a few millimeters of space between them again.

"What are you doing?" His voice was a deep, dark rumble. Sexy. Enticing. She'd never imagined wanting someone like this—with every fiber of her being. But she did. She wanted him so badly it was impossible to stop reaching for him. Impossible *not* to take this chance.

"Trusting my instincts."

He inhaled sharply. "Leya…"

She leaned in, bringing their mouths closer. His fingers tightened around her wrists, burning into her skin, and her pulse banged against them.

"I'm going to kiss you, and it's going to have nothing to do with your job and everything to do with what I'm feeling," she said, twisting his words from yesterday and tossing them back at him. "If you get your hopes up, that's up to you…" she trailed off and gave him a chance to push her away, to stop her, but he didn't. His nostrils flared, and his pupils darkened as his gaze lazily dragged down her face to land on her mouth.

She set her lips against his. Soft. Tantalizing. A mere taste, just like he'd started with the day before. A tease of everything that could come if they just let go. The slight touch combined with the heady scent of him crashed through her in a rush of desire. Everything about this moment was a reverse of what had happened mere hours ago. His groan was like her moan, the slide of her tongue along his seam just like his had been. She moved her hands to settle around his neck, and his arms surrounded her waist, pulling her into him. And just like yesterday, soft and sweet turned to a desperate hunger in seconds.

Tongues tangled and pulsed and lunged, seeking the inner recesses, sipping at each other. Their mouths were wet and hot and delicious. Her body shivered, goosebumps littering her skin, and she pushed herself impossibly closer, fingernails sinking into his neck.

His hands slid under her pajama top, thumbs circling her sides and causing her core to ache. He broke the kiss, and a whine escaped her before she could help it, but he didn't push her away. Instead, his lips slid down her jaw to the tender spot below her ear, layering open-mouthed kisses until he landed on the throbbing pulse in her neck, sucking and claiming each beat of her heart as his own. She wanted him to claim her. She wanted to be branded by him in every way, but she also wanted to mark him back. Something permanent. Something he'd never be able to deny.

His hands slid up and barely grazed the underside of her breasts, and a gasp escaped her. She'd fallen asleep with her bra on, and now she regretted it. She wanted his hands on her bare skin. Ached to have those strong fingers pulling and tugging at the tips. Craved his hot mouth devouring her. Greedy and hungry.

Her hips rocked involuntarily, slamming into the thick length of him. She needed friction. She needed release. She needed him.

But just like yesterday, the motion stalled him.

He didn't freeze completely, nor did he step away and claim it was a mistake, but his hooded, lust-filled gaze met hers with a warning. One she didn't heed. Instead, she moved her hips again, this time knowing exactly what she was doing as she stared into his eyes. His lids fluttered, heat flaring in the blue storm, before he uttered another pained warning, "Leya…"

"I've never felt this way, Holden. I've never wanted someone so badly it tossed every thought, every caution, every reasonable excuse out of my head. I need to experience every burning ounce of it. I feel like if I don't, my life will always be some mirage. Half-lived. Half-experienced."

"Jesus," he groaned, and she watched the desire and duty battle in him. She felt a moment of remorse for pushing him. For the selfishness of asking him to step beyond the boundaries of his honor and pride. But hadn't Landry's death and Paisley's and Fee's attacks proven that life was too short to sit around and let something you wanted slide by? She could be gone tomorrow. Even *Nani* had been there one day and then collapsed with a brain aneurysm the next. She wanted to grab these feelings with both hands and hold on. To douse herself completely in the sensations roaring through them.

Leya had lived too long in the shadows of other great people, and now she wanted to be the sun. She wanted to be the light. The flame. The one burning, demanding others take notice. Even if it meant never again having her mother's approval. Even if it meant they both had to walk away from things they'd thought they wanted.

Wasn't it worth it?

Maybe he didn't understand she wasn't talking about simply losing themselves in each other for a night, giving in to passion and lust. Maybe the idea of life partners and soulmates was terrifying to a man approaching thirty who'd been a lone wolf most of his life. They'd shared two kisses. Two kisses and a handful of longing touches and looks. Perhaps she was the only one feeling inexplicably tied together. That sent pain through her worse than anything she'd ever felt.

She started to step back, and his fingers dug into her skin, holding her. Hope banged against her rib cage. She had to be brave. She had to tell him what she saw, and what she wanted, and then leave it to him to accept it or walk away. She placed the pad of her thumb on his lips, shifting over skin way softer than she would have expected from the firm, set line they normally formed.

"This isn't me being a flighty rock star, wanting to fall into bed with some sexy superhero, Holden. I see a lifetime ahead of us. That might scare you. I know it scares the hell out of me, but what terrifies me even more is the idea of losing you completely. Of never again feeling this alive. So, just know that if you want this too, if you're willing to take the leap that asks you to risk one future for a completely different one, then I'll be here, ready to jump with you."

He inhaled sharply at her words but didn't respond, and it twisted and turned inside her. But she also understood this wasn't as easy as asking him for a forbidden kiss.

She turned and walked back into the bedroom, shaking from the rush of adrenaline it had taken to stake her claim and trembling with fear that she'd pushed too far, too fast. Afraid that he'd deny them both what she thought the universe had offered them—an infinity of lives tied together.

# Chapter Twenty-one

## *Holden*

***THE POWER OF LOVE***

*Performed by Huey Lewis and the News*

*As Leya walked away, his heart* slammed violently into his chest. A piece of him was screaming to go after her. To finish the molten kiss. To go further. To take every piece of her she'd offered and make them his. To give her everything she'd asked and more in return. He wanted it so badly it burned through his chest and limbs.

Her courageous offer twisted and turned with his thoughts from the day before about relationships and keeping her. It taunted him with a glimpse of a different life, and now his brain wouldn't let it go. Scenarios and tasks scattered through his mind as he desperately tried to figure out a way to have them both—to have her and his job.

But the truth washed over him. He was never going to be able to keep her even if he gave up his job. Because there was no way his boss, the vice president, or her mother were going to stand by and watch as she twined her life permanently with some Secret Service agent who'd taken advantage of his position to have her.

So, there would be no more kissing. No more tantalizing touches and heated stares.

He had to shut it all down.

He had to walk away now because if he couldn't have something permanent, he couldn't have her at all.

Because nothing else was good enough for her.

He shoved his gun at his back, untucking his T-shirt so it covered it, and stepped out onto the tiny balcony to clear his head. To try and rid his body of the sensations of her pressed against him and the taste of her tongue in his mouth.

A thin mist had settled low over the frost-covered fields, but it was slowly dissipating as the sun strengthened. A field dotted with horses and cows dipped away into what appeared to be a small ravine. On the other side of it, willow and magnolia trees blended together at the base of a craggy hill.

The air was fresh, but the smell of hay and dirt and animals hung at the edges of it. He turned his head the other way and saw a row of cabins behind the barn. They looked as rustic as the rest of the ranch, and yet they had an elegance to them as well. People were sitting on a few of the porches, coffee cups in hand, enjoying the morning.

A tractor started up somewhere behind him, and pretty soon, one came into view, heading out toward a field of plants Holden couldn't identify. The man in the seat was tall and broad-shouldered with a cowboy hat blocking his face.

Eva had said it was a working ranch, but he hadn't really considered what that meant—lots of people who might see Leya and recognize her just like Camp had inferred about his grandparents' place. His stomach churned. Maybe this wasn't the hideaway he'd thought it would be. Maybe it would be another mistake.

He'd already made so many. Lost focus so many damn times. His chest was a knotted mess as he wondered if he'd ever be able to keep his concentration enough to protect her. Doubt turned to disgust and then anger that was all self-directed. He was the only one here. He couldn't trust anyone else with her, not after the way they'd been followed the day before. He had to put his dick away and do the job.

The door opened behind him, and Leya came out in jeans and a sweater that clung to her curves. It was a rich shade of orange that bordered on red, reminiscent of her cherry brandy daisy. Below the cowboy hat, her wet hair had been twined into a long braid that rested over her shoulder. She had the bag he'd rescued from the crash over a shoulder, the bomber jacket looped through the handles.

"Where do you think you're going?" he demanded. He wanted to shove her back into the apartment, out of view, out of his senses, until he was sure he could keep everything in control again.

She met his gaze, and he saw pain in her warm, brown eyes that she hid from him by turning away. She thought he'd rejected her, but it wasn't because he didn't want to accept what she'd offered. There was no way he could tell her that without giving her hope, without her arguing in her typical Leya way that they could make it work.

She looked away, running a hand through the row of bracelets before saying, "I can't stay inside without losing my mind. Can we take a walk? Explore the ranch and maybe find a place where I could draw?"

"Staying inside is safer," he said, eyes scanning the cabins once more and the people lounging around them.

"And do what?" she asked, glance darting to his mouth and then away again.

Jesus. She was right. If they stayed inside, he'd lose his mind as well. How would he keep from touching her? Spending a day with her on the couch in a tiny apartment would be ten thousand times more difficult than it had ever been standing at her door.

A hike would be better. Safer in at least one way.

"Step back inside while I grab a few things," he said.

She did as he asked, and he grabbed his hat, his sunglasses, and a couple of water bottles he shoved into a duffel he emptied of clothes. Then, he picked up one of the brochures from the counter. It had a map of the ranch and surrounding area with hiking trails and vista points listed. He palmed a few more painkillers and looked up to find her eyes had narrowed in on the bottle.

"You should probably rest."

He shook his head. "No, you're right. Sitting around doing nothing isn't going to be good for either of us."

She swallowed at his perceived rejection, and he hated that he was hurting her.

"But your ribs—"

"Let's go, Lita Rae," he said, cutting her off and heading out the door. At the base of the stairs, he turned to take her in, catching his breath at how beautiful she was. "Keep your head down until we're farther out."

She sighed but dropped her chin.

He studied the map and then strode past the cabins to a well-worn path meandering through cows and horses who were grazing lazily, tails swatting at flies. At the edge of the field, they reached a gate leading them along another rambling trail to the ravine he'd seen from the balcony. A creek that was nothing more than a slow trickle at the moment twisted through a gravelly riverbed, but in the winter, he imagined it would run fast and furious.

They hopped over the stream and wound up the other side where the path passed through a dense grove of willow trees, limbs draping to the ground. The air was clean and fresh, and Holden felt his entire being relax as the quiet serenity of the countryside enveloped them. Birds twittered somewhere far to the right, a bee buzzed past his ear, and all sounds of humanity seemed to disappear except for the crunch of their boots.

Leya stopped, closing her eyes and turning her face to the sun as it flickered through the leaves, and his heart expanded as the light seemed to halo her in a golden haze.

"You okay?" he asked, studying her carefully. The knot on her temple was nothing more than a bruise today, but she'd been tossed around in the car accident too.

She opened her eyes, scanning him like he normally did her, and then nodded.

"Keep going?" he asked.

"Yes. I may be a citified rock star, but I can still handle a little hike over mostly flat terrain," she teased with a small smile he was relieved to see.

She could handle more than a little hike. She may not work out as rigorously as Adria, Nikki, and Paisley, but she used yoga and meditation to keep in shape. And their concerts were a full-body workout that left them all exhausted and yet amped up. He knew because it took them several hours after being onstage before they were relaxed enough to go back to their hotel rooms. He'd stood by through it all.

He turned and continued along the path. They eventually emerged from the trees onto a hilltop scattered with large boulders looking over a valley. Trees and animals dotted the countryside, and in the far distance, another farmhouse much like the Hatley's glimmered. They were facing west, which meant at sunset it would be a stunning collage of colors. Even now, the sky was its own masterpiece filled with puffy white and gray clouds that the sun ducked behind briefly before reappearing.

"Here," she breathed out, climbing up one of the large boulders and pulling a sketchpad from her bag. She rested it on her knee and started drawing with a charcoal pencil.

He wanted to sit behind her, drape his legs around her, and pull her up against his chest while she worked. He longed to lean his chin on her shoulder and watch as she created her art. He had to clench his hands into fists to remind himself of the promise he'd just made out on the balcony a handful of minutes ago.

He was there to protect her. That was all it could be. He climbed up on a boulder one over from her, facing the path, listening for any telltale signs of footsteps.

"How do you do it?" she asked, drawing his eyes briefly to her as she added broad strokes to her page.

"Do what?"

"Stay alert every minute of every day."

"I used to be able to say it was my training." The words were out before he could take them back. But they were also the truth. Staying focused had seemed easy before her. He'd never understood when others had found it difficult

"Used to?" she asked, not even looking up from the scene she was drawing.

"I lose my way with you." More truths burst from him. Frustration and desire breaking the calm he was aching to find again. He had to find it, or he'd cost them both everything.

"I used to hate the way you made me feel," she breathed out. "Passion wasn't something I wanted. Not like this…not the way I feel with you. I wanted to build something slow and steady, a partnership built on respect and family."

He still didn't say anything for a long time, but when he did, his question was deep and guttural. "Why can't you have it all?"

Her fingers slipped as her gaze met his. Heated. Full of longing. Why couldn't he stop himself? He wanted to say he hated it just as much as she did, but there was a voice inside him that denied it. That loved every damn moment of it.

# Chapter Twenty-two

## *Leya*

***UNLESS IT'S WITH YOU***
*Performed by Christina Aguilera*

*Did he understand? If she couldn't* have it all with Holden, she'd never have it with anyone. There was only one true soulmate for every person. You didn't get three or four or even two. He hadn't denied her outright after she'd laid everything out for him, but she'd seen him move back behind his broody agent exterior, closing the doors that had opened and hiding away.

He was the one to turn away now as well, eyes shifting back to the path that had brought them here. He looked relaxed, stretched out on the rock, lying with his long feet pointed toward the trees, cowboy hat beside him, but his hand was near his waist, keeping his gun in easy reach. Still on alert.

The sun played peekaboo above them, drifting in and out of the gray clouds. When it emerged again, the light turned his hair into an array of shimmering golds and silvers. Before she thought much about it, she turned the page and began sketching him.

Normally, she drew with one hand on her subject, and the other on the page, eyes closed, a string of abstract lines and curves. A general shape and texture that she explored on the page, adding a single, dominant hue of the aura she saw around them. But with Holden, it didn't seem like enough. As if it was only in capturing every light and shadow, every groove and arch, that she'd be able to do him justice. Except, instead of drawing the sunglasses he wore and the firm set of his mouth, she drew him smiling, recalling the shape of it from memory. The way it had crinkled the corners of his eyes and made a tiny dent appear in his cheek.

It had been so long since she'd done a realistic sketch that she felt rusty, but the longer she drew, the looser her hand became, and the more confident she felt about it. While she captured him in great detail, she drew the sky, the rocks, the trees, and even his hat as vague impressions. It made him stand out even more, drawing extra attention to the stunning beauty that was Holden.

They were quiet while she worked, the twitter of birds and the whoosh of the breeze the only sound accompanying them. Her legs grew stiff, her butt cried due to the hard granite below it, and yet still she drew. The sun became lost, hiding completely behind ever increasingly dark clouds.

She worked for so long she thought he might have fallen asleep, but a sharp crack of a twig had him on his feet in an instant. His gun was in hand and pointed toward the path as heavy footsteps broke through the tranquility.

"Get down behind the rock," Holden grunted.

Her heart raced, panic taking hold in a pattern that carried over from the day before. She grasped her pad and slid down in between the two boulders they'd been on. But she could still see the trail as a tall man broke through the trees. He was wearing a khaki-colored uniform shirt, green pants, and a tan cowboy hat. A bronze star glowed on his chest, and a gun belt hung around his waist. Above her on the rock, Holden lowered his gun but didn't put it away.

The man strode toward them, confident and sure. He picked his hat up, swept his hair back, and then replaced it as he came to a stop in front of the rocks. His hair was a shade darker than Holden's but not by much, and his eyes were also blue. In some universe, they might have been brothers. Except, Holden was broader and thicker while this man's muscles were all long and sinewy.

"I'm Maddox Hatley, the sheriff. You got a license to carry that?" he asked Holden.

"As I'm sure your mother told you who I am, I don't think I need to answer that."

"I'd like to see your badge myself, if you don't mind," the sheriff said, eyes darting down to where Leya was hidden. Holden stepped so he had a foot on each boulder, partially blocking her as he dug in his pocket and came out with his badge.

Sheriff Hatley took it from him, eyed it, and handed it back. Then, he pulled out his phone and started typing.

"I'd prefer if you didn't do that," Holden grunted.

The man pulled his gaze up from his phone, fingers stalled, eyes narrowed. "Check your badge number? What am I going to find? It isn't real or that you've gone rogue?"

It was said half-tease, half-serious as the two men assessed each other.

"I'm on a protective assignment, and we're afraid we might have a leak. I could have you call my boss, but even he's asked me not to tell him where I'm at until we close the gap. If you call or start poking at my badge number, someone's going to trace us here."

"So, I'm supposed to just believe someone who shows up at my family's place beat up and on the run with a weapon he has no problem drawing?"

The tension between the men grew, swirling and growing until it almost took shape.

"Take off your glasses nice and slow," the sheriff demanded.

Holden did as he was asked, and the man inhaled sharply. "What happened?"

"Hit-and-run in Virginia as we were leaving town. We were rammed from behind, and it wasn't an accident."

The man's eyes narrowed, and she wasn't sure this standoff was going to end well for anyone. So, she did the only thing she could. She dragged herself back onto the boulder next to Holden, pulled off her cowboy hat, and faced the sheriff.

"Get back," Holden growled, hand to her waist, but Leya stood her ground.

"Do you know who I am?" she asked the sheriff.

His eyes grew wider before flipping from her to Holden and back again. "I do," he said.

"You'll have heard about the bombing at my sister's school, then."

He gave a curt nod.

"The people who did that are looking for me."

"Jesus, Ley—Lita Rae," Holden grunted his disapproval.

The smallest of smirks formed on the sheriff's face, but he shoved his phone into his back pocket before glancing at Holden with a more serious expression. "You bringing something bad to my family's doorstep? We've been through a lot in the last year and don't really need more trouble."

It was Holden's turn to frown. "As long as no one shouts to the world that we're here, there should be no way for anyone to find us. Like I said, not even my boss knows."

Another tense beat was broken by the sheriff glancing up at the dark clouds.

"It's gonna rain soon. You might want to take cover. Mama has invited you to our family dinner so you don't have to eat in the restaurant. It's at seven. Don't be late."

The man turned on his booted heel and headed back toward the trees just as a drop of rain fell and landed on Leya's hand. She scrambled to her bag, shoving her drawings and pencils inside to keep them dry.

Holden had his hand out to help her off the boulder when she turned back around. She took it, hopping down, and they both sprinted toward the line of trees with their fingers entwined. The shelter of the branches held off some of the water, but once they'd emerged by the creek, it started to come down in a steady stream. Warm and heavy, like her heart.

They were drenched by the time they raced across the field and up the staircase to their little apartment. They dropped their bags inside the door. Her sweater was clinging to her, showing the black bra she had on underneath it. She tossed her hat aside and yanked at her boots while Holden did the same. His pale T-shirt was more see-through than her sweater, plastered to his ridged stomach in a way that caught her breath. It was like seeing him as he'd stepped out of the shower all over again, and her body reacted to it. She shivered, nipples hardening even though she wasn't cold.

Holden's gaze strolled down her just like hers had him, and when his eyes returned to her face, the heat in them almost burned her from a foot away.

A loud boom of what sounded like a gunshot ricocheted through the air, and he reacted instantaneously, sweeping her into his arms and dropping them to the floor with him on top of her and his gun facing the door. The same panic and fear that had spread through her on the boulder took over as another loud bang hammered through the skies.

How had they found them? She buried her head in his neck.

They lay there, waiting for the worst, but no footsteps thundered up the staircase. Another thunderous shot sounded off, deadly and cold, sending a quiver of dread through her.

A scattered flurry of honks and loud beating of wings filled the air, and she pulled her eyes from Holden's shoulder in time to see a bevy of birds scattering into the sky out the window. A man's deep voice yelled, "Get the hell out of my field, you monsters!" And another shot filled the air, sending more birds bolting.

Her pulse slowed ever so slightly. Holden's entire body softened, the weight of him settling down on her completely and making her heartbeat increase for a different reason.

"Fuck," he exhaled quietly and placed his forehead on her chest.

"Wh-what was that?"

"My guess, it was a farmer scaring the birds off his crop."

The words were calm, but beneath them, she heard his tortured regrets. She brought a shaky hand up to run it through his short hair, trying to find a way to soothe him like he always did her. His warm breath coasted over the swell of her breasts above the sweater's neckline, making her skin tingle, and all thoughts of the shots and the birds and ranchers left her head.

When he lifted his eyes to hers, they were tormented. His gaze bore into her as everything around them disappeared. The only thing she could focus on was how their mouths were inches apart and his body felt deliciously heavy on top of her. His belt buckle was pushed into her stomach, and his thick thighs caged hers, sending spirals of lust into her core and filling her with images of undoing the clasp and pushing his jeans down.

The rapid beat of his heart reverberated through her, and when he spoke, it was with a pained rasp. "I don't know how to do this."

"Do what?"

"Want you and protect you. I just keep screwing it up."

The anguish in his voice grew as if he hated himself. As if he was failing. But to her, it was just the opposite. A gift he was giving her. She'd promised herself she wouldn't touch him again after putting everything on the line. Wouldn't push if he needed to retreat, but every particle of her being ached to kiss him, to ease the remorse and contrition pouring from him.

She didn't let herself think about it further.

She placed her mouth on his.

And just like both times before, it felt perfectly right. Felt like it was what she was supposed to do and where she was supposed to be. Kissing Holden, being completely covered by him, not just his mouth and his body but his soul…it felt as if they were sliding together after thousands of years of searching. Her *jeevansathi.*

For a long moment, it was just her lips that danced across his, closed mouth and tentative, waiting for him to pull back. But as heat twirled and expanded between them, he groaned, and then, he was plundering her with a ferocity that was more intense than either of their kisses before. This wasn't just him being unable to stop himself. This was as if he no longer wanted to. As if he'd finally accepted everything they were.

Her heart soared as their tongues finally met, dancing out a beautiful beat.

He dropped his gun, cupping her neck with one hand as if to draw her mouth even closer. His opposite palm slid up under the hem of her wet sweater, and the combination of the cool fabric and his heat sent a sensual thrill over her body.

Her core ached, and her hips rocked involuntarily into his. The motion had caused him to stop every time they'd been tangled like this before, but now, it seemed only to add another log onto the already burning fire, and his hips thrust back with a joyous rhythm that filled her soul.

He kissed her deeper, fiercer, capturing every breath and making them his, making her lungs burn. She willingly gave him each inhale and exhale, begging him to never stop taking them, silently pleading with him to take every piece until there was nothing left for her to give.

# Chapter Twenty-three

## *Holden*

***SECRET***

*Performed by Heart*

*How had he gone from promising* himself he wouldn't do this again to devouring her like a starving man? But he couldn't stop himself. For the first time in his life, he'd completely lost control, understanding what addiction truly felt like, being drawn over and over again to the one thing you knew could tear your world apart. Except, this wasn't some unhealthy habit. This was him, worshipping a goddess.

His thumb found and pushed against the pulse point on her neck, and a perverse feeling of pleasure filled him at the way it beat wildly. Wings of a bird. No, wings of the firefly she'd always been to him. His other hand slid underneath the damp sweater, touching her smooth stomach, sliding upward and over the top of her bra, finding her hard tips. He plucked one through the thin fabric, loving the way she whimpered at the touch.

She was hot and wet and nothing he'd ever experienced. It felt like he was burning from the inside out. Like his chest was going to explode along with the other hardened parts of him. He was a black hole bursting into a universe.

When her hips rocked into him, he didn't pull away this time. Instead, he thrust back like a green teen, almost letting go fully clothed. She had her hands twisted in his shirt, and she tugged it up until he had no choice but to pull it over his head in order to continue ravishing her mouth. His ribs screamed at the motion, but he didn't care. He only cared about the soft gasp that escaped her as he swooped back in to take every single breath she gave. They were his. He was never giving them back.

She drove her core at him again, twining a leg around his body, rubbing to relieve the ache building in them both. His knee hit the hard wooden floor, and it broke through the passion-infused haze. He was manhandling her on the goddamn floor, savagely rocking into her in a way that would likely leave a bruise. And yet, he didn't want to be done with her. He didn't want to stop touching and kissing and licking until she'd come apart under his caresses.

He moved, and she moaned in protest. In two smooth motions, he was standing with her in his arms. His bruised body hollered again, but it was nothing to the pounding in his groin. He walked with her wrapped in his embrace toward the bedroom. She peppered kisses along his collarbone, sucking and nibbling until a hiss of pleasure escaped him.

He sat on the bed with her in his lap, and their mouths fused together again. Hungry. As if they'd been apart for months…decades…years instead of mere seconds. His palms slid against warm skin as he raised her sweater, and they had to break their kiss yet again as he pulled it from her body. He undid the clasp on her bra and flung it aside, pausing to take in the sight of her, eyes hooded and lust-filled. Cheeks flushed, lips red from his savage kisses, chest heaving. The large swells of her breasts rose and fell with each sharp intake of breath.

"Please, Holden," she whimpered. "Please don't stop." It sounded lyrical and rhythmic, as if she was singing.

He needed to stop—a tiny voice in his brain was shouting warnings—but he couldn't. Not yet. He filled his hands and mouth with her, making her moan as he played with her rosy peaks. The sound not nearly enough to satisfy him. He wanted her screaming his name.

He flipped them around so she was on her back and he could unbutton and pull down her rain-logged jeans, taking her underwear with them and chuckling with her as they stuck to her legs. And then, they were gone, and he could take in all of her. The beauty of every single curve. His gaze locked with hers, wondering how far she was willing to let him go, but there was nothing in her look but desire…desire and an adoration he wasn't sure he'd earned.

He lay down beside her, aching to be inside her, but he wouldn't go there. Not today. Maybe he'd talk himself into some sense before it happened, but not now. Right now, he was going to finish what he'd started.

His hand skimmed her bare stomach, trailing lower and watching her face as he made slow swirls through her curls. Her hips rocked into his hand, brown eyes turning almost black as his index finger made contact with her wet heat.

"Kiss me, Holden," she demanded.

And he did. He kissed her, lunging into her mouth as his finger dove into her sweetness. She whimpered again, a pleasure-filled sound that spurred him on, finger and tongue echoing each other, slower, faster, a dizzying mix of speed and pressure until she forced her mouth from his, gasping for air, and chanted his name as her body spasmed around him.

He watched, entranced. Honored to be the one touching her. Knowing he'd finally thrown his old life away and not having the coherency of thought to care. He'd find a new one that allowed him to worship her every day. To be the man making her gasp and cry out and shudder in pleasure.

A slow smile spread across her face. Her nails were digging into his sides, and he hadn't even noticed because his complete focus had been on her. She loosened her hold, palm sliding up and down his chest, taking extra time on each ridged line of muscles and lingering slightly on the black and purple bruises.

She leisurely made her way down past his buckle, cupping and stroking him through his jeans, and his body pulsed. He pulled her hand up, kissing the palm. “No.”

Her eyes turned sad, as if he was rejecting her again, turning her way. He leaned in and kissed her, deliberately and tenderly but with a fierce, unspoken promise.

“Not yet. Not now. We need to slow down,” he told her, his voice deep and lust-filled.

“Why?”

“Because I need you to be sure every single step of the way.”

“I already told you I want this.” She looked down at their bodies. “I want the feeling you just gave me over and over again. With you above me, under me, and inside me.”

He bit back a groan and kissed her again briefly—a gentle adoration.

“I want that too. But, Leya, there isn’t a way back from this. For me or you. So we’re going to be sure every step we take is the right one.”

It wasn’t, ‘I love you,’ but it was damn close. Words he’d never said to anyone but family. Words he’d never wanted or imagined saying to a woman.

“I don’t want a way back,” she said, all firm determination. All Leya.

He was overwhelmed by the emotions on her face that matched the unfamiliar ones in his chest. He rolled onto his back, and she curled into him, head on his chest, arm over his waist, feet tangled. The sensation of her next to him and the heady honeysuckle scent of her almost sent him over the edge.

Instead, he tried to focus on what he’d said…on what she’d said…on the truth, which was that in taking her, trying to keep her, he could actually lose her.

“You don’t understand,” he breathed out.

"Then, explain it to me."

"Breaking my oath in order to keep you will strip away everything I could actually offer you."

"You have yourself to offer. That's all I care about."

"But what about your parents? Will that be all they care about? Do you want to be the cliché? The rock star who fell for her bodyguard?" He tried to keep the bitterness out of his voice, but he knew it was there. He could taste it in his mouth as it settled uncomfortably in his heart.

He felt her cheeks pull upward on his chest, and a small huff coasted over his skin that might have been a chuckle. "I didn't really think of it that way. It's actually like a romance novel, isn't it? But I guess it's the truth. We *are* romance, Holden."

His heart hammered at her words. The pure acceptance he heard in them eased the bitter taste and filled him with something sweeter. He rubbed her back slowly, her soft skin doing nothing but make him want her more.

It was a long moment before she finally spoke again. "No one that my aunties or my mother could find in their piles of biodatas could ever make me happy now, and I believe, in their hearts, my parents want that for me—happiness."

"They won't believe you can find it with me. Not when I'm jobless with a black cloud following me. What kind of partner would I be? Certainly not anything they expected when they presented Krish Arya to you. But even worse than that…even if I somehow find someone to hire me, how could your parents ever trust me after I took advantage of you…broke every vow…" his voice cracked with emotions.

She leaned up on her elbow, cheek in her palm, and met his look with a heated smile. "I believe I'm the one who took advantage of you." When he didn't smile back, she turned serious again. "I hate that you feel like you have to choose. What you said on the rocks, about having everything, that should be true for you as well. You should have everything in your life you want. Duty and honor *and* love. But let's get one thing straight. You aren't breaking your oath, Holden." When he started to deny it, she covered his mouth with her fingers. "Would you ever let someone hurt me?"

"No." It came swiftly to his lips. An eternity of promises shoved into that single syllable.

"Then, you're keeping your promise. *I* trust you. The rest…the rest is just window dressing."

Jesus…he wanted to believe her words—heard the truth in them—but still, unease settled in him. The heavy weight of the decision he'd already made lodged in his chest. Choosing her, choosing them, meant walking away from every dream he'd ever had, walking away from the service he'd promised himself to at only seven years old. A life he'd wanted so badly he'd cut everyone but his family from his world.

But there really was no other decision to be made.

He couldn't give her up.

Not for her parents, or his boss, and definitely not to send her careening into another man's arms just because his bank account and his star chart read a certain way.

For the first time in his life, as the pages of his goals and to-do lists emptied, he accepted the blankness. He didn't know how he'd fill them back up, but he knew they belonged to her.

♫ ♫ ♫

Holden jerked awake, heart pounding, reaching for his gun. Jesus. His stomach clenched as he realized he'd actually passed out with his weapon laying on the floor in the front room and their bodies exposed to whatever could have come through the door. The light shifting through the window told him it was early evening. He'd been asleep for hours.

When his gaze settled on Leya, he realized she was no longer bare next to him. At some point, she must have gotten out of bed to slide a T-shirt on, and he hadn't even heard it. Frustration mounted inside him. He'd let everything spiral out of his control when he was renowned for having it. He hadn't lied when he'd told her he didn't know how to do this—to be both the fierce protector and lover. But he had to figure it out and fast. He'd keep at least this one damn piece of his oath intact.

He sat up, feet sliding over the edge of the bed, and she made a displeased sound as it dislodged her legs and arms from where they'd been tangled with his. When he looked back at her, Leya's eyes were wide and alert as if she'd been awake for a while. She'd unwound the braid, and her long hair was splayed out around her like a dark halo, making her look exactly like the goddess he'd thought her. She had one hand tucked under the T-shirt at her waist, and it exposed her taut stomach, tempting him to lean down and kiss it. Lick it. Taste her again. To taste every piece of her.

"I'm sorry I fell asleep. I shouldn't have," he said, voice husky and layered with slumber but also the lust he'd kept hidden for too long and that now refused to go back behind the barrier where he'd once kept it.

"You needed the sleep. Your body won't heal if you don't rest."

"Did you watch over me, Lita Rae?" He attempted a tease, but the idea of her staying awake to watch over him shot warmth through his chest. Deep feelings of tenderness…love… Jesus. He was so far gone.

"Maybe," she said with a half-smile that lit her eyes. "Or maybe I was just trying to unravel the puzzle of Holden Kent. But you keep yourself as tucked away in your sleep as you are awake."

He returned to her, body half covering hers, elbows bracing him. The now familiar tug of pain in his ribs only woke him further. He ached to place his mouth on hers. He barely held back by asking, "What were you hoping to discover?"

"I wondered what would happen when you opened your eyes. Would you pull away and tell me it was a mistake? Would you insist we're wrong for each other even though our souls know better? Or would you simply kiss me like you did earlier? Like we'd been apart for a century."

He stared for a moment, heart still pounding fiercely, coiled desire threatening to unwind without his say…and the only response he knew how to give was to lower his lips to hers. He was hit with a wave of sensations that filled the empty cracks in his heart he'd never known were there. When had they shown up? When had his dedication turned into loneliness?

He infused the kiss with a deep promise, one he hoped he could keep even as he was breaking the ones he'd made to himself, his job, and his team. It tore and mended all at the same time, and he didn't understand how it could do so. How she could be both his ruin and salvation.

"Does that answer your question?" he asked, brushing against her mouth again, wondering if he'd ever get enough of doing it. If he'd ever feel like he was sated and full or if the yearning growing inside him would always be there.

She smiled, one of the largest, most stunning smiles he'd ever seen on her face—and he'd seen a lot of them while he'd hovered in the shadows. She put both palms on his cheeks, stroking the rough stubble of his unshaven skin.

"I think so, but maybe you should kiss me one more time to make sure I got the message."

He obliged, intending only another soft embrace, but he craved her too much, and soon, his tongue was parting her mouth, and he was slowly devouring her inch by inch until their hips were rocking once more.

The only thing that stopped him from taking everything he had earlier and more was a rumble that exploded from her stomach, vibrating into his, and he broke away with a chuckle. The sheriff had basically demanded they show up to dinner, which was fine by Holden as it would give him a chance to make sure the lawman was on his side.

"Let's go, Lita Rae. We've got a dinner date with the Hatleys," he said, kissing her temple and dragging himself away from her warmth to the edge of the bed. His body groaned for multiple reasons, and when he stood up, the look she sent him only added to them. He pulled his Miles Green twang back out to tease her. "Darlin', you don't get up, and I won't be able to leave this room for days."

"Maybe Lita Rae likes that idea," she said, but her stomach grumbled again, loud enough for him to hear it at the edge of the bed. He grinned, and she inhaled sharply before saying, "You look stunning that way."

His brows drew together in confusion.

"Now you've ruined it. Bring the smile back. The one you hand out so rarely," she said, taunting him, lips quirking.

A deep laugh burst from his chest. She was right. He didn't smile or laugh often. The determination and focus driving him hadn't allowed for many light moments in his life. Her smile joined his, and it hurt almost worse than his ribs to turn away rather than crawl back in bed with her.

He grabbed his things, made a quick stop in the living area to pick up his gun, and then headed for the bathroom. As he cleaned up, he thought about her watching over him while his weapon had been abandoned in the other room. He needed her to know how to use it. Needed to know she could protect herself if he failed to stand watch.

He dragged on a black T-shirt and a fresh pair of jeans and then stared at the man who was reflected in the mirror. Who was he? This unshaven misfit with a smile quirking at his lips and eyes sparkling. Who would he be when he handed in his notice and showed up at Number One Observatory Circle in a different capacity? As Leya Singh's what…boyfriend? Lover?

His breathing grew shallow, pulse hammering.

God, he couldn't even label them, and yet he was tossing everything in his life aside just to be at her side. Maybe they'd let him stay in the USSS on the investigative side. He couldn't be the only agent to have fallen for someone in their care, could he?

He shook his head and palmed more pain meds before going back into the bedroom. She hadn't moved. She was still curled up on the bed, looking wonderfully sexy and watching him with a hooded gaze.

"Leya." It was a warning because he knew he'd break if she kept looking at him that way.

She smiled. "I think this might be my new favorite thing." He raised an eyebrow in question. "Tempting you."

He growled, "You're damn good at it."

He swooped her up into his arms as she squealed a half-hearted protest while his ribs screamed a real one. He stalked into the bathroom and then set her down in the shower, reaching for the knob, only stopping when her hands settled over his wrist.

"Don't do it, Holden. If you do, I can guarantee you'll be in here with me," she said, voice sultry and thick. He turned to find their lips inches apart, and his gaze locked with hers.

"We only have fifteen minutes before dinner, and I can guarantee you, the first time we shower together, it's going to take longer than that."

Her breathing turned ragged in a heartbeat, and he got a secret thrill out of it, of knowing he could make her tumble out of control as quickly as she did him. He kissed her gently before stepping away, moving until he was at the doorway, leaning against the frame. He watched her pull the shirt over her head, her bracelets jingling as they fell down her wrist with the motion. Something tugged at the back of his brain with them, but he couldn't hold on to it as Leya's bare body became the focus. Curved and soft. Luscious and warm. And even though he was across the room from her, he swore he could smell the sweet floral scent of her.

She tugged the shower curtain closed before peeking out around the edge at him. “Change your mind, Avenger-man? Going to join me?”

He swallowed hard and left with her laughter following him.

# Chapter Twenty-four

***YOU'RE TOO POSSESSIVE***

*Performed by The Runaways*

*BLOCKED: The tracker stopped pinging.*

*ISABEAU: Where was it last?*

*BLOCKED: I'm not sure. I needed to give them a little room after he saw us in Knoxville. I expected to be able to open the app and find them again like you promised.*

*ISABEAU: Sounds like they found it. I told you to use the one that recorded. You'd at least have a last known location before it went dead.*

*BLOCKED: Which would have left a trail for them to tie back to us.*

*ISABEAU: You. Tie back to you. The boss has made it clear you are no longer to receive our support.*

*BLOCKED: You're the one who put the tracker in play, or did you forget that?*

*ISABEAU: I wouldn't have helped you if I'd known you were going off the rails.*

*BLOCKED: I'm handing him the winning card. The sign we've all been waiting for. He's going to thank me. I need you in Knoxville.*

*ISABEAU: I can't help you anymore. No one can. Didn't you read what I wrote? The boss has cut you off.*

*BLOCKED: No one cuts me off! No one. My files are long, and my memory is longer. Remember that little incident in Houston? The police have an unmatched DNA source for the murderer, right? What would happen if I gave them the missing DNA?*

*ISABEAU: I was defending myself!*

*BLOCKED: If that's what you have to tell yourself to sleep at night. I don't want this to get ugly, but I need someone I can trust.*

*ISABEAU: You don't want me. They'll recognize me.*

*BLOCKED: Don't worry. You'll be out of sight, and then you can continue to play chicken for the infidels.*

*ISABEAU: You're a bitch.*

*BLOCKED: I'm the arrow that's sat in the crossbow too long.*

*ISABEAU: I'll find someone else to help you, but then I'm done.*

*BLOCKED: You're done when I say you're done.*

# Chapter Twenty-five

## *Leya*

***SO DONE***

*Performed by Alicia Keys w/ Khalid*

*FOUR DAYS BEFORE*

*When Leya woke the next day*, the sun was already high in the sky, and the space beside her was empty and cold, but it smelled like Holden. She curled into it, cherishing the scent. Her heart felt like it had expanded and grown overnight. As if she'd finally found her wings and been freed from her cage but also found a place to land that she could finally call her own.

The murmur of the television in the other room told her he hadn't gone far. The smell of coffee he didn't drink but made for her sent a little thrill that matched all the ones she'd felt every time her fingers had brushed his at dinner last night. They'd come back from the Hatleys and lost themselves in each other again. He'd brought her bliss with hungry kisses and slow, tantalizing fingers. She'd had him groaning and calling her name as she'd learned the muscled contours of his body with her mouth and hands. But he'd stopped them from going all the way again.

He insisted they take things slow. He said it was so she'd be sure every step of the way, but she had no doubts about them, even if she still carried remorse for the things they were both giving up in order to be together—her family…his job… Still, she didn't push him because she'd already pushed him into leaping across the abyss to join her. Maybe they both needed time to adjust to the new versions of themselves they'd finally become.

In the meantime, she'd revel in the tantalizing feelings of passion and desire she'd never felt before. Explore every moment and stoke the burning flames.

A smile grew on her face just thinking about every kiss and every touch. She was suddenly desperate to see him again. She pulled herself from bed, tugging on his black T-shirt and stepping out of the bedroom.

Holden did what he always did when she appeared, looking her up and down, assessing and appreciating her. He no longer hid the heat in his gaze. Instead, he let it burn between them, and her pulse picked up.

They'd just taken a step toward each other when a familiar name from a reporter's lips on the television behind him drew her eyes to the screen.

"Mr. Smythe, what's your response to the accusations that FGT was behind the bombing at Ria Singh's school?"

Her stomach flipped nastily at the sight of the blond-haired man who hated her family enough to try and kill her. He tugged at the sleeves of his expensive suit as if the reporter's question was irritating, but he gave her a snake-charmer smile that didn't reach his cold, gray eyes.

"For Greater Tomorrows is being blamed because we aren't afraid to speak the truth about the sins of our leaders. Our country has stumbled far off the path our forefathers set for us. Our character and strength have withered as we let the rats in the field run us out. While FGT feels strongly about the misguided direction our country has taken, we had nothing to do with the bombing at Ria Singh's school. Just like we had nothing to do with the car accident and the disappearance of Leya Singh. Maybe the authorities need to be asking themselves why she's on the run."

Leya's palms began to sweat, and her heart sped up at the cold insinuation Smythe had tossed into the air, knowing the haters would pick up the thread, twisting it into something bigger. Her knees wobbled, and then Holden was there, lacing their fingers together, pulling her into his side, making sure she didn't fall.

"What do you mean?" the reporter asked.

"Look at the people she hangs out with. A murdered friend and one attacked supposedly by her own bodyguard. The kidnapping of Adria Rojas's sister. Maybe the inner circle of The Painted Daisies knows the truth about these women. Maybe someone is simply ensuring their disease doesn't spread around the globe." His hateful words were spoken with so much charm you'd think he'd just uttered a compliment.

Leya's stomach heaved.

The woman's eyes widened. "Are you saying The Painted Daisies are responsible for all of the things that have happened to them?"

His fake smile grew, showing off perfect, white teeth. "What I'm saying is FGT had nothing to do with any of it. We're a simple organization run by simple men and women who want a kinder, gentler, cleaner world. We work within the bounds of the government our founding fathers set for us. Our real work will begin when I win the next presidential election."

"You're officially announcing?"

"Yes, Lynn, I'm absolutely announcing." He directed his gaze to the viewers. "And every single person who wants this country to be the one they read about in their history books, the country that led us through two world wars, the one who turned a ragged shamble of a continent into the number one superpower, will be voting for me."

Holden used the remote in his hand to flip the television off, dropped it on the table, and then pulled her tighter into his embrace. Nausea swam through her, and she fought a shiver that had nothing to do with desire and everything to do with fear and disgust. She pressed her head into his chest.

"He's so evil, Holden. I can feel it radiating from him out of the television. How can people not see it? How can they believe the fake smile he gives them? It's terrifying to think of what he'd do to this country."

"He'll be held accountable for the things he's done. We just have to find the final nail to put in his coffin."

She scoffed. "How long has the Secret Service been after him?"

His throat bobbed before he said, "Too long."

She was frustrated by law enforcement's inability to put the man out of business just like she was upset they hadn't arrested Landry's killer or found Adria's sister. She'd been terrified and guilty and sad for so long, but now rage grew inside her as well.

She pushed away from him, hands on her hips, and demanded, "When will it stop? When will they all get what's coming to them?"

Holden crossed his arms over his chest. "We're working on it."

"I hate how it makes me feel completely and absolutely powerless."

"You're not powerless."

She rolled her eyes, hand going to her empty wrist. The bracelets had been drenched in the rain the day before, the leather ones more so than the silver, and she'd left them all drying on the sink in the bathroom.

"Have you ever shot a gun?" Holden asked. Surprise filled her, and she shook her head. "Yesterday, after I fell asleep, I was thinking I should teach you how to use mine."

Killing wasn't what she believed in. She didn't even want to see John Smythe dead. She wanted him arrested, put in prison for decades, and unable to harm her or her family again, but she certainly didn't want to be the reason he was sent on to his next life. There was no good karma in that, no way for her to move toward *moksha* and be rejoined with Brahman.

As if he read her hesitation, he added on, "Knowing how to use a weapon doesn't mean you have to take the kill shot. But you can stop someone from hurting you."

His face was grim and solemn, and she suddenly understood. He'd said he didn't know how to be her protector and her lover, and this was his way of trying to find a balance. To keep her safe even if it wasn't by his own hands.

She returned to him, wrapping her arms around him, lifting up on her toes and kissing him lightly, a rush of tears hitting her eyes not because she was sad but because she was moved that this beautiful man was risking everything to be with her, and she didn't know how to even the scales. Her voice was choked as she whispered, "Thank you."

His hand cupped her neck, the other tightening on her waist as he looked deep into her eyes and said, "Stop feeling guilty. You didn't handcuff me to a chair and take advantage of me, Leya. I chose to give in. I chose to take the leap."

He said it with such surety, with such deep emotion, that it was impossible not to believe him. She brushed a thumb over his mouth, wanting to remove the somber expression from his face, aching for the stunning smile that stole her breath. So, she funneled a little piece of Fee into her voice and tossed back, "Are the handcuffs an option for later?"

His eyes widened, and the beautiful smile she'd been hungry for lit up his face. He tipped her face toward his, kissing her with a ferocity that made her doubt the slow and tantalizing pace they'd been keeping themselves to. She never would have stopped kissing him if he hadn't pulled back.

"Keep talking like that, Lita Rae," he growled, "and we'll never leave the apartment."

"You keep saying that. But there's no backing out, Special Agent Kent. You promised to show me how to use your gun, and now all I want to do is handle it." She was proud of herself for the innuendo. Not anything like the tween ones Fee always accused her of dropping. She knew it was a good one, because his nostrils flared, and his pupils expanded, the black taking over the blue.

"Jesus…"

Her heart skipped several beats, joy filling in behind the worry and anger and frustration in her heart. She was safe. She was with Holden. She'd concentrate on those good things instead of the bad lingering just outside their door.

He put his arms on her shoulders and set her away from him. "Go get dressed before I change my mind."

She laughed, heart easing even more.

He headed for the door and said, "I'm going to ask Eva for some directions. Don't open the door for anyone. Not even that sweet little girl we ate with last night."

She laughed, replying, "We're safe, Holden. There's no way they could have found us here."

He didn't look as certain, and it made her stomach flop.

"They shouldn't have been able to find us in Knoxville either. I can't figure out—son of a bitch!" he barked, and Leya's eyes widened. He dragged his wallet from his pocket and pulled out a business card with a single number on it—the card Angel Carter had left with the keys to the Camaro.

Holden stalked into the kitchen with a look of anger and disgust on his face. He doused the card in water, rubbing it between his fingers until it turned to a pulpy mush.

"No tracker," he breathed out with frustration and relief. He tossed the mess into the garbage and then ran a hand over the short stubble of his hair, and she knew the weight of everything they were running from had landed on him all over again.

"Holden," she said softly, and he lifted his eyes to meet hers. "We're safe here."

She repeated it for him, but it was also for herself. She had to believe that they'd stepped into a little bubble where no one could find them. Neither of them had made a call since the first night. No one had followed them through the dark of night as they'd left Knoxville. The Hatleys might have known who they were, but they seemed as determined as Holden to keep her secret from the other guests. Had even assured her that this was the last week of their regular season. The cabins would be vacated over the next few days and left empty until spring.

The tension in Holden's shoulders eased ever so slightly as he stepped back toward the door. "Go get ready, Lita Rae."

"Miles is bossy," she tossed back.

"Yeah, but Lita likes it."

It was true. She loved when he took command. Loved that he knew exactly what they both needed to take them over the edge. She trusted him with every single part of her in a way she never would have trusted Krish. The star charts had all been wrong, or maybe Aja Aunty had just seen in them what she wanted to see, because there was only one person who was perfect for her. Maybe no one else in their lives would be able to see it, but they did, and that was all that mattered. They were tied together. Their bodies and souls had already promised each other forever, just like they'd done in their past lives and would do again in their future ones.

# Chapter Twenty-six

## Holden

***ANSWER***

*Performed by Sarah McLachlan*

*Holden was cursing himself as he* locked the door and stomped down the stairs toward the restaurant. He should have thought of the damn business card well before now. He was lucky there hadn't been a tracker inside it, but it didn't mean they were in the clear. He hadn't talked with Camp since they'd arrived at the ranch, and no one but his sister and the Hatleys knew they were there, but he couldn't help the way his neck prickled as if he was still missing something, as if they were just in a waiting pattern that would eventually burst.

Losing himself in Leya was everything he shouldn't be doing and yet nothing he'd stop. Not now that he'd gone over the edge with her. The best thing he could do was prepare them both.

Inside the restaurant, he asked Eva for a place they could shoot safely, and she pulled out the map, drawing with a marker to a ridge well away from the ranch above the lake that bordered their property on one side. Then, she insisted on grabbing them a bagged lunch to take on the long hike.

When she came back, both her hands were full. She handed him a backpack, saying, "It's not as romantic as the wicker one, but we prep these lunches for our adventurous crowd." Then, she waved a clear bag full of empty cans at him. "And if you're anything like my sons, you'll want something to shoot at."

He thanked her and headed back to Leya, who was waiting inside the door for him, fully dressed with her boots and hat on. For two seconds, he debated throwing aside all his plans to divest her of everything she'd put on just to see her naked again.

Instead, he pulled her with him out the door, hitting the longer trail Eva had showed him toward the lake, and veering off the clearly worn path into the brush and trees as she'd instructed. The terrain was rockier, tougher going, and it was quiet with only the hum of insects and the twitter of birds in the air. They'd left the flat farmland far behind, and there wasn't a hint of humanity.

They kept going as the sun beat down on them until he had to shed the flannel shirt he'd put on, and she was pulling off her sweater to reveal a tank beneath it. A tank and lots of skin that bumped his pulse up more than the hike.

Eventually, they crested the top of a ridge. There was plenty of tree cover, but also a long line of rocks that made an almost perfect makeshift gun range. He pulled a couple of water bottles out of the backpack, and while Leya sat down on one of the rocks, drinking, he set up the empty cans on the boulder at the end of the natural corridor.

When he rejoined her, he slid behind her, legs surrounding her just like he'd wanted to the day before on the rock while she'd been drawing. Except, this time, he put his gun in front of her instead of pencil and paper. She stiffened.

"Don't be afraid of it," he said before showing her how to empty the weapon, how to slide it open and closed, and how to put the clip in. Then, he handed it to her. She grabbed it hesitantly, as if it was a snake going to bite her. He closed his hand around hers, forcing it onto the grip fully, saying, "It can't hurt you. Being afraid of it is worse than using it."

She inhaled sharply, but then he felt her fingers clench the grip tighter.

Determined to get her fully comfortable with it, he helped her load and unload the weapon half a dozen times until she finally pushed him off and did it on her own with confidence. Then, he showed her how to stand and how to aim, shifting her hips and feet, wrapping his arms around her to help her point, and explaining about the recoil. He pushed her arms into her chest, imitating the force. His breath coasted along her ear as he talked, and she shivered in his embrace. He couldn't stop himself from placing a quick kiss along her jaw, and when it made her drop the gun, he chuckled.

He repositioned her and then stepped back a little, nodding at her to shoot. Even prepared for it, the kickback still jerked her arms, and the shot went wild. They spent another thirty minutes shooting, and he was grateful he'd had the foresight to stock up on ammunition when they'd been at the store. She wouldn't be able to hit anything far away, but if someone was close, she'd get a piece of them.

When she was done, he reloaded the Glock and cleanly shot out each of the targets.

"Show off," she teased.

He chuckled. "I've had a lifetime of practice that you haven't. "

"Who taught you to shoot?" she asked.

"My dad. He taught my sister, mom, and me. Other kids went to the bowling alley on the weekend. We went to the shooting range."

He pulled the food out of the backpack, and they ate in silence for a few moments.

"So, your dad was an agent also. Is that what made you want to be one?"

"I was seven years old on 9/11, and I saw my dad on the television, standing behind George W. It felt like the whole world was crumbling, but there he was, ready to defend our leader. I didn't recognize it as pride then, but I was overwhelmed with it. After that, it was all I ever wanted to do, even when my dad stepped away."

"Why did he?" she asked softly.

"For my mom," he said. Their eyes met, long and steady, keenly aware of the similarity to their situation. "Or at least I always assumed it was for her. It was a lonely life for a wife. My dad tried to bring us on assignment sometimes, sticking us in the same hotel as him, but even then, he really didn't get to be with us. When his contract was up, he got out."

He wondered now if his dad had missed his mom more than he'd wanted to do the job. If he, like Holden, had made the choice not only for the woman in his life but because it meant filling in the lonely cracks that had taken over his soul.

"What did they think when you joined?" she asked.

"They've always supported Gia and me in whatever we did. But I think Mom's upset that I've been on my own for so long."

"She wants you to have a girlfriend?"

"According to her most recent comment, she wants grandkids." He knocked her shoulder with his knee. "Sound familiar?"

She smiled. "A dozen?"

He laughed softly. "I think she'd be happy with one or two."

She didn't say anything, closing her eyes and scooting down to sit in the grass along the boulder edge and leaning her head back against the rock. The sun was lower in the sky, the light filtering in through the tree branches and dancing over her face. She was so damn stunning. He let his hand drift over her exposed neck, settling on her chest and the swell of her breasts. She turned, watching him as he stared at her.

He ached to kiss her, but he was afraid if he did, he'd never stop. The sun would set, and they'd still be on top of the hill, miles from the ranch. So, he simply placed a kiss on the palm of her hand and then headed to the end of the makeshift range to pick up their trash.

He led the way back down the mountain, picking the easiest way, holding back branches so they didn't smack her in the face, and eventually coming out in a little different spot than where they'd gone up. The lake shimmered below them. It wasn't very large. No motorboats were racing around it, but there was a dock lodged in the middle of it, and there was a group of teens jumping off it as he and Leya made their way on the path around it.

He looked back at her as they got closer to the people, tapping the brim of her hat as a reminder to keep her head down, and then continued toward the ranch. The sun had dipped even lower by the time they reached the ranch gate. They had to dart around a trio of cows to get into the field, and Leya laughed.

As they skirted around them, she asked, "Did your grandparents have animals on their farm?"

"It's not really a farm like this, mostly rows of apple trees. But Gram has egg chickens and a couple of goats who keep the grass by the house trimmed."

"If I didn't see you here"—she waved at him in his jeans and hat and then at the pasture of animals—"I would never have believed you could have worked on one."

When they reached the plank fence near the barn, he pulled himself up onto the rail, one leg on either side, and then held out a hand to have her join him. She sat facing him, boot-clad feet tangling with his.

"Pops was hoping Gia or I would want to take it over at some point, but I think he's resigned himself to the orchard being sold once they're gone."

"She doesn't want it? Even though she's into all the agricultural stuff?"

Holden shook his head. "No interest at all in being tied to one place. She's a wanderer. Although, she has him test out new technologies here and there."

"Did you like working there?"

He thought back to his college days. He hadn't hated it. The hard work kept him fit and busy. But he'd been so focused on getting his criminology and psych degrees and getting into the Secret Service that he'd always seen the work as something temporary. If he'd known back then that he'd be tossing his career aside at not even thirty, would he have looked at it as something different? As something permanent? Could he imagine himself living like this, as a farmer? Concerned with the weather and frost patterns and pests and nothing else? It still didn't seem to fit him.

"I never thought to like it or not, if that makes sense," he said.

She considered him for a moment before nodding.

"What about you?" he asked. He grabbed her fingers, lacing them together. "Where did you see yourself settling down?"

She looked down at their joined hands. "Ever since I was fifteen, I thought I'd move from my parents' home into one with Krish. So, I guess, like you, I never saw anything else for myself. I didn't have to."

"You were only fifteen when you got engaged?" The surprise hit him in the chest at the same time as a bout of jealousy, feelings he shouldn't have for the man she'd already turned down but that he couldn't help.

She smiled at him. "We weren't engaged. It was more like…a promise of a promise. And it isn't as scandalous as you just made it sound."

No one he knew had gotten engaged or promised or whatever that young. Not even his grandparents. But she'd said it had been a relief to know her future, and he understood that. He'd known his future at seven—or at least, he'd thought he had.

"Did you know him before? Or was it completely arranged?"

"I knew him. He was Rishik's friend, but that's all I really saw him as until *Nani* took me with her to *Maha Kumbh Mela*."

Holden frowned. "What is *Maha Kumbh Mela*?"

"It's a religious festival—more like a pilgrimage, really—that happens every twelve years in India. Millions of people come from all over the world to bathe in the Ganges, hoping to have their sins washed away. The celebration lasts for almost two months. Great stories are retold, offerings to the gods are made, and there's plenty of food and entertainment."

"It sounds pretty amazing."

She nodded, her beautiful smile lighting her up from the inside so she glowed in the fading light. "It was. It is. *Nani* was desperate to go because she hadn't been in a long time, and she wanted me to go with her. But my parents didn't want us to travel by ourselves. They were tied up in their careers, and Rishik had started medical school, so there was no one to go with us until Krish and his family said they were going. He and I were together so much that it was inevitable for us to become friends too. We took long walks, and he bought a few gifts for me, but nothing more. Like you said, I was only fifteen, and he was much older. Plus, I was there to learn from *Nani*."

"Learn what?"

She looked out over the field, a faraway look in her eye. "Everything. About India and music and life. When my great-grandparents came to the U.S., they wanted nothing more than to look like they fit in here. They gave up a lot of their culture to do so, keeping their religion and their celebrations hidden away. They started dressing and eating and acting like the people they saw in the movies. *Nani* was the one to bring our heritage back to us. She went to college in India, spent several years there, studying music and folklore, and came back with an appreciation of her homeland neither her husband nor her children ended up being overly interested in. I was the first one to soak it up like a sponge."

Her eyes turned watery thinking of her grandmother, and Holden eased closer to her, spreading his hips wide so he could encompass her fully, wrapping his arms around her waist.

"She was your hero."

She nodded softly, leaning into him more, but her eyes were still turned toward the hills that were fading from green into purple as the sun dropped more. "I loved everything about her. The way she dressed, and talked, and all the stories she told. Everything in my life felt so much more colorful with her there, and I don't mean that in just the stereotypical way about the saris and the kurtas she wore. I mean she was bright and vivid—an explosion of color." Her voice turned soft and quiet. "She's the only portrait I've ever drawn with more than one color because I couldn't decide which one of her auras was the brightest."

"You actually see colors around people?" he asked, sucking in a surprised breath.

She turned to take him in, but it was unfocused, as if she was looking at the air around him. "Yes, and not just people. Animals and even sometimes objects, especially if they're well-loved or have strong emotions tied to them."

He brushed his hands up and down her arms, tucking her braid behind her shoulder and drawing her chin so she was forced to meet his gaze. "What color am I?"

Instead of the sadness she'd shown talking about her grandmother, a smile reemerged, twisting up the corners of her mouth and making her cleft all but disappear. "You change. It's varying shades of greens and blues. Right now, you're flickering from green into aquamarine. Not just regular aqua, but the indescribable shade you can only find at sunset. Like that," she said, pointing at the colors above the hills.

When he looked at the sky, he didn't see anything like the color she'd mentioned. All he saw was a fiery orange turning almost black as a partial moon and a handful of stars came to life around them. His brows drew together in a frown. "I don't understand."

She looked at him with wide eyes before saying, "See how the colors are stacked, like layers of a mile-high cake, the deep orange fading into golds and yellows? And there, just before they disappear completely, they turn into a delicious shade of aqua right below the midnight blue."

He shook his head in awe, and she flushed as if embarrassed before saying, "Someday I'll be able to capture it fully on the page, but whenever I try, the oranges are too tangy and the aqua and blue fade together into one layer that's nothing but a dim denim."

"I don't even know what you're looking at. All I see are orange and yellow and dark blue."

She leaned into him so their cheeks were touching as she pointed at the sky. "Here, next to the clouds, it looks like neon pink, right?"

He shook his head. "It looks orange. Maybe red."

She huffed and continued to point, naming colors as she slowly moved up from where the sun had gone down toward the black. "Here, right here, for a brief moment, this is the aquamarine. Brighter than even the Caribbean Sea. An almost indescribable shade. That's you most of the time, but especially when you kiss me. You don't see it?"

He cupped her neck with one hand, turning her face to his. "What I see is how the sunset is reflected in your eyes and how your body is caught in its golden glow."

His thumb landed on her pulse point, and he was happy when he felt it skitter into a faster pace.

"That sort of makes me sad," she said. "There's so much more to everything around you. So many more shades and colors and tints."

"Maybe I need you to help me see what my eyes don't."

She let out a sharp breath as if his words had hurt, and then their lips were together. Hot and fiery like the sun that had faded. Heat zipping between them, the bright electric energy humming through his veins. He drew her even closer until she was in his lap, legs wrapped around his waist. Tongues invaded, her hand skimming under his shirt, and passion that felt bigger than anything he'd seen in the sky invaded every muscle in his body.

Her hat fell off, and his joined hers on the ground, and all he did was continue to kiss her, as if this was the last moment he'd ever get to do so, under a sky all the colors she'd described with only a handful he could see. And the truth beat through him over and over again, as it had since he'd finally given in yesterday, that he'd do anything and everything to be with her. To keep her. To have these kinds of moments for the rest of his life.

Holden stroked her jaw before tangling in her hair, twisting and pulling and adding another log to the fire burning inside them. They were in the middle of the field, tucked together on a fence rail, but he didn't once let up the onslaught against her mouth. He kissed her until he'd taken every breath and made them his. His body coursed with need. Achy. Greedy for things he couldn't have. Not tonight. But he could lose himself in her for a little while. Ease the hunger with a taste.

He didn't stop the onslaught on her mouth until a burst of laughter from the cabins not far away brought him back to his senses. He scanned the area, berating himself for leaving them both exposed for so long in the open yet again. He set her down on the ground, jumped off the rail, picked up both their hats, and stuffed them on their heads.

He led her toward the main house, looking in all directions, assessing the few people milling around, and then aimed them in the direction of their room with her tight up against his side. Once the deadbolt clicked into place, Leya tossed her hat to the ground, tugged his from his head, and then slid up against him.

Her gaze held all the fire of the sunset. Warmth spread from her and covered him, and even though he'd just scolded himself for getting lost in her, he did it all over again. Mouth finding a home on hers. Drowning them both in deep, tangling kisses that only built the flame growing inside him. They stood that way, holding each other while their mouths spoke to each other, for a long time. His hand went to her braid, tugging it gently so her head bent backward, and he had access to the enticing pulse that fluttered in her neck.

Her hands moved, palms sliding up under his T-shirt, dragging the soft cotton with them until he was forced to let her go and haul it over his head. While he did, she took off her sweater and then stepped back into his embrace. The heat of their skin burned everywhere it touched. She placed hungry, open-mouthed kisses along the smooth contours of his chest, fingers grazing the scattering of light hair journeying down toward his jeans. She followed the lines, unclasping his belt, and he almost broke. He almost gave in and lost himself to everything she was offering him.

Instead, he jerked himself back from the edge, placed his hands under her arms, and lifted her back up so he could continue to devour her lips. But this time, it was with gentler kisses, slowing them down, trying to infuse into them just how much he cherished her. Honored her. Loved her.

"Holden…" she gasped. "I need…I need you…all of you."

He groaned, hands settling on her hips before cursing himself and picking her up. Her legs went around his waist, and he carried her into the bedroom, kicked the door shut, and set her down on the bed. He put distance between them, trying to slow them down, trying to calm his hard dick. He placed his gun on the nightstand and turned back to her. She was sprawled on the bed, long braid flipped forward, hiding one breast still tucked behind a cheap cotton bra. Her chest heaved. Her eyes were so dark they were almost black.

His body reacted to it, to all of her. He needed a taste. Just a taste with their bodies skin to skin. He'd hold back. He had to. He had that much control and that much self-respect left, didn't he? He abandoned his jeans and then moved to the bed to make short work of hers. When he finally lay down next to her on the quilt, they were in nothing but their underwear.

His hands coasted over her skin, and he watched as a trail of goosebumps emerged. He was enchanted by them. Lost in them. She shivered again, fingers sliding over his chest and side before stopping atop the black and purple marks.

"Are you still hurting?" she asked.

"You'd know I was lying if I said no, but honestly," he replied, brushing his hand along her arm and collarbone, "being with you…it all fades. It's like just feeling this…" His palm settled on her chest where the beat increased into a crescendo, as if her heart was as desperate to be caressed by him as the rest of her. "Makes everything else in the world disappear, including the pain."

She cupped his face, gaze locked with his. They'd been this way so many times in the last few days. As if staring allowed them to see into each other's inner souls. As if just a glance allowed the pieces that belonged to the other to collide back together.

"You're so beautiful," she said softly.

He scoffed. "I'm just a guy, Leya. You…you're everything stunning about that damn sunset we watched. Light and dark. Beauty and grace. I feel like I've been wandering around in a too-bright light for too long, unable to see anything but a single, blinding direction set before me, and now…now I have the chance to see every shadow, every nuance, every color…as long as you're still there leading the way."

She leaned in and kissed him again, their bodies twining, rocking, blending. And even though there were mere wisps of cotton between them still, it felt like it was too much. He ached to be buried inside her. Ached in a way he couldn't describe. As if it had been a century since he'd had the chance to do so.

But when she went to tug at the waistband of his boxers, he stopped her, setting her hand back on his chest.

"What's wrong?" she asked, heavy brows drawing together in a crease he attempted to smooth with his finger.

"I know enough about you, Leya, to know you were waiting. That you wanted to be married before you did this."

She inhaled, holding her breath before she let it out slowly. "Things change. I've changed."

He shook his head, untwining the band around the bottom of her braid, spreading his fingers through it so he could curl the dark tendrils around his fingers.

"Even if you feel that way at this moment…" he said, voice deep with emotions he'd never felt but now dragged through every pore and every nerve. He'd die for her. Not because it was his job, but because he couldn't imagine a life without her in it, a world that didn't have Leya Singh spreading her light all over it. "I don't want this to be where we make love for the first time. I don't want it to be on the run, hiding from our real lives, unsure and uncertain. I want it to be after we've gone back to reality, when you've seen your parents' faces, and I've felt Camp's disapproval. If we can get past those things, and you still want this as badly as I do right now, then maybe."

"Maybe?" she gasped, voice tinged with frustration and disbelief. "Holden, I'm never going to stop wanting this."

He didn't respond. He just played with her hair.

She pulled his chin up so their gazes locked.

"You doubt me…" her voice cracked, tears filling in those beautiful eyes, and he hated himself for it.

"I don't doubt that you feel all of this right now. I even believe that when we drive back into D.C., you're going to claim me to your family and the world."

"But?"

"This moment still feels pretend. Like it can simply disappear. You know, 'What happens on the run, stays on the run,'" he said, trying to make her laugh by twisting the famous quote about Las Vegas, but it didn't work.

She pulled away from him completely, moving to the edge of the bed, sitting with her legs crossed but facing him.

"I'm not some teenage girl offering herself up to her first boyfriend. I may not have done this before, but it doesn't mean I don't know what I want or that I'm unsure of my feelings. I'm never going to regret this. Maybe your hesitation is less about me and more about you."

He sat up, a growl escaping him. "No. I don't doubt what I'm feeling, Leya. I love you." It seemed to shock them both that he'd said it aloud. But then, he plowed forward. "I love you, and because I love you, I am not going to let you disregard everything you've valued for one moment. Not when we can wait and have even more. If we're truly forever, if you want me—want us—to last, then you know, deep in your heart, that waiting is the way to prove it."

Anger flashed over her face, or frustration, or both.

"I'm not changing my mind. You're my *jeevansathi*, Holden." He frowned at the word, and she explained, "My life partner. I'm never going to stop feeling this way. There is only you. For the rest of my life. For all my next lives. Until time stops."

He stared, his heart hammering at her words. The beauty of them. The gift of them.

"If we have the rest of our lives, the rest of eternity, then that's even more reason to wait. To prove we can. To prove what we have is not lust and that it really is two souls joining forevermore."

She stared for a long moment, shock and then awe crossing over her face. Then, she fell into him, mouth finding his again.

"This…" she murmured against his lips. "This is why I love you."

They lost themselves in the kiss for a long moment, and while the heat and desire curled deep inside him—inside them both—it was as if the kiss was doing something else. Something more. Binding him to her. Building something permanent neither of them would be able to break, even if they wanted to. Fate, the gods, whatever you wanted to name the powers of the universe, came down and sealed them together. A bond that could never be severed no matter what time or man sent their way.

# Chapter Twenty-seven

## Leya

***WHAT WE DID IN THE DARK***

*Performed by Imelda May w/ Miles Kane*

The rush of love Leya felt for Holden was larger than anything she'd ever imagined. How could she have ever thought she'd mistake lust for love? Maybe other people did. Maybe if they'd only experienced a physical passion, they'd think the rush of adrenaline and soaring release were what poets and dreamers wrote about. But the desire she felt for Holden was only amplified by the feelings of love that rushed through her.

She'd never wanted the romantic fairy tale that books and movies offered, and yet she was living one. A dreamy existence that spread across the next few days, a montage of sweet moments that wove the strings binding them together tighter and tighter.

They slept in late, hiked all over the valley, and practiced shooting hidden away on the mountaintops. They talked about their pasts and their futures. Their families and their friends. She told him about pretending to be someone she wasn't to gain her mother's approval. He told her about the people he'd left behind in search of his career.

The only thing that broke through the bubble of bliss they were living in were the news reports Holden watched daily, looking for a sign that his team had arrested Astrid or Smythe or both. The longer Leya was out of sight, the more

FGT threw hate her way, trying to blame her for the bombing at a minimum and hinting at more. She shuddered every time she saw Smythe on the news, an acid-like substance growing in her stomach that Holden washed away with a touch and a kiss and promises she knew he'd do anything to fulfill. Safety. Love. Family.

But as the fourth day ticked by with no change, their sweet dream was broken with anxious thoughts. She needed to get back to the band, and he didn't want to hide forever. He was a man of purpose who needed to check things off his list and move on to the next goal. She just reveled in knowing she was at the top of his list. The one thing he wanted to keep over all the others.

After another disappointing morning news report, Leya suggested they go back to the boulders where she'd drawn his picture the first day. As they walked, he pulled her hand into his, fingers lacing together, a sense of completeness filling her. He was hers. She was his.

When they got to the rocky hilltop, she set her drawing pad on her knees, flipping until she found a blank page. There weren't many left as she'd filled them up with sketches of him. She'd drawn him a couple of times with her eyes closed and only fingers exploring, but most of the images were like the first day, with him in great detail and the things around him abstract and blurry.

Once in a while, she took out her colored pencils and added a blending of blue and green to the black and white. But even though she'd said aqua was the color she saw most around him, she still felt something was missing. As if her body knew that once they'd finally fallen together with him completely inside her, she'd discover another secret color to him. To them.

The sun was shining, but it was chilly that morning. The wind whistled through the valley, whipping her hair around her face, and she tugged the bomber jacket closer. When Holden went to sit behind her and pull her against his chest, she shook her head and handed him the pad.

He raised an eyebrow.

“I seem to remember a conversation where you insisted you were good at everything, including drawing,” she said, the dare laid out with a smile.

His lips quirked, but he didn’t laugh as he took the pad and the pencil from her hand. He put some space between them, turning so she couldn’t see the page and concentrating on the sketch. His eyes kept journeying from her to the mountains and trees and back to the paper. His brows were pinched together, his long fingers scratching and scraping away, and she was dying to see it, wondering if he could capture the love in her gaze.

“Was your mom really an artist, Holden?” she asked.

“Shh. Don’t break my concentration,” he said.

“Come on, you can talk while you draw. Seriously, what does your mom do?”

“She was a stay-at-home mom while we were growing up, but her real love is gardening. Every home we ever lived in had a yard you could swear the fairies played in. She could turn nothing but dirt and old wine barrels into a fantasyland.”

“She must have hated giving them up whenever you moved,” Leya said softly.

He hesitated, looking up over the pad at her for a moment before looking back down. “Maybe, but she also liked the challenge of starting over. Making something new. Where they’re at now, the entire neighborhood pretty much has yards she’s designed.”

“Are your grandparents in Grand Orchard her parents or your dad's?”

“Dad’s. They hated that he joined the military. It actually caused a little rift between them for a few years. But—and this is according to my mom, so don’t think I’m bragging or anything—once I came along, it healed everything.”

Leya laughed softly. “Superhero from birth.”

He grinned at her, putting the pencil down. "Ready for this masterpiece?"

"You're done already?"

"Does time really matter when you're capturing beauty?" His smile was sexy and contagious. She felt lucky to have seen so many of them over the last few days.

"Just show it to me, Captain Annoying."

He chuckled and slowly flipped the page. She stared for a moment and then burst out laughing. It looked like a preschooler had drawn it. She was a stick figure with wild lines for hair, and she was sitting on a circle that was supposed to be a rock. Behind her, the mountains were upside-down V's, and the trees were mere lines with broccoli-like tops. The sun was a circle with straight lines for rays. It was the worst drawing she'd seen in a really long time, and yet, she loved it.

"Are you laughing at my masterpiece, Lita Rae?" he said, lips smirking as he set down the pad and pencil and closed the distance between them. He pushed her back on the rock, his body half on her, his palms holding his weight, and their smiles matching.

"I think we found your weakness, Avenger-man."

His smile slipped away, and his gaze turned hooded, eyes darkening. "Yes, I think we have."

And then, he was kissing her as he had every moment since he'd started. With everything. All his passion and intensity and focus. As if she was the only thing that mattered in the entire world. As if they'd never have another moment to do so. The kiss went on forever. It felt like time stopped, the drift of the sun over the rocks and the changing shadows the only proof that it hadn't.

Eventually, they came up for air. He helped her up, jumped down, and then put his hands on her waist to lift her to the ground.

"Let's head back. I don't like the look of those rainclouds. I certainly don't want to repeat the mad dash we did the other day," he said.

They loaded her bag up and headed toward the ranch. When they got there, the parking lot held half a dozen work trucks. With the ranch closing for the season, the Hatleys had begun annual repairs. It had made Holden nervous to find more people coming and going, but they'd just avoided being seen as much as they could.

The truck Holden had bought in Knoxville hadn't moved since they'd gotten there, backed into a space not far from the restaurant entrance. They hadn't had to leave once. They'd done laundry together in the card-operated machines at the back of the barn and been fed by Eva Hatley and her staff. Sadie had invited them to the bar in town for line dancing, but Holden had declined, and she hadn't pushed.

Hiding her face had become second nature to Leya, keeping the hat on and her eyes to the ground whenever others were around. But she felt safe here, and she knew Holden did too, because his shoulders weren't as tight as they'd been when they'd first arrived.

So, when they unlocked the door to the apartment to find the place had been tossed, they both froze. Shock billowed through them at not only the physical invasion into their world but into the peace they'd found.

Holden reacted first, shoving her back onto the balcony just as a man in a black ski mask came out of the bedroom. Time stopped in a completely different way than it had on the hilltop. This was watching the worst part of a movie in slow motion. Fear hit her veins as the man raised a gun at them.

Holden twisted, shielding her while yanking his Glock from his back. She couldn't see what happened because his body was covering hers, but she heard the bang of the assailant's gun, and she felt Holden's body jerk into hers.

"Get to the truck," he barked, pushing her toward the stairs. He returned fire as she scrambled down the staircase, slipping and sliding before jumping over the last two steps. Holden was right behind her as they sprinted for the parking lot.

She yanked on the door handle, surprised to find it unlocked, and jumped onto the bench seat as the ping of metal on metal had her screaming and ducking. Holden slid in behind her, flipping the visor and letting the keys fall into his lap.

Her heart slammed against her rib cage, and her lungs almost collapsed as adrenaline and terror rushed through her. The engine jumped to life, and Holden was flooring it as another shot hit the glass behind her, shattering the back window. She screamed again, leaning forward so she was doubled over.

As the gate came into view, Holden cursed at the work trucks blocking their path with the gates half hung. Leya peeked over the seat, shocked to find a dark sedan skidding into place behind them, wheels screeching on the asphalt. Holden stomped his foot on the gas, and the motion threw her against the seat.

"Put your seat belt on," he grunted out. She reached for the passenger belt but never grabbed hold as her eyes landed on him. There was blood pouring from his shoulder, and her heart fell to her stomach, new fear snagging and dragging through her like a knife.

"You're bleeding! You were shot?!"

More gunfire exploded in their direction from the vehicle chasing them. Holden jerked the wheel and skidded off the road between two trees and into the fields. The bumps and grooves tossed her around the seat as he sped up instead of slowing down over the rough terrain.

His left hand gripped the steering wheel like a vise while he returned fire with the Glock in his right hand. She'd barely been able to hold herself steady whenever she used it, and yet, here he was, driving and shooting after a bullet had torn through him.

Her eyes filled. Fear. But also sorrow. He'd been hurt again…because of her.

They approached the fence that led down to the creek and then out to the ravine, and still, he didn't slow.

"Holden!" she cried as the truck barreled right through it. Wire and wood slammed against the hood, flying over the roof. They dragged some of the debris behind them for a few feet before it bounced free and hit the vehicle behind them.

Holden changed directions on a dime, spinning the steering wheel, and she slid into the side of the truck as gunfire, heavier and faster than his handgun had ever sounded, scattered over the back of the truck. She peeked over the seat top and saw the man from the apartment leaning out the side window of the car with a rifle of some kind.

The tailgate became a sea of bullet holes, and she squawked, ducking again.

"Get your belt on! And stay the fuck down!" he growled as he tried again to return fire.

He couldn't do both. He couldn't drive and shoot.

Before she even considered what she was doing, she'd yanked his gun away and aimed out the shattered window. She used the seatback to steady her two-handed grip. He grunted his disapproval but put both hands on the wheel and spun it again, turning them toward the main road that ran along the side of the ranch.

She was too far away from the chase car to hit anything. She hadn't gotten that good, but she could at least give him some kind of backup.

"Hold on!" He slammed through another fence, this one all wood. The noise was almost deafening. The truck shuttered and jerked as they skidded onto the road.

The sedan had lost ground, ill-equipped for the dirt fields that their four-wheel drive had taken with relative ease, but they were still back there. Still coming.

"Reload!" Holden said. "There are bullets in the glove box."

Her hands shook so much she almost dropped the clip when she ejected it, and she did drop the box of bullets. They danced around the floorboards, and she scrambled to pick some of them up, trembling as she shoved them down and reloaded the clip.

"You're doing great," he said.

"You're shot, Holden! You're bleeding. We need to get you to a hospital."

He didn't reply, just glanced in the rearview mirror. The sedan had reached the road and was closing the distance again. The truck barked and growled almost as much as Holden as he gunned it again, putting the beefy engine to the test.

Leya risked looking up over the seat again and was rewarded with another rush of gunfire coming their way. Holden cursed, and she ducked down. She'd gotten a glimpse of the driver. Long, blonde hair. Ice-blonde. The man in the passenger seat was still covered in a ski mask, but the woman wasn't.

"She's there, Holden. She's the one driving."

"I know!" he grunted.

Sirens filled the air over the sound of the gunfire. Leya looked into the side mirror. Behind the black sedan was the sheriff's truck with its lights ablaze.

They approached an intersection—a four-way stop with cars already there—and when Holden still didn't slow down, her lungs gave out, air leaving her completely as a new terror filled her. They were going to crash.

At the last moment, Holden swerved into the wrong lane, racing around the stationary cars and through the intersection. The sedan did the same thing as more shots rained toward them, and she tried valiantly to send a few back, knowing it was useless.

"Just get down," he ordered, and she looked over to see blood had dripped from his arm onto the seat. She didn't know how he was still driving. Didn't know how he hadn't lost consciousness.

A sharp curve came into view, and Holden took it without easing off the gas at all. Her heart almost stopped as the right-side wheels came up off the ground, and dread rolled through her. They were going to flip, just like they had in the intersection in Roanoke. Except, this time, neither of them was strapped in.

Just as she thought the vehicle was going to tip over, the wheels slammed down onto the pavement, screeching and squealing. She looked behind them. The sedan didn't have the same luck. The woman wasn't nearly as trained as Holden, and the sedan hit the guardrail, flipping and turning, the noise behind them deafening.

"They crashed!" she screamed.

Holden took his foot off the gas, glancing into the mirror again. The sheriff's truck had been joined by a second police vehicle that skidded to a stop at the crash site, but the truck was still barreling after them.

Holden slowed more until he could flip a U-turn and head back the way they'd come. "Wh-what are you doing?"

"Making sure they capture the bastards."

Hatley's truck screamed past them, and she caught a glimpse of his pissed-off face as he hit his brakes and whipped around to follow them.

At the corner where the car had gone over the guardrail, Holden skidded to a stop. He eyed the gun in her hand. "Get down on the floorboard. Stay here!"

He waited as she slid off the seat, ducking as best she could under the dash, with loose bullets and glass glimmering all around her. Sirens roared, stopping behind the truck.

"What the fuck, Kent!" the sheriff's voice shouted out followed by a car door slamming.

She couldn't see what was happening tucked under the dash, and she hated it with every fiber of her being.

A voice she didn't know hollered, "Passenger's here, driver's gone!"

"She couldn't have gone far!" Holden's voice drifted farther away, and Leya panicked at the idea of him leaving her. The puddle of blood on the driver's seat was proof he shouldn't be anywhere but a damn hospital. She crawled out from her spot, eyes searching the accident scene until she found him. He'd jumped the guardrail and was leaning into the flipped car with a sheriff's deputy at his side. Then, Holden rounded the vehicle, hopped over a tiny creek, and hit the grass on the other side at a dead run.

A face leaned into the truck window, and Leya screamed, shut her eyes, and pointed the gun in the person's direction.

"Fuck! It's me. Sheriff Hatley!"

She opened her eyes and saw anger and a flick of fear coast over his face.

"Put the gun down, Leya," he demanded.

She shook her head.

He eyed her for a moment.

"Stay there!"

She didn't. As soon as he walked away, she was out of the truck, and the first thing she saw was the masked man lying partially under the overturned sedan. He wasn't moving. Blood poured from him. She tried not to vomit, forcing herself to turn in the direction Holden had gone, raising her hand to shield her eyes from the sun and scanning the field until she locked on to him again.

She saw him stumble, and her stomach lurched violently. "Holden!" she screamed as he hit his knees. Just as her vision started to spin and swirl, hard metal hit the back of her head, and a quiet female voice said, "Drop the gun."

She didn't at first. A terrible agony at the thought of Holden on the ground with blood pouring from him like the man under the vehicle had her stomach heaving. She wanted to cry out in frustration and fear. She wanted to run to the field and fall on the ground beside him. To check for a pulse. To make sure the partner she'd sworn to keep for eternity didn't leave this world before they'd been allowed to truly share it.

The hammer of a gun clicked. "I'm not joking. Drop the gun, get back in the truck, and get behind the wheel."

Her hands were shaking as she tried to turn. The gun at her head slammed into her temple, the same spot that was barely healed from the car accident days ago. The world spun.

"You've got two seconds, or I blow your brains out right here."

The gun in Leya's hand clattered to the ground, the sound loud, echoing like a gate to her future shutting forever. She pulled herself into the truck and glanced at the woman who climbed in beside her. Her blonde hair was streaked with blood from a gash on her cheek, but it was the hatred blazing in her blue eyes that slammed into Leya's chest. Astrid had a gun smaller than Holden's pointed at her.

"Drive," the woman said.

Leya did as she was told, turning the key and hitting the gas. She had to scoot forward on the bench seat because Holden was taller than her, the pedals farther away, making it awkward and risking another crash. How long had it been since she'd driven herself anywhere? A long time. She'd barely learned to drive before she'd been shuttled around in a tour bus and in Secret Service vehicles.

"Wh-where are we going?" Leya asked.

"Shut up!" Astrid howled, anger and disdain dripping from each syllable.

Leya looked in the rearview mirror and saw Sheriff Hatley running back toward her across the field with his gun pointed in their direction, but she was already too far away. Her heart screamed for him to go back to Holden. To make sure he was okay. To make sure he lived. That was all that mattered. She didn't want Holden to die for her…for this…for hatred and cruelty.

"Turn left at the stop sign."

Leya did as she was told, risking another glance in Astrid's direction. Leya had thought she was beautiful when she'd seen her at EchoBar. Had thought so every time she'd seen her when Leya had worked with D.C. Avenue Writers. Astrid had the classic, endless kind of beauty the world seemed to adore. White. Blonde. Petite. The kind who could rally men with a single tear. The kind who could cry and move a nation.

All Leya could see today was evil.

Leya's heart hammered, and tears threatened to fall as Astrid's dark energy pulsed through the truck. She glanced over, and Astrid's red-hot aura shot like flames from a burning building touching the sky, her eyes dilated so only a hint of blue showed.

They approached the tiny, picturesque town of Willow Creek, and Astrid finally spoke, "Pull into the deli lot."

Leya did what she was told, parking in the first spot she found. Instead of opening the passenger door, Astrid slid over toward her, stuffing the barrel of the weapon into Leya's side. "We're going to do this nice and slow. You try to run, you try to get anyone's attention, and I'm going to shoot your brownie brains out. Nod if you understand."

Leya did. Her body was shaking so hard as her feet hit the ground that she almost crumbled. Thoughts of Holden collapsing in the field spotted her vision even more than the pain of the gun hitting her ribs. Astrid flung an arm around her shoulder, and Leya barely caught herself from jumping back as nausea traveled through her.

From a distance, it looked like they were good friends…lovers, even. But no one was looking anyway. The few people in the lot were on their phones, busy with their lives.

"Walk slowly to the silver Passport in the corner," Astrid said.

Leya did what she was told. If Holden was hurt…or worse…who was going to come for her? The Secret Service didn't even know where they were. Sheriff Hatley had seen her disappear. Would he come? Would he contact the Secret Service? Her heart thudded, fear and anger spiking through her. But also determination. She needed to figure this out on her own. A way to escape…or at least a way to leave a trail.

Leya took in their surroundings. A bank across the street. They'd have cameras, right? For the first time in days, she lifted her face and hoped someone around them might recognize her. A woman coming out of the sandwich shop did a double-take but then kept moving toward the sidewalk out front.

At the SUV, while Astrid was distracted pulling the fob from her pocket, Leya slowly and carefully slid off one of her leather-and-silver bands and let it fall to the ground. She toed it under the vehicle with a barely perceptible motion.

"Get in the passenger side and climb over the console to the driver's seat," Astrid commanded, her voice scarily calm for someone who'd just been in a gun chase, survived a car flip, and was now kidnapping the vice president's daughter. What kind of human being did you need to be to have no emotions through all of it?

Leya adjusted the driver's seat, pushing it back and willing her shaky hands to do their job. She got the seat belt on and the car started all while her heart beat so fast she thought it might burst. She maneuvered the vehicle out of the spot and toward the parking lot exit as her body trembled and quaked.

"Turn right," Astrid instructed.

Leya drove onto the street and had to stop almost immediately at a stop sign. The woman who'd done the double-take at the deli was waiting to cross and her gaze landed on Leya again. She turned her head fully toward the driver's side window, hiding her face from Astrid, and mouthed, "Help."

The woman's eyes widened.

They'd barely pulled away from the stop sign when a police car sped toward them from the other direction, lights and sirens blaring. It didn't slow until it hit the parking lot where they'd left the root-beer-colored truck Lita Rae and Miles had bought. Lita Rae was gone now, and who knew what had happened to Miles. A sob escaped her before she could help it, and Astrid let out a disgusted sigh.

"Don't fall apart on me now. We've got a long drive ahead of us. I want you alive. I have a point to prove showing up with you, but I won't hesitate to dump your dead body in some lake on the way if I have to."

Leya gripped the wheel, hoping somehow, someway, she'd find a way out of this. Hoping Holden was alive and that when they found each other, they'd be able to return to the fairy-tale world they'd lived in for a handful of days.

# Chapter Twenty-eight

## *Holden*

***DEAR AGONY***

*Performed by Breaking Benjamin*

As Holden sprinted across the creek and into the field, eyes scanning for any sign of Astrid, his vision started to blur. It was his first realization that the gunshot wound was more serious than he'd thought. He glanced down to see his right arm covered in blood. With the adrenaline pumping through him, he couldn't even feel it.

Jesus.

He needed to find Astrid before he passed out.

He'd fucked up again. Let his goddamn guard down.

His feet stumbled as dark spots spread across the landscape.

Damnit. He could not lose consciousness.

He ordered his body to turn around, to go back to Leya, but instead, he hit his knees.

In the distance, through a layer of what felt like cotton gauze wrapped around his ears, he heard her scream his name, heard the fear and panic in her voice, and his heart lurched.

And then, there was nothing.

♫ ♫ ♫

A needle stabbing him jerked him awake. He was on a gurney, and the sheriff was leaning over him. He reached for the hand with the needle and yanked it away.

"Get off," he growled, fighting waves of nausea and pain that spiraled through him as he sat up.

There were two EMTs hovering around him along with Hatley. They were on the side of the road, behind an ambulance. The sharp corner where the sedan had crashed was visible from his gurney, with a blanket covering the body of the shooter. The realization of what was missing from the scene had another wave of nausea hitting him—the truck was gone.

"Where the fuck is Leya?" he asked, swinging his feet over the edge.

"You need to lie down, sir," one of the EMTs said with an edge to his tone.

Holden ignored him, standing and wobbling. Jesus. He needed to get a handle on this. His eyes met the sheriff's, and his heart stopped, lungs tightening until he couldn't breathe. He forced air into them and repeated, "Where's Leya?"

Hatley swiped his hat off his head, brushed his hand over his hair, and then replaced it. "The driver of the sedan took her."

His stomach bottomed out. The black spots returned, and he fought his way through them by biting his tongue and gritting his teeth. He took two steps toward the sheriff's truck.

"Where the hell are you going, Kent?" Hatley matched his strides in two steps.

"After her."

"You've been shot. You passed out. You need a hospital."

"I need Leya!" he barked.

"I get it. I do. A year ago, someone kidnapped my daughter, and those were the worst fucking moments of my life. But you aren't going to do Leya any good if you pass out again."

Holden looked down at his arm. The EMTs had cut off the sleeve of his shirt, and blood was caked on it. They'd applied a compress to the front and the back of his right shoulder—a through and through—but who knew what kind of internal damage had been done to muscles and bone as it had torn through him. He squeezed his right hand, and all he felt was pins and needles behind the wave of pain. No matter how messed up it was, it didn't matter. He'd gladly cut the damn arm off if it meant finding Leya.

"Just tell me what happened," Holden growled.

Hatley stared at him, brows drawn close together.

"I was coming after you when she screamed your name. When I turned back around, I saw a blonde-haired woman get in the truck with her. They tore off down the road. I put an APB out on her and the truck immediately."

The sheriff's radio squawked, and he turned it up and spoke into it, "Repeat that please."

"They spotted the truck at Daisy Mae's Deli. No sign of either woman," a voice on the other side said.

Holden's chest ached worse than the bullet hole. "I need to get to that scene, and I need to call it in."

Hatley stared at him for a moment before heading toward the driver's side of his F-150. Holden climbed into the passenger seat as the EMTs scrambled and called after them.

"You pass out on her or me, and it's just going to be worse," the sheriff growled as he turned the key in the ignition.

Holden ignored the last statement, nodding toward the cell phone in the cupholder. "Mind if I use your phone?"

Hatley handed it to him and then turned the lights on, racing in the direction of Willow Creek. He put his foot on the accelerator in a way Holden appreciated as he dialed the number he'd memorized. Guilt, anger, and frustration burned through him, but it was a sickening sense of fear that held him in its grips the most. This was his fault. He'd lost focus. He should have realized way before they'd mounted the steps that there was someone in their room. He should have planted cameras. Should have planted temporary alarms. Fucking tin cans that rattled. Anything.

Instead, he'd spent the morning on a stupid stick figure and lost himself in her mouth and her body, and now… Goddamnit, now Leya was out there with a hate-filled extremist. A domestic terrorist who saw her as nothing but a tool to send a message to the world.

Camp's voice was hesitant when he picked up. "Assistant Special Agent in Charge Camp."

"It's Kent." He gulped. "Firefly has been taken. APB has been issued."

Silence. And then Camp barked out, "What the fuck happened?"

"Barrows showed up with a gunman, and we fled the safe house. Barrows's car flipped, and I went to pull her from the car, but she must have doubled-back on me. Took Firefly and the truck where I'd stashed her. The local sheriff was right behind us and put out an APB. The truck was found abandoned in Willow Creek, Tennessee. I'm heading there now."

"How long?"

Holden looked at the sheriff. How long had he been out? Hatley growled out, "Fifteen minutes, tops."

Fuck. Fifteen minutes was a lifetime. Bile burned in his throat. He couldn't lose her. Not now. Not after everything they'd been through. Everything they'd become to each other.

"Fifteen minutes."

Camp swore. "Where's the gunman?"

"Dead. Locals are bagging him. Sheriff Hatley is the man in charge. I'll get him to send us an ID once they have it."

Doors slammed on Camp's end, and then he hollered, not to Holden but to the entire D.C. field office, "I need a counter-assault team in Willow Creek, Tennessee ASAP. Firefly has been taken. Fifteen minutes since last seen. Move! Now people! I need visuals of every camera in that goddamn town, and I need every agency in the area doing nothing but this."

Holden could envision the scrambling that was happening in the office. The quiet, controlled chaos. None of it came close to what he needed them to feel. He needed them as desperate as he was.

"I'm en route now," Camp said to Holden. "Establish a command center at the sheriff's department, and I'll join you."

"Do you have anything new on Barrows?" Holden asked.

"Got a hit on a credit card issued to Penny Waylin at a hotel in Knoxville. When we got there, staff identified Barrows as the woman who checked in."

"They're working together!" Holden bit out.

"Uncertain. Penny Waylin was pretty upset when we pulled her back in, denied ever having that particular credit card or having anything to do with Barrows. She'd have to be a damn good actress if she's lying."

"Like father like daughter," Holden growled.

"We're holding her until we're sure. Call me when you get to the truck."

Camp hung up, and Holden's fist squeezed the phone until he thought it might shatter. He'd had the vague notion there might have been a slim chance for him to maintain an investigative position in the agency before this, but the truth was, his career was over, and he didn't even give a shit. All he cared about was Leya. Finding her unharmed. Getting her back. He'd hand her over to her family and the USSS and take whatever consequences came his way.

"They're scrambling a team?" Hatley asked.

Holden nodded.

Even with the sheriff's lights blazing, it seemed to take an eternity to get to where the truck had been abandoned, but it was really less than ten minutes before Hatley tore into the parking lot. He'd barely braked before Holden jumped out and headed toward an officer near the truck he and Leya had bought. His shoulder rippled with pain, and all he could do was hope he'd stay on his feet.

The deputy was talking to a small cluster of people by a string of yellow crime-scene tape that was holding them back. Sheriff Hatley caught up to him just as Holden demanded, "What do you got?"

The officer looked at him with narrowed eyes and then over to Hatley. "Sheriff," the man said, sending a raised brow in Holden's direction.

"This is Special Agent Holden Kent, U.S. Secret Service," Hatley explained. "Let's step over here, and you can give us an update."

They moved toward the back of the C10, and the officer pointed to a woman in her mid-forties dressed in workout apparel. "Nancy James came out of the deli at 1:04 p.m. Saw someone she thought might be Leya Singh with a blonde woman walking away from the vehicle. They were tucked together. The blonde had her arm around her shoulders, so Nancy thought they were a couple and that she was mistaken about Miss Singh. Nancy headed back toward her apartment off Main. She'd only gotten to the crosswalk when a silver Honda Passport braked at the stop sign. The woman she identified as Miss Singh looked out the window, and Nancy swears she mouthed, 'Help.'"

Holden's stomach turned, but a surge of pride welled through him as well. She hadn't shut down. She hadn't curled up into a ball and given up. She was fighting back the only way she could, with her face and her notoriety.

"She get a plate?" he demanded.

The officer shook his head.

"I need every available video in the area. Any photos anyone happened to take, even from inside the deli. If they thought they were taking a picture of their sandwich, they still might have gotten something out one of the windows." Holden's gaze settled on the bank across the street. "Looks like they have a clear shot of the lot, right?"

He ran across the street, horns honked, and he dodged one car and then another before hitting the sidewalk and bursting through the bank's doors. A security guard took one look at him, shirt torn, bloody bandage hanging from his shoulder, and stepped forward with a hand hovering over his weapon. It was only the sheriff coming in behind him that stopped the man from drawing it.

It took barely two minutes for Holden and the sheriff to be inside the bank's security office, pulling up the video feeds. His heart lurched as he saw his truck pull into the lot with Leya at the wheel. She looked scared…worried…her brows were drawn together. She parked and slid out from the driver's side with Barrows right behind her. The angle of the camera didn't show a gun, but the way the blonde threw her arm over Leya's shoulder, and Leya's corresponding grimace, told Holden it was shoved into her rib cage. Rage filled him along with a sudden desire to end a life when he'd never, ever felt that way before. He wanted to send Astrid Barrows somewhere she'd never be able to touch Leya again.

The two women crossed the lot and got in the passenger side of a silver Passport just like Nancy had said. When the vehicle came up to the lot's entrance, it was Leya behind the driver's seat, hand gripped tight on the steering wheel. The SUV's bumper was in full display of the camera, but there was no front plate. He watched as it pulled out and headed south.

Holden picked up Hatley's phone he hadn't given back and called Camp as he sprinted out of the bank, looking both ways down the street for another video camera that might have picked up the rear plate.

"Camp."

"Silver Honda Passport. 2021 or newer. Headed south on Main out of Willow Creek. No front plate. Still working on the back plate. Been on the road for at least twenty minutes. I need a helicopter in the air." He hung up without waiting for a response, only partially listening as Hatley barked things into his radio.

His stomach twisted and turned, wondering what Leya had been thinking. Did she think he was dead? Did she think no one was coming for her?

Holden's gaze landed on the spot where the SUV had been parked. Something glimmered on the ground, and he jogged over, swiping it up. One of Leya's leather and silver beaded bracelets. It hit him in the chest like a punch.

Had it fallen off? Had she left it on purpose? A trail she hoped he could follow?

He slid it over his wrist and stalked over to the sheriff standing by his F-150. "You got a map?"

Hatley dug in the back and pulled out a topographical map of the state.

"They're likely driving the speed limit or close to it so they don't risk being pulled over." Holden did the math in his head, making a circle with his finger on the map. They'd been headed south, but that could have changed as soon as they hit any of the main roads. The only thing north was a mountain range, and Astrid Barrows didn't strike him as a camper. He dialed Camp back. "Nothing north but mountains. They have to be headed south." His fingers landed on the border of Tennessee and Alabama where a town name jumped out at him. "Doesn't Smythe have a compound in Scottsboro?"

"She wouldn't be stupid enough to go there," Camp said. "But I'll send a team out of Birmingham to check it out."

He hung up with Camp, and the sheriff said, "I have a search-and-rescue copter setting down at the hospital in five minutes."

Holden didn't respond, just turned and climbed into Hately's truck. The sheriff's foot was heavy on the accelerator again as they sped down the road. The tires squealed as they pulled into the parking lot of a small building that looked more like an office building than a hospital. Hatley drove to the back of the lot where space had been marked off for emergency landings.

As soon as the vehicle stopped, Holden slid out again, ignoring the throbbing in his shoulder and the black that spotted his vision. His anger was worse than the pain. Anger at himself. At FGT. At Astrid Barrows.

The flurry of an incoming helicopter filled the air, and Hatley leaned in to say, "I'm going to stay here, continue canvassing other cameras and witnesses."

Another squad car pulled into the lot, and an officer emerged, jogging over to join them. The two men exchanged something that the sheriff then handed over to Holden. "I'd like my phone back. Wilks here got you a burner."

Holden swapped phones with him and watched as the sheriff pulled a gun from his back waistband. It was his Glock that he'd left with Leya. His throat bobbed as he took it. An agent who lost his gun… Jesus, he was such a wreck. A screwup. But he'd known as soon as he'd gotten in the truck at Number One Observatory Circle that he was screwed. Known it and done it anyway.

"I'll keep you posted on anything new we find here, and as soon as we have an ID on the dead man, you'll know."

"My boss is on his way with a CAT team. He wanted a command center set up."

The helo landed, and the womp-womp-womp of the blades made conversation nearly impossible.

Hatley hollered over it, "I'm on it. Good luck!"

Holden ignored him. He needed more than luck. He needed those damn gods Leya believed had bound them together to help him find her safe and unharmed. It was the only option.

# Chapter Twenty-nine

## *Leya*

***TORNADO***

*Performed by Lea Michele*

*Leya's heartbeat had slowed to a* more normal pace, but every time she looked over at Astrid and the gun gripped in her hand, it picked up again. Worry for Holden churned into a furious knot inside her. If he was okay, he'd be looking for her. He'd be coming after her…but what if he wasn't? What if the bullet had—she couldn't even think it. Her throat closed, making it hard to breathe, and a choking sound erupted from her again.

Astrid blew out a frustrated breath. "You cry, and I might shoot you just because."

For a moment, Leya debated crashing the SUV and taking her chances on foot, but the road Astrid had directed her onto was windy, going through mountains and farmland with houses dropped sparingly in between. Would she be able to make it to one before Astrid caught up to her? What if she got hurt trying to crash the car? With so few choices, she didn't know what else to do but keep driving. She wished she could open her window and drop more bracelets like a gingerbread trail for those that were coming after her to follow.

"Why are you doing this?" Leya asked, even though she already had a pretty good idea. Hate. Racism.

Astrid scoffed. "Somebody had to stop you from spreading your disgusting seed all over the place."

Leya swallowed back the waves of nausea that hit her. She breathed out, "I'm not interested in Lincoln. We're just friends."

Astrid glared. "He's been poisoned by you already. It's too late for me to save him now. It required me to change my plans, but I'll achieve them anyway—without him."

"Did John Smythe put you up to this?" Leya asked.

Astrid straightened the red blazer she had on over a blue, silk tank top. She fished a mop of napkins from the glove box and cleaned the blood from the cut on her face. If you ignored the gun, she looked like the normal writer Leya had first met.

"If you turn yourself in and testify against him, I'm sure they'll give you an easier sentence," Leya continued, not knowing if any of it was true, but just hoping to somehow talk her way out of this. To forge a connection. Isn't that what negotiators did?

"Stop talking," Astrid said. "You can't poison me. I'm immune to your brownie *charm*."

"What will your family think of you being arrested and put in prison for kidnapping the daughter of the vice president?" She stressed her role in a vague hope that the seriousness of what she'd done would make Astrid think twice about keeping her. She could even just let Leya out here and go on her way. Leya didn't care, as long as she got out of the car with her life in her hands so she could find Holden.

"Who cares what Mama thinks? She doesn't have a hint of ambition. Spent her life waiting tables and cleaning houses because all the immigrants stole the work she was more qualified to do, and she didn't even care. Just kept her shitty minimum-wage jobs that barely put food on our table."

"And your dad?"

Astrid's face turned into a solid block, icing over with a chilliness that honestly scared Leya almost as much as the gun.

"Stop talking."

They drove in silence for a long time. The miles between them and Holden grew at a disturbing rate that made her chest hurt.

As a sign for a gas station came into view, Leya said, "I have to use the restroom."

Astrid rolled her eyes. "Hold it."

"Unless you want me to pee all over your nice little SUV, you're going to need to let me use the bathroom."

"Fine, but if you pull any stunts, I'll not only shoot you but anyone else who's there, and I'll make sure everyone thinks you did it."

As Leya turned into the gas station, Astrid added on, "Pull up to a pump. We'll fill up while we're here." When they'd parked, Astrid slid out first and had Leya climb over the console again. She kept the gun tucked close to her body, but she waved the barrel in the direction of the pumps. "You fill up."

"I don't have any cash."

Astrid pulled a credit card from her pocket and tossed it at Leya. She grabbed it and then eyed the machine. How lame was it that she didn't know how to do this? She'd never had to fill her car. Ever.

"Oh my God, you don't know how to do it," Astrid said with a bitter laugh. "The princess hasn't ever had to deal with mundane things like filling her gas tank."

Leya stuffed the card into the reader and followed the directions that appeared on the screen. She hit the gas button and lifted the handle, fighting with it and the gas tank's door before eventually getting the nozzle in, all while Astrid snickered.

When they were done, they headed for the store. Inside, they followed the signs to the restrooms. Once

Astrid realized the women's room was empty, she locked the door behind them. For a second, Leya thought she was batty enough to follow her into a stall and sighed with relief when she let her go in by herself.

While Leya peed, she slid a bracelet off her wrist, wishing she had paper and a pen, wishing she had anything. She placed it on the purse hook on the back of the door. Someone might take it, thinking it was a lost item, but she'd have to risk it.

She flushed and left the stall, washing her hands while Astrid watched, gun tucked into her blazer pocket.

They headed back into the store, and Astrid stopped by a shelf with camping gear. She picked up a box and then stopped by the drink case, grabbing two waters.

"When we get to the counter, use the credit card to pay."

Leya was happy to do so. She met the clerk's gaze with a wavery smile, hoping beyond hope that the man with his country musician T-shirt would recognize her.

His motions did slow down as his eyes landed on hers, but then he just went about the business of ringing them up, asking, "Want a bag?"

"No, thanks," Leya said as Astrid picked up the items and pushed Leya toward the door.

Once they were back in the car, Astrid pointed to the box they'd bought. Leya looked down and realized it was plastic zip ties.

"Take one out," Astrid said, "And tie your left hand to the steering wheel."

"I've done everything you asked. There's no reason to tie me up."

"Do it, or I can shoot you, roll you out of the car, and keep going."

"Where are we going?"

"Stop talking!" Astrid waved the gun at her, and Leya swallowed hard. She opened the box of zip ties and took one out.

"I can't do this one-handed," Leya said.

"Use your teeth."

Leya struggled to get the zip tie around the steering wheel and her wrist, using her mouth to tighten it the best she could. When she was done, Astrid leaned over and tightened it a little more so it bit into Leya's wrist every time she moved it.

"Let's go," Astrid said.

Leya pulled out onto the road, hoping the clerk recognized her. Hoping someone was coming for her. Anyone. But more than anything, she wanted it to be Holden because then he'd be okay. She didn't know what she would do if he lost his life for her too. Like Landry might have if FGT had thought it was Leya standing on the shore of Swan River Pond that night. Tears returned, and her stomach flipped.

"Did you kill my friend because you thought she was me?" Leya asked, voice shaky and unsure.

Astrid frowned. "What?"

"Landry Kim. Did you kill her?"

Astrid snorted. "No. Although, whoever did get rid of her did the world a favor. One less curry muncher in the world."

Leya's stomach rolled with anger and disgust before she asked, "Are you working with Angel Carter? Is that how you found us?"

"You talk a lot for someone who was told not to. If I didn't want you to drive, I'd just smash you over the head and throw you in the back."

"Maybe your dead friend in the ski mask would have done it for you," Leya said dryly.

"He wasn't my friend. Just one of the many minions who couldn't perform as he'd promised. That's the problem with so many men, right? Performance issues. Take your Secret Service friend. He wasn't up to his job either."

Leya's heart clenched. She'd know if he was dead, wouldn't she? She'd feel it deep in her soul if her life partner had left this world. They were bound now, and she should be able to feel the severed strings. She swallowed the nasty reply hanging on her tongue, focusing again on trying to build a relationship with the disgusting excuse of a person next to her. "You're right. Most men couldn't handle half the stuff women put up with. If you want something done, you gotta do it yourself, right? Is that how you found us? Holden didn't do his job?"

Astrid's gaze fell to the bracelets on Leya's wrists. "You got my gift, I see."

Leya's eyes landed on the dragonfly bracelet she'd gotten from Adria the day before they'd left D.C. In the chaos of everything going on, she'd never been able to thank her for it. If Leya had, she would have known the truth. It wasn't a leak at the Secret Service that had given them away…Leya had. This was on her. She'd led Astrid straight to them.

"It went dead for a few days, and I thought you'd found it, but then, my luck returned, and it started transmitting again. Almost as if it wanted me to find you." Astrid's eyes got far away. "It's fate."

"How did you even get it into the residence?"

Astrid looked pleased. "Wouldn't you like to know."

Leya's stomach turned. Maybe there was someone in the Secret Service after all. Otherwise, the device surely would have been noticed when it had been brought through the X-ray machines.

"Was it just me you bugged?"

"John wanted me to spy on you. Get some dirt he could use to blackmail your father with, but you've been sneaky with your sins, pretending to be so damn innocent. When I saw you at EchoBar with Lincoln, grinding up against him, I knew we couldn't wait anymore. The time to stop you is now." Astrid's voice turned cold and hard. "John's been waiting for a sign, and I'm going to deliver him one."

"I don't think he'll see it as a sign, Astrid. I think he's going to be angry with you for bringing me to his door. He wants to be the next president. Do you think he can do that with a kidnapping and murder rap hanging over him?"

"Shut up!" Astrid screamed. "Shut up, shut up, shut up!"

The gun waved violently in her direction, and Leya did as she was told.

They drove in silence, but Leya could feel Astrid fuming next to her. Could feel her ire building. Another round of terror melted its way through every vein in Leya's body, making her hand shake so much she had to tighten her grip on the steering wheel to make sure she didn't start weaving.

Eventually, Astrid put the gun on the seat between her legs as she drank from one of the bottles of water. Leya thought again about purposefully crashing the car, but even if Astrid lost the gun, she'd find it before Leya could free herself from the steering wheel. There was nothing to cut the zip tie off with, not even a car lighter, like in the old days, to try and burn it off. No key to try and saw it off. Astrid had a fob that started the vehicle with the push of a button. She had no way of escaping.

Astrid took a phone out of the pocket of her blazer and typed a message. She waited for a response and scowled when it came.

"He's already unhappy," Leya said softly.

Astrid glared at her. "He used to want to burn every last piece of the government down and start over. He wanted me to help him. He promised me…he promised me I'd be sitting at his side…"

Leya's stomach clenched as realization struck. "You love him."

Astrid shot her a glare. Anger that became longing filtered over her face before the rage settled back in. "Don't make it sound like that. He isn't sleeping with me. I'm the daughter he always wanted. His daughter by blood didn't want anything to do with him. She sent him away, but me…I loved him from the moment I met him. I did everything he asked. Believed in him! Right up until he told us he was running for president. How can he burn everything down if he's sitting atop it? We had plans to bring this country to its knees. All he had to do was say the word. A single word and every cell spread out around the country would activate. The United States would shudder to a halt."

Leya cringed inwardly at the rant as Astrid's tone got wilder and wilder. She was beyond reason. Beyond being swayed by logic. She was living in some alternate universe where only an apocalypse could result in a better future with John Smythe leading the charge.

# Chapter Thirty

## *Holden*

***KNOCKOUT***

*Performed by Bon Jovi*

The rescue Blackhawk was staffed with four people. One of the men in the back was a medic, and he insisted on looking at Holden's wound again. Through the headset covering his ears, he heard the man say the bullet was a through-and-through to his outer deltoid muscle. Without surgery, he'd likely have permanent damage to the arm. Even with surgery, there was no guarantee he'd recover fully.

"This isn't a damn movie, man," the medic groused. "You aren't going to get the bad guy and wink at your boss at the end of the story with this injury."

Holden didn't have a choice. He needed to be exactly what Leya had teased him about being. A robot. Captain Avenger…a superhero.

"Just keep me in the game," Holden barked at him.

The man looked like he was former military. He was muscled and contoured with a nasty scar down the right side of his neck, and he seemed to not only read Holden's determination but understand it. He gave a curt nod before repacking and wrapping the entire shoulder from clavicle down almost to his elbow. Then, the man pulled a T-shirt from somewhere in the back, handing it to Holden. The shirt had the words Winter County FD scrawled across the back. Pain spiked through him as he tugged his torn and bloody one off and slid the new tee on.

Then, he turned his eyes to the ground outside, scanning the roads for a silver SUV.

They should have caught up to it by now. Leya and Barrows had only been, at most, forty-five minutes ahead of them, but the sea of freeways and highways below them leading into Knoxville made it almost impossible to identify them from the sky, even when the helo dropped low over the causeways.

Deep in his gut, Holden knew where Barrows was heading. She was going to Smythe. She had to be. Either at his command or like a cat bringing a mouse back to its owner, hoping for praise. For a pat on the head and a "good job."

He opened the map app on the phone Hatley had handed him, eyeing the different routes to Scottsboro. Holden tapped the screen over a smaller freeway leading south and showed it to the medic. "She'll go here."

"You sure?" the man asked.

He couldn't be one hundred percent certain, but he was doing what he'd been taught and following his instincts. "This is where they went."

The man relayed the message to the pilot, and the helo banked to the right, flying away from the city and out to the smaller highway winding straight through the trees down toward Chattanooga. The road wasn't completely desolate, or the SUV would have stood out, but it also kept the number of people seeing it down. It was a smart choice, and for some reason, he couldn't get out of his head that everyone, including the USSS and John Smythe, had underestimated the twenty-four-year-old blonde.

Holden had two options. He could continue to scan the highway, hoping to catch sight of them, like trying to identify an ant from a rooftop, or he could go with his gut and fly ahead of them to set down in Scottsboro. Nausea crawled through him, and his chest tightened, the decision crawling through him and tearing at his soul. Could he risk Leya on instinct? But maybe those ties binding him were what was tugging him there. Both his years of experience and the essence of her. The lives they'd lived together before now that she insisted made them life partners…*jeevansathi.*

"Get me to Scottsboro," he spoke into the headset. He brought up the address of Smythe's location on the map. "As close to this address as you can."

♫ ♫ ♫

"You need help?" the medic asked Holden as they jumped out of the helo at a tiny airport on the north side of Scottsboro.

Holden met the man's stare. "I don't think that's a good idea."

"You're on your own. You got backup coming?"

"From Birmingham, but I'm not waiting for them to show."

The man considered him for a long moment, wavering, and then he locked all his emotions away. "I did two tours in Afghanistan. I understand not waiting. I don't have a weapon, but I can be another body with eyes, ears, and hands.

"You going to get in trouble with your team?" Holden looked back toward the other three men on the helo.

The man shrugged. "We all served. We all understand the importance of rescuing the vice president's daughter."

Holden's chest tightened at the reminder of what Leya was to the world. A symbol. A symbol FGT wanted to snuff out. He needed all the help he could get. "I appreciate the extra hand," he said before sticking out his left hand. "Holden Kent."

"Raul Garcia," the medic said, shaking it.

While Raul updated his team, Holden headed for the airport's main hangar. He flashed his badge around and commandeered a mechanic's truck, and within minutes, they were on the road to Smythe's place.

He called Camp.

"I'm heading to the Smythe compound with a former military man from the search-and-rescue team. How soon is the team from Birmingham going to get there?"

Camp swore. "You'll blow every single investigation we have if you show up and ram through the gate."

"Get me a warrant."

"Get me proof Leya Singh is on site, and we won't need a warrant."

Holden wanted inside and in position before Barrows showed up. He didn't want to wait for proof.

"Get me backup," Holden groused and hung up. It didn't really matter if he pissed Camp off. Not only was his career over, but no one was going to hire him after this, private security or otherwise, permanently injured or not. He glanced over at Raul, and said, "You want out at any time, you just say the word. Otherwise, I'll take any legal consequences and say I ordered you to assist."

"Appreciate that, but I know what I'm doing."

"How much action did you see?" Holden asked him.

"Enough. You serve?"

Holden shook his head. "No, but my dad was Army, then Secret Service, and now works for the National Guard."

"Good men, the National Guard. They don't get the credit they deserve. Like the Coast Guard. Everyone just assumes they're some knockoff of their Navy and Army buddies, but some of the toughest men and women I know serve in both."

Holden grunted his agreement, and they ate up the rest of the miles to Smythe's in silence. Holden did a drive-by along the front to get an idea of what was waiting for them. The gate had a guard on duty with plenty of cameras along the top of a wide stone wall extending for at least a football field's length on either side. He redialed Camp as he pulled onto a road marked private property running south of the compound, parking the maintenance truck in the dirt.

"We got plans on Smythe's property?" he asked without greeting.

"Should already be in your inbox. I'm twenty minutes out from Willow Creek. You hear from your sheriff buddy yet on the I.D. of the shooter?"

"No. But he was busy searching for cameras that might have gotten a shot of the back license plate of the SUV."

"You're sure this is where they're headed?" Camp asked, the doubt clear in his voice. "I don't see what he gains from having this go public after he just announced his bid for the presidency."

Holden's stomach swam again. "Maybe he'll be as surprised as we are that Barrows shows up. Maybe she's gone rogue trying to prove something to him."

"Sounds familiar." Camp's voice was dry, the message clear.

"I'll get her back," he said, trying to reassure himself as much as his boss. "I'll get her back, and she's going to be fine."

He hung up, logged into his USSS account, and pulled up the plans on Smythe's entire estate. They had architectural drawings for the house and outbuildings as well as landscape plans and details on the security measures in place. Holden wasn't sure who'd hacked into what system to get the security plans, but they had a list of cameras and placement. Could all have been bullshit. Could have been changed twenty times by now, but it was a start.

He and his new pal, Raul, looked them over.

Raul pointed to the screen and said, "I can climb the wall here, take this one out, and they'll send someone over to look at it. You take out this one and this one a few seconds later, and they'll think the entire line is failing. You might get over the wall here before they sound an alarm.

Give me this number." He tapped the phone. "I'll tell you when the SUV shows up out front."

They exchanged numbers, climbed out of the maintenance truck, and headed toward the wall in separate directions. Holden examined the wall for footholds. It was at least ten feet up to the top. If he was a hundred percent, it would have been a piece of cake, but with a bullet hole in his shoulder, he had to roll a fallen log over to help him up. He waited for Raul's call and then jumped up, hooking the top of the stone wall with his left hand.

He dragged himself onto the top, biting his tongue so he wouldn't scream as pain spiked and a gush of liquid came from his wound again. He forced his feet to move to the camera before it swiveled around, cut it, and then sat, catching his breath and forcing the world to stop spinning. Seconds slid by, and he knew he needed to get his ass moving again before the next camera looped around. He barely made it, cutting it just as it was about even with him, and then he used his good arm to swing off the wall, dropping the last four feet. Pain jolted through him, but it pushed at the spots in front of his eyes, keeping him from passing out. He took cover behind a large oak tree while he watched the drive to his north as it curved through a bank of trees and hedges before winding down to Smythe's colonial mansion.

There was adequate tree coverage, and Holden used it to his advantage, keeping low and moving from trunk to trunk until he was closer to where the drive ended in a circle around a bronze statue of Poseidon at the front of the house. It was an almost two-hour drive from Willow Creek to Scottsboro. With the time he'd wasted chasing the truck down at the deli, his time in the helo, and then getting to the estate, he figured Leya and Astrid should be showing up in the next few minutes. If he was right…

He couldn't let himself think otherwise.

Holden eased to the ground, leaning his head back against a tree trunk, weapon in hand. Adrenaline, anger, and fear had been driving him—were still driving him—but coming to a dead stop allowed his body to think it was time to rest…heal…recover. His eyes fluttered, but he forced them back open. He pulled up the sleeve of his T-shirt to see blood had seeped through the fresh bandage. Using his right hand was nearly impossible now. He couldn't grip anything with it, and he'd lost enough blood to be dangerous.

He had one shot at this. One shot to rescue Leya before he probably collapsed for good. He couldn't fuck it up like he had everything else with her. Like everyone helping the Daisies had fucked up along the way.

Leya had said she couldn't trust any of them, and he'd insisted—promised—she could trust him, and yet he'd still allowed her to get kidnapped. He'd gone after Barrows instead of staying with his protectee. You never leave your protectee! Guilt and frustration had him banging his head against the bark.

He'd always considered himself a decent enough human being and a damn good agent, but after all the ways he'd screwed up and broken the trust of his team, his boss, and Leya's family, he wasn't sure decent was going to cut it anymore. Not when Leya deserved so much more. He'd be jobless. He eyed his arm…a broken man. What could he offer her?

Love. That was it. Was it enough? She sounded so sure about them. Life partners…

He swallowed hard. The ache inside him to be twined with her in every possible way was more painful than the arm that had gone numb. He wanted to see the colors of the world through her eyes.

His phone vibrated, an incoming text from Raul's number.

*RAUL: They just pulled up to the gate.*

Relief flew through him. He'd been right. He hadn't screwed up one more time.

Holden used the tree to drag himself up off the ground, gripped his gun in his good hand, and slipped through the shadows of the trees, easing closer to the front doors.

As the SUV came closer, his heart leaped seeing Leya in the driver's seat. She was alive and driving, so she couldn't have been hurt…not too badly. But even at a distance, she looked pale and exhausted. Her brows were drawn together, hands clamped on the steering wheel in a death grip. As he slid to the last tree before the drive, his legs gave out like they had in the field. His vision swarmed, and he hit the ground on his hands and knees. Pain ricocheted through his shoulder. He gritted his teeth, trying to push up.

He wouldn't leave her there alone.

He wouldn't pass out.

He'd damn well get up and go after her.

# Chapter Thirty-one

## *Leya*

***AFTERLIFE***
*Performed by Hailee Steinfeld*

*TWO HOURS AFTER*

The large black double doors of the mansion swung open as Leya parked the car in front of it. John Smythe emerged in a gray suit that was pressed to perfection, and her stomach flipped over. If she was right, he'd be pissed Astrid had brought them here, but he hated Leya and her family enough that maybe she was wrong. Maybe he'd do exactly what Astrid had said and use her arrival as a sign to kick off his plans to bring the government down…to bring the U.S. to its knees.

Except, deep in her heart, Leya wasn't convinced he had terrorist cells in place around the country as Astrid had said. She believed he was exactly the conman she thought he was. A carnival magician convincing everyone he could make everything disappear. A liar.

His blond hair was slicked back, and his face was blank. A little furrow sitting between his pale brows was the only hint of any emotion as he watched Astrid step out of the car. She left the door open and had her body twisted so the gun at her side wasn't visible to Smythe.

Leya's heart slammed harder in her chest, blood pounding through her veins and dimming the noises around them. How long could you live in this high-adrenaline state before your heart gave out?

"You need to leave," Smythe said to Astrid, and Leya heard the anger in every syllable that his calm posture didn't reflect.

Astrid's shoulders stiffened at the words, but her voice was cajoling, almost begging as she said, "I brought you exactly what you need. This is your sign, John. Say the word and let it all come tumbling down."

"The plan has changed," he spoke through gritted teeth.

"What he means is that he never had that much power, Astrid. He pretended to have the dominoes lined up to get followers. To get you on his side," Leya said quietly.

"Shut up!" Astrid said, shoving the gun in Leya's direction. Leya's pulse jumped and skittered, and she tugged at the zip tie, but all it did was cause the plastic to cut into her skin more. Her wrist was already bleeding from driving with it tied so tightly. Astrid shifted, allowing John to see the gun she'd aimed at Leya. "Give the signal, John, or I shoot her here and end any chance of you ever being elected to any government office."

"What were you thinking, Astrid?! I told you we were done after the bombing and the accident, and yet you continued to use my men anyway. Enough is enough. This will not achieve anything." He waved at the car with Leya inside it, and a sense of relief washed over Leya. Never in her life had she thought she'd be happy to hear any of Smythe's words. "You've given me no choice. No choice but to reject you. To tell the world how *I* saved Leya Singh from my daughter's friend who lost her way."

The door behind him opened, and another woman stepped out with two burly men in security garb. Surprise had Leya looking twice and then again.

This blonde's hair was darker than Astrid's, and it was up in a smooth ponytail that she tightened before sliding her hand onto Smythe's arm. Leya's stomach sank.

"Mirabel?" Leya croaked just as Astrid said, "Hello, chicken."

Her mother's assistant didn't cast a single look in Leya's direction. Instead, she pressed herself closer to Smythe and turned toward Astrid with a look of pure triumph. "You said you wanted to be the arrow, but I think you've missed your target."

Astrid waved the gun in their direction. "John…you can't be serious. She's a little mouse. Scared of her own shadow. You think she can make the tough decisions? You think she'd kill for you?"

"I already did, didn't I?"

"Enough!" Smythe barked. "This has all gone too far." He turned toward the men. "Take care of this." The guards stepped forward with ominous faces just as another voice had everyone swiveling toward the drive.

"Secret Service! Everybody freeze! Put down the weapon and back away." Leya's heart jumped, even though she didn't recognize the voice. Her gaze took in a dark-haired man striding down the road in a Winter County Fire Department shirt. He held a gun in their direction, but the incongruity of his words and appearance confused everyone, including Astrid and John Smythe.

Astrid swung the gun back toward Leya, finger resting on the trigger.

"Don't any of you come any closer, or I will shoot her," Astrid said.

"Try it and you're dead," the man on the drive said.

Leya's heart pounded as her stomach fell. Holden wasn't here. Some unknown agent was. Did that mean...? No. She shook her head. He couldn't be dead. But a sob broke free. Shiva, please not him…not Holden…please don't have taken him just as we found each other.

"Come, my dear, give me the gun. As you can see, the situation has spun completely out of your control," John said, his tone sickly sweet. A father talking his toddler out of a tantrum.

"Has it?" she said, chin raised, and she turned her gaze to the men behind him. "Watership."

The men's eyes widened. They unholstered their weapons and aimed them at Smythe, who caught the movement out of the corner of his eye. He spun around to look at them, eyebrows drawn together, before a weird smile came over his face, and he turned back to Astrid. "Lovely check, Astrid."

Mirabel, her mother's sweet, quiet assistant, blew out an exasperated noise as she turned to the guards and said, "Whatever she promised you, we can easily double it, quadruple it. Do you want to go down with her"—she waved a disgusted hand at Astrid—"or be at our side when we're in the Oval Office?"

"I promised them only what John said he was giving us. A new world!" She looked at the men. "What are you waiting for?"

While they'd hesitated, the man who'd claimed he was Secret Service had taken five steps closer to the car.

"Stop," Astrid barked. A week ago, before Leya had been out shooting with Holden, she never would have noticed how Astrid's finger pushed down on the trigger. But she did now. It felt like the world slowed as she jerked her head and shoulder down toward the center console. Her zip-tied wrist shrieked in pain as the gun went off, shattering the driver's side glass where her head had just been.

Leya's eyes landed on the engine start button. She punched it on, and her foot hit the accelerator. Gravel from the drive kicked up behind her just as Astrid shot again, and the back window splintered. Fear…adrenaline…tears all took over, and she risked a glance in the rearview window. Someone stepped from the trees…a body she knew…gun raised… She heard the report of his weapon and saw Astrid's body crumble. As she spun the car around the Poseidon statue, Holden wavered and slid to the ground.

"Holden!" she screamed. The passenger door swung wildly as she drove the SUV toward where he'd fallen.

The Secret Service agent she didn't know was suddenly there, throwing a shoulder under Holden's left arm and all but tossing him into the car before he jumped into the back seat and yelled, "Drive!"

More gunfire erupted around them. From the men in the security uniforms behind Smythe, from the sky, and from a pair of black SUVs barreling down the drive toward them.

She thrust the car into reverse, sliding backward past the fountain where Astrid's body had fallen, and saw John Smythe stumbling toward the door with blood pouring from his chest. Mirabel fled into the house, and Leya slammed her foot onto the gas, skipping over the edge of the grass, overcorrecting, and causing the back end to fishtail as the wheels hit the paved drive. Her pulse banged, but she kept going as the dark-windowed SUVs flew past in the opposite direction. The front gates were wide open, the security guard lay slumped against the guardhouse, and she floored it past him onto the main road.

A groan from the passenger seat had her eyes cutting to Holden. Blood trailed down his arm again. *Hey bhagwan.* How much had he lost?

"We need to get him to a hospital." The man in the back leaned over the front seat, checking Holden's pulse. "Now."

Tears streamed down Leya's face. "I-I don't know where I'm at."

One of the black SUVs from the Smythe compound squealed into place behind them. The PA system from the car instructed them to pull over. She didn't. She couldn't. Not if she wanted to save Holden like he'd just saved her.

The man in the back seat pulled out his phone and shouted out directions that she followed unquestioningly. The SUV behind them repeated the command to pull over, the loud volume causing her to jump.

A phone vibrated somewhere on Holden's body. The man felt around until he found it.

"Raul Garcia speaking."

Someone was yelling and growling on the other end. The man who'd identified himself as Raul eyed Leya, gaze stalling on her wrist tied to the steering wheel and down her body.

"Leya Singh is secure and unharmed. We're on our way to Jackson County Hospital. We'll need a surgical team on standby. Holden Kent is bleeding out from a gunshot wound to his right deltoid."

More harsh words on the other end, but Raul just hung up in order to give Leya more directions. The vehicle behind them continued on their tail, but no more demands to pull over came from it. Finally, the hospital came into view, and Leya slammed on the brakes in front of the ER doors just as they slid open to reveal a hospital team wheeling out a gurney.

She tugged on her wrist again, sobbing at being caught and unable to get to Holden. Raul jumped out and opened the front door. Holden almost fell out, but Raul and the hospital team caught him, pulling him onto the gurney just as her driver's side door was yanked open.

She screamed, and Raul turned back in her direction, gun pointed over the roof of the SUV.

"Secret Service!" the woman at her door shouted. She had a Secret Service pin stuck to her lapel that she pointed to, and with a finger to her ear, she spoke, "Firefly secure. I repeat, Firefly secure."

The woman pulled a combat knife from the pocket of her black suit, flicked it open, and sliced through the zip tie with ease.

Leya pushed her away, ready to round the car to get to Holden's side, but the woman stopped her, gripping Leya's bicep.

"We need to get you out of here," the agent said.

Leya wrenched her arm away and continued to where Raul was talking to the hospital staff. "Took a bullet approximately two and a half hours ago. Bleeding temporarily stopped. I shot him up with painkillers and antibiotics about an hour and a half ago. Uncertain when the bleeding restarted, but I'd say at least thirty minutes."

A man in scrubs looked up from Holden, gaze stalling on her before taking in Raul, the black SUV, and the four Secret Service agents who'd emerged from it. But then, without a word, he yanked on the front of the gurney, and the entire hospital team took off at a jog. Leya and Raul followed them down the beige hallways trailed by the rest of the USSS agents.

At the doors of the operating room, the doctor stepped forward with a hand out.

"This is as far as you can go. There's a waiting room down the hall," he said.

"We need a private location," the woman told the man.

"I don't have time for this if you want me to save his life." The doctor turned, punched in a code, and slid back through the doors.

The woman's gaze settled on one of the male agents who'd accompanied her. "Go find the administrator, and get us a secure location." She turned back to eye Leya from her head to her toes. "And get someone to come look at Firefly's injuries."

The man set off at a clip down the hall, dress shoes tapping on the polished floor.

"I'm Special Agent Sheridan West from the Birmingham office," the female agent said to Leya. "Can you tell me if you've been hurt anywhere I can't see?"

Leya's wrist stung, a bloody bracelet that would likely scar and be a permanent reminder of today's events, and her head was pounding from where Astrid had slammed into her already bruised temple. But the thing that hurt the worst, the injury that wouldn't stop screaming at her, was her heart. All she could see was Holden's body slumped in the seat, blood pouring down his arm… The way he'd fallen out when Raul had opened the door…

Tears streamed unchecked down her face. Her chest and lungs were so tight her breathing was labored.

He'd come for her. He'd come for her, risking his own life just as he'd promised he would. And she hated it. An anguished cry escaped her chest, even as she shook her head at the agent, trying to say she was unharmed.

"West, we've located and emptied a staff lounge." The other agent came back down the hall at a jog. West put out her hand as if saying Leya should go first.

But she didn't want to go. She didn't want to leave the doors where she'd last seen Holden. Raul seemed to sense this, and he stepped closer, as if to console her, and West was immediately there, putting a hand out to stop him from touching Leya.

"My colleague, Special Agent Castle, will be taking you in for debriefing. Your assistance is no longer needed," West told Raul.

Raul's eyes narrowed, glancing toward the four men in suits and then back to Leya. He gave a curt nod. As West took Leya's arm gently, guiding her down the hall, she looked back and mumbled through her sobs, "Th-thank you, Raul. Thank you for h-helping H-Holden."

The man's jaw clenched, but he nodded again.

Then, she was around the corner and being shuffled down corridors until she was drawn through a door labeled *Doctors Only*.

The room had a circular table with cushioned chairs, two couches, a small kitchenette, and a TV blaring in the corner. She saw her face flash over the screen before one of the agents reached up and turned it off.

She sank onto the couch, put her face in her hands, and let herself cry.

She was free. She was safe…but at what cost? To Holden? Her dad? Her friends?

"Miss Singh. I need to understand the extent of your injuries so we can have you treated," West's voice was soft, kind.

Leya looked up, eyes really noticing the agent for the first time. The woman's dark-brown skin was smooth and clear but drawn tight. Her brown eyes were intense and sharp below thick brows drawn together with concern. Her coiled ebony hair was pulled back with a pair of sunglasses tucked into the strands. She was tall, maybe even six feet, but she felt larger somehow. Larger…and safer—like someone she could trust.

"I'm not hurt," Leya said, waving her wrist. "This and a bump on my head. A few bruises from the crash, and cuts on my palms. Nothing serious."

West's face smoothed out, concern fading. "We've got someone coming to do an assessment just in case."

But Leya only heard half of it because she'd closed her eyes, sending all her energy into prayers, hoping that through her words to Shiva and Vishnu, Brahma would hear her and spare Holden's life. Keep him alive so they could have more than just the handful of moments they'd had together.

# Chapter Thirty-two

## *Leya*

***BURN WITH YOU***
*Performed by Lea Michele*

Leya felt the exhaustion dragging at her as she sat on the uncomfortable couch in the staff lounge. Her body was demanding rest, but she didn't dare sleep. Didn't dare let up her silent prayers. Not with Holden still in surgery. She stood, pacing the small space to keep herself awake. A doctor had come to the room and said she was dehydrated and had a slight concussion, but other than that, she was whole and unharmed. He'd wrapped her wrist with gauze and then left. West had procured an enormous bottle of water from somewhere, and Leya had drank almost all of it in a matter of minutes.

Now, she needed caffeine. Something to keep her from slipping away into the oblivion that threatened every time she sat down.

It had been two hours already, and still, there was no word on Holden.

She'd been debriefed by West and told Astrid Barrows and John Smythe were dead and that Mirabel had been taken into custody. But all of it had happened in a haze, as if the low clouds that had greeted them in the mornings at the ranch had wrapped around her, holding her in their midst.

West put a finger to her earpiece at the same time as the other three agents did. They all stood, and that was Leya's first clue that one or both of her parents were there. The door swung open to reveal them both. Their suits were perfectly pressed, hair done, Mom's makeup carefully applied, but their eyes…their eyes were wild, and when they landed on Leya, Mom broke into a sob.

And then, Leya was in their arms, surrounded by both of them, a tangle of love and relief and sorrow. Kisses were littered along the top of her head as they murmured soothing words, not just for her, but for all of them.

"You're safe now, *beta*," Dad said. The agents in the room slipped out to join Leya's parents' agents in the hall, giving them privacy.

"I'm fine…but Holden…" her voice cracked, and more tears ran down her face even though she'd thought she'd finally gotten them under control.

Their grip on her loosened. Her mother took Leya's face into her hands, searching her eyes. "Special Agent Kent did his job. This was his job, *beta*. Protect you at all costs."

Leya's hands settled on her mother's wrists, their gazes locked. "No, Mom. He…" She struggled for the right words. To tell them what she thought and felt.

Her mother inhaled sharply, and her dad's eyes narrowed.

"*Beta*…please tell me you did not fall for this man," her mother said.

Leya sobbed. "He is my *jeevansathi*."

Mom dropped her arms as if she'd been hit, but her father pulled Leya to his chest, and she was surprised when his words were kind and gentle but also held a tiny tease. "This is serious, then."

She hiccupped in reply, squeezing him. When she risked looking up at her mom, it was to see her rubbing her fingers along her forehead—a clear sign she was troubled, or irritated, or perhaps both.

"I told you, Ved. I told you sending her off alone with a single male agent was not wise."

"And I told you, Zaira, the seeds had already been sown long before."

Leya looked up at her father in surprise. "Wh-what?"

He laughed softly, kissing her on the temple. "I may be busy, *beta*, but I'm not blind."

"But you would have let me marry Krish?"

His eyes softened. "Why do you think I forced your decision? It was as much for Krish as for you. He deserves to find someone whose heart doesn't belong to someone else."

She turned to her mother who still didn't look happy.

"Mom?"

Her mother made a disgusted noise in her throat, and Leya felt the single string she'd had in common with her mother snip in half. "You know how I feel about this nonsense, Leya. And this man…he is nothing like you. Nothing like our family. He's watched from the shadows and now wants a piece of the cake."

Leya's heart squeezed tight, worry and fear that her mother would take her anger out on Holden and cost him even more than his career. "He fought it, *Maa*." She used the Indian word for mother that she hadn't used since she was a little girl, and she saw her mother's eyes soften at it. "He fought me…fought us…but it is like *Nani* used to say… Once you are stuck in the riptide, fighting it is not a choice. Instead, you must let it sweep you away until you find steady ground to stand on once more. You may end somewhere you never expected, but it doesn't mean it isn't where you belong."

Her mom looked up at the ceiling. "*Bas, Maa*, do you see what you have done to my daughter? You've filled her head with garbage."

Leya's dad grabbed her mother's hand and raised it to kiss her knuckles. "You say this as if we are not our own love match, Zaira. As if I did not sweep you off your feet and make you leave your logic and science behind as I wooed you."

Leya gasped. "No!"

Her mother's lips twitched slightly as she pulled her hand away, patted her father's cheek, and then looked at Leya. "We were an arranged marriage first, *beta*. Our lives, and our values, and our goals matched. Our star chart was nearly perfect. The love came after."

"That's what your mother will tell you," her father said with an unfamiliar wink. "Me…I fell for her the moment she strode into the room."

An unexpected laugh escaped Leya, easing the heavy, twisted agony inside her. "Why have you never told me this?"

"Because your mother, and you, are also right. Many people mistake lust for love, and the marriages end in divorce. I wanted better for my children. I gave each of you time to find it on your own, but when you didn't, I hoped we would find partners who would bloom into the same thing for you that your mother and I have."

"But not with Krish. You've encouraged that relationship since I was fifteen," she said with a frown that he returned, darting a look at her mother who was still rubbing the tell-tale V's between her brows.

"You have always been guided by your emotions. I knew we needed something stable for you before you did something impulsive…like fall in love with your bodyguard," her mother said dryly, the scold clear, and it frustrated Leya.

"You told me you wanted me to be happy. To have a partner. That you wanted a dozen grandchildren. Does it really matter who it is with?"

"You are smart enough to know it does," her mother snipped back. "I want what is best for you, not some temporary bliss. Besides, this is not just about you. It is about the family. Who you are tied to impacts all of us."

"You don't believe in the *kundali*! You told *Nani* she was ridiculous for using her *Vedic* signs during father's campaign."

"I'm not talking birth charts and astrology, *beta*. I'm talking about our family's image in this country. In the press. Who is his family? Will they hurt your father's bid for reelection? How will it look when you turn your nose at everything you've said about arranged marriages? Everything we've said together. You'll look ridiculous, and the press will use it against all of us."

"Enough," her father said, sending Mom a look she simply shrugged at.

Leya withdrew, sinking onto the sofa. She glanced at the door and thought of the hours Holden had been in the operating room, and fear thundered through her veins all over again. "It may not matter. H-he may…may not make it."

Her entire being recoiled at that thought, and tears fell down her cheeks in waves. She clutched her stomach. The pain was visceral, as if she was being stabbed repeatedly. She rocked back and forth. She could not lose him. She returned to her silent prayers and almost missed the sharp inhale from the other side of the room that was followed by her mother sitting down and wrapping her arms around her.

They sat there for a moment, Mom moving her hand in small circles along Leya's back, as she had many times when Leya was sick as a little girl. Soothing. Loving.

"If he is truly your *jeevansathi,* he would be foolish to leave this earth after having just found you," her mother said, and it made Leya snort in a very unattractive way, but it also gave her hope. Hope that maybe the love she felt from her mother would allow them to find a new island to stand on together. A different bond.

Leya set her head on her mother's shoulder and let the soothing scent of Chanel and the motion of her mom's hand on her back bring a momentary peace from the waves of intense emotions that had lived inside her for the last week.

Before she knew it, her eyes were drifting shut, and she was dozing off into a dream where Holden was healthy and safe, and he was on the back of a white horse, arriving at their wedding in complete Indian garb.

♫ ♫ ♫

The door clicking shut brought her awake. In the windowless room, it was hard to tell how much time had passed, but her father was at the table with a computer, and her mother was on her phone. They all looked up as the doctor who'd taken Holden into surgery emerged.

"He's made it through. Lost a damn lot of blood, and he might never recover the full strength of his right arm, but he's alive."

Relief flooded Leya's veins. Relief and heartache and more relief. He was alive. But injured…maybe permanently. She'd already known his career as an agent was over. He'd said it to her as much as she'd thought it, but this would mean the door was shut for good. You couldn't remain in the USSS if you couldn't pass the quarterly fitness tests. She ached for him. She wanted to be with him. To comfort him. To help him see that as that door closed, there was still this one with her that was opening. Not just opening but welcoming him in with all his vibrant colors. The force of him would always be there, injured shoulder or not.

"Can we see him?" she asked, body aching to run down the corridor and slide into his arms.

"They're preparing a room for him now. Once he's been moved, we'll make sure your detail gets the information."

He turned to leave, and Leya called out to him, "Thank you, Doctor. Th-thank you so much." Her voice cracked and tears came again.

He gave her a long stare before his chin bobbed, and then he left.

She wondered if it would be all over the news now. If the doctor and the nurses and other staff at the hospital would tell the media how Leya Singh was in love with her Secret Service agent. Her stomach turned because her mother was right. The media was going to drag her beliefs across the fire, twisting every word she'd ever said in favor of arranged marriages, using it against her father in any way they could.

She couldn't risk looking at the *I told you so* in her mother's gaze.

Holden had told her that he didn't doubt she'd claim him to her parents, and yet he'd made them wait before making love. He'd known that when reality invaded their world, it wouldn't be as easy to choose each other. But he'd promised to be there. To protect her. To allow them to have the choice.

He hadn't let her down. She couldn't let him down either.

Not if she truly wanted to be with him for the rest of her life.

She needed reinforcements. People who would remind her that she was making a wise decision and not a foolish one.

She turned to her parents. "I need to call the band. Can I borrow a phone?"

"I'm trying to clean up this mess that Mirabel has made," her mother said, and Leya could see the hurt and guilt in her mom's face. Someone she'd trusted had turned on them in the ugliest way.

Leya stepped toward her mom, hugging her and saying the words Holden had repeated to her over and over in the last few days. "It isn't your fault."

"She knew everything… I didn't keep anything from her." Her mother's voice was tired and pained.

"Zaira, if the Secret Service didn't know her connections to Smythe, how were you to know?" her father said.

Her mother already had trust issues. Huge ones. And this would only add to them. Her father pulled her mom away from her and into his arms. "Let Leya use your phone. Give yourself a moment."

To her surprise, her mother handed it over without hesitation, and Leya slipped out into the hall. Special Agent West was at her side immediately.

"I need a moment to myself," Leya told her softly.

"There's a bathroom, down here," West said, leading her to a single-stalled room the agent cleared before letting Leya into it.

It smelled like bleach and antiseptic. Clean but sterile.

The opposite of how Leya felt. Inside, she was a jumble of mixed, messy emotions.

She stared at the phone for a long moment. She wanted to talk to Fee or Paisley because it was reassurance about love that she needed, but then she realized she needed to call Adria first. For two years, Adria's family had looked for her sister without success, and now Leya had been kidnapped. It was too close to home. Too sharp and bitter.

Adria picked up immediately, thinking it was Leya's mom. "Mrs. Singh, have they found her? Is she okay?" The fear in Adria's voice made Leya's heart hammer and stomach sink.

"Ads, it's me," Leya breathed.

"¡*Dios*! We were so worried. What the hell happened?" Adria said, the relief in her voice followed by fear and then anger.

"A lot…but I'm okay… It's just Holden…" her voice cracked. Would the tears ever stop? Would she ever feel like she had them back in control?

"Oh, Ley… I'm so sorry." Sorrow dripped from Adria's words, and Leya realized she'd made her friend think Holden had died.

"No. No. He's alive. But he got shot. He just got out of surgery."

More voices shouted over Adria in the background, a cacophony of them that sounded like…all the Daisies.

"Wait? Are you all together?"

"As soon as they took you out of D.C., we all flew back. You were in trouble, Leya. Of course we came back together," Adria said. "I'm putting you on speaker."

"Hey, everyone," she finally choked out, and there was a chorus of *I love yous* and demands to know what happened that burst through the speaker. She ached to be with them again. To be on tour. For the only worry she had to be about getting onstage that night.

"Tell us what happened!" Fee demanded.

And so she did. All of it. The ugly accident, and Angel Carter, and the chases, and the ranch. She skipped over the piece about her and Holden. She wasn't sure why. But then she told them about everything that had happened today, ending with Holden.

"Holy shit," Nikki said.

It was Paisley who picked up on the name Leya had used. "Holden? What happened to calling him Special Agent Kent? Or Captain Annoying? Or jerkwad?"

Leya's skin flushed, the heat coating her neck and cheeks. She played with the handful of bracelets she'd returned to her wrists, pushing them up and down, twirling them. She'd given the dragonfly one to Special Agent West, and it had felt like a weight had left her.

"Ley?" Adria prompted.

"I don't think he's going to be a special agent for much longer," she finally breathed out.

A stunned silence was followed by laughter on the other end.

"You did it with Captain Avenger?" Fee said with a chuckle. "I wish you were here so I could high-five you, and squeeze you, and then give you a noogie."

"We haven't 'done it,' Fiadh. Isn't that the kind of childish language you harass me about?" Leya tossed back, and her friend laughed more.

"What happened to Krish?" Paisley asked, cutting into Fee's mirth.

"I called it off."

"Yes!" Fee cried out, and Leya smiled, imagining her friend wiggling her entire body in joy.

"This is…a lot happening all at once," Nikki said. She was always the calm voice of reason in the group. "Ley, are you really okay?"

"Maybe not right at this moment, but I will be." She took a deep breath and said the words that she'd been wanting to say aloud for days now. "As long as I have all of you, and Holden, I'll be okay."

"We're coming down there," Paisley announced.

"I don't know how long I'll be here. I'm sure I'll be back in D.C. soon."

"We're not in D.C. Asher flew us to Willow Creek, where a very handsome sheriff is trying to find a place for us at the dude ranch you'd supposedly been staying at," Fee announced.

Leya's heart swelled. Her friends had come for her, not only when they'd thought she was in trouble but after she'd been taken. They'd gone to Willow Creek to look for her…to be there when she showed up. "Don't let Asher hear you say that about the sheriff," Leya said, a watery smile pushing at her lips.

Fee laughed. "Asher has already befriended the man. It's like they've known each other their whole lives. If anyone should be worried, it's me."

A knock at the door startled Leya. West's voice came through. "Kent is in a room, awake, and demanding to see you."

Her heart leaped…a spike of joy through the anguish. He was awake! Awake and alive and wanting to see her.

"Give me the night to figure out where I'll be, and I'll let you know."

They weren't happy, but as she told them she needed to go, they let her off with a chorus of *I love yous* ringing through her ears again.

Leya opened the door, and West led her down twists and turns of corridors to a room near the back of the hospital. Leya's eyes found Holden's as soon as she entered. Relief coasted over her, and it was mirrored in his gaze. They assessed each other in the way he'd always done but that she now returned. His right arm was in a cloth sling-like contraption that held his arm close to his body with a cap over the ball of his shoulder. The blankets were tugged about his waist, and the hospital gown had been loosened so that it was partially baring his muscled torso. The sharp lines and hard curves were on display but covered in blood and the orange antiseptic used in surgical rooms.

She rushed over to his left side and hugged him. He used his good arm, hand at her back, to pull her tighter into his chest and whispered in her ear, "Thank God you're safe. I'm sorry, darlin'. So fucking sorry. I left you on the side of the road—"

The tortured guilt in his voice was as large and clear as the relief, and it tore through her as the tears fell unchecked down her cheeks. How many times had she cried in the last few hours? There was a tangled warren of relief and love and uncertainty burrowing inside her.

"You couldn't have known. None of that matters," she choked out, and even though she believed it was true, she knew he'd never let himself off the hook that easily. He felt responsible. But all that mattered was him being alive. When she'd thought he may have been dead… *Hey bhagwan*, it had been the worst pain she'd ever felt. "I thought… I thought you were…" She couldn't even finish the sentence as she sobbed into his neck.

He stroked her hair gently, kissing her temple. His voice was low and guttural, full of his own unshed tears. "We have too much unfinished business for the gods to tear us apart yet, Leya. You have too many colors still to show me."

His words were as beautiful as they were agonizing. She lifted her head to meet his gaze.

"I love you, Holden. Don't you ever do this to me again. No more getting shot. No more running around with blood pouring out of you. Do you understand?"

His eyes were haunted and tired, remorse and uncertainty stirring below the exhaustion that pulled at his lids. Finally, he growled out, "Don't get kidnapped again, and I can keep that promise. Otherwise, all bets are off."

His gaze shifted to the four USSS agents waiting at the door, and hers followed. While the agents' faces were blank, she knew by the way his jaw ticked that he was thinking of the disapproval roiling through them. For a man who'd lived his entire life with honor and dedication, it would be like a knife stabbing him.

The dreamlike world they'd lost themselves in had burst. Reality was setting in. It wasn't just the terror of the day. It was her mother's disapproval and the agents lined up at the door. If the media found out about them, they'd come for her...not him. They'd toss her words about marriage back at her. They'd scorn her for falling for one of her detail. All of it would test the tentative bonds they'd formed.

But even facing all of that, her life would be relatively unchanged. She'd go on singing with her band, creating her art, and visiting her family, whereas he'd had his world pulled out from under him.

"I'm so sorry, Holden. I-I..." She didn't know what else to say. Agony tore through her because of what she'd done to him, and yet she also knew she couldn't give him up. As selfish as loving him was, she did. She loved him and needed him as much as she needed air. Life would never be the same if he wasn't with her. The people in their lives—hell, the entire world—would have to adjust. The gods had given them to each other, so far be it from humanity to tear them apart.

# Chapter Thirty-three

## *Holden*

***EMPTY HANDED***

*Performed by Lea Michele*

Exhaustion and grogginess from the anesthesia were eating through his veins as much as the guilt from having lost her and the overwhelming relief that she was there. But as he looked at the torment on Leya's face, his only thought was to ease it. He'd do anything to make sure she felt only love and happiness for the rest of her life. Just like he'd do anything to protect her. She could have a dozen Secret Service agents following her around, and he'd still be first to step in front of her if a bullet came.

"No matter what happens from here, Leya, it was worth it. You'll always be worth it," he said with a certainty he felt deep in his bones.

She flushed, glancing down, stilling for a second before tugging at something on his good arm. He was surprised to find her leather-and-silver bracelet he'd picked up from the deli parking lot still on his wrist.

"You found it," she said softly, tears filling her eyes.

"I promise I'll always come find you," he said and meant it with every fiber of his being. He started to slide the bracelet off to give it back to her, and she stopped him.

"Keep it. I'll feel better knowing there is a little piece of me with you right now."

"Still looking over me, Lita Rae?" The intensity of that thought rippled through him like a sledgehammer.

"If you'll let me."

He barely had to lean up to brush his lips against hers, but it still sent knifelike pain through his wounded shoulder. It was a brief, tender kiss, but it was packed with everything he was feeling. Love, first and foremost, but also joy that she was relatively unharmed, and worry because he didn't know what happened next. And at the back, there was still fear that the world could tear them apart.

"I don't know what happens now," he said gruffly, hating that, for the first time in his life, he didn't have a mile-long list in his head, guiding him.

"You don't have to figure it out alone, Avenger-man. We'll figure it out together," she said softly, brushing her hand over his jaw.

Jesus, he loved her. So much he wasn't sure it wouldn't burst from him, leaving him scarred in ways much worse than his arm. But he'd spoken the truth to her. She was worth the risk. Loving her would always be worth it. Even the judgment wafting over him from the agents at the door was worth it. If he got to touch her and kiss her and be the one at her side, lifting her up when she had moments of insecurity, he'd deal with their glares and her parents' disapproval.

He put his good hand over hers, heavy logs weighing his lids down. He fought it, but sleep was claiming him. "Don't leave," he growled.

He'd know if she did. Even in his sleep, he'd feel her absence, and he wasn't sure he could take it after the tortured hours without her. Seeing Barrows with the gun, seeing the way the car window had shattered where her head had been, had filled him with the worst pain he'd ever experienced. He'd barely dragged himself to his feet from where he'd hit the ground at the Smythe compound in time to take the shot at Barrows. He barely remembered it…a hazy recollection of Leya hitting the gas on the SUV and him taking aim before he collapsed again.

He shuddered at the memories, and her soft, lyrical voice whispered through the nightmare, "I'll be here, Holden. Just rest. Heal."

He felt her slide into the bed with him, aligning her body with his good side, and for the first time in what felt like days, he relaxed completely. She was there. Barrows and Smythe were dead. They were safe and together. That was all that really mattered.

♫ ♫ ♫

*ONE DAY AFTER*

As he came awake, confusion ran through him. He heard his dad's deep voice and his mother's light one laughing at something. Other voices mingled with theirs. Was he at his parents' house? He shifted on the bed, and the pain in his shoulder had his eyes popping open. A hospital room filled his vision.

Everything hit him at once. The days on the run. Leya. Getting shot.

He searched the room for her, and when she wasn't there, panic filled him.

"Leya!" He sat up, and everything spun wildly.

The four adults sitting and standing in the room turned toward him. He hadn't been hallucinating. His parents were there, along with the Singhs.

The vice president was the first to step toward the bed, saying, "She's at the hotel. We had to practically carry her from the room to get her to shower and rest, so I'm sure she'll be back soon."

The reassurance did nothing to ease the worry inside him.

His mom rushed forward, running a hand over his hair that, even as short as it was, was probably a mess, whereas all four of them looked completely put together.

"You gave us quite a scare, Holden," his mother said, hugging him carefully.

His dad joined them, tapping his good shoulder with a closed fist. "Damn good to see you awake." He searched Holden's face, eyes drifting sideways toward the Singhs and back. "Fine mess you landed in." But there was a twist to his lips that took the bite out of the words.

Holden closed his eyes briefly before meeting his dad's again with a curt nod.

His dad's voice was deep with a well of regret as he said, "I knew you were conflicted when you came to see us last… I wish I'd—"

"I wouldn't have been ready to talk to you about it or hear what you had to say. Circumstances had to happen to put things in perspective for me," Holden responded.

They stared at each other for a moment, unspoken words drifting between them.

Their silent conversation was broken up by the vice president saying, "Thank you for saving our little girl." Gratitude traveled through each syllable, and it stabbed at the guilt Holden still felt for having broken this man's trust. He'd been tasked with protecting his daughter, and instead, he'd spent days touching her. Devouring her. Doing everything but the last final act that would tie them completely together.

Holden gritted his teeth. "I'm sorry, sir. For everything. For not keeping her safe. For break—"

Ved Singh waved his hand, eyes boring into him as he asked, "Do you love her?"

The energy and command wafting from the second most powerful man in the United States was undeniable even if it was understated. The vice president was known for his friendly, easy demeanor, whereas the president was known for his charismatic intensity. But below Ved's soft words today, Holden heard a different message. A warning. If he wasn't all in, he needed to back away now.

He held the vice president's gaze and spoke from his heart with certainty. "Yes, sir."

A disapproving huff came from Zaira Singh standing on the other side of the room. The second lady was going to be harder to win over than her husband. She didn't acknowledge Holden at all as she stepped toward the door.

"We'll discuss this more when you're well," the vice president said, joining his wife, who raised a single eyebrow as if displeased by his words. They left the room, and a sea of agents went with them.

"That could have gone worse," his mom said with a chuckle.

"What did they say before I woke up?" he asked.

"We were just commiserating. Two sets of parents who'd almost lost their children," his mom answered, tears swarming in her eyes and her chin bobbing.

When his gaze found his dad's again, uncertainty wavered in them. Unable to sustain the look, Holden let his lids slide shut, suddenly overwhelmed by his reality. The loss of his job. The disdain of his peers. The doubts his parents felt. The even larger doubts of the Singhs. Normally, he'd have a list of actions assembled that would take him through unsteady ground, but today, his pages were blank, just as they'd been since he'd chosen Leya over everything else. For a moment, a raw ache filled his gut, but then, it eased as new goals started to appear. Objectives he shouldn't have but did anyway, including finding Leya, kissing Leya, and never letting her go.

It eased his troubled heart to have a few immediate tasks to complete, but it still troubled him that there was nothing appearing in the columns for next week, or next year, or even five years. All his plans had withered away. What would he do with himself besides love Leya? It wasn't like he could sit around, eating bonbons. He had skills he'd spent a lifetime honing but would do him little good in any law enforcement capacity now. But he still had a mortgage. Bills to pay. Jesus.

As if reading the turmoil in him, his dad's hand landed on his shoulder again. "You'll figure it out, Holden. It doesn't have to be right this moment or even today. Just concentrate on healing."

And he realized, for the first time maybe in his life, it was true. He didn't need to stack the deck with a list of tasks and find all the answers. Time would unravel the choices for him. He just had to let it happen instead of forcing it to come.

♫ ♫ ♫

Holden was in and out of sleep the rest of the night. Whenever he came awake, one or both of his parents were there, but also Leya, looking decidedly more like her rock-star self and less like Lita Rae. She was dressed in designer jeans, a soft white sweater that made her skin glow, and heeled boots that showed off those long legs he adored. Her eyes were warm, her smile genuine. She was relaxed in a way she hadn't been in the last week except for the brief moments when she'd come apart in his arms, chanting his name. He needed her that way again, with pink in her cheeks and fire in her eyes. Instead, he settled for chaste kisses and fingers twined.

About the time he really started to get antsy, the doctor discharged him.

He'd gotten a brief respite from his boss and the Secret Service, but it was now over. He was due back in Washington for a debrief…and likely dismissal. He'd resign first, if they let him.

Somehow, nothing had hit the media about him and Leya yet. Her kidnapping and rescue were all over the place, but nothing about him. Details were spotty because the Secret Service was keeping it that way. The world knew Smythe and Barrows were dead and that other members of the FGT, including Mirabel, were in custody, singing like blue jays. Loud and hard. But there was nothing about the agent and the single firefighter who'd saved her. Nothing about love that had bloomed between an agent and his protectee.

As Holden dressed in jeans and a T-shirt his mother had brought him and reattached the weird contraption that kept his right arm hooked tight to his body, Leya watched. She was nervous for some reason. He knew because he could read all her emotions these days…or maybe he always had been able to read them.

"What's wrong?" he asked, stalking over and pulling her to him.

"I'm not going back to D.C."

His stomach churned, fear and conflict hammering through him. He needed to be at her side, but he was expected in Washington. "Where are you going?" he finally asked.

"The band is in Willow Creek," she said, and surprise shifted through him. "They came as soon as they found out I'd been taken. Even though the ranch had shut down for the season, the Hatleys have welcomed them anyway. We have less than two weeks left of our break before we're due back on tour, and I think it'll be good for us to be together there. See if we can forget some of the trauma we've been through lately."

As much as he hated to admit it, she was right. It would be good for all of the Daisies. The problem was, he couldn't go to Willow Creek—not yet. And he hadn't wanted her to leave his damn hospital room, hadn't wanted her to ever be away from his side again, let alone be hundreds of miles from him. His body tightened, frustration and concern leaking into every pore. She saw it, read it, and leaned toward him, placing a soft kiss on his lips that wasn't nearly enough, wasn't anywhere near the devouring he wanted to do to her.

"I don't want to be apart either," she said. "It terrifies me in more ways than I can even describe, but my family doesn't want me to face the media yet. And the truth is, I don't want to talk about what happened, and if I'm in Washington, the press will find me."

His finger ran over the bandage around her wrist. He hated she'd been scarred by this. Hated that it was his fault. He wasn't sure he'd ever forget it or forgive himself completely. He'd been so angry. So determined to end Astrid. He'd been wild and out of control. Everything he knew he shouldn't have been and yet was unable to stop it.

He'd feel that way again if Leya wasn't at his side.

But the things he had to do, the list that had slowly been coming together, would be easier accomplished without her. And she needed her friends. Needed the love and companionship of the Daisies to help her forget what she'd been through.

"I'll come to you when I'm done in D.C.," he grunted out.

She smiled, one of her radiant smiles that felt like the sunset was glowing around him. "I know. You promised to always find me, and I know here"—she pressed her hand to her chest—"that you always will."

Hand in hand, they left the hospital through a back service entrance. A dark SUV waited for them and took them to the small airport where the helo had landed almost two days ago. Two small planes sat on the runway, waiting to send them in different directions. His insides were knotted, and it felt as if his lungs were compressing. He didn't know how to walk away from her, even temporarily.

"I'm going to be okay," she said softly, running her hand over his good shoulder.

He nodded, but panic was in his heart. Not only because they were going to be physically apart, but because there would be time for others to come between them. Everyone knew Leya Singh deserved someone better than an agent who couldn't keep his dick in his pants. Even if he had, the world didn't know that.

Her fingers slid over his chin, turning his face so their gazes met.

"Stop overthinking this, Captain Annoying. You. Me. That's all that matters. Not what others label us. Not what our parents think. Not our jobs, or where we live, or who the media thinks we are. Just us."

He let out a shuddery breath, inhaling the scent of her, letting the confidence in her eyes soothe him. He missed the days of Miles and Lita Rae on their own. Missed being able to touch her, claim her, make her his.

"Kiss me, Holden."

He did as she commanded, mouth landing on hers, losing himself to anything but the softness of her lips and the heat of her tongue tangling with his as if they'd been doing it for centuries. He groaned, drawing her closer with his good arm, fingers pressing into the hollow of her back so every curve aligned with his hard ones.

Her fingernails dug into his scalp and neck as the kiss went from soft and gentle to hot and demanding in a second. They'd gone too long without being joined this way. Too long without feeling those strings binding them, tightening around them, pulling them closer.

A knock on the glass broke their lips apart.

She was smiling, a dazzling display that made everything else disappear. Like in the drawings she'd done of him, she was etched in fine details, every line and shadow popping while, behind her, the world blurred into abstracts.

"Hurry, Holden. Hurry back to Willow Creek. Lita Rae wants her husband back."

Then, she pushed herself away and out the door.

He wanted to growl and argue. He wanted to demand she come back, but then he realized the truth. If he wanted to finish what he'd started with her, he had to close the door on the other pieces of his life first.

# Chapter Thirty-four

## *Leya*

***NOBODY'S BUSINESS***
*Performed by Sheryl Crow*

*TWO DAYS AFTER*

*LEYA: I miss you.*

*AVENGER-MAN: It feels like a lifetime already. How long has it been?*

*LEYA: An hour.*

*AVENGER-MAN: Jesus. This is going to be impossible.*

*LEYA: Just think how desperate we'll be. Think of what it'll be like when our lips touch again.*

*AVENGER-MAN: Screw the debrief. I'm coming now.*

*LEYA: ***laughing emoji*** Don't come until there's nothing left standing between us, Holden.*

*AVENGER-MAN: ...*

*LEYA: Don't you dare do that. I deserve a response.*

*AVENGER-MAN: You leave me speechless, darlin'. I don't have the words to express what I'm feeling.*

*LEYA: I don't want words. I want to feel your body and your lips and know for myself the truth of us.*

*AVENGER-MAN: I'll be there as soon as I can.*

*FOUR DAYS AFTER*

*LEYA: I need to know how it went. I need to know you're okay.*

*AVENGER-MAN: I'm not going to lie. It hurt to hand in my badge. Seven-year-old me would be disgusted. Seventeen-year-old me would be furiously ranting. Even twenty-seven-year-old me heading toward Grand Orchard for my second protective assignment would have had a few harsh words for this version of me.*

*LEYA: I wish I knew what to say besides I'm sorry.*

*AVENGER-MAN: You know what twenty-nine-year-old me has to say?*

*LEYA: No.*

*AVENGER-MAN: Hurry, idiot. Lita Rae is waiting.*

*LEYA: I love you.*

*AVENGER-MAN: That's all I'll ever need to hear.*

*FIVE DAYS AFTER*

*LEYA: You're on your way?*

*AVENGER-MAN: Soon. I have a stop to make, and then I'll be on my way.*

*LEYA: Hurry, Miles. Hurry.*

# Chapter Thirty-five

## Holden

**_TWO_**
*Performed by Heart*

*FIVE DAYS AFTER*

*Holden had a duffel and a* gift bag in his good hand as he exited his building and headed toward the Firebird he'd parked down the street after returning from the Washington field office minus his badge and his gun yesterday. It had hurt. So had the disdain of his boss and his peers, but every time it had started to tear at his soul a bit, he'd thought of Leya, and everything had cleared. He'd made his choice. He'd chosen Leya, and he didn't regret it.

Now, he just had to make sure she didn't either.

It wasn't his nearly empty to-do list or the savings account that would only last a few months that were on his brain today, though. Instead, it was the words that had been on repeat ever since she'd typed them. *Don't come until there's nothing left standing between us*.

And there was one thing still left. He didn't know if he could fix it, but he'd at least try before he left the city and went to her.

The gray skies that had hung over Washington all day, darkening the Capitol building and dimming the monuments, cast heavy shadows as he scanned the street out of habit. He clocked the white-haired man even before he'd pushed off the wall and headed toward Holden. Rafe Reinard was ancient, with gray eyes and an attitude that matched his background in French special forces. Broad-shouldered and narrow-waisted, Holden had only ever seen the man on a computer screen.

"Kent," Reinard said, his French accent sliding through each syllable as he stepped into pace with Holden.

"Reinard," Holden clipped back. "What brings you to the States?"

"Angel Carter and the Daisies," Reinard said.

Holden stopped and turned toward the man. "You get a bead on him?"

"No, but we have a sketch of someone he was meeting with in Boston. We might know who he is, so we're chasing it down."

Holden itched to know more and to follow the lead, but it wasn't his job anymore, even though he wanted to find answers for Leya and her friends. He turned and started to walk away when Reinard's voice halted him again. "Ever heard of the *Cavalieri d'Oro*?"

Holden shook his head.

"It's a secret society. English translation is The Golden Knights. Maybe even older than the Knights Templar. I've heard rumors they're in the U.S., searching for someone."

"Someone who? The guy meeting with Carter?" Reinard shrugged, and Holden had the distinct feeling the man was holding something back. "How does this involve the Daisies?"

"Not sure yet."

Holden gave a disgusted sigh and finished walking down the sidewalk to his car. "I can't help you anymore, Reinard. You need to send what you've got to Leya's new detail."

"I don't trust the new detail, but I do trust you."

Holden scoffed, dumped his bags on the ground, tugged his car key from his pocket with his one useful hand,

and unlocked the Firebird's door. Reinard leaned his elbows on the roof across from him and said, "You see yourself as having failed. Your former bosses probably told you the same thing, but you know what I think?"

"Do I care?"

Reinard's stare cut through him. It ate at Holden that he did care. Just like it ate at him that the entire Secret Service saw him as one of their worst mistakes.

"I think," Reinard went on, "you have extra motivation now to keep Leya Singh safe. To keep them all safe. The Painted Daisies need someone like that around them. People who are motivated by something more than a paycheck and honor. Those women need someone who would literally die if one of those women lost their lives. That's why I'm offering you a job."

Holden's eyes narrowed. There was no talk about him and Leya in the press, so he wasn't sure exactly how the man had heard about them. Reinard met his gaze with a twinkle in his eye and tapped the roof, the dull thud vibrating across the car. "Not as Leya's personal detail. I agree, you're too close to stay focused when on duty. I want you to oversee the entire team. Garner Security's men are overlapping with mine, and the Secret Service are crawling all over the place. It's a mess of people pissing all over each other to show who has the most say and the biggest stake. I need you, someone who understands what's been happening from the beginning—from before Landry Kim was murdered—to be the go-between. Coordinate with all of them. Make sure that, between all the posturing, there isn't a gap someone's going to crawl through again."

Holden understood exactly what the man meant. He'd seen it coming to a head before the band's scheduled break in the tour. After Fiadh had been hurt and Garner Security's men had come back on board along with Reinard's team, it had been a nightmare of who was doing what. No coach guiding the entire mess of men and women on the field who all had egos the size of the Washington Monument. Former military, former police, people who all thought they knew what they were talking about and wanted things their way. As Secret Service, he'd been able to play the trump card multiple times, but he wouldn't have that anymore. In fact, he'd have to negotiate with the USSS and each of the security teams to try and figure it all out.

His mind leaped into overdrive. Plans and schedules. Meetings filling in the empty spaces. It would keep him close to Leya. It would give him a purpose. It would give him money to pay his mortgage.

"Let me think about it," he told Reinard, but he was pretty sure the other man knew he was going to take it.

"I'll send you a contract. Look it over, and if something doesn't add up, I'm willing to negotiate. The Daisies need this. I'll be damned if another one of those women gets hurt on my watch."

The man turned and headed down the street.

Holden threw the bags in, climbed into his car, and by the time he turned the ignition over and looked out the rearview window, the white-haired man was gone. He'd literally disappeared. But everything about Reinard and what he'd said made the back of his neck itch. He needed to know more about all of them. Reinard. Carter. The *Cavalieri d'Oro*.

He'd let all of it whirl around in his brain while he drove to Tennessee. But first, he had another stop to make, and he wasn't sure they'd let him in.

♫ ♫ ♫

It was Marv who walked him up the staircase to the family den at the vice president's residence. The man still had a cut on his cheek from the accident in Roanoke, but he was at least on duty again. Even if Holden hadn't chosen Leya over the Secret Service, it was unlikely he would have been accepted back with his injured arm.

But it didn't stab at him as much as it had when he'd woken up this morning.

He had the possibility of a job.

He had Leya.

Now, he just had to convince her mother he was the best thing for her daughter.

When he walked into the family den, Zaira was on a floral couch, teacup in hand and an eighteenth-century tea service in front of her. She looked over the rim at him with dark eyes. Ones that reminded him of Leya. Thick lashes, thick brows, and a fire in them.

"Thank you for seeing me," he said, stepping into the room.

She put her cup down, dragging her eyes over the suit he'd worn for just this purpose.

He set the gift bag down next to her and then stepped back.

She raised a brow. "What's this?"

He shrugged, and she was curious enough to open it, pulling out a beautiful golden statue of a woman with ten arms, hands full of weapons, riding on the back of a lion.

"Do you even know who this is, Special Agent Kent?" she asked.

"It's just Holden, as I no longer work for the Secret Service. And yes. It's the goddess Durga. She represents protection, strength, and motherhood, but also destruction."

"And you thought this was appropriate for me?" Her lips twitched.

"I see her as Leya. My destruction, and yet I cannot stop worshipping at her feet because she's also my creation. I also know the goddess comes from Mahadevi, who like you, is the female center of the family."

"Many would say it's bad taste to gift her to others, but I don't suppose you knew that," Zaira said, and Holden's gut turned.

Had he made everything worse? But then, she waved him into a wingback chair near her, and relief coasted through him.

"Do you know what *vakdaanam* is?" she asked. He shook his head, and she explained. "It's where the groom-to-be sends two elders to the bride's father to ask for her hand. It is part of a traditional wedding ceremony. You had a *vakdaanam* of sorts appear on your behalf today."

"Excuse me?"

"Your parents came to see me."

His breath caught. "I didn't ask them to."

She hmm'd.

"And what did they have to say on my behalf?"

"Nothing…and yet everything. Nothing that changed my mind. I told them it was up to you to do that, and now here you are, giving me Durga. Interesting, no?"

He could see the doubts whirling in her brain. "I can promise you I didn't know they were coming. This"—he waved at the little statue—"had nothing to do with them."

She seemed to consider his words for a moment before moving on. "Neither Ved's family nor my father were very traditional. Our grandparents had all done their best to assimilate into America, and our families had lost many of our traditions. It was my mother who brought them back to us, and I promised her I would not lose them again."

"Leya told me something similar. She's told me a lot about *Nani*," he added.

"From the moment my daughter came into this world, Maa understood her better than I did. They had a very special bond." Zaira looked away from him for a moment, something akin to sadness crossing the second lady's face. When she turned back to him, it was gone. "My point is, my family is not ready to give up what we've fought to gain in order to fit into anyone's expectations."

He swallowed back his immediate reaction. "While I don't understand all your traditions, it doesn't mean I don't want to or that I'd ask Leya to give them up or expect her to change."

"But you already have."

His eyes widened, body stiffening.

"You are the reason she turned Krish away, are you not? Broke an agreement that had been in our family for ten years."

He shook his head. "No. I was nothing to her then."

She hmm'd again.

"Regardless of how it came about, your daughter and I love each other. Would you have her throw away her happiness…love…because I'm not the person you expected for her?"

She surprised him by laughing. "I know my daughter better than she thinks I do. She is nothing but stubborn, Spec—Holden. If I tell her I do not approve, she will only do everything in her power to insist I do. If I ask her to give you up, she'll dig in her heels and hold on stronger."

"I love that about her. Her determination. Her loyalty. Her utter commitment to the things and people she believes in."

"Whereas you seem to have problems following through on your vows."

It hurt…and yet it was fair. He looked her in the eye and said with as much strength as he could, "If you think walking away from my oath was easy, you know nothing about me."

"Exactly. I know nothing about you."

"For twenty-two years, I saw my future one way. Designed every event, every goal, every task to make sure it happened. And then Leya walked in and wiped it all away. Refashioned my world before I'd even realized it."

"And in another twenty-two years, will something—someone else—make you decide Leya is no longer the focus of your life?"

"No."

"How can you be so certain?"

"Because I have faith in what your daughter has taught me. That *jeevansathi* means we've been tied together across multiple lifetimes and will be together in the next."

A knock on the door revealed her new assistant, a man in his early twenties. "The reporter is here, ma'am."

Zaira rose, and Holden did as well. "My mother would have loved to hear you say that. She would have been tickled to death by you thrusting that word at me with your chin raised and fire in your eyes."

Holden's gut churned because he wasn't sure anything had come of this conversation, except for him feeling like he was swimming in a sea he didn't understand. His resolve to fix things with her parents before going to Leya wasn't going as he'd hoped.

At the door, she turned back. "My daughter has given you her heart, Holden. Don't disappoint me by breaking it."

She disappeared, and relief washed through him.

It wasn't exactly acceptance, but it was a command. One he'd gladly follow.

# Chapter Thirty-six

## *Leya*

***LAVENDER HAZE***

*Performed by Taylor Swift*

*It had been three days since* she'd left Holden at the airport in Scottsboro, but it seemed like it had been twenty. Even with her friends distracting her, Leya felt restless and achy. It was as if she was missing an organ…a piece of her that she needed to breathe.

Every day since she'd arrived, she'd spent her mornings drawing out on the boulder she thought of as hers and Holden's. Then, she spent the afternoons with Paisley, working out lyrics to go with the rhythms Lita Rae had discovered on a country station in an old truck.

The pickup sat at the ranch with its back window boarded and bullet holes in the tailgate after the sheriff brought it back from the crime lab. It was a harsh reminder of what had happened and symbolic of what Leya had done to Holden's life. She'd crashed it. Wrecked it. Shot it all to hell. And while he was out there trying to piece it back together, she was in hiding again.

She felt like a coward. She'd evaded the media, leaving it to her parents and the Secret Service. She'd even avoided her parents for the most part, taking calls here and there but mostly trying to forget everything that had happened. Everything but Holden.

Him…she was waiting for.

He'd handed in his badge the day before, and she'd sensed his heartache through the phone. His job had been more than just a paycheck. It was who he was. Honor and trust. Service. Try as she may, she couldn't shake the worry that someday he'd become embittered at having given it up for her. And the longer she went without him at her side, the worse it got.

Festering. Growing.

She needed to touch him. To feel him up against her so the threads binding them drew tauter instead of looser.

And then, her mother called.

"Your boyfriend was here, *beta*."

Her breath caught. "Holden came to see you?"

"Yes. And before that, his parents."

Leya didn't know what to say. Confusion swarmed. "What did they all want?"

"His parents? To insist on the honor and good intentions of a man who broke his oath."

"Mom—"

"And then he came to reclaim it. His honor, I mean."

"He is honorable, Mom. One of the most honorable men I know."

Her mother hmm'd before saying, "We've kept it out of the press as much as we can. Neither the Secret Service nor our family wants the world to know one of their agents was sleeping with his protectee."

"Mom! We didn't… He wouldn't…" Leya trailed off, her cheeks warm, the blush going down her neck and into her stomach.

Her mother snorted. "Interesting. Even your father and I didn't wait."

Leya made a choking sound. "Too much information. Way too much."

Her mother chuckled but didn't offer anything more. Leya's heart was tight as she played with the strands of bracelets up and down her arm. When she finally couldn't stand the silence, she asked, "What did you say to him?"

"I told him not to break your heart, of course."

Leya's soul leaped, a wave of relief coasting over her and a weight lifting from her shoulders, tears hitting her eyes. She choked out, "I know I disappointed you—"

"Just because we do not always understand each other or agree doesn't mean you've disappointed me, *beta*."

"I threw away our tradition, and…" Leya's heart stopped and started again before she breathed out the rest. "I will never change the world or save someone like you, and Rishik, and Dad."

"Is this truly what you think?" Her mother sounded surprised. It was Leya's turn to stay quiet, and it was her mom who spoke again. "Have I ever told you that when I was a young girl, I wanted to be one of The Runaways?"

Leya made a noise of disbelief, and her mother laughed.

"A so-called friend told me not to be ridiculous, that a person like me could never be a rock star. And after that, everywhere I looked—television, magazines, movies, music—there was no one like me. It made me feel less for so long. It's the rare little girl who wants to be a neurosurgeon, Leya, but there are millions who want to be a rock star. And now, when they open a magazine or walk into a store, there you are, proving to them that they can be. Proving we aren't less. That we belong. It's important work."

Leya's throat closed, emotions filling it, and she thought she heard her mother sniffle on the other end. A rarity. Zaira Singh did not cry.

"Now, see what you've done," her mom said. "Made me smudge my mascara, and I have a reporter coming in five minutes. I need to go touch up my makeup."

"I love you, Mom."

"I love you too."

♫ ♫ ♫

After dinner in the restaurant at the ranch, Sadie convinced Fee to go line dancing at her uncle's bar, and once Fee decided to go, she wheedled and cajoled until they'd all been dragged into it. Dancing was the last thing Leya felt like. She hadn't heard from Holden since that morning, and even though her mother had said she'd seen him, basically told him it was okay for them to be together, she needed to hear it from Holden's mouth. She'd sent a few texts that had gone unanswered, and now she was getting worried all over again.

Leya waited until everyone but Nikki had piled into the SUVs, and then she pulled her friend aside, knowing she'd be the least likely to insist she go. Nikki respected everyone's privacy. Her life, of any of the band's, had been kept out of the spotlight the most.

"I'm going to stay here," Leya told her.

To her surprise, Nikki wrapped an arm through hers and shook her head. "No, Ley, we need this. Us together, letting off some steam. We haven't been able to do that in a long time. The after-parties on the tour are full of VIPs, and we're exhausted from being onstage. Whenever we have time to ourselves, Paisley is off with Jonas, and now Fee up and got married and is a stepmom, to boot. As soon as your man arrives, you're going to be lost to us for weeks. Tonight, we need to celebrate you being okay. Celebrate all of us being alive and together. Life is so short…" Nikki's voice cracked. "Even before all the shit that's happened to us, I knew that. Look at what happened to my dad. He left the house with a smile one morning and never came back—some random holdup at a gas station…" She paused to get a hold of herself. "We need this."

It was the fact that Nikki was emotional, when it was as rare as Leya's mom showing it, as much as her little speech that had Leya moving toward the vehicle. Calm and steady had always been Nikki's way. Logical to a fault, she'd been a stabilizing force whenever things got tilted too far off center.

Nikki squeezed Leya's hand.

They drove into the quaint downtown where the lights, fashioned to look like old gas lanterns, cast a warm glow onto the brick buildings and cobblestone streets. Their security team hated when they went to a bar almost as much as the USSS did, especially when they hadn't had a chance to send an advance team to check out the location, but Leya had a feeling the local joint would be decidedly easier to secure than EchoBar.

McFlannigan's was an Irish pub, reflecting an old-world elegance. The back of the bar was delightfully full of stained glass, beveled mirrors, aged wood, and carved pillars. The lighting was dim, barely shining on the crystal decanters on the shelves, but it still felt rich and luxurious.

Tonight, the bar had been retrofitted to resemble a country barn. Hay had been scattered around the dark mahogany tables and green leather booths. Only the space cleared for dancing had been left bare of the straw.

Their security detail spread out around the room and near the exits as Leya and her bandmates moved toward a large booth in the corner that Sadie had grabbed and shoved another table into. There were enough seats for all the Daisies plus Jonas and Asher and a third man who'd joined them. Unfortunately, it wasn't the one Leya was desperately waiting for.

Adria's feet came to a halt next to Leya as she groused, "*Dios*! What's the Hollywood Player Prince doing here? He wasn't supposed to be back until we were on tour again."

"He's Asher's best friend, Ads," Fee said with an apologetic smile. "I'm afraid Ronan's here for us."

"Well, then, I'm going to need something much stronger than beer," Adria said, stomping off to the bar.

A band was up onstage, warming up, the twang of the country music already filling the air as the group crowded around the tables. Ronan's gaze shot to Adria at the bar, and a look came over his face—annoyance mingled with something else Leya couldn't place. She thought it might have been remorse, and she wondered, for the millionth time, what had gone on between the two that had caused Adria to hate him so much. It hadn't been that way until after The Red Guitar tour was over. Before that, they'd been full of snark and flirtation, like Ronan was with everyone of the female persuasion.

"Who's been line dancing before?" Sadie asked, drawing Leya's attention from Ronan and his puzzling relationship with her friend.

Only Fee raised her hand.

"Okay, everyone onto the floor. I'll give you a quick lesson, but I promise it's easy."

The men declined, happily sipping their beers while watching the band and Sadie on the dance floor. As she walked them through a series of steps, their little group was joined by some of the locals who Sadie harassed and tormented in the friendliest kind of way.

Pretty soon, the music started in earnest, and they were clapping and stomping and twirling around on the floor. Every time they made a mistake, they'd run into one another, laughing. Fee was glowing, shooting eyes in Asher's direction where his gaze was hooded and dark. Paisley kept dancing back and forth to the table until she'd finally convinced Jonas to join them. He towered over her friend but seemed happy to have his hands joined with hers as they moved together.

Leya's heart ached. She wanted that. She wanted Holden looking at her with his heated gaze and fingers that couldn't stray far from hers. Where was he? Why hadn't he answered her last text? It was nearly midnight, and something akin to panic ran through her veins.

And that was when she saw him, moving through the crowd of locals, one arm still in the sling that held it up tight against his body, good hand shoved into the pocket of his snug jeans. He was wearing Miles Green's cowboy hat and the boots that they'd bought together, and those, as much as his wall of muscles that were on display in the light-blue Henley clinging to him, made her body hum.

He stopped at the edge of the dance floor, watching her with the somber look Special Agent Kent had always sent her way and not the soft look Holden had given her while they'd been tucked away at the ranch. But then, he smiled. The most relaxed, beautiful, handsome smile she'd ever seen on his face—or maybe just because it had felt like months since she'd seen it last. Regardless, it was directed at her—belonged only to her.

Her steps faltered for a moment, and then she was running toward him.

His good arm caught her, swinging her around just as his mouth found hers. The kiss was thunder. Full of the aftershock of a lightning strike. Heady and warm. Strong and vibrant. Flickering as the electricity built up around them. Just like storm clouds hitting the mountain, they were going to need a release soon, or they'd burst.

"You're here," she breathed against his lips.

"Did you miss me, Lita Rae?" he asked. She tapped the edge of his hat that was now askew from their kiss. His arm was still banded around her waist, holding her tight up against him, his hard body pressing into her soft curves.

"You know I did, Miles Green. Your wife doesn't like being left behind."

His smile slipped ever so slightly, blue eyes taking in every inch of her face, boring into her gaze. His voice was serious when he asked, "What about Leya Singh…how would she feel about being Holden Kent's wife?"

Her hands settled on either side of his face, stroking the stubble that was so much shorter than when she'd seen him last. She kind of liked the stubble. It blurred the straight-laced edges of him into something more.

"We're already bound. Don't you feel it?" she asked softly. He stared for a long moment before he nodded, but his jaw ticked, as if he was upset she hadn't responded to his actual question. "Yes, Holden, I'd be honored to marry you."

"You're sure?" he asked, deep and guttural, as if he was giving her one last out.

"I don't know how you can doubt me."

"Even though I have nothing to offer you now?"

"You have everything to offer me. A lifetime of love. An infinity of time together."

He inhaled sharply, kissing her furiously, as if those simple words had been said in front of the fire, taking the seven circles and sealing their fates together.

Holden lifted his head and smiled as his hand at her back pushed her tighter against him. "What do you say we go home, Lita Rae?"

He removed his hat and placed it on her head. It slipped low over her eyes, and she had to shove it back up to see him.

"By home, I hope you mean our little love nest above the barn at the ranch because I don't think I'll make it all the way back to D.C. before I combust."

He chuckled, tapped the brim of the hat, and then tangled his hand with hers, heading for the exit where West and her other USSS agents had settled. Leya looked back at her friends on the dance floor. Fee winked, Paisley waived, and even Nikki smiled a wide, knowing smile.

They slipped out into the night with Holden scanning the street just like the agents in front of them did, but the street was completely quiet. She said a silent prayer of thanks, hoping it would remain quiet for all of them—for all the Daisies. The only response was a burst of laughter from the open door of the bar.

She shivered. The cool air was such a contrast from the heat inside, and she leaned into Holden for warmth. He squeezed her tight before opening the door of an old muscle car painted a vibrant blue that sparkled in the streetlights.

"Is this yours?" she asked.

He nodded as she climbed in.

"I think Miles would like this car."

He kissed her fingertips before shutting the door and jogging around the back to the driver's side. Once he'd started the engine, he waited for her detail to bring around their vehicle before shifting out onto the street and heading back toward the ranch. There was no moon tonight, but the stars were bright and sparkling as she glanced out into the fields running alongside the empty road to the Hatleys'.

The scene outside the vehicle was quiet, but inside was loud. Her heart was thudding fast, and her body ached, hungry for more kisses. More touches. Just more. She glanced at Holden, his face doused in bluish haze and shadows from the dash lights, and itched to draw him again, like this. Relaxed and with the natural aura around him enhanced by the car lights.

"I've been offered a job," Holden said, breaking the silence.

It took a second for his words to hit home, and when they did, her stomach fell. She was a mix of happiness and wariness. Where would he go? How could she stand being apart from him for days…weeks…months at a time? The last three days had been torture. Now that she'd found her soulmate, she didn't want to be away from him ever again.

"This is good, right?" she said, trying to hide the uncertainty shifting through her.

"To be honest, I wasn't sure I'd ever find a job again. I thought I'd have to sell my condo and…I don't know…go with my tail between my legs to beg my granddad to hire me at the apple orchard."

She breathed in sharply at the pain in his words over losing his career. Losing a piece of him.

"I'm sor—"

He shook his head and cut her off. "No. Don't say it. I've already told you. I'm not sorry, and you shouldn't be either. This…" He looked between her and him, trying to lift his arm that was in the sling and then grimacing with frustration. "This between us is everything, Leya. The rest…it's just a way to pass the time until we're alone again." She didn't respond, and a soft smile hit his lips. "Reinard offered me a job."

Her eyes widened as she listened to what Reinard wanted him to do. Basically, captain the team. It made her smile because he was going to be the leader, the Captain Avenger the band already saw him as—the person guiding them to safety.

The ranch came into view, and he pushed a code in at the gates, waiting as they swung open before driving through and winding down the tree-lined drive to the buildings. Holden flipped around and backed in beside the bullet-ridden truck. He stared at it for a moment before jogging around the car and opening the door for her.

"It pisses me off that this classic got shot up."

"Miles is cursing the gods," Leya said, twining her fingers into his good hand as they walked toward the stairs leading to the room over the barn.

Special Agent West joined them at the foot of it. "You're in for the night?" Her question was addressed to Leya, ignoring Holden, and Leya saw his jaw tighten.

She nodded, feeling both Holden's and West's eyes on her as she mounted the stairs in front of him, anger brewing inside her at the slight sent his way. As soon as they were inside with the door locked, she tossed the hat aside and put her arms around his neck.

"Is that how they all treated you?" she asked quietly, scanning his face for clues on his emotions.

His shoulder barely shrugged.

"That's rid—"

He cut her off with his mouth on hers, hard and soft all at the same time, and her body reacted, arching into his. His tongue danced along the seam of her lips, and she opened, letting him in, savoring the taste and smell and feel of him. A wild chorus of notes and lines filled her, merging with black-and-white ink and stunning colors.

He pulled back slightly, the pale blue of his eyes almost invisible in the dark of the room, as he took in all the pieces of her she'd never shown anyone before.

"It doesn't matter, Leya…what they say, or do, or how they act…because I get to do that. I get to kiss you and touch you and hold your hand. Stop apologizing. You think I've stepped away from the Secret Service for you, but it's not just for you. It's for me also. I get to have a life now where you're always at my side. Not just for an assignment. Not just for a few years or until I'm too old to meet the fitness requirements, and they stick me at a desk or toss me out of the service altogether. I get to do this…" His hand ran along her arm, up her collarbone, and cupped the back of her neck, drawing her face to his and gently kissing her. "Until I die. It may not be the life I had planned, but it doesn't mean I've traded down…that my life will be somehow less. Quite the opposite. It's going to be so much more than the one I'd ever envisioned. I didn't know it could be this way because I didn't know what love was. I didn't know I could be this person…the one I am at your side. So much more than the lonely man with the badge I'd become."

His words eased the stranglehold that doubt and worry had locked around her heart. She went up onto her tiptoes and returned his kiss, but instead of being gentle, it was demanding. Insistent. Pushing when she rarely pushed. Strong when she often felt weak.

Her body melted, a heavy, coiled feeling growing inside her belly.

Hot and greedy.

Hungry.

She'd waited too long for this time with him. Regardless of the vows said or unsaid, they were tied together forever. And at this moment, she didn't want to wait any longer to be twined with him. She wanted him inside her, taking the last step to seal their fates once and for all.

# Chapter Thirty-seven

## Holden

***RUNAWAY***

*Performed by The Corrs*

When Leya broke their heated kiss in the darkened room above the barn, Holden groaned. He wasn't anywhere near being done with her tonight. She stepped back, a knowing smile twisting up her full, pink lips as she pulled her top over her head. His body had already been tight and hungry, and the sight of her in nothing but a bra wound it up another notch. When he reached for her, she smiled wider and moved farther away. She tugged off her boots before sliding the zipper of her jean skirt down. The damn thing had tormented him from the time he'd seen her long legs in it at the bar. The denim fell to the floor, and his heart banged wildly in his chest as he took her in. She wore black lace, much sexier than the simple cotton she'd bought at the box store, but in some ways, he missed it. Just like he missed the simplicity of Lita Rae and Miles. He and Leya would never be that uncomplicated.

But maybe that was what made them better. Made it all worth more. The hurdles they still faced would make them stronger. He moved, hand landing on her waist, fingers stroking over the soft curve, and watching as goosebumps broke out over her entire body.

He wished he had use of both hands. Wished he could lift her up and stride with her into the bedroom like he had when they'd arrived at the ranch and the rain had thundered over them while lightning zipped between them.

"Make love to me, Holden," she said softly.

His hand dropped to hers, twining their fingers and leading her into the bedroom. He lost his boots, his shirt, his jeans, and then sat on the edge of the bed, pulling her onto him. She straddled his hips, cores aligning, the hard length of him pressing into the lace hiding the wet heat he'd thought about the entire drive from D.C.

He kissed her, open-mouthed, tongue finding hers, licking at the inner recesses, stroking and igniting. She met each movement with her own, more confident than she'd been when they'd first started kissing. Knowing just what he liked…what she liked. They'd spent a handful of days locked like this, tongues and fingers finding pleasure. He'd reveled in the memories, but the reality was better.

Her hips rocked into his, making his dick swell to an almost painful level. Hard. Aching. Needy. He flicked open her bra, tossing it aside, and lost himself in her breasts. The nipples pebbled, turning into sharp peaks at his touch, and she let out a delightful little moan that ricocheted through him.

He gripped her waist with his arm and flipped them over. He dragged her underwear down and tossed them aside before settling his hips between her thighs. He pressed her into the mattress with his weight, loving the feel of her below him. Soft to his hard. Gentle to his rough.

The sweet scent of her surrounded him, drowning him with a need he was no longer prepared to stop. His fingers found her core, stroking, curling, plunging, and she broke away from his mouth with a sexy little gasp. "More, Holden. I need more."

It burned through him, turning up the fire flaming through him.

"Come for me first, Leya," he demanded, circling his fingers one more time and watching with pleasure as she shattered. He continued moving until he'd ridden out every last quake of her body. Then, he rolled off her, pulled a condom from the pocket of his jeans, tore it open, and rolled it on while she stared at him.

"Everything about you is so beautiful," she said in a voice loaded with lust. "Hard lines I ache to draw every time I see them."

He settled back between her thighs, brushing away tendrils that had fallen over her cheek. "You paint me like this, darlin', and your parents will never let me through the door again."

She laughed. "Think of the scandal… *'Vice president's daughter paints a nude portrait of her former Secret Service agent.'*"

Only the joy in her voice allowed the stinging reality of her words to not hit him. He'd told her the truth before. This life he was now forging from the ashes of his old one…it was better than anything he'd ever imagined for himself. But he knew enough to grieve the loss of the old one. Grieve it so he could let it go completely and be a hundred percent present in this one with her.

He kissed her, sucking her lower lip into his mouth, nibbling, and then sliding his tongue down her neck to the tender spot at the corner of her jaw and ear. She shivered again when he kissed her there. He moved down, massaging a beautiful breast with a hand while his tongue devoured the other before returning to her mouth, staring into her dark eyes as his hips hovered at her entrance.

"You're certain?" he asked.

She thrust upward. "Now, Holden."

"It's going to hurt at first," he said softly.

Her lips twitched. "I know."

He couldn't help smiling back at her as he pushed inside, hitting her barrier, slowing his movements, and waiting for her to adjust to him. Jesus…she felt good. Tight and hot and all his. He could stay here forever, just like this, and be happy. Her eyes fluttered shut, and then she moved again, opening her lids and leaning up to take his mouth with hers.

He moved farther inside. She gasped, clutched his good shoulder, and then wrapped her legs around his hips, angling so he was forced deeper until he bottomed out, and she let out the sweetest sigh he'd ever heard. Pure joy. Happiness.

He slid out and back in, her wet heat coating them both, making him want to lose himself already. He kissed her furiously before burying his head in the crook of her neck, increasing his pace, unable to slow back down, unable to wait any longer for the pleasure at the end. She moaned at the same time he did. A beautiful sound that filled the room with a heady combination. They found a rhythm, the silence of the room only broken by the carnal sounds of skin on skin, bodies joined and tangled, moving together toward tantalizing heights.

"Leya—" he grunted, not wanting to come before she did.

"So close, Holden. Yes…yes…there."

He reached down, sliding his finger over her again as he pushed into her, and she crested, body convulsing in beautiful waves that sent him over the top as well. The dam broke, and a golden light burst around them as he thrust into her one last time. Joy he'd never experienced before filled him. Complete and utter peace. The lights people said they experienced at death were nothing compared to this. Instead of death, it brought him salvation.

When the dark of the room pushed at the golden hue, bringing him back to Earth, he rolled to his side, bringing her with him. His good arm was latched around her waist, his legs tangled with hers to ensure she didn't escape. He kissed her forehead and looked down to see her smiling with her eyes closed. She was happy, and he vowed to keep her this way forever.

"Are you okay?" he asked.

Her lids slowly flickered open, meeting his gaze, smile growing even wider. "Perfect. I don't think I could be any more perfect than at this moment. Are you okay?"

He chuckled. "I think I died there for a moment. Pearly gates and all."

Her laughter rang out through the room, filling in the dark spaces with more light.

"I saw colors, Leya."

Her smile disappeared, face turning serious. "Yeah? What color did you see?"

"It was all around you. Gold. Like the haze of a sunset reflecting against glass or a pond. You're gold."

"Aqua and gold…they're good together."

"We're good together." His voice was deep and guttural, the truth of it in every syllable.

She nodded, resting her head on his chest.

They fell asleep that way. Tangled together. Invisible threads wrapping around them, knots twisting and tightening in a beautiful way. A way he'd never regret because it meant she'd never be far from him again.

♫ ♫ ♫

When Holden woke, he was alone, and his heart banged to a start. He jumped up and slid into his jeans from last night. Bare-chested and bare-footed, he made his way into the main room. The door was open, and she was out on the balcony in his Henley and her cowboy boots, leaning against the rail, face turned toward the sunrise, eyes closed. She was bathed in gold again.

He eased out behind her, legs going wide so her rear was settled against his already hardening body. His eyes scanned the view in front of them. The cabins to the right were quiet. The main house was out of sight to the left. The only soul they could see was the silent, dark-suited man at the foot of the stairs, his mirrored glasses reflecting the sun as it burst over the trees, flooding the sky with vivid color.

He kissed her by the ear, and she sighed softly, and it lodged in his chest as a memory he'd never forget.

"What colors do you see this morning?" he asked.

She pointed at the sky and clouds and said, "Magenta and rose and carnation blending into honey and tangerine and ginger."

He thought maybe he could see a faint distinction between the pinks and oranges and wondered if someday he'd see them all because she'd showed them to him.

"Sounds like the perfect combination to start your birthday."

She turned slightly, lips finding his in a soft, tender kiss. "I shouldn't be surprised you remembered. You know everything about me."

"Not everything… I like to think there are some mysteries I have left to explore."

"Would you be bored if there weren't?"

"Bored is not an adjective I will ever be able to associate with you, darlin'. Miles is going to have his hands full meeting all your needs."

Her lips quirked upward, and a stunning smile took over her face as she teased, "It's a rough job, but someone has to do it."

He growled, eyes narrowing as his gaze slid over her body before saying, "I'll take an oath to do it well. I hereby promise to uphold and defend the body and soul of one Leya Singh against all enemies, and that I will bear true faith and allegiance to the same. I take this obligation freely, without any mental reservations or purpose of evasion. I will well and faithfully discharge—"

"Shut up and kiss me," she said breathlessly.

"As you command, my lady." And he did.

He kissed her like he would for the rest of his life. With heart and soul and a vow to keep her happy and loved and glowing. Just like she was now, with all the colors he couldn't see and all the colors she could washing over them.

# Epilogue

## *Leya*

***SUPER LOVE***
*Performed by Dami Im*

*THIRTEEN MONTHS AFTER*

The park along the Hudson River in New York City was packed as the sun faded along the skyline. Traditional Indian music weaved through the trees and the booths lining the shoreline. The smell of curry and a sweet hint of cardamom was heavy in the air. The mood was light and expectant amongst the thousands of people enjoying the celebration. Laughter broke out, drawing her eyes to a man and a woman trying to straighten the braids on a little Indian girl. She had on a delicate pink-and-blue sari that made her warm-brown skin stand out. She was a beautiful little thing.

Leya slid her hand over the deep-orange sari she wore. Her hand and eyes slowed over her flat stomach before continuing down her hips. When she glanced back up to where Holden had disappeared into the crowd, searching out the *kaju katli* she'd asked for, her eyes found Special Agent West first. The woman looked out of place in her dark suit, just like the rest of Leya's detail. She'd almost declined Secret Service protection recently, no longer feeling the need for them, not when everything had finally come to a head with The Painted Daisies. Not when they'd found Landry's murderer, and nothing was hanging over them anymore. But now… Her hand slid down her body again. Now, she felt protective in a different way.

Holden's dark-blond head showed up above the crowd, and his eyes landed on her as soon as he broke through, finding her and assessing her as he always had. Her pulse picked up, stomach tightening in swirls of pleasure. He looked handsome, if slightly unlike himself, in loose linen pants and shirt. It wasn't quite the traditional sherwani and fitted pants he'd worn for their wedding this summer, but it was something in between. A blending of his heritage and hers…a way to honor her and her traditions.

He strode over to her, that confident presence swirling around him, causing people to move out of his way without even knowing it. In his hand, he had a plate with the star-shaped treat. Her mouth watered at the thought of it. Of him.

When he reached her, she was already on her toes, and her mouth landed on his in a kiss that was far from sweet. It was intense. Hot. Full of the love and passion they'd spent the last year exploring.

He stepped back, eyes twinkling. "Is it me or the *kaju katli* you're really happy to see?"

"Can't it be both?"

He laughed. He did so much more of that these days. The somberness would always be a part of him, but the smile came more readily to his lips, especially when they were alone together.

They turned to the water, sharing the treat, fingers covered in powdered sugar they licked from their hands in a decidedly un-PG way. A display someone would probably capture and post on social media with the hashtag #leyas-swoony-husband if anyone recognized her. But maybe with the dark kohl on her eyes, and the henna down her arms, and her hair tucked away, they wouldn't see Leya

Singh of The Painted Daisies, but just an Indian woman celebrating Diwali with her husband.

"We're going to be late to the boat if we don't head out now," he said, even though he made no effort to move away from the railing.

Her parents had chartered a boat so they could watch the thousands of candles being lit along the shore before the fireworks were set off over the harbor. The *diyas* were used to celebrate the victory of light over darkness, good over evil, and Leya felt it was even more symbolic after the year they'd had. The final black cloud that had hung over the Daisies was gone.

"Before we join my parents, I wanted to talk to you about something," she said.

His gaze narrowed, taking her in again. "What's wrong?"

She shook her head, barely containing her smile. "Nothing."

"Leya," he grunted, knowing her too well, knowing something was eating at her. But this was all good. At least…she hoped he'd think so. They hadn't talked about this in a long time—since before the wedding.

"Truly, nothing is wrong, Holden. I have some really—"

"I'm so sorry to interrupt," a man said. West was at their side in a heartbeat, putting herself between Leya and the stranger. It was the father with the little girl in the pink-and-blue sari. His eyes grew wide as West's hand settled on the butt of her Glock. He pushed his child behind him. "I'm truly— She just wanted…"

The little girl peeked from behind him. "Can I have a picture with you?" she asked.

Leya smiled, waved off West, and then squatted down. "I'd love one. You look beautiful today."

The little girl blushed as she took a hesitant step forward. "You're my favorite Daisy. It isn't just because you're Indian like me. It's because you're the prettiest and because you draw like I do."

Leya had finally allowed Lincoln to display her art in his studio after they'd had a long talk about everything that had happened with FGT, the paintings, and his press conference. He'd insisted he hadn't meant he loved her in a romantic sort of way, but she wasn't sure she believed him. There was a sadness in his eyes whenever he saw her with Holden that made her heart hurt for him. She wished she could use Aja Aunty and her biodata sheets to find someone as perfect for her friend as Holden was for her.

"What do you like to draw?" Leya asked.

"Flowers. Lots and lots of flowers."

"Maybe you can send me one?" she suggested, and the girl's face broke into a huge smile, her brown eyes lighting up.

The girl's mother held up her phone, and Leya pulled the child close, cheek to cheek, while photos were taken. The girl skipped over to her mom and waved goodbye to Leya as the dad said, "Thank you. I'm sorry to have interrupted your day."

Leya watched the little family unit meld into the crowd.

"We're due at the docks," West said.

Leya nodded. "Give us five minutes."

West walked away a few feet, finger to her ear, talking into her mic.

Leya turned back to Holden. "I probably should have found a better time to tell you this. But I just found out for sure yesterday, and I don't want to wait."

Holden's brows drew together. She took his hand and laid it over her stomach, setting hers on top. "I'm pregnant."

His eyes widened and then closed, fingers flexing and tightening over the sari. Then, he moved, grabbed her by the waist, and spun her around. His right arm was weaker, as it always was these days, even though it was stronger than it had been. He may never get the full strength back, but it was still much better than what the doctors had thought it would be.

He'd barely set her down when his mouth found hers, kissing her as if there was no one around. As if the earth and the sun and the moon were the only things looking down on them.

"You're glad, then?" she asked, breaking their kiss to gaze up at his smiling face, which caused a return smile to fill hers.

"So happy my heart feels like it might break free of my chest."

"We said we were going to wait."

"I didn't want to pressure you. You have plans and goals and an entire life that isn't about being a mom. I trusted you to know when it was the right time."

"Apparently, that's now."

He laughed. "Apparently."

She turned serious. "It's a lot…adding a baby to our already wild lifestyle."

"Just one more little daisy to add to the band. It might change how things are done, change who you are a bit, but it won't stop you from making music with your friends."

Her heart pattered a strong and scattered beat. He always knew what to say to make her feel better. But he also always told her the truth. This would change everything, and yet it would change nothing. After all, they were already tied together in every way possible. By man. By the gods. By the weaves of time and space.

Just Leya and her *jeevansathi*.

♫ ♫ ♫

I hope you loved Leya and Holden's bodyguard, on-the-run story as much as I did. If you missed the bonus material, ***SWAN RIVER***, that showed what was going on with each of the Daisies the night Landry died you can get that here:

***https://BookHip.com/NQWSQLF***

But if you're ready for the clues in Landry's murder to continue while you find out just why Adria dislikes Ronan so intensely, keep reading for a first look at book four in the series, ***BLUE MARGUERITE***.

***She'll never forgive him for humiliating her. Not even when he offers answers her family desperately seeks.***

# The Painted Daisies – Book Four

# Blue Marguerite – Sample

## PROLOGUE

# *Adria*

### ***WOULD'VE, COULD'VE, SHOULD'VE***

*Performed by Taylor Swift*

*SEVEN YEARS BEFORE*
MOVIE SET
BURBANK, CALIFORNIA

*RONAN: What the hell have you done to me? Every look you sent my way today had me ready to go off like a pubescent teen.*

*ADRIA: Looks? You're accusing me? What about that whole finger stroll down my neck?*

*RONAN: I had two minutes before my dad called action again, and I had to touch you.*

*ADRIA: You can't say things like that.*

*RONAN: Get over here, Adria. Get to the hotel before we both spontaneously combust without ever being twined together.*

Twelve hours later.

*RONAN: I woke and you were gone.*

*ADRIA: We have one last day in the studio. I couldn't be late.*

*RONAN: We need to talk.*

*ADRIA: We already agreed this was a one-time thing. We have lives that will never touch again.*

*RONAN: No one should lose their virginity in a one-night stand, Star. No one.*

*ADRIA: This is why I didn't tell you. You wouldn't have had sex with me, and we both would have combusted—your words. But that's all it was, Hollywood—sex.*

*RONAN: Liar.*

*FOUR YEARS BEFORE*
BURBANK, CALIFORNIA

*RONAN: Meet me at my place? Seven o'clock?*

*ADRIA: No.*

*RONAN: I can't go another day watching you from behind my camera while you beat on those drums with your skin glistening and those hot-as-fire blue eyes calling me home. I'll lose my goddamn mind. I need to be inside you.*

*ADRIA: Don't you mean Landry? Or Fee? Or Nikki?*

*RONAN: You're jealous? If I didn't flirt with them, they'd see right through me—us—and you told me you didn't want them to know.*

*ADRIA: So, your excuse for hitting on my friends and bandmates is so you wouldn't flirt with me?*

*RONAN: Yes. I did what you asked. Now do what I ask. Show up.*

*ADRIA: I'm not sure it's a good idea.*

*RONAN: Coward.*

*ADRIA: Excuse me?*

*RONAN: You're afraid. You're afraid you'll remember what making love really feels like. I'll ruin you, just like you've already ruined me.*

*ADRIA: ***Eye roll emoji*** Hollywood's Player Prince wants me to believe the best sex of his life was with a random virgin? I'm not sure what that says about you.*

*RONAN: Making love, Star. Not sex. Sex is just bodies finding release. What we did to each other left scars. Permanent marks. Gouges in my soul only you can fill, damn it.*

Twenty minutes later.

*ADRIA: I'm at the door. Buzz me in.*

*THREE AND A HALF YEARS BEFORE*
NEW YORK CITY

*RONAN: Can you leave?*

*ADRIA: What? Why?*

*RONAN: You know why.*

*ADRIA: Landry wants to take pictures with the VMA award front and center. She plans on sending it to that dick critic who told her to give up singing and become a phone sex operator.*

*RONAN: The award is pretty amazing. But you and me, skin on skin, that's unforgettable. Stars-bursting-into-existence kind of unforgettable.*

*ADRIA: I hate when you say shit like that.*

*RONAN: Because you FEEL the words. Your body knows the truth of us.*

*ADRIA: How many women have you used that line on, Hollywood?*

*RONAN: I don't need to use lines with anyone else, Star. Only you.*

*ADRIA: I can't leave the party yet.*

*RONAN: Fine. I'll meet you in my room in thirty minutes. But I'm not sure how long I can hold off….*

Ten minutes later.

*RONAN: *** Image of Ronan's bare upper body that ends just below the divots above his hips. His muscled torso ripples, and his arm extends past the edge of the photo, hand flexed, gripping something out of sight.*

*ADRIA: You fight dirty.*

*RONAN: Fighting is the last thing I want to do. Hurry.*

*THIRTY-FOUR MONTHS BEFORE*

*RONAN: I'll be at the concert tonight, and I'd like to see you after.*

*ADRIA: You're in Washington?*

*RONAN: I was meeting with a production studio in Vancouver.*

*ADRIA: The after-party will last hours. We're celebrating the end of the tour with the crew.*

*RONAN: Get me backstage. We can duck out as soon as you think Landry won't miss you.*

*ADRIA: Lan will notice no matter when I leave.*

*RONAN: She's not your mom or your boss. I know you've missed me as much as I've missed you.*

*ADRIA: ***Eye roll emoji*** Neither of us has been lacking in companionship in the year since we've seen each other.*

*RONAN: I've told you before, and I'll tell you again, Star. Sex is sex. What we do...you know it's more.*

Fifteen minutes later.

*ADRIA: I'll leave you a backstage pass at the will-call window.*

Ten hours later, she'd barely joined him in the back seat of the SUV when Ronan's hand slid underneath the hem of her little black dress. His touch along her inner thigh was like an electric shock to her system, sending waves of hot desire through every molecule in her being.

She wasn't sure if she loved it or hated it.

What she did know was she had to stop this. It had gone on too long.

This had to be their last hookup.

She'd told herself the same thing the last time, and yet, here she was. He'd reeled her back in with a handful of swoony words.

She wasn't weak, damn it, but he made her feel that way. Needy and desperate.

Even now, when she was physically and mentally exhausted from being on the road for over a year with barely a break, he had her amped up and ready to go with a single touch. She should have gone back to the hotel and slept for a dozen days with their tour finally finished. Instead, she was here, letting him turn her body into liquid lust.

She was pretty sure Fiadh had finally caught wind that something was up between them. Adria had been able to keep whatever this was under all her friends' radars until Landry had noticed her ducking out of the VMA party. When Adria had shown up at the airport the next day with beard burn on her jaw and neck—and down below where no one could see—Landry had said, "We need him, Ads. We need him so we can keep winning awards, so don't fuck it up."

Which was exactly why she shouldn't have agreed to meet up tonight. Because Adria was most certainly going to screw it up. The over-the-top satisfying release they found together was never going to be a relationship. It couldn't be. He was the heir to Hollywood royalty, slowly making his own mark in the industry. Adria was one of six women in a band whose fame and demand were rolling downhill and picking up speed. Neither of them had time for more when they were rarely on the same side of the country.

Even if she hadn't promised herself, ages ago, that she'd never be in a relationship like her parents, spending more time apart than together, she couldn't be what Ronan really needed. Someone who wanted love and happily ever afters. Someone who fit into his family's squishy, cuddly mold that looked like a 1990s sitcom.

As Ronan's long fingers flicked against her panty line, she had to clamp her mouth shut to keep herself from letting out a breathy moan. She glared at him, darting an eye up front to the driver and her bodyguard in the passenger seat.

Ronan just smiled. His sexy smile that was plastered all over the tabloids on a regular basis. He would have made it on the covers of magazines regardless of his mom being an Academy-Award-winning actress and his dad being an Oscar-winning director. He had those timeless good looks Hollywood adored. Chiseled, square jaw. Cinnamon-burnished hair, silky and thick, with just a hint of a wave to it. Intense, stormy, gray eyes that made you feel like you were the center of their universe. A nose that plastic surgeons put on the screen for others to choose from even though his had never seen the underside of a scalpel. And below that perfect face, the corded veins of his neck led to broad shoulders and sharply cut biceps and triceps. His entire body was sculpted as if an artist had carved it out of stone, all sinewy power.

Ronan leaned in, the tip of his nose barely skimming her jawline. His warm breath sent goosebumps over her skin, and her nipples hardened. His lips lightly caressed the side of her mouth. "Hello, Star."

Yet another thing she hated and loved—the nickname he'd given her the first time they'd ended up twined together. From the moment their fingers had collided on a soundstage, she'd been flooded with a desire she'd never thought possible. She'd been sought after, pursued by boys in high school, even men around the pageant circuit she'd been on, but she'd never had her body light up for someone. Not until him.

And now, years later, it still lit up whenever he was in the same room.

She ground her teeth together, knowing those kinds of thoughts were the ones that would damn them both. She grabbed his hand, pulled it from under her dress, and set it back on his thigh. The curve of his grin pushed against her cheek.

"Shy isn't your style," he whispered.

"Neither is banging some guy in the back of a car while my detail watches," she hissed.

He pulled away slightly.

"God, I've really missed that growl."

Her heart tugged at the idea of him missing her. Of anyone missing her attitude and snark. For most of her life, it hadn't been seen as a positive. Hadn't she lost more than one beauty pageant because she didn't say what the judges wanted to hear? Hadn't her mom begged her to soften her tone?

The car stopped at a back entrance of the hotel the band and Ronan were staying at, and he alighted first, extending his hand to help her out. All gentleman. It would disappear when they were in the room. He would be masterful and commanding but hardly polite, and it made her entire core clench. He was an addiction she couldn't stop feeding even though she knew it would end up with one or both of them broken. They'd give each other just a hair too much of themselves and never be able to get it back.

In the elevator, with her bodyguard at the front, Ronan tilted his head and kissed her temple while his hand slipped up the back of her thigh, under her dress, and squeezed a cheek left bare from her thong. Her insides convulsed. She was almost ready to explode from a handful of touches.

¡Díos! She was a lost cause.

A ding announced their arrival on Ronan's floor, her bodyguard cleared the hallway, and then Ronan held the elevator door open as she exited. His eyes strolled down every inch of her, his grin growing wider and wider.

The door to his hotel room had barely clicked behind them before he slid her dress off, and she ripped his T-shirt over his head. Hands, fingers, and tongues were in a battle to find every last groove and valley that they'd been without for over a year. Hot. Wet. Needy. His pants were gone, her bra and underwear were gone, her shoes flung somewhere, and he had her on the bed, hovering over her with his lean muscles straining. His mouth trailed down her body, and every single nerve ending burned as if a stick of incense was being dragged along it.

She was gasping, panting, craving exactly where he was going and the heaven he'd bring when he was there, and then suddenly—

He was gone.

Air and space between them.

"Fuck. Hold on," he said. He stared down at her, eyes dark and heated, before wheeling around and searching in a messenger bag thrown over a chair. She lifted herself on her elbows, breath uneven. Desperate longing beat through her veins as she waited for him to come back with a condom.

When he turned around, his boxer briefs were straining to contain him, and her heart hammered as she took in the entirety of him. His muscles rippled over his entire frame as he moved. Stomach. Thighs. It was the thighs that made the ache in her grow even more. She wanted them encasing her, pushing into her.

He sat on the edge of the bed, setting down the foiled wrapper she'd expected, but it was the other items that caught her attention—a key, a piece of paper, and a pen.

Confusion bled through the lust.

"This isn't how I wanted to do this," he said, rubbing a hand over his short, clipped beard. "I had plans of champagne and strawberries before we ended up skin on skin. I wanted to start with this and not the naked bodies." His lips twitched upward as he waved the key in her direction.

"What is it for?" she asked, reaching for it.

He bent toward her, nuzzling her jaw again, and it sent another fiery wave through her, blending in with the inferno already blazing. "It's a key to my condo—our condo."

Her heart tripped at his words. They had to be a mistake.

She pulled back, scanning his face, managing to get out a choked, "What?"

His smile faltered, and it pricked at her soul. This…this was exactly why she should never have agreed to meet up with him. Not tonight. Not the last time. Not any of the times after that first one.

His hand skated over her thigh, eyes soft and pleading. "Your tour is done. I'm between gigs and actually considering making a movie. I thought LA would be the perfect home base while we figured it all out."

She closed her eyes against a rush of tears. The word home…the idea of coming home to someone, or someone coming home to you…it was too much.

She pushed his hand away and picked up the document, and that was when a chill filled in behind the layers of desire and panic. It was a non-disclosure agreement. And not just the standard one the people who worked for The Painted Daisies signed. This one was deeply personal. It was them promising to keep all aspects of their relationship and their lives, from hygiene to food habits, confidential. Worse, it stated any arguments or disputes they had that couldn't be resolved directly between them would be mediated by his agent. His agent! And the coup de grâce was the paragraph where she agreed to remain on birth control until he signed a waiver agreeing she could come off it. Fury sparked as her eyes flicked to his signature already at the bottom, and her entire being iced over. Every last ounce of desire disappeared in one rapid beat of her heart.

She stood up, searching for her underwear, as her body shook with a sea of emotions. If, for some godforsaken reason, she'd even been willing to contemplate an actual relationship and sharing a home together, she wouldn't, simply because of the NDA. It was like saying, I care about you enough to ask you to move in, but I don't trust you enough to not secretly get pregnant. What kind of screwed-up way to start a relationship was that? Even more screwed up than her parents being married and never living in the same city.

"Star?" For the first time, there was a hint of concern in his voice. Confusion.

She couldn't have this conversation naked, but when she went to step into her thong, he was there, pulling it away. He put one hand on her waist and the other on her chin so she was forced to meet his beautiful, hopeful gaze.

"Talk to me."

"I'm not moving in with you, Ronan." She went with the simple fact because it allowed her to keep her emotions hidden just like she'd been taught to do for decades.

"Why not?"

"We've had a handful of one-night stands. I don't even know you."

"That's bullshit and you know it," he said. "We know each other."

"Do we?" She tried to pull away, and his grip tightened. She had to fight to keep her voice calm. "If you really knew me, you'd know I don't want any kind of long-term commitment, and you sure as hell wouldn't need to ask me to sign an NDA to know I'd never sell your underwear online."

His jaw ticked as he scoured her face, looking for the emotions she was desperate to hold back. "Is this really about the NDA, or is this about your parents?"

"Don't." One word was all she could manage. She jerked away from him and was finally able to put her bra and underwear back on all while he watched.

"Where are you going?" he demanded as she picked up her dress from where it had fallen. When she didn't respond, he continued. His voice was low with frustration carved through it. "I never thought I'd see the day the badass rock star ran chicken."

She tried to ignore his attempt at goading her, but it still pricked, and she tossed back a response before she could help it. "Just because you turned this into something I never agreed to, doesn't mean I'm chicken. You're too used to everyone pandering to you. Do you ever think about what someone else wants, or do you just expect them to fall in line?"

She'd struck a nerve, because his eyes narrowed, and he crossed his arms over his chest.

"You want it, Star. You want me, us, the whole shebang. This, what you're doing right now…it's not about moving in with me or being pissed that I tried to protect us both with an NDA. It's about you loving your parents, and them not being around long enough to show you how much they love you back. You think by not getting close to anyone, by walking out before they can, you can protect yourself."

It tore apart scars she pretended she didn't have. Her parents were good parents! They'd loved her. They'd said the words. She'd been hugged and held and kissed goodnight…or goodbye. She and her siblings had everything they'd ever wanted. *Except them*, a little voice chided, but she shoved it away.

She wasn't sure what was worse, that he'd torn open her hidden wounds, that he was right about them, or that he didn't understand just how hurtful the NDA had been. Like a wounded cat, she struck back, nails and all. "Don't go all psychologist on me, Hollywood. Stick to what you're good at."

"And what exactly is that?" he demanded.

"Charming your way into people's panties and using Daddy's name to help you make a video or two."

His face reflected the pain her words had caused, and she regretted the words as soon as they were out. But then again, she regretted everything about tonight. From acknowledging his text, to agreeing to meet, and walking into the unsuspecting trap he'd laid.

She pulled on her dress, shoved her feet into her spiked heels, and stormed to the door. She'd barely gotten it open an inch when he reached over her head and slammed it shut before she could escape. His arms caged her, and she flipped around to glare at him.

"Damn it. Don't leave. Not like this," he said, his tone a command and a plea all rolled together. "Fight with me. Tear up the NDA. But don't go until we've settled it."

"That's the problem right there. We have settled it. You just don't like the way it landed," she tossed back, and he was already shaking his head as if to disagree, which just frustrated her so much that she threw out another jab. "For heaven's sake, it was just sex! And not even that great."

His eyes narrowed, a flush of irritation coating his cheeks. They both knew it wasn't true. The sex had been off the charts. Addicting. A candy you couldn't turn down whenever it came within reach. Even her first time had been life-altering. Her friends all said losing their virginity had been so painful and awkward they'd barely been able to get through it. Not her. Ronan had ignited her until she felt like she was coming apart in the very best kind of way. Pleasure and sin wrapped in one heady package.

"Liar," he growled.

To prove it, he trailed a hand down over her breast hidden under the thin dress and flicked a finger over one taut tip. She had to bite her tongue before she let out a longing gasp.

"It was never just sex between us. If it was, you wouldn't still be wet and hungry for me right now. You're going to ache for days if you walk away."

"Any dick will satisfy me. Hell, even the toy in my drawer or my fingers will do just fine, and they won't ask me to sign a stupid NDA," she said, lifting her chin in defiance.

"Star," he growled out in a tangled mix of something like remorse but also a warning.

The nickname curled in her stomach, an ache for something she'd never get back. Not after tonight. But then, it had never truly been hers to begin with. It had been a mirage she'd let herself hold on to for a handful of hours whenever their worlds crossed.

"Don't ever call me that again."

She pushed his hand away from her chest, ducked under his other arm, and jerked the door open. He didn't stop her this time, and somehow, that hurt almost as much as walking away did.

"I hate to break it to you," Ronan's voice, full of condescension and anger, carried down the hall, "but putting someone else inside you, putting anything inside you, won't make you want me any less, Beauty Queen. Just like running chicken won't fix the hurt of your childhood."

His hotel room door banged shut, and she realized, with a flush of humiliation, that there was a little group of people at the elevator who'd just heard everything he'd said. They were all making a good show of not staring by darting surreptitious looks under their lashes. Her cheeks turned red, and she hated that almost as much as the fact everything he'd said was right.

One of the men in the group cleared his throat.

She knew he was going to ask for her autograph. A picture. Hell, maybe he was going to offer to try and fill the void Ronan had promised couldn't be filled. This god-awful, mortifying moment was going to be all over the news. Daisy Drummer storms from hotel in a cloud of sex-filled innuendos. And if they'd recognized Ronan, it would be worse.

She whirled on her feet, heading for the stairs with her bodyguard on her heels.

She was already halfway down the flight of stairs when Ronan's new nickname for her hit her in the chest. Beauty Queen. He'd used it as a sneer when being a beauty contestant was hard work. It took talent and smarts, but he'd used it as a dagger. A way to strike back when he hadn't gotten what he wanted. And the Hollywood Player Prince always got what he wanted.

But he couldn't have her.

Not now and not ever again.

# *CHAPTER ONE*

## *Ronan*

***SOME OF US***

*Performed by Starsailor*

*EIGHT DAYS BEFORE*

Ronan rolled his suitcase out the door of the guest cottage on his parents' estate and headed for the main house. Skirting the infinity pool looking over the Hollywood hills, he let himself in through the back door and into the kitchen. It smelled like burnt toast, which meant they were between cooks again. Every other year, his mom, or his dad, decided they could make their own meals and let their private chef go. It would last maybe a month before they hired one back.

His mom looked up from buttering a piece of black charcoal. Born Gayle Benson, his mom had long ago legally changed her name to her Greer Bennett after two of her all-time favorite movie stars. She was in her early fifties but didn't look much older than him. Ronan had inherited both her willowy frame and her cinnamon-colored hair and hoped he'd inherit her agelessness as well.

She looked up and smiled until she saw the suitcase. "You heading out again? I feel like you just barely got home," she said.

"Off to two more concert stops in Texas," he said.

"You ever plan on finishing the documentary?" his dad asked, walking in and kissing his wife on the cheek.

The question stabbed into Ronan's chest where an aching wound had long ago begun to fester. Two and a half years was an eternity to spend on any film, let alone a documentary on a rock band. But he never could have predicted that everything would go to hell weeks after he'd started filming. When he'd first pitched the exposé to Asher for the streaming service his best friend had kicked off for Ridgeway Media Industries, it had seemed like a cakewalk. A way of killing two birds with one stone.

Now, he couldn't let it go for more reasons than he could count.

He owed it to himself, to Landry, and all five of the brave women who were getting onstage every day to show the world they wouldn't let murder and mayhem stop them.

"I'm close," he said. It was only a partial lie. He had almost all the footage he needed, while at the same time, it didn't feel like he'd ever have enough.

His dad saw through him, raising a dark, bushy brow in his direction. Strong and fit for a man who'd just turned sixty, his dad had barely any white in his beard, but the wrinkles around eyes as gray as Ronan's made him look his age in a way his mom's face didn't.

"No matter how much we're enjoying a project, we still have to call it quits at some point. Either the money or our energy will run out if you don't," his dad said.

Ronan would never admit how right his dad actually was. Just like he wouldn't tell him that the budget for the documentary had long stopped coming from RMI's cups and had been bleeding into his profits from his movie, *The Secret of Us*. He was hoping to recoup the losses with a sequel to the film. The new movie was going to be the first thing the production studio Asher had bought and handed over to Ronan would make.

His gut flipped with anticipation, thinking about everything he was going to accomplish as president of Ravaged Storm Productions. With the scripts, the decisions, *and* the money fully in his hands at last, he wasn't going to have to listen to a sea of rejections before doing what he really wanted. He just had to finish the damn documentary, hire an assistant, and get to work.

"Is your head hurting?" His mom's concerned question drew him back to the fact he'd been rubbing the scar on his temple.

A flicker of panic ran through him that he'd gotten good at pushing aside. His injury hadn't truly hurt in months, but the nightmares and the waves of anxiety still threatened to pull him under on a regular basis. The powerlessness he'd felt the day of the attack would wash over him at unexpected moments, and he'd live through it all over again. He'd obsess over ways he could have prevented being cuffed, taped, and thrown into a tub by Paisley Kim's attacker. He was still working through it.

Therapy and hand-to-hand combat had helped.

"Not really," he told her.

Both his parents were staring at him with that look—the one that said as much as they cared about him, they had some tough-love speech to deliver.

"We feel like the longer you stick around the band, the harder it's going to be for you to move on," his dad said gently.

Ronan didn't feel like he was ever going to move on. Not because of what had happened in Albany, but because of a blue-eyed, black-haired drummer who'd stolen his heart and never given it back. A woman he'd hurt and who hadn't let him close enough to her again to apologize.

He'd almost found a way in with Landry's help. They'd concocted a scheme that would have given him a fighting chance, but then she'd been murdered, and Adria's sister had been kidnapped. While Ronan hadn't felt the loss in the same way as Landry's family had, he'd still been shaken up by the events of that awful night at Swan River Pond long before the attack in Albany ever had impacted him. He'd considered Landry a friend, and when she'd died, he'd wanted to mourn her with the rest of the Daisies. But they'd scuttled into the woodwork. Adria had disappeared to Colombia with her mom, and Ronan had been forced to give up on any ideas of reconciliation.

By the time the band got back together earlier this year, he'd convinced himself he was finishing what he'd started only because it was what Landry would have wanted. She'd believed in the documentary. Believed it would bring them closer to the fans, allowing them to be seen as real people and not just vague, unattainable superstars. Every fiber in Ronan's being wanted to honor her and her wishes. But as soon as he'd seen Adria again, he'd known the truth. He'd needed to do this for much more than Landry. This was his last chance to apologize for pushing too hard and too fast. For the fucking NDA he hadn't even read until it was too late. It was his last chance to find the part of his soul that had shriveled up when she'd stormed out of a hotel room in Seattle.

A chance that still hadn't happened. He'd been with the Daisies for months now, and she continued to push him away—maybe even more than before everything had gone to hell in her world.

"Ro," his mom called to him, and when he looked up, her eyes were concerned, pleading with him. "What's really holding you up?"

*A long-legged former beauty queen.*

Ronan tugged at the beanie on his head. He almost hated wearing it these days. The image consultant he'd hired to convince the world he was more than just a pretty face, more than just his parents' son lucking into every open door in Hollywood, had insisted it made him look artsy and hip. But these days, it seemed to remind him of all his mistakes. With Adria. With Landry. With an attacker who had nearly killed him.

Worse, he couldn't get out of his head that if he hadn't gotten sidetracked by his grand gesture that awful day at the pond, he might have been able to save Landry's life. But he supposed the truth was that he might have wound up dead too. After all, he hadn't been able to save Landry's sister either. Paisley had all but saved herself while he'd lain useless in a tub with his hands tied.

His chest grew heavy, and his entire body felt weighed down.

Nothing good would come of reliving any of those memories.

Maybe his dad was right. Maybe it was time to call it quits.

His heart screamed in objection. His heart wanted what it had always wanted—the wild connection he felt when he was tangled with Adria. They'd seen beyond the false faces they both presented to the world to the real people beneath. But it was the fact he'd seen the truth of her that had sent her scrambling in the first place. She was terrified of anyone actually seeing her, of wounding a heart that had already been scraped too many times as a child.

But he knew, with a certainty he could never explain, that what bound him and Adria, the ties that went all the way to the bottom of his soul…he'd never find that again with anyone else.

So, he'd go back on tour with them for one more concert.

But because his parents were right, because he had to stop at some point before his pride and his heart were completely obliterated, he'd make this his last effort. If she still hated him, if she still refused to even meet with him to finish her interview for the documentary, then he'd find a way to walk away. He'd put this part of his life behind him.

He crossed the kitchen to his parents, kissed his mom on the cheek and gave his dad a one-armed hug. "Thanks for looking out for me. I think this will be the last trip. I have a studio to pull together, after all. And a house to buy."

"You're moving out?" His mom's eyes grew wide. "That's not… You don't—"

"I've left the Oscar-winning actress tongue-tied," Ronan laughed. "I know. You like having me here, but it's about damn time I flew the nest, don't you think?"

"I like my nest full," she said softly.

She hugged him to her, and he hugged her back before stepping away.

He was so close to having all his dreams come true. It was missing an important chunk, but this trip would have to be his last attempt to fill it. The longer he chased after Adria, spinning his wheels, the more it jeopardized the other things in his life that mattered. Asher and Asher's dad had trusted him with the production studio, and he wasn't going to let them down. If he couldn't have Adria, he'd have to be satisfied with accomplishing his professional dreams and not his personal ones.

♫ ♫ ♫

By the time Ronan got off his flight in Arlington, he was antsy as hell. He'd had to play nice with his seatmate in the first-class cabin, listening to the man drone on about all the things Ronan's dad had gotten wrong in his *Stilleto* movies. The guy had acted like he was a spy himself and had been personally offended by the inaccuracies.

But more than his irritation with the guy tearing into his parents' films, what had bugged him even more was how the man had looked decidedly like the asshole who'd attacked him in Albany. Or maybe hadn't looked like him as much as there had been a vibe coming off him that screamed *unhinged stalker*.

So, once Ronan checked into the hotel, the first thing he did was change into his workout gear and head for the hotel's exercise room, hoping to find a sense of control through the martial arts moves he'd recently learned. The two men in the black uniform of Reinard Security at the door had him simultaneously wanting to beat his head against the wall and go storming inside to see which of the Daisies was in there.

"Gym's closed. Come back in an hour," one of the men said. The guy was new and didn't recognize Ronan. Or maybe he did, and he'd been given the "Don't let Ronan near me" speech.

Before he could respond, she was there, stepping up behind the bodyguards, looking like the pageant winner she'd once been, even with sweat glistening over her forehead and dripping down her chest. She looked completely and deliciously hot and bothered. Just like she'd looked coming apart beneath him as they moved together in a sea of white sheets with her black hair spilled across the pillows. Her brilliant blue eyes had burned for him back then. They'd warmed him up like a fire that would never die—except it had. Now, as those lapis eyes landed on him, all he felt was ice.

Her tiny pair of workout shorts and sports bra showed off every line of her lean frame and every curve that bordered on being too much for her fragile bone structure. And yet, every piece of her was goddess-like perfection with naturally red lips, high cheek bones, and a classic oval face. She was an enchanting image that had haunted his dreams from the first time he'd seen her on set in a Burbank studio.

"I'm done, Red. Let the man in," she said, easing past her guards and into the hall.

Her hand accidently brushed his arm, and they both jumped as a shock wave rushed through them. It shouldn't have pleased him as much as it did that she still felt the same overwhelming rush, but he couldn't help it. He was sick. He had an addiction. He needed her. As if nothing in his life would truly be right if she didn't agree to be the person at his side.

It was ridiculous.

When the media had labeled him the Hollywood Player Prince, it had been for not needing anyone. For leaving a string of hearts behind him as he'd moved from one to the other. But the truth was, those past conquests…they hadn't really wanted *him*. They'd wanted the suave exterior the world saw as Greer Bennett and Quentin Hawk's son. The few people he'd let past the façade had been confused by the moody, sensitive artist they'd found there. Of all his friends and girlfriends, only Asher had stuck once he'd seen past the shiny surface.

Ronan watched as Adria moved down the hallway without a word in his direction.

"Nice to see you, too, Adria," he called after her, chest hammering and body aching.

What he got back was a one-fingered wave.

His jaw ticked. They'd both been at fault that night in Seattle. He'd pushed too hard and had stupidly not read the NDA ahead of time. But she'd also overreacted. Words had been said that they'd both regretted. The hard truth was, Adria didn't want him to apologize. She was still running scared. She didn't trust him to stick when that was all he wanted to do.

Her bodyguards followed her down the hall, and he entered the gym with yet another layer of frustration to burn off. He went to the boxing bag first, pounding on it for a few minutes, and then turned to the mat jammed up against the mirrors and worked through a sequence of punches and kicks.

"Jerome show you that move?" a quiet voice asked.

Ronan turned to see Nikki standing there dressed in workout gear similar to Adria's. As tall as her bandmate and with hair just as black, Nikki was the leaner of the two. Adria was toned and shaped with strong arms from pounding on her drums, but Nikki was defined everywhere. Ronan didn't think there was an ounce of her that wasn't muscle.

"He did," Ronan answered.

Jerome Barry was a former Green Beret who was a friend of Nikki's family. After the attack in Albany, she'd put Ronan in touch with the man, promising he'd be discreet. Barry had been more than discreet. He'd been a godsend. He'd helped rebuild Ronan's confidence in a shorter amount of time than he thought therapy ever could have.

"Feel like sparring?" she asked, closing the distance to face him on the mat.

He raised a brow and ran a hand over his beard before glancing toward the door where her bodyguards waited.

"They're not going to come after you for working out with me," Nikki laughed.

"Fine, but I'm not going easy on you because you're a girl."

She huffed. "As if."

Then, she swirled and kicked at him. He barely blocked it. He moved on instinct, batting each offense that she sent his way, but just barely. They moved around the floor in a dance that surprised the hell out of him. He'd known she was strong, but this was skill from years of practice.

When he finally ended up on the floor with her elbow up against his throat, she laughed. She rose and then offered him a hand. When he got up, she was still smiling—something he didn't see often in Nikki these days. She'd been quiet even before Landry had died. Not shy in the way Paisley had been, but just reserved. As if she saved all her words for when they really mattered. But now, she seemed to have a shell around her that was all but impenetrable, even by smiles.

"Barry teach you also?" he asked, uncapping a water bottle and taking a long drink.

"My dad and Jerome. These days, I mostly workout with my stepmom."

He frowned. "She's here with you?"

He had a vague recollection of a tall woman with plain brown hair and thick black eyeglasses who'd shown up at the farmhouse that awful night when Landry had died. But he didn't remember seeing her on the tour with them.

Nikki shook her head. "No. I just mean when we're together. She might be joining me for a few concerts stops, though. She's in between jobs."

"What does she do?" he asked.

"She's worked mostly as an executive assistant for a couple of CEOs and studio execs. But in the last two years, she's had some bad luck. Positions being downsized, that sort of thing."

"You know I'm looking for a personal assistant, right?" he said.

Nikki glanced over, wide-eyed. "No, I didn't."

He chuckled. "Serendipitous, then. When Asher fired the Ravaged Storm president and put me in his place, the guy's assistant took it personally and walked out. I need someone and soon. Have her send me her résumé."

He headed for the door, and Nikki called after him, "You're done? Was I too much for you, Hollywood?"

His chest tightened at the nickname, wishing with all his being it was her friend saying it instead of her. Nikki was beautiful, stunning even, but she wasn't Adria Rojas. She'd never be able to make his blood pressure spike and his groin ache. He didn't even have it in him to flirt with Nikki anymore. What did that say about the player prince? When was the last time that name the paparazzi had coined for him had even truly applied?

Years. Maybe since Seattle.

"I'm man enough to admit that if we kept going, you'd continue to whip my ass," he said, shooting her a hand wave as he left.

Her laughter followed him into the hall.

And just like he'd wished it was her friend's voice, he wished it was Adria's laughter. Wished he'd been able to share half as many words with her as he'd just shared with Nikki. Maybe then, his Star would finally hear and accept the truth. They'd both been wrong. But it wasn't too late to fix it.

**Keep Reading *BLUE MARGUERITE* now on Amazon**

And then get ready for the stunning conclusion in ***Royal Haze***.

# Message from the Author

Thank you for taking the time to read the third book in *The Painted Daisies* series inspired by Heart's "Secret." I hope the way Leya's and Holden's souls came together brought a smile to your face, and that the mix of music and words in this story leaves a memory you'll think about every time you hear one of the songs from now on.

***Cherry Brandy*** is the third book in a connected, standalone series. While each couple will have their own suspense plot line and their own happily ever after, you'll need to read the entire series to find out just what happened that day at Swan River Pond with Landry. The good news is the entire series is releasing this year, and you can get the next book, ***Blue Marguerite***, now.

If you're like Leya and Zaira Singh, you might be wondering how we can work together to fight against child brides and forced marriages. Here's a list of some charities that do good work in this arena and a website that helps you identify a charity's score based on transparency, percentage of money going to its actual cause, etc.

Too Young to Wed

Girls Not Brides

VOW for Girls

Unchained at Last

Plan International

Breakthrough

World Vision

https://www.charitynavigator.org/about-us/

If you like talking about music, books, and just what it takes to get us through this wild ride called life as much as I do, maybe you should join my Facebook readers' group,

**LJ's Music & Stories**, and join the conversations there today. Hopefully, the group can help ***YOU*** through your life in some small way.

Regardless if you join or not, I'd love for you to tell me what you thought of the book by reaching out to me personally. I'd be honored if you took the time to leave a review on BookBub, Amazon, and/or Goodreads, but even more than that, I hope you enjoyed it enough to tell a friend about it.

If you still can't get enough (ha!), you could also sign up for my newsletter where you'll receive music-inspired scenes weekly and be entered into a giveaway each month for a chance at a signed paperback by yours truly. Plus, you'll be able to keep tabs on all my stories, including fun facts about The Painted Daisies and more.

Finally, I just wanted to say that my wish for you is a healthy and happy journey. May you live life resiliently, with hope and love leading the way!

# Acknowledgments

I'm so very grateful for every single person who has helped me on this book journey. If you're reading these words, you ***ARE*** one of those people. I wouldn't be an author if people like you didn't decide to read the stories I crafted, so THANK YOU!

In addition to my lovely readers, I'd be ridiculous not to thank these extra folks who've made this journey possible for me:

My husband, who means more to me than I can explain in one or a thousand sentences, and who has never, ever let me give up on this dream, doing everything he could to make it come true, and then CHEERING from the rooftops at my tiniest success. Here's to you being a "Kept Man" someday, my love.

Our child, Evyn, owner of Evans Editing, who remains my harshest and kindest critic. Thank you for helping me shape my stories and reading this one a million and one times until I got it right.

The folks at That's What She Said Publishing, who took a gamble on me, this wild idea I had for a series, and then were determined to see the best in all of it even when I chewed my lips to smithereens, worrying that it would fail.

My sister, Kelly, who made sure I hit the publish button the very first time and reads my crappy first drafts and still loves my stories anyway.

My parents and my father-in-law, who are my biggest fans and bring my books to the strangest places, telling everyone they know (and don't know) about my stories.

The beautiful Shabnam Arora, Paramita Patra, and Oindrilla Sarkar who shared their culture and their personal lives with me in order for me to get Leya's story right. I'm forever grateful to you for reading with kindness and correcting my mistakes.

The talented Emily Wittig, who made the perfect covers for this heart-wrenching series.

Jenn at Jenn Lockwood Editing Services, who is always patient with my gazillion missing commas, my hatred of the semicolon, and scattered deadlines.

Karen Hrdlicka, who ensures the final versions of my books are beautiful and reminds me hyphens aren't always optional. You're a beautiful soul.

To the entire group of beautiful humans in LJ's Music & Stories who love and support me, I can't say enough how deeply grateful I am for each and every one of you.

To the host of bloggers who have shared my stories, become dear friends, and continue to make me feel like a rock star every day, thank you, thank you, thank you!

To a host of authors, including Stephanie Rose, Kathryn Nolan, Lucy Score, Erika Kelly, Hannah Blake, Annie Dyer, and AM Johnson, who have shown me that dear friends are more important than any paralyzing moment in this wild publishing world, MWAH!

To all my ARC readers who have become sweet friends, thanks for knowing just what to say to scare away my writer insecurities.

And I can't leave without a special thanks to Leisa C., Rachel R., and Lisa K. for being three of the biggest cheerleaders I could ever hope to have on this wild ride called life.

***I love you all!***

# About the Author

Award winning author, LJ Evans, lives in Northern California with her husband, child, and the three terrors called cats. She's been writing, almost as a compulsion, since she was a little girl and will often pull the car over to write when a song lyric strikes her. A former first-grade teacher, she now spends her free time reading and writing, as well as binge-watching original shows like *Wednesday, Ted Lasso, Veronica Mars,* and *Stranger Things*.

If you ask her the one thing she won't do, it's pretty much anything that involves dirt—sports, gardening, or otherwise. But she loves to write about all of those things, and her first published heroine was pretty much involved with dirt on a daily basis, which is exactly why LJ loves fiction novels—the characters can be everything you're not and still make their way into your heart.

Her novel, ***CHARMING AND THE CHERRY BLOSSOM***, was *Writer's Digest* Self-Published E-book Romance of the Year in 2021. For more information about LJ, check out any of these sites:

www.ljevansbooks.com

FaceBook Group: LJ's Music & Stories

LJ Evans on Amazon, Bookbub, and Goodreads

@ljevansbooks on Facebook, Instagram, TikTok, and Pinterest

# Books by L J

## Standalone

***After All the Wreckage***

A single-dad, small-town romantic suspense

He's a broody bar owner raising his siblings. She's a scrappy PI who's loved him since she was a teenager. When his brother disappears, she forces aside years of pining and family secrets to help him.

***The Last One You Loved***

A single-dad, small-town romance

He's a small-town sheriff with a secret that can unravel their worlds. She's an ER resident running from a costly mistake. Coming home will only mean heartache…unless they let forgiveness heal them both.

***Charming and the Cherry Blossom***

A contemporary, new adult romance

Today was a fairy tale…I inherited a fortune from a dad I never knew, and a thoroughly charming guy asked me out. But like all fairy tales, mine has a dark side...and my happily ever after may disappear with the truth.

***Perfectly Fine***

A Hollywood, second-chance romance

He's a charming, A-list actor at the top of his game. She's a determined, small-town screenwriter hoping for a deal. They form an unexpected connection until secrets ruin their future.

## My Life as an Album Series

***My Life as a Country Album*** — Cam's Story

A boy-next-door, small-town romance

Cam's diary-style, coming-of-age story about growing up loving the football hero next door. She vowed to love him forever. But when fate comes calling, will she ever find a heart to call home? Warning: Tears may fall.

***My Life as a Pop Album*** — Mia & Derek

A rock star, road-trip romance

Bookworm Mia is trying to put years of guilt behind her when soulful musician Derek Waters strolls into her life and turns it upside down. Once he's seen her, Derek can't walk away unless Mia comes with him. But what will happen when their short time together comes to an end?

***My Life as a Rock Album*** — Seth & PJ

A second-chance, antihero romance

Recovering addict Seth Carmen is a trash artist who knows he's better off alone. But when he finds and loses the love of his life, he can't help sending her a host of love letters to try to win her back. Can Seth prove to PJ they can make broken beautiful?

***My Life as a Mixtape*** — Lonnie & Wynn

A single-dad, rock star romance

Lonnie's always seen relationships as a burden instead of a gift, and picking up the pieces his sister leaves behind is just one of the reasons. When Wynn enters his life just as her world is disintegrating, their mixed-up pasts give way to new beginnings neither of them saw coming.

***My Life as a Holiday Album*** – 2nd Generation

A small-town romance

Come home for the holidays with this heartwarming, full-length standalone full of hidden secrets, true love, and the real meaning of family. Perfect for lovers of *Love Actually* and Hallmark movies, this sexy story intertwines the lives of six couples as they find their way to their happily ever afters with the help of.

***My Life as an Album Series Box Set***

1st four Album books plus an exclusive novella

In the exclusive novella, *This Life with Cam*, Blake Abbott writes to Cam about just what it was like to grow up in the shadow of her relationship with Jake and just when he first fell for the little girl with the popsicle-stained lips. Can he show Cam that she isn't broken?

## The Anchor Novels

***Guarded Dreams*** — Eli & Ava

A grumpy-sunshine, military romance

He's a grumpy Coast Guard focused on a life of service. She's a feisty musician searching for stardom. Nothing about them fits, and yet their attraction burns wild when fate lands them in the same house for the summer.

***Forged by Sacrifice*** — Mac & Georgie

A roommates-to-lovers, military romance

He's a driven military man zeroed in on a new goal. She's a struggling law student running from her family's mistakes. They're entirely wrong for each other…except their bodies disagree. When they end up as roommates, how long will it take before intense attraction shatters their resistance?

***Avenged by Love*** — Truck & Jersey

A fake-marriage, military romance

When a broody military man and a quiet bookstore clerk end up in the same house, it isn't only attraction that erupts. Now, the only way to ensure she gets the care she needs is to marry her.

***Damaged Desires*** — Dani & Nash

A frenemy, military romance

A grumpy Navy SEAL reeling from losing his team fights an intense attraction for his best friend's fiery sister. Until a stalker put her in his sights, and then he'll do anything to protect her, even if it means exposing all his secrets.

***Branded by a Song*** — Brady & Tristan

A single-mom, rock star romance

He's a country-rock legend searching for inspiration. She's a Navy SEAL's widow determined to honor his memory while raising their daughter. Neither believes the intense attraction tugging at them can lead to more until their futures are twined by her grandmother's will.

***Tripped by Love*** – Cassidy & Marco

A broody-bodyguard, single-mom romance

He's her brother's broody bodyguard with secrets he can't share. She's a busy single mom with a restaurant to run. They're just friends until a little white lie changes everything.

***The Anchor Novels: The Military Bros Box Set***

The 1st 3 books + an exclusive novella

Heartfelt reads full of love, sacrifice, and family. The perfect book boyfriends for a binge read.

## The Anchor Suspense Novels

***Unmasked Dreams*** — Violet & Dawson

A second-chance, age-gap romance

Violet and Dawson had a heart-stopping attraction they were compelled to deny. When they're tossed together again, it proves nothing has changed—except the lab she's built in the garage and the secrets he's keeping. When she stumbles into his dark world, Dawson breaks old promises to keep her safe.

***Crossed by the Stars*** — Jada & Dax

A second-chance, forced-proximity romance

Family secrets meant Dax and Jada's teenaged romance was an impossibility. A decade later, the scars still remain, so neither is willing to give in to their tantalizing chemistry. But when a shadow creeps out of Jada's past, seeking retribution, it's Dax who shows up to protect her. And suddenly, it's hard to see a way out without permanent damage to their bodies and souls.

***Disguised as Love*** — Cruz & Raisa

A chemistry-filled, enemies-to-lovers romance

Surly FBI agent, Cruz Malone, is determined to bring down the Leskov clan for good. If that means he has to arrest or bed the sexy blond scientist of the family, so be it. Too bad Raisa has other ideas. There's no way she's just going to sit back and let the infuriating agent dismantle her world… or her heart.

## The Painted Daisies

Interconnected series with an all-female rock band, the alpha heroes who steal their hearts, and suspense that will leave you breathless. Each story has its own HEA.

***Sweet Memory***

Paisley and Jonas's opposite-attract, second-chance romance.

The world's sweetest rock star falls for a troubled music producer whose past comes back to haunt them.

***Green Jewel***

Fiadh and Asher's enemies-to-lovers, single-dad romance.

He did it. She'll prove it. Her body's reaction to him be damned.

***Cherry Brandy***

Leya and Holden's opposites-attract, forbidden, bodyguard romance.

Being on the run with only one bed is no excuse to touch her… until touching is the only choice.

***Blue Marguerite***

Adria and Ronan's celebrity, second-chance, frenemy romance.

She vowed to never forgive him... Not even when he

offers answers her family desperately seeks.

***Royal Haze***

Nikki and D'Angelo's bodyguard, on-the-run romance.

He was ready to torture, steal, and kill to defend the world he believed in. What he wasn't prepared for… was her.

## Free Stories

FREE with newsletter signup

https://www.ljevansbooks.com/freeljbooks

***Perfectly Fine*** – A Hollywood, second-chance romance

He's a charming, A-list actor at the top of his game. She's a determined, small-town screenwriter hoping for a deal. They form an unexpected connection until secrets ruin their future.

***Rumor*** – A small-town, rock-star romance

There's only one thing rock star Chase Legend needs to ring in the new year, and that's to know what Reyna Rossi tastes like. After ten years, there's no way he's letting her escape the night without their souls touching. Reyna has other plans. After all, she doesn't need the entire town wagging their tongues about her any more than they already do.

***Love Ain't*** – A friends-to-lovers, cowboy romance

Reese knows her best friend and rodeo king, Dalton Abbott, is never going to fall in love, get married, and have kids. He's left so many broken hearts behind that there's gotta be a museum full of them somewhere. So when he gives her a look from under the brim of his hat, promising both jagged relief and pain, she knows better than to give in.

***The Long Con*** – A sexy, antihero romance

Adler is after his next big payday. Then, Brielle sways in with her own game in play, and those aquamarine-colored eyes almost make him forget his number-one rule. But she'll learn… love isn't a con he's interested in.

***The Light Princess*** – An old-fashioned fairy tale

A princess who glows with a magical light, a kingdom at war, and a kiss that changes the world. This is an extended version of the fairy tale twined through the pages of *Charming and the Cherry Blossom.*

Made in United States
Orlando, FL
02 October 2024

52253136R00246